The Deliverers

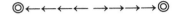

The Deliverers

◎←←←← →→→→◎

Suzanne Akerman

ISBN 978-1-7379805-0-6 (print)
ISBN 978-1-7379805-1-3 (e-book)

First paperback edition September 2021

Cover credit Adam Botsford

"...it's no use going back to yesterday, because I was a different person then."

— *Lewis Carroll, Alice's Adventures in Wonderland*

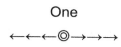

One

She chose to be Tuesday Devlin. When she shed her old identity and crafted her new one for the new world, she wanted to be Tuesday. The second day of the week, a chance to be the person she wasn't on Monday.

Tuesday lay flat on her back in the loft of her tiny house, staring at the knotted wood of the ceiling that hung only two feet from her face. Her heart was racing—she'd had the dream again. Tracing the wavy lines of the wood grain on the ceiling with her eyes, she breathed deeply. Long, straight line, swerve to the left, through a smear of pine tar, back to straight. A vibration from her phone on the mattress interrupted her meditation. She rolled over and read the message from GoferGoods.

"Can't turn that down, can we, Oz?" Tuesday said, swinging down from the loft without using the ladder. Oz sat up and cocked his head. Tuesday stepped over the big dog's bed and opened the mini fridge that occupied much of the room's available floor space. Canned water, cheese sticks, yesterday's three-bean salad, vegetables harvested from the tiny garden next to the tiny house. Tuesday grabbed a carrot, and scratched Oz behind his ear, "Let's just eat while we're out." Her unruly brunette waves in a loose braid down her back, her eyes the color of a stormy sky, and the unpretentious swagger in her stride gave Tuesday Devlin a presence larger than her 5' 5" frame.

She slipped her dagger into its holster along the thigh of her leggings, pulled on her tunic vest and belted it around her slender waist. Oz shook out his silvery fur and stretched, vaguely wagging his wolfish tail. He glanced at his bright red working vest hanging on a hook on the wall, his pointed ears at attention. "Not today," Tuesday said, and opened the door for Oz to trot outside. She followed with the laces of her boots still untied. Oz lifted his leg on the small weeping willow Tuesday had planted two years ago when she decided they would stay and put down roots at the tiny house on top of Alabama Hill in Bellingham. "Why do you have to pee on my symbolism?" she asked around a mouthful of carrot.

While Oz patrolled for rabbits in the shrubbery, Tuesday focused her eyes on the sliver of Lake Whatcom visible from her plot of land. From this vantage point, she could almost believe the city below was still sleepy Bellingham, a college town near the northern border of Washington State. She could almost believe that the pandemic had never happened, that it had never erupted across the globe, ravaging populations unchecked for nearly seven years. She could almost believe that the disease hadn't claimed two billion lives, hadn't exploded governments into chaos and rendered twenty-first century economics completely useless. Almost.

In the city below, Tuesday and Oz passed their usual haunts, a term that now carried extra heft. Many of the old shops in the town of Bellingham remained, even just as vestiges of the era before the pandemic started ten years ago. The three-story independent bookseller with a cafe and gift boutique retained its regal brick exterior and white plaster letters exclaiming, "Village Books." Inside, the top floor now housed an antiques and oddities dealer, run by a pair of former accountants. The only evidence of the defunct bookstore was one nook in their shop where volumes of all types were crammed onto disorderly shelves. The restaurant in the lower level of the building had long since been converted to a soup kitchen and food bank, operated by the former Village Books employees themselves. Many times Tuesday had connected the food kitchen with farmers whose crop of onions, cabbage, or zucchinis was about to spoil. It wasn't as humanitarian as it sounded; she got paid.

Tuesday and Oz approached the once-coveted bay view condominiums, now occupied by organized squatters who had formed their own community called "Boundary Land," a bastardization of Boundary Bay and the housing community's pre-pandemic name, "Morse Landing." Someone had graffitied an extra letter "o" on the sign down the block so it read, "*Morose* Landing, next left."

One of Boundary Land's residents, a woman about Tuesday's age, early thirties, came out of the building's glass door, followed by a boy of about ten. The woman stopped and silently watched Tuesday pass, but the boy asked, "Is that one of them? It's wearing the collar! That's one of them, isn't it?" While his mother stood stoically, the boy leaped toward Oz, arms spread wide, and blurted to Tuesday, "Can I meet your dog? I've never met a Deliverer! What kind of dog is it? What places have you been to?"

Tuesday half-smiled. "His name is Oz. He's not a special breed— probably a German shepherd mix. We've traveled to lots of places. Nepal, New Zealand, Ecuador, a bunch of islands most people have never heard of. And some places not so far away—Colorado, Arizona, British Columbia..."

The boy knelt in front of Oz with one knee up and the other foot tucked beneath him. "Hi Oz. It's so great to meet you." He didn't reach out to touch the dog's thick fur, but he was barely containing himself. Oz sat patiently. He was a serious dog, but accustomed to attention. He always kept Tuesday in his view, checking for visual cues, even when he wasn't on a job. Her manner told him to be relaxed, alert, or playful.

"You can pet him if you want," Tuesday allowed, seeing the boy's restraint. He put his hand on Oz's neck and stroked it.

"Wow."

Tuesday looked at the boy's mother while he continued to prattle on conversationally to Oz, "Were you ever scared? I've seen some of the videos. I'm sorry some of your friends died. How many vaccines did you deliver?"

The boy's mother met her gaze, and Tuesday answered, "Forty-eight thousand, six hundred and thirty-seven."

"Come on, Theo," the woman said, her eyes still fixed on Tuesday. "Let them go about their day."

Theo bounced away exclaiming, "Wait until Dad hears about this!"

"Thank you," murmured the woman.

3

"You're welcome," answered Tuesday.

As Tuesday and Oz walked on, they passed several more buildings, one a housing complex like Boundary Land, one an imploding mansion, and another that was a fitness center converted into a shelter for homeless and orphaned youth. The open space and large showers at the gym were a luxury compared to some accommodations during the pandemic, and the facility was a safe haven for dozens of needy teens, even ten years later. The old exercise apparatuses rusted nearby, as if someone had ridden the rowing machines and stair-steppers straight through the gym walls, screeching into the parking lot, and then left them there to deteriorate into skeletons of black piping.

At a bend in the road Tuesday came to a gated housing development with a security bot at the entrance. She flashed the tags she wore around her neck, breezing past the bot's retinal scanner and interrogating questions. "Deliverer detected," said the bot to no one.

Manors, villas, and haciendas were more accurate descriptions of the residences than "houses." Tuesday had thought so even a decade before, when she had been a student at Western Washington University, walking and training dogs to pay for tuition, books, and beer obtained with a fake ID. Dog walking had paid for the fake ID, too. In those days, the lawns were manicured to mimic Japanese gardens or tropical paradises, with palm trees or bonsai that took hours of hired attention. Today some of them had overgrown to look like secret passages to fairylands, some had simply died down to bare soil, and others, like the one she approached, were an expanse of barely tamed native plants and wildflowers. Tuesday didn't need to knock because the security camera would have alerted the home's residents when she punched in the code to open their iron gate. They also would have been alerted when, like the tiniest of military tanks, a Jack Russell terrier exploded out of the dog door, assaulting Tuesday and Oz with gleeful barking. Oz wagged his tail in greeting and Tuesday couldn't help but kneel down to hug the still spry little dog.

"Your arrival is always a celebration like the return of the Prodigal Son

4

to him," said the figure at the door. He was a man in his sixties, dressed as only serious men attempting to be casual can, in loafers, a pressed t-shirt, and what were perhaps his third-best khakis. Ten years ago, he had just retired from a distinguished military career when he had acquired the terrier puppy, Fauci, and hired Tuesday to train him.

"Fauci has always been a celebratory dog," Tuesday agreed. "And you should celebrate too, considering what I bring." Tuesday handed him a cloth bag, "The usual." Two pounds of freshly roasted single-origin Sulawesi Arabica peaberry beans, and a bottle of medication. To herself, Tuesday referred to this customer as Captain Caffeine.

"The only two things besides Joan that make my heart beat," Captain Caffeine cracked the same joke every month. Sometimes Joan Caffeine accepted the delivery, her delicate hand glinting with jewelry, her hair diagonally parted and frozen framing her face. She reminded Tuesday of a news story where three women in Georgia had been having tea when a hurricane hit, and afterward the porcelain teapot sat right where they left it on the picnic table, inexplicably carrying on, steeping tea in its floral painted belly. Joan was a teapot in a hurricane.

When Fauci was a puppy and Captain Caffeine was paying for daily walks and puppy manners sessions, Tuesday learned the intimacies of rich people's lives. She learned where spare keys and cash are kept, where people shop, what they eat, and what they throw away. Back then, the pandemic was just on the fringes of people's minds like a niggling hangnail, and everyone could still get their own coffee, medication, liquor, acid reducer, citrus fruits, sneakers, and motor oil. As the disease evolved and surged closer, supply chains shriveled and dried up entirely or sporadically appeared and disappeared, leaving people desperate for soy milk one day, a new bra the next, and a replacement hose for their vacuum cleaner the next. Tuesday discovered she could earn just as much beer money by finding things for people as for walking their dogs. Like many children growing up in the U.S. foster care system, Tuesday had learned to barter, to source important items from unlikely places, to

5

massage an ego or tear it down to get what she needed. She excelled at finding things.

Eventually, finding things became more than just beer money—it was her livelihood. Tuesday brought Joan nail lacquer in Velvet Haven purple and hair dye called Garnet Shine. She found a steady supply of galangal root, black truffle sea salt, and true vanilla extract for the foodies who lived one street over. She could find Guess jeans in the right size, antibiotics, light bulbs, or a fuel filter for a Porsche 911 for the right price. Tuesday became invaluable to members of the community who buttoned themselves up in their homes and never came out, terrified that the sickness would find them. She learned that people paid just as well for small luxuries as for necessities. By the time GoferGoods enhanced the network of people finding things and people needing things, Tuesday already had a large customer base, and used the app as a supplement to her other business activities.

Captain Caffeine was not a small talker, thankfully. "Have a nice day, Ms. Devlin." Fauci bounced with them to the gate and wagged goodbye. After ten years of societal turmoil, Captain Caffeine was nearly the only hold-over from her college days of supply running, and even he switched to using her new name. Now she was Tuesday Devlin to everyone.

"Okay Oz, now that the usual is out of the way, let's find Myles and get to the fun part."

Across town at the college where Tuesday spent so many days in classes and nights at parties, the brick buildings stood largely unchanged. The familiar exteriors though, belied the bizarre upheaval in post-high school education. Instead of residence halls full of freshmen living in close quarters sharing lounges, kitchens, and showers, each wing of the halls could be leased by a single student at a cost only heirs to pharmaceutical fortunes or foreign royalty could afford. Other would-be students could earn their degrees online in some cases if they could obtain a stable internet connection and enough cryptocurrency for tuition.

6

The harder part of earning a degree online was somehow maintaining the headspace required to study, learn, or create while the world was daily a different mish-mash of rubble and rebuilding. And of course, online degrees did not lend themselves well to some fields where labs or in-person internships were essential. Virtual microbiology could only go so far before a student would have to build a microscope, scrape a sample from the toilet tank onto a glass plate of homemade agar compound—assuming there was any gelatin to be found, which there probably wouldn't be because the meat packing plants shut down. Even shooting a deer and boiling the bones for homemade gelatin would make a better profit being sold at the market so people could indulge in precious fruit jellies or cosmetics. After all that, an online degree starts to feel pretty ludicrous.

Tuesday had graduated college the year in-person classes had halted and universities didn't know what to do. So they just granted seniors degrees, shrugging and sending the students into a reality no one had ever described when answering the entrance essay question, "where do you see yourself in four years?" At the time, Tuesday thought she was lucky to have the final semester grades waived, and her B.A. bestowed, since she had been failing her anthropology course. She hadn't wanted to walk in a pompous robed ceremony anyway. But in the new reality, unpredictability reigned, and degrees lost much of their meaning, as the economy became hugely stratified. A few companies raked in billions, while others deteriorated into nothing. Graduates might end up working for Zoom from home in a palace like Captain Caffeine's, working as a bicycle repair mechanic, or selling homemade soap at the People's Market.

Today the campus appeared peaceful and mostly deserted, as it generally did. Tuesday knew Myles would be running on the track today, but she decided to make a stop at one of the administration buildings before interrupting his workout. Again, Tuesday bypassed the security check, and as always ignored the "no dogs" sign. Though the first floor of the building still housed a handful of university staff and faculty, many of the offices were leased out to entrepreneurs, graphic designers, website developers, and others who could afford to rent shared office space. Most of the campus buildings now served dual purposes; Oz's veterinarian ran her practice from one wing of the science building, and the auditorium—no longer needed as a medical clinic as it had been during the height of the pandemic—hosted a bustling marketplace twice a week.

Tuesday passed a row of cubicles and peeked into an office with a hand-written sign reading "Realtor" taped to the door. "Knock knock," said Tuesday as Oz waltzed in.

"Who's there?"

"Oh, I didn't mean to start a knock knock joke."

A petite woman with chestnut hair spun in her office chair to face Tuesday and removed her ironic horn-rimmed glasses, "Oh, how disappointing. It's...Miss Thursday, is it?"

"Ugh," Tuesday rolled her eyes and came into the room, closing the door behind her. "Hey Sharon, just passing through and wanted to see if you needed anything. I know you're not a fan of GoferGoods."

"Yes, they say the app security is top level, but—call me old-fashioned—I like to look my gophers in the eye when I ask for something," Sharon winked.

"I'm not a rodent," Tuesday replied, more amused than she sounded. "I have your standing offer for Reese's peanut butter cups, and I'm expecting to get my hands on some at the end of next week. Anything else?"

Sharon feigned concentration and then her face lit up, "Ah, I know! An ace pilot with skin the color of hot chocolate and a good sense of humor please."

Tuesday cleared her throat, "I don't know any of those. And if I did, I probably would keep him miles away from YOU" she joked dryly.

"Miles away? *Myles* away?" Sharon laughed.

"Have you always been like this?" Tuesday asked, "I don't remember you being like this when you were the registrar."

"Lighten up. Take a seat." Sharon gestured to the combined chair and desk unit so common in university classrooms. Tuesday reluctantly sank into the chair, and the desk panel immediately clattered to the floor. Oz came to see what the fuss was about. "Oh right," Sharon said, unsurprised. "Forgot we're missing a screw."

"The chair's not the only thing with a few loose screws," Tuesday said, trying to reassemble the desk and chair.

"Ha! See, I knew you could crack a joke!" Sharon was delighted. "And I *was* always this way but had to hide it when I was the one holding the fate of your semester schedule in my grasp. Can't be ridiculous and play God at the same time. Now I'm powerless, so I just get to be ridiculous."

"Lucky us." Oz sat down next to the rickety chair-desk and fixed his earnest brown eyes on Tuesday. She instinctively put her arm around his muscular shoulders.

"Seriously though, I don't suppose you could get your hands on a bottle of full-bodied cabernet from Woodward Canyon?" Sharon asked.

"Oh definitely, but Woodward Canyon is outside of Cascadia so that's extra. If you'd settle for Vartanyan or Shrugging Earth that would be more affordable."

"If I wanted to settle, I'd put on my pioneer outfit and hitch a plow to an ox."

Tuesday shook her head, "You could be very successful with an operation like that these days."

"I am not Laura Ingalls Wilder, and we are nowhere near Catan; therefore, I will not settle."

"Sorry I offered!" Tuesday couldn't help smiling now.

"No, I'll take Woodward Canyon when you can get it. Bonus if you can get a 2014 charbonneau red."

"Done."

Sharon winked and faked a Southern accent, "If you can milk the cows

9

and bring in the firewood before supper, I'll give you a nickel, Miss Ingalls."

Tuesday raised an eyebrow and took that reference to be her dismissal. "C'mon, Oz," she said.

Sharon swiveled her chair around so her back was to Tuesday again, "Why Oz?" she asked, "Like the Wizard? The Great and Powerful?"

"Something like that," said Tuesday, closing the door behind her.

At the track, Tuesday scanned the red dirt ring, shielding her eyes with her hand. There was no sun, but the thick sheet of clouds still made her squint. She spotted the figure she was looking for and watched him approach, admiring his gait, still smooth and easy, even though she was sure he'd already run the loop ten times by now. As he came closer, she could see a shine on his skin, the only evidence of effort. Myles acknowledged her with a tilt of his head, and Tuesday hopped onto the track and began jogging alongside him. "I didn't wear my running shoes."

"Why come to the track then?" Myles played along. "Javelin throwing? High jumping?"

"Pole vaulting."

"Hmm, I'd never have guessed." They slowed to a stop while Oz ran playful circles around them. "Did you just come from visiting the Suits?" Myles asked. The term Suits formerly referred to business people who wore suits to their high-powered office jobs as lawyers or CEOs, so it was a natural transition when these same people began wearing literal suits of fibers synthetically engineered to protect them from the virus in the days before the vaccine rolled out. Only Suits could afford suits.

Tuesday shrugged, "They're good people."

"Sure, there are good suits: birthday suits, leisure suits, hearts and spades..." Myles listed.

"You too? I stopped to talk to Sharon on the way here and I've have had enough punnery for today."

"Suit yourself."

"Jesus, Myles."

"All right, I'm done. You want some lunch? Or are we doing a job? I'll need to fuel up first if you need a plane, but we're good to go if you need a truck," Myles offered.

"Plane. But not today. I need a couple of days to sort out details. You want to meet Jeff Brogan?" Tuesday asked expectantly.

"THE Jeff Brogan? The founder of Ultimate Fighting Forever? Are you kidding and please don't be kidding because that would be cruel."

Tuesday smiled, "Yes, THAT Jeff Brogan, who is also a House of Commons representative from L.A. And I'm not kidding. I guess I've got a reputation."

"And you're so humble too," Myles joked. Then he added, "Well, Brogan's politics aside, I'm a huge UFF fan, so you know I'm in."

"I knew you would be."

"Wait, Jeff Brogan uses GoferGoods? Or he's one of those under-the-table-can't-tell-you-details deals?"

"Not important," Tuesday answered. "But I'm going to need to get a Chihuly glass chandelier and a Hoyt Carbon RX 10 with locking rear stabilizer and bow release."

"I don't know what those words mean, but I'm still in."

"That's the great thing about hanging out with you in post-apocalyptic times, Myles. You're always in," Tuesday said. "Well, that and your cooking."

"Huh," said Myles, "I thought maybe it was my sparkling personality."

"We both know it's your airplane."

"Yeah, it's the plane."

When they arrived at Myles' RV near the shores of Lake Whatcom, Tuesday noted a strand of new patio lights strung along the awning. "Adding a little atmosphere?" she asked.

"Yes, and I'm proud of them because it took me like two weeks to get them working. They look better in the dark, obviously."

"I'm sure the ladies will approve," Tuesday teased without smiling. Skilled young men with property and sanity were a hot commodity in any era. Tuesday found Myles attractive, but she had always kept her distance in this regard. Just before the pandemic struck, Myles had been a newly licensed pilot with a job offer from Alaska Airlines in hand, but when the airline industry collapsed, he became one of the millions without employment, and largely abandoned by the government. In the wake of the pandemic though, he'd been resilient, resourceful, and in many cases just damn lucky; over time he obtained a variety of vehicles and now ran his own marginally successful transport business. Myles' services were invaluable to Tuesday. He even had an airplane in a secure hangar nearby where Tuesday was able to store goods from jobs she completed. They had been working together almost as long as she'd been calling herself Tuesday, and Myles had earned her trust time and time again. They had traveled together, met foreign diplomats together, and buried bodies together. Some relationships were more important than sex.

Inside the trailer Myles laid out an array of simple foods, mostly procured through bartering for his services. It could be handy to get paid in cheese by the dairy farmer, paid in homemade peanut butter by the produce farmer, and paid in curry powder and honey by the Suits who wanted to fly to a ski resort in Oregon.

"Ooh, next time I'll add some of the lime juice you got from that job last week. That would definitely improve my salsa! All the jugs are still in the hangar."

"We'll need to get some things from the hangar anyway, I think," Tuesday said. "I'm going to need to do some wooing to make this deal."

"Yeah, what exactly do you have up your sleeve this time?"

"Eventually we're taking fragile glass art and a hunting bow to a TV personality-turned-politician in the Republic of California."

"Ah, and as the preeminent gopher for glass art and hunting

12

equipment, you were the first gopher on Jeff Brogan's list? Well done," Myles approved. He put down a plate of shredded chicken and diced carrots for Oz, who waited politely for Tuesday's nod before digging in.

"First though, I need to get some classy wine from the other side of the mountains, and figure out what to bring as a little... incentive for the Chihuly glass. I was thinking of some of the champagne and cigars, but I'm not sure if that'll be good enough," Tuesday mused.

"Coleman knows you. He'll make the deal even if you don't sweeten him up first. But we've got the Goldwin Metropolitan cigars we picked up in Beverly Hills if you're willing to part with them."

"A few, absolutely. I'm not sure I'm ready to part with the champagne though. I *miss* champagne! Damn France and their grape vine blight!" complained Tuesday.

"Climate change is a bitch."

"Let's save a bottle for ourselves. Or maybe two. For when we have something to celebrate," Tuesday suggested.

"It's ours. We can keep it all if we want it," Myles smiled. "For the moment, let's toast to the next prosperous adventure," he raised his Mason jar of water.

Tuesday clinked her jar against his, "To the next adventure."

Tuesday excelled at packing. After nearly five years of trips running medicine and vaccines for the World Disaster Relief Organization, plus another two years in business for herself, she could easily prepare to take Matchiqua seeds to Cuba or honeybees to Norway. She had systems and lists and protocols for transports. She was meticulous in her work. Clients on GoferGoods appreciated the no-nonsense efficiency; those hiring her for jobs through more opaque means appreciated her discretion.

To prepare for the upcoming journeys, Tuesday gathered materials for packing and transporting the delicate glass sculpture and hunting bow, retrieved items from the airplane hangar that might facilitate smooth transactions, and packed supplies for herself, Myles, and Oz. There was never any question about whether Oz would join them. As a Deliverer for the WDRO, he was allowed access anywhere Tuesday went. Of course, with the advent of the vaccines (seventeen different vaccines, in fact), and global herd immunity achieved, Tuesday and Oz's official status as Deliverers was mostly honorific, but it still entitled them to luxuries such as unfettered border crossings.

Travel plans always hinged on the tenuous availability of fuel. Tuesday paid careful attention to the supply's ebb and flow; it was like gambling in the stock market. Buy low and know when to hang on to what you've got. Gas stations operated intermittently, and often the attached convenience stores had been converted into living quarters for the owners and their families. Most of the gas stations in Bellingham had been creatively repurposed for entirely different endeavors. One became an appliance repair shop, another became a small brewery, and another housed a seamstress' clothing boutique and thrift store. The gas station nearest the college now operated as a virtual reality depot where VR junkies could rent time using a visor plugged into one of the former fueling kiosks to experience something other than this version of the world.

At one of the more reliable fueling stations in town, Myles loaded barrels of gas for the plane into the truck bed, though the bulk of their journey would be powered by bio aviation fuel. Meanwhile, Tuesday paid the attendant for the gas. When applying Tuesday's discount to the fuel purchase, the attendant, an elderly Indian man, prompted, "I know you, but you must show me the tags, like every time." Tuesday pulled out the two small metal tags hanging from a stainless steel chain around her neck and the man nodded. Tucking them back into her shirt, Tuesday absent-mindedly touched the silver locket hanging with her tags. "You wear that necklace always," the man observed, printing her receipt from a handheld machine.

"I do," Tuesday didn't offer more.

"From a boyfriend?"

"No. It's a gift from a long time ago," Tuesday lied. She didn't say that she never took it off or that the previous owner was dead.

"Ah. Pretty necklace, pretty lady," he smiled. "Where is Oz today?" the attendant asked amiably.

"He's here, just behind the truck, don't worry," she reassured him. Some less fortunate Deliverers had lost their dogs during or after the deliveries, some through dangerous missions dropping vaccines in war-torn cities or thick jungles, and some through old age and the passage of time. Oz had been hardly more than a puppy when he and Tuesday earned their title and joined the WDRO seven years ago. Tuesday's breath caught in her throat from the combined thought of losing Oz and the question about her locket.

"I'll see you another time soon, Mr. Modi." Tuesday smiled because she couldn't afford to let her antisocial tendencies cause a fuel supply connection to fizzle. Back at the truck, she hoisted herself into the passenger seat and dropped her head back against the headrest. She closed her eyes and tried to conjure the meditative wood grain lines on the ceiling of her loft. Long, straight line, swerve to the left, through a smear of pine tar, back to straight.

Myles appeared on the driver's side and tipped the seat forward for Oz to jump into the back of the cab.

"This plus the biofuel we've got in the hangar will be more than enough—are you asleep?"

Tuesday kept her eyes closed, "Yes."

"Okay, but tomorrow on the long drive you'll need to stay awake to keep me company because Oz never says anything back."

"That's what makes him such a good listener," Tuesday said. She opened her eyes and suggested, "If we're done doing business, let's go to The Rabbit Hole."

"You can't keep your eyes open, but you want to hang out at a shinery?"

"I'm not tired, I was...meditating. I want to people-watch, and I have credit there for bringing them a packet of dried orange peel last week."

"Ah, do you want to "people-watch" or are you actually looking for someone from Chum?" Myles smirked. Tuesday had a sparsely-detailed account on Chum, and the casual encounter app had provided her with a few liaisons, but she wasn't in the mood today.

"Don't judge. And I haven't used Chum in months."

"No judgement here," Myles assured her, pulling out of the fuel station parking lot, "If Chum and a shinery keep you sane in this world, you're better off than most."

"Oz." Tuesday said. "It's Oz that keeps me sane in this world."

The entrance to The Rabbit Hole peeked out from between two buildings in downtown Bellingham, just a shadowy dip into the pavement that revealed a staircase if you got close enough. While not likely to be a high priority for government law enforcement, shiners operated outside of the liquor control board's regulations, selling small-batch, often home-brewed alcohol to anyone who could pay. Shiners risked being raided and shut down if they earned reputations as violent street gang headquarters or hubs for drug deals, which provided incentive enough for establishments to self-regulate however they saw fit. The peacekeepers at The Rabbit Hole belonged to a street gang who carried spiked billy clubs like miniature medieval maces on their belts, and who claimed this small sector of Bellingham as their own.

At the bottom of the concrete stairway a man and a woman, each with a mace at their waist, shared a hand-rolled cigarette. Tuesday held up the tags around her neck as they passed and the man patted Oz on the head. Inside the dimly lit space, a hodge-podge of light fixtures hung from exposed piping and ancient graffiti added ambiance to otherwise empty walls. There were classier places in Bellingham, with real liquor licenses, consistent menus and coordinated furniture, but Tuesday preferred The Rabbit Hole because it felt like what she imagined a speakeasy from a century ago would have been like. A place to both relax and not, to meet people without really knowing them, or to fade into the dimly lit corners watching others wind up or wind down. A tense card game proceeded quietly at a large table. Most of the other patrons were alone or couples, each with one hand on a Mason jar of moonshine.

Myles pretended to order from Tuesday as he sat down, "Miss, I'll have the catch of the day on a bed of linguine with paprika-roasted cauliflower on the side. And my friend here will have the dog food," he patted Oz's muscular shoulders.

"I'm sorry sir, we're out of everything except the dog food," Tuesday answered, sitting down next to him so both of their backs were to the wall. Oz tucked himself under the table at Tuesday's feet. The bartenders were an unlikely pair of men, one slight with glasses and the other bulky with caterpillar eyebrows.

The thinner man brought a bowl of water and set it on the floor next to Oz. "On the house," he said amiably.

"Hey, don't give away shit for free!" joked the larger man loudly from behind the bar.

"Don't pay attention to him. He was so thrilled with the orange peel you brought that he's been making old fashioneds all week. I'll bring you two."

"Thanks, Nicholas," Tuesday said.

"Have you *seen* Nick's outfit?" called the larger man, "He's too trendy to bring old fashioneds; he only brings NEW fashioneds!"

"Yes, Gabe, I watched every episode of *Project Runway* growing up," Nick called back. He pointed to his crisp hemp shirt, "He thinks my clothing budget is extravagant, but it evens out because he spends a preposterous amount collecting old music. Does anyone really need Adele's *Hello* on vinyl?"

Gabe crossed the bar carrying two drinks with the cleaning rag still in his hand. He put the drinks down and draped an arm around Nicholas. "Hello," he used a sing-song voice, both as a greeting and as the first line

17

of the song. He continued, "It's me."

Nicholas shook his head good-naturedly, and played off the lyrics in monotone, "No, I do not want to meet after all these years!"

Myles obliged, "Not even to go over everything? You know they say time's supposed to heal."

"I ain't done much healing," Tuesday finished the stanza. "So that song might be a load of shit."

Gabe made a show of snapping the rag in the air and turning back toward the bar. He looked over his shoulder at them. "That's why we have to watch sportsball or depressing news on the bar TV. Because you don't appreciate listening to good music."

"Give the patrons what they want," Nicholas said. With a roll of his eyes, he continued, "These news programs exhaust me. I don't know why people want them on. I'd be watching *Transformers* reruns if it were up to me."

Tuesday glanced toward the TV above the bar. An impassioned man shouted into a microphone in front of a crowd, leading the chant, "Unite for life and liberty!" Tuesday stopped with her glass halfway to her lips. The headline "PULL takes hold in Utah" ran along the bottom of the screen. She took a swig of her old fashioned, set the glass down firmly and sucked her teeth. Myles turned to see what had caught her attention.

"People United for Life and Liberty is rallying again? I thought those wackos all disappeared into the mountains of Utah." He glanced at Tuesday, "You know there's hardly anyone who buys that load of crap. PULL's beliefs have only gotten crazier." The news camera zoomed in on the throngs with homemade signs. One banner read "Vaccines Kill!" and another depicted a horned devil brandishing a syringe. Dripping black letters read "Infused with Lies!" underneath the image.

When the camera panned to a crude painting of a dog in a red vest, tipped over with x's for eyes, Nicholas and Gabe exchanged a look. Nicholas muted the TV and announced, "Hits from the 10's 20's and today, coming right up!" Innocuous pop music faded in through the bar's sound system.

"Hey, I was watching that!" protested a patron at the card table.

"Sorry, we're playing music by request," Nicholas said politely.

"Whose request?"

"Mine!" boomed Gabe. The players at the card table grumbled or scoffed and returned to their game.

Tuesday kept watching the screen, the silent angry faces, mouths still shouting and fists still pumping.

"I'm fine," she spoke low enough for only Myles to hear.

Before he could respond, a young woman from the card game stood up, ran a hand through her short spiked hair and tugged her miniskirt into place. She approached Myles and Tuesday with a nervous smile, looking younger the closer she came. "Sorry, my friend didn't see you guys here," she nodded toward Oz under the table. "I mean, I know he doesn't support PULL. He just likes to watch the news."

Tuesday stared blankly, tapping her finger on her Mason jar. The girl continued, "I was riveted the whole time Deliverers were out there. I followed all the missions I could. The one to the Indigenous people of the Amazon was just so...heart-wrenching. All those people saved and the Deliverer and his dog both got chased by that caiman in the river...Epic."

Myles smiled in a way that made the girl blush and run her hands through her hair again. He reassured her, "Of course."

Encouraged, she asked him "You don't have a dog with you, but I know a lot of them have passed on by now. Are you a Deliverer too?"

Myles touched his chest, showing he wore no tags like Tuesday's. "No, not me. But I was a pilot. I flew them in on some missions."

"Oh wow." She touched Myles' arm, "Well, that's really brave too!"

"I like to think I delivered Deliverers," Myles said.

The man who had complained about muting the TV appeared behind the spiky-haired girl. "Ready to go?"

Her eyes were fixed on Myles, "You both have so much to be proud of." She peeked under the table, "And you do too!" The man nodded curtly

19

to Myles and Tuesday, clearing his throat as the girl said, "Okay, we're headed out." Pointedly at Myles, she purred, "SO nice to meet you."

"Thanks," said Tuesday flatly as the couple slipped away.

"You don't always have to be fine," Myles turned to Tuesday. "Sometimes I'm not fine," he shrugged.

Tuesday met his gaze, "No. You're always fine. What's that saying? Oil off a duck's back? Water rolls off a duck?"

"I don't give a flying duck?"

Tuesday forced a smile, "Duck you, Myles."

Back at her plot of land on Alabama Hill, Tuesday let herself and Oz into the tiny house, which, in the darkness, looked just like a cozy cottage and not at all like a converted metal freight shipping container. She hung her tunic on the hook next to Oz's red vest, took her knife out of its holster, and started water boiling for tea on the burner in the kitchenette. While she waited for the water, she invited Oz to sit by her on the little padded bench in the nook by the window. She kicked off her boots, tucked her feet under her and pulled out her phone. She accepted a couple of jobs from GoferGoods that she knew would be simple deliveries, just a matter of knowing who to ask. Then, even though she knew she should resist, she pulled up the Deliverers website. It hadn't been updated in over a year, but much of the content was still there.

"Water's boiling," she said to Oz. "Can you make my tea?" He looked up, but stayed on the cozy bench while Tuesday crushed some leaves and added a mixture of dried herbs to her mug. She picked up her phone again as she sat back down. "Don't look at this site, Oz. It's probably not healthy." She scrolled through the history of the Deliverers, how they had accepted 50 trainers and their dogs when the program launched as part of the new World Disaster Relief Organization in.

She didn't need to read the Deliverers' bios; she knew them all, but looked at the photos anyway. None of the other forty-nine Deliverers had been recent graduates with dogs who'd barely lost their puppy teeth. One

20

was a former cop with his dusky canine unit, another an ex-marine with his blue-tick coonhound. A professional softball player from Cleveland and her low-slung basset hound, a German immigrant predictably with a German short-haired pointer, several mixed breeds with similarly checkered owners—hunters, a white-water rafting guide, a zookeeper.

When the program launched there had been no vaccine. The Deliverers at first had delivered other medications for managing the disease or for purifying water. On missions, the dogs wore tiny cameras mounted on their red vests and responded to precise voice commands from their trainers who sometimes directed the dogs from miles away. The coordination had to be impeccable. Tuesday clicked on a brief video from one of the dog's vests. It was Dirk and Nina in a vast tundra. The camera showed a dog's-eye-view of patchy snow and impassable crevasses of glacier water. She could hear Dirk's heavy breathing and the crunch of Nina's paws in snow booties as they jogged. At the edge of a deep fissure with an icy stream rushing below, Dirk skids audibly to a stop and gives the command, "Go alone." The camera jostles as he pats Nina, steps back and calls, "Jump, Nina!" She does. The ravine sails into and back out of view, as Nina easily clears the water. Dirk is now only audible through the speaker on Nina's vest, "Good girl! Fast, long, straight!" The terrain flies past while Nina sprints until the clip cuts to her arrival at a village. The footage is blurred and shaky as people swarm to greet her and unload the medicine from her packs. The clip ends with the villagers cheering and a child's mitten covering the camera with his hug.

Oz sighed in his sleep and Tuesday realized her tea had grown cold. "That's a lot of lives, pal," she whispered. "Atta boy." She rose gingerly so as not to disturb him and climbed the ladder to her lofted bed. Before closing her eyes, Tuesday exhaled, and traced the pattern of the wood grain: long, straight line, swerve to the left, through a smear of pine tar, back to straight. She turned off the light and tried not to dream.

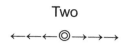

The next morning, Tuesday awoke with the gray dawn and reached for her phone before rolling over in bed. No alerts, texts or holographic messages, though her data connection wasn't strong enough to receive a Holo most of the time anyway. When she swung down from the loft, Oz, who had moved from the bench to his bed during the night, stretched without standing up. His soft brown eyes watched Tuesday as she washed her mug and started water heating for her tea. "That's the kind of morning you're having, huh?" She tousled his ears on her way to the tiny bathroom.

After her shower she stood in front of her steel basin sink and wiped her hand across the foggy mirror, looking herself in the eye through the steam. Between sips of tea she finessed her hair into a loose braid and wrapped her hands for her workout. The tiny shipping container house didn't have eaves, but she'd screwed a post into the side near the kitchen window to hang a punching bag. She never turned down a job because she might have to take or throw a punch. The combination of boxing lessons from Myles, a couple of Krav Maga courses for P.E. credits in college, and growing up in a volatile foster care system meant Tuesday didn't have to be choosy about work. Oz poked his nose into the foliage around the house while Tuesday drummed out a beat on the punching bag. When she reached the sweet spot where exhaustion and exhilaration intersect, she sank onto the wooden step by the front door and unwrapped her hands while she caught her breath. Oz came to the step and looked at her, his tongue lolling in a grin. "C'mere," Tuesday smiled and scratched under the big dog's neck. "You're nothing but a big puppy. No one would guess you're seven; you don't look a day over five!" Tuesday sat for a few minutes watching the draping arms of the weeping willow sway in the gentle breeze before turning her eyes to the city of

Bellingham below. "Time to go, pal," she said to Oz.

At the airplane hangar Myles was drilling the final screws into the hefty crate Tuesday had built from old pallet wood the day before. "Oh thanks," she said. "The drill didn't have enough solar charge left to finish that last panel yesterday."

"You can thank an unusually sunny Northwest morning," he replied. "And I think we're all set to go now since we're just doing the one pick up in Tacoma today."

"Museum of Glass, here we come," Tuesday said.

With the crate gently resting on a layer of straw in the truck bed, Tuesday stuffed the inside of the crate with cotton batting and wood wool. In exchange for a few luxuries, the merchants at the market ensured Tuesday didn't run out of materials for delivering delicate items. "I miss bubble wrap," she said, not for the first time. "Who'd have guessed the Sealed Air company would go out of business as soon as the postal service went under?"

"I don't even care about packing with it," Myles admitted." What I miss is popping it. Everything about that was so satisfying. The sound. The sensation."

"Children today will never know that joy," Tuesday said wistfully.

"Do you think there's something primal about popping bubble wrap? I mean...it's a universal human pleasure," Myles mused.

Tuesday shook her head, "Get in the truck, Myles."

"Okay," Tuesday started as she pulled the truck out onto the highway, "If I'm lucky and Coleman has a piece he's willing to part with for the price Representative Brogan is willing to pay, we should be in and out in about… forty-eight hours."

"I guess you should feel privileged Coleman likes you so much. He wouldn't let just anyone walk away with precious fine art."

"I know," Tuesday agreed, "And I like him too. And his wife. I just don't feel much like socializing lately."

Myles smirked, "Do you ever?"

"No."

"Me, on the other hand—" Myles started.

Tuesday interrupted, "Oh, speaking of socializing, were you going to stop in to see your brother while I'm at the museum?"

"If it's going to take you forty-eight hours, *yes*," Myles confirmed.

"It was a joke," Tuesday smiled, "Sort of."

"Should I have packed a weekend bag?" he asked.

"No," Tuesday laughed, "But..."

"We're set for overnight, no problem," Myles anticipated. "Except that I already ate all the jerky."

"We've only been driving ten minutes!"

"Okay, not ALL the jerky," he turned to Oz in the back of the cab, "Don't worry, I didn't eat your treats."

"You'll have to save room for your own treats," Tuesday said, "Isn't your brother's wife the best baker in Tacoma? She'll stuff you full of scones and pies."

"Yessss," Myles put his hand over his heart. "She's a saint," he sighed.

"Category?" Tuesday initiated a game they often played.

"Cars named after cities," Myles suggested.

She paused. "Santa Fe. Rode around in one of those at foster home number four."

"The Tacoma, of course."

"Durango. There's one in Mexico AND Colorado" Tuesday flaunted.

"Is the Soul named after Seoul, or after the immortal essence of being?" asked Myles as he watched the passing landscape out the window.

"I do not know," Tuesday shook her head. "Tesla."

"Doesn't count—it was a car before it was a city."

"Fine."

"Drone," Myles pointed to the sky.

"Is a drone a type of c—Oh. Drone." Tuesday looked into the rearview mirror, "What kind?"

"Trooper, I think."

"All good then," she tapped the Deliverer tags hanging around her neck and then pulled them out to rest over her shirt.

"I did all the paperwork and registration for the transports, but it's impossible to tell what's out of date or which government to submit anything to," Myles complained.

"Can't stop me anyway," Tuesday shrugged.

"And when I tried to send in a request to visit Utah next week, I might as well have sent smoke signals. Or a mail delivery owl...Let's get an owl."

"No."

"Speaking of Utah," Myles began, "Do we really have to go all the way out there to get the fancy hunting bow Jeff Brogan wants?"

"Yes. And I know you're thinking about PULL and their damn rally, but I don't care. No stupid anti-science cult is keeping me from doing a job."

"I didn't know you were such a Brogan fan."

"I'm not. It's the principle of it. I'm not changing plans or sitting on my ass waiting for something to blow over. Not just this time, but always. Regime change, rallies, riots, whatever. I'll do what I need to, and I'm not going to cower in a corner waiting for "normal" or "safe" any more than I'd sit around and wait for my fairy godmother."

"I think *Regime Change, Rallies, Riots, Whatever* is a great title for a book," Myles said.

Tuesday tightened her grip on the wheel and started angrily, "You're not hearing me—"

"Sorry, just a joke," Myles conceded. "I hear you. You don't let other people's bullshit get in the way. I can be on board with that."

"Thank you." Tuesday was appeased.

26

"I can also help make sure your head stays attached to your shoulders while you stand so tall on principles."

Tuesday looked at Myles out of the corner of her eye. She wanted to protest, but instead answered, "Thanks for that too."

Tacoma's renowned Museum of Glass hadn't operated as such for a number of years, but the exterior remained unchanged. The unusual structure was an enormous tilted cone, as if someone had plucked a giant calla lily and dropped it face down onto the Tacoma waterfront landscape. When Tuesday pulled up to the loading dock, she grabbed her knapsack, hopped out of the truck and let Oz out of the cab.

"Say hi to the family for me, Myles."

"You could meet them someday you know," he answered, sliding into the driver's seat.

"Someday."

Tuesday pressed the button at the door marked "deliveries" and heard the buzzer sound. A few moments later, a groan rumbled out from the loading dock's huge garage door and it began to rise, screeching as it opened. When it ground to a halt and the reverberations faded, a figure sauntered into view, framed by the giant door, his arms outstretched. Coleman announced himself to the silent museum parking garage, "Hey, hey! Look who's here!"

"Do you mean you or me? I've arrived, but YOU'RE the one making an entrance. I was just trying to quietly use the side door!" Coleman managed to bring out Tuesday's more affable side.

"You're no fun," he said, wrapping her in his arms.

"You're a showman," she answered, smiling into his shirt.

Just how Coleman came to reign sovereign over the Museum of Glass and its contents was a mystery. He and his wife were the sole inhabitants of the museum and the final word on fine art dealings of all kinds in the

Pacific Northwest. Coleman himself used the museum's glass blowing hot shop to produce twisted spirals of bright glass, both graceful and aggressive in their beauty. His wife, Elora, painted. The sprawling galleries of the museum now housed her own works among the other art exhibitions that had been on display when the pandemic struck and the museum had closed. In the cavernous entryway she had painted an entire two-story mural dedicated to the spring when the pandemic first shocked the world. In her medium, the sickness swirled into a frenzy that clashed with the earth-shaking "big one" that struck Bellingham, Tacoma and the whole state of Washington. The earthquake followed too closely on the heels of too many other disasters, and similar catastrophic chains played out across the globe. But through the turmoil, there was hope. At least, that's what Tuesday always thought when she looked at the mural.

When Tuesday and Coleman arrived in the entryway from the loading dock, Elora met them and embraced Tuesday. "Tuesday Devlin, make yourself at home! Stop at the mural on your way to the lounge," she said, "But don't dawdle too long, his spicy bourbon meatballs just reached perfection!"

"Elora Coleman, you just can't stop talking about my meat, can you?" Coleman winked at his wife.

Unfazed, Elora answered, "Nope. I'll tell Tuesday all about how you rubbed the oil and spices on it before—"

Tuesday broke in good-naturedly, "I'll just have to get the recipe later, thank you!" She stood in front of the mural while the Colemans plated a meal in what used to be the museum's cafe. Tuesday's visits were infrequent, but each time, she stared at the expanse of colors mingling into meaning on the wall. She felt, rather than saw, the rising tide of the pandemic, and her stomach always turned to stone when she looked at the earthquake. For her it was the mark of death and the beginning of reeling into dark oblivion. Emerging from the darkness though, eventually, came a certain brightness, a bursting finality of light and air and truth. If she looked back at the earthquake, Tuesday could see that the

28

brightness was there the whole time, first as a thin golden thread and then a pale swath, obscured, but shining its hardest behind the shadows. Each time Tuesday studied the mural she found some new wisp of color she hadn't noticed before. This time her eyes were drawn to a sharp stroke of red, just at the heart of the earthquake, amidst the confusion.

"Golden Metropolitan cigars!" Elora called excitedly from the cafe, interrupting Tuesday's reverie, "You must have a big-ass favor to ask!"

"Maybe," answered Tuesday.

Tuesday and the Colemans spent the evening in a variety of activities throughout the former Museum of Glass. They reclined on the patio and blew smoke rings from the cigars, watching the rings expand out of existence over the waterfront. They projected old grunge music videos onto the wall like a movie screen and played chase with Oz in the lobby. They competed to see who could catch a tossed blueberry in their mouth from the farthest away.

Later, Tuesday watched from the hot shop viewing deck as Coleman coaxed form out of molten glass. A 10-foot-tall beast of a furnace, easily the size of a downtown apartment, occupied a commanding central space in the building's giant cone. Coleman spun brilliant bulbs of liquid glass on the ends of poles in a set-up clearly intended for an entire team of artists. He set one pole spinning as if on a spit, while he pressed another glob with paddles of graphite, and pulled tendrils out of a third blazing ball. He worked like an athlete, focused and confident with sweat from the furnace's heat glistening at his collarbone. From the arena deck, he looked like a firedancer, twirling the glass and poles rhythmically, pressing, pulling and fusing until he bowed to signal his creation was complete. Tuesday applauded for the final creation, a five-foot sculpture of what appeared to be a radiant carnivorous sunflower.

Finally Tuesday and Coleman went to the museum's skybridge, formerly the pedestrian connection to the building from the street below. They lay on their backs, staring up at the hundreds of multicolored glass pieces, spirals, disks, spheres and curlicues, suspended from the skybridge ceiling like an alien botanical garden.

"This is the best way to do business," Tuesday said.

"It's better when you're high," answered Coleman.

"Which of these did you make and which are genuine Chihuly designs?" she asked.

"Chihuly was a hack."

Tuesday laughed. "Okay, then choosing a chandelier for my client should be no problem?"

"Ooh, working for some Suit again then, huh? You know there are hardly any Chihuly sculptures intact. He'd stopped designing even before the sand shortage. Do they want a refurbished one? I'll fuse some upside down vases together; they'll love it," Coleman suggested.

Tuesday made a non-committal sound.

"Or *I'll* just make a full chandelier and you *tell* them it was made by Chihuly. The Suits won't know the difference."

"You're probably right, but I'm going for authenticity on this one. Don't want to take the chance of pissing off the wrong people, you know."

Coleman snickered, "I didn't know you cared who you pissed off!"

"Oh stop it. So, can we make a deal?"

"No doubt, Sourpuss. No doubt."

When the deal was decided, Tuesday slipped out of the museum into the night with Oz. She would sleep at the Coleman's guest loft in an adjacent building, but not before making one more stop. Instinctively she tapped her dagger, holstered snugly at her thigh as usual. Oz was unconcerned with the deep night and its on-goings, trotting with his tail in the air, which put Tuesday at ease. They passed a gas station like the one in Bellingham, converted into a virtual reality hub with junkies curled up against the kiosks or pacing and whispering to themselves. As Tuesday turned down a more brightly lit street, she might as well have stepped into another era. Cobblestones paved the narrow road and music from a corner violinist floated into the air. A few cafe tables under glowing lanterns dotted the sidewalks. In front of a green door with a curved iron handle stood a hand-painted sandwich board sign reading "Gilman House" in dreamy cursive.

The violinist's song faded out behind Tuesday and Oz as they stepped into Gilman House. She surveyed the venue quickly, scanning the cascading red curtains and velvet oval-backed chairs that lent an ambiance of the 1920's to the room. Suddenly Oz's tail began to wag and he whined eagerly, his mouth open in a wide doggy smile. Generally he reserved this behavior for greeting only Tuesday's dearest friends, so she was aggravated when she spotted sitting at the bar, the only person about whom she and Oz disagreed.

Oz bounded across the room to a man in a long leather jacket sitting alone on a low-backed barstool. The man faced away from Tuesday, but when he turned to look at Oz, the handsome angles of his features, high cheekbones and arched brows were unmistakable.

"Mox," muttered Tuesday.

Oz's whole hind end wagged along with his tail for a few moments before he couldn't resist putting his paws up on Justin Mox's knees. Mox's hair was either bleached or so blonde it was nearly white, and shaved close along the sides, leaving the top long enough to be slicked into a small wave over his forehead.

Mox put down his drink and said, "Alright, you big lug!" in his British accent. He thumped Oz's sides and continued talking to the dog while Tuesday took a breath and crossed the bar.

"Oh, you brought that trollop along, eh? Ah well, I won't hold it against you, lad."

"Hello, Mox," said Tuesday icily. "I see they've significantly lowered their standard of clientele at Gilman House."

"Yes, you just breezed right in," Mox replied.

"What brings you here—did someone need a knife in their back?" she

31

asked.

"Hm. I don't think I see that sort of job on GoferGoods," Mox answered drily. Damn, he was hot. "No, I'm here because we both know this is the only joint in Cascadia with real gin since the juniper blight. Put your hackles down and let this gentleman pour you a drink," Mox gestured to a bartender in a fez.

Tuesday looked down at Oz, who had flopped contentedly at Mox's feet. "Fine, but only because Oz is so comfortable." She scooted her barstool slightly away from Mox and perched on the edge. "And because of the gin."

"I always recommend the Shambler, but it would be sexier to hear you ask for a London Buck," Mox said, looking her straight in the eye.

"Does that line *ever* work?"

"All the time."

Tuesday held his gaze while she ordered. "Gilman Gimlet, please," and added, "I'm picking up a hunting bow later this week, so London Bucks will want to steer clear."

"Mm, would you say you'd like to bag a buck then? I like the sound of that." Mox's smile was slow and self-assured.

"Too bad England wouldn't take you back," she said. "A semester overseas turned into a decade overseas. Your horizons must be SO broad by now." Tuesday curled her fingers around the stem of her gimlet glass as it arrived.

"Cheers," Mox tipped his glass toward her.

"To what?" she asked. "To former friends who accidentally got into the same line of work and who Fate insists on occasionally tossing into odd situations together?"

"Friends?" Mox paused contemplatively, "Is that what we were?"

"I never thought much about what we were," Tuesday said.

"You lie," Mox said pleasantly.

Tuesday couldn't let it slide, "That's a very pot-kettle-color-identifying statement, I'd say."

"Fair," Mox conceded. "Cheers to being human then."

"To being human."

After a long pause during which Oz stared enthusiastically at Mox, Mox stared stoically at Tuesday, and Tuesday stared uncomfortably at her drink, Mox asked, "So what's the girl who can get anything for anyone been up to these days? Snagged the Hope diamond and delivered it to Atlantis with Fido? Why are you picking up a bow? I thought you didn't do weapons."

"I don't do *firearms*."

"Still playing by your own arbitrary rules, I see. Well, you're missing out. There's good money in firearms," Mox said. "Especially if you're not fussy about rules. Or a little blood."

"Depends on whose blood," Tuesday said simply, "But no, I don't do guns. I don't want that on my conscience. And I don't want to talk about work."

"Then you pick the topic," Mox said with mild exasperation."Where's your dashing pilot? He's easier to talk to."

"He doesn't like you."

"All right, so the Flying Fool is off somewhere not liking me, and you're here for the gin and maybe a job but we don't want to talk about it," Mox summarized.

Tuesday glanced at the door for what she realized was the third time since she'd sat down.

"Are you waiting for someone?" Mox asked. "Oh, is a Chum on the way? That's why you didn't bring your pilot along, I see! Interesting, I'd have thought he'd be an excellent...wingman."

"Really?" Tuesday lifted her eyebrows and tried not to smile at the pun. Mox started his slow smile and Tuesday gave in. "Fine, I want to talk about my love life even less than I want to talk about work. I've got a couple of big deliveries, but nothing like the backstreet shit you get into.

No firearms or human trafficking…"

"I don't do human trafficking," Mox brushed her off. "Sometimes I might move people around—human shuffling, if you will."

"I won't," said Tuesday, starting to warm up after half a gimlet. "I've got a Suit who shall remain nameless waiting for high ticket items with a lot of red tape."

"You always did enjoy ducking under red tape," Mox acknowledged, "Or cutting through it, or painting it blue…"

"Truth."

"So, Utah," Mox paused. "Seems like a bloody stupid idea right now."

"I didn't ask you," Tuesday shrugged. "I'm not afraid of anti-intellectual PULL philistines."

"Philistines!" Mox smirked. "You sound like you're back in Anthro 201."

"I REALLY don't want to talk about Anthro 201," she spat.

Mox backed down, "Right, right. Shouldn't go digging up fossils."

"Damn right you shouldn't," Tuesday said earnestly, adding under her breath, "Back-stabbing bastard."

He pretended not to hear. "I know you don't exactly keep your finger on the pulse of political on-goings Just thought I'd mention there's some relevant unrest."

"Right. The guy who looks like a vampire from the 1990's is lecturing me about current events?"

"Vampires are the sexiest of the undead," he said.

"And, hang on, I didn't mention Utah to you," Tuesday narrowed her eyes.

"You didn't need to." Mox leaned toward her, "I hear things."

She frowned, "Well, that's creepy. Thanks for your concern."

"And the back-stabbing was for your own good," Mox said out of the side of his mouth, bringing his glass to his lips.

"Which time?" Tuesday jeered.

"Every time."

She made a disgusted sound, "I'm going to need another drink if I'm going to endure you any longer."

"I'm not holding you here with anything except my charms," Mox nodded his head toward the door, "Feel free."

He was right, which made Tuesday clench her jaw. That smooth British accent. "Oz and the gin are keeping me here."

"Hold on, getting a Holo," he interrupted, touching his wrist and turning away.

"Ooh, you've got high class clients too—sending Holos," she said to his back as her second drink arrived. "I'm not the only one working for Suits."

"Not important," Mox turned to face her again. "Where were we? Oh yes, Oz and gin and I'm just icing on the cake of your evening."

"I always preferred ice cream," she replied, but let herself give him a hint of a smile.

"Speaking of Oz, how's the old boy? Looks chipper as ever."

Tuesday glanced down at Oz lying near Mox's feet, "Yeah, he's happy to be—" when she glanced back up, she caught just the slightest movement of Mox's hand. "What was that?" she demanded.

"What?" he asked, sounding surprised.

"When I looked down. You did something."

"I'm always doing something. Breathing. Blinking…"

Tuesday stood up in alarm, "No, you did something!"

"Just stay calm," Mox soothed, "There's nothing to be worked up about."

She pushed her barstool back with her boot and stepped closer to Mox. "You put something in my drink," she growled.

The look on his handsome face told her all she needed to know. She swung her fist toward his jaw, but he caught her wrist and stood up, stepping so close she could see the flecks of gold in his eyes.

His voice was low, "Don't know how to use that dagger on your hip,

35

then?" He squeezed her wrist tighter.

"Hey!" The bartender with the fez intervened, charging across the room "None of that in my bar—get the hell out!"

Tuesday was enraged now, "It's him!" she shoved Mox with her free hand, "He put something in my drink!" she accused.

The bartender's fist landed where Tuesday's had been aiming, sending Mox stumbling backward, tripping on his barstool. Oz began to bark and the bartender grabbed Mox, dragging him to the door and sending him sprawling onto the pavement. "I never want to see you in here again!" he shouted, and pushed Tuesday out the door after him, "You either!"

"What the fuck is wrong with you?" Tuesday looked down at Mox, who propped himself up on his elbow and touched the blood trickling out of the corner of his mouth.

"Dammit, I really liked that bar."

She kicked him in the stomach.

Mox groaned and Oz started to bark again. "C'mon Oz," she turned on her heel.

"I'm sorry, Birdie," he said just loudly enough for her to hear.

Something about the words, softly spoken, hit Tuesday. Hard. She stopped with her back to him, feeling her racing heart rise up in her throat. He'd always called her Birdie when they were in college, but after the day of the earthquake, in the times they'd crossed paths, he'd never used it again.

She resisted the urge to turn back and kick him again. Instead she ran. Oz loped along after her as she darted down the cobblestone streets, past the glowing lanterns, and idyllic cafe seats under the stars. Tuesday ran until she reached the Colemans' outbuilding near the Museum of Glass. She flung open the door and slammed it behind Oz. Standing in the middle of the spacious flat, covering her face with both hands, Tuesday felt her breath coming in deep gasps. The room seemed to spin. Finally the pressure and warmth of Oz leaning against her knees brought her back.

Tuesday buried her fingers in the fur of Oz's neck. "We're okay," she said. She inhaled slowly and forced herself to notice the old hardwood floors, polished to a sheen, the houseplants with vines weaving up the window frames set into cheerful yellow and teal walls. "Everything is fine," she told herself weakly. She found the filtered water in the kitchen and poured herself a glass, imagining the liquid sliding down her throat, into her stomach and through her veins. She still felt on fire. The bedroom nook held a four-poster bed with a makeshift canopy of rose-colored organza, and a nest-shaped wicker chair. Falling back onto the bed, Tuesday patted the plush comforter beside her to invite Oz to join her, an indulgence never allowed in her tiny house, since the bed there was on a platform only accessible by a vertical ladder. Oz snuffled around in the blankets while Tuesday willed the adrenaline to leave her body, longing for the woodgrain ceiling of her own shipping crate home. "Glad you're pleased," she said sincerely to Oz, who stretched and sighed.

She curled into a ball in the expansive bed, squeezed her eyes shut, and tried to sleep.

The dream always started the same way. Blurred nighttime shadows of trees racing by, the sickly sensation of curves taken too quickly. The steering wheel cold under her white knuckles. Her vision fogging up from the edges. The world becoming dark and formless. She could feel the engine roaring as she pressed the pedal harder. Suddenly a flash of a figure, pupil-less eyes reflecting like bright coins in the headlights, the silver canine staring, a harbinger. Screams from the seat beside her. There is always screaming.

Three

It had been happening more lately, the dream. Maybe this time it was the rumbling of the train station near the flat reminding her of the earthquake, or maybe it was contemplating Elora's museum mural again that triggered the nightmare. Maybe it was Mox. The dream always shook her, and when she awoke twisted in the clinging blankets of the four-poster bed, she was doubly rattled. She should have been disturbed by Mox's gall and villainy—she should have been outraged that he'd tried to spike her drink. Instead, it was his final utterance that haunted her. Through the graveyard of her subconscious, the words clawed to the surface and burst out of the earth. The tone, the accent, the timbre of his voice. *I'm sorry, Birdie.*

Even now Tuesday felt she had to gulp air into her lungs to calm herself. She sat up and looked down at Oz, who had moved to the floor during the night, probably because Tuesday made an unpleasant bedmate when she dreamt. Dawn had not quite arrived, and even though only a couple of hours had passed since she'd run through the streets to escape Mox's words, she knew sleep would evade her. She tried to appreciate the space and solitude of the Colemans' flat, moving to the nest chair where she wrapped herself in a robe Elora had laid out for her to borrow. "Make me some coffee, Oz," she demanded straight-faced. Oz did not. "You're right, coffee would make my heart explode," she conceded. "You're always so reasonable." Oz yawned.

Tuesday thought back to the last time she'd seen Mox—on that job in the heat of the Arizona desert. They had each gotten what they needed. No one died. The year before that there had been the run-in with an Eastern Washington rebel militia. Again, she and Mox had been forced to work together; it hadn't been pleasant, but again, everyone had survived. A couple of years before that, when Tuesday and Oz were at the height of their Deliverer days, there was the time Mox had rerouted vaccine distributions to suit his whims. Maybe that time people had died. It was the first betrayal though, that really stung.

The first time Tuesday had seen Justin Mox was during their junior year at Western Washington University. She had noticed his physique, slender but muscular, as she followed him into the lecture hall for the first day of anthropology class. She caught his eye during the lecture and he rewarded her with an alluring raised eyebrow. The next day before class she beelined for him, slid casually into the desk beside him and asked, "What do you know about being human?" "Too little and too much, Birdie," he had replied.

Looking out the window of the flat onto the empty street below, Tuesday watched as sparse raindrops began to fall, plastering stubborn leaves to the pavement. A train whistled in the distance, signaling that somewhere in the early dawn life charged onward.

Tuesday knew a con artist when she met one. The term seemed so apt for what it described— manipulating people was indeed an art. Mox was other things too, of course. An excellent photographer, an avid soccer fan. But most endearing to Tuesday was that he had dazzlingly illustrated the difference between articulate and silver-tongued, between intelligent and cunning. Back then she had thought she was perpetually in step with him, or perhaps even a half-step ahead. During the last quarter of their senior year, they schemed together to steal the answer key to their Anthropology 201 final.

Tuesday realized she was famished. "Hungry?" she asked Oz, who was investigating a potted ficus tree by the built-in bar. "Please don't 'water' any of the plants." She slid out of the robe and willed her body to take her to the kitchen, where she discovered sun-dried tomatoes, some sort of salted fish, and cubes of gelatinous microalgae. "There's even jerky for you, buddy." Tuesday got Oz's attention and tossed him a palm-sized flap of dried meat. "No pepper, just how you like it."

With the tomatoes, canned fish, and a mug of steaming hyssop tea, Tuesday returned to the robe and nest chair by the window. In the end, when Mox ratted her out to the university authorities for cheating, and she'd been threatened with expulsion, it hadn't mattered in the awarding of her degree. After all, the semester had progressed alongside a metaphorical tsunami of disease, and had concluded with a literal shaking of the earth itself. But it had broken Tuesday.

She had thought the risky part was stealing the answer key. It was not. It was loving someone.

Oz gnawed on his breakfast near the window where Tuesday watched the sun begin to rise into the heavy sky. Eventually, she saw a familiar truck roll to a stop along the curb in front of the building, and she watched an even more familiar man get out of the cab. She was yanked back into the present. Thank God for sensible, solid Myles. She exhaled slowly and imagined slamming the nightmare and Mox's words into the glove box of an abandoned vehicle, carried but forgotten.

Before Myles reached the curb, Tuesday pried open the old window and called down, "What time zone are you IN?"

"Soft, what light through yonder window breaks," Myles answered from the street, his arms open wide.

"Screw you." She was smiling.

"Oh, speak again, bright angel!"

She shook her head "Hang on, I'll come let you in."

"Tea?" she offered, when Myles entered the flat and examined the room.

"No thanks."

"I'll be ready by six, right on schedule," she said, combing her fingers through her hair.

"Yeah." He studied her. "You sort of look ready now. Did you sleep?"

She deflated. "Not much. I had a...rough night."

"Was it that dream?" he knitted his brow.

"Yes..." she faltered.

"Feel free to tell me about it anytime," he said, half-joking.

Tuesday considered what it might be like to finally unburden herself of the weight she had carried for ten years. What would it be like to divulge everything to someone? "Later," she said slowly, trying out the feeling of the word on her tongue. "I can talk a little bit. On the drive."

Myles froze with a sun-dried tomato halfway to his mouth. He blinked. "Okay."

"Don't be so shocked."

"Okay," he repeated, then forged ahead, "Well, there's still plenty of time to finish your tea before six. And I have pumpkin oat cakes in the truck for you. My brother knows how much you like them."

"Why does he know that?" Tuesday stopped straightening the covers on the bed and looked at him.

"Because I told him," Myles shrugged. "And his wife, Gwen, she—"

"I ran into Mox," Tuesday blurted.

"Your unscrupulous frenemy ex who we can't seem to avoid? Damn, you did have a rough night."

"And I need a *really* good apology gift for Gilman House if I'm ever going to be allowed back in there," Tuesday threw her arms in the air.

Myles winced for her and sat down heavily in the nest chair. "What happened?"

Tuesday faced him, but tilted her head back and addressed the ceiling, "I was bitchy; he was a dick, we argued and got thrown out. I guess."

"You guess?"

"Basically."

"Well, things didn't turn out so badly last time he swooped out of his lair to interfere."

"Are you comparing him to Batman or Dracula or...?"

"Not sure. He just seems like the type who would swoop."

"Well this time it turned out badly." She thought for a moment about his "lair." Mox lived somewhere on Antique Row near Gilman House, in a space above one of the abandoned old curiosity shops, that much she knew. One more gimlet, one more slow smile, one more light touch of his forearm against hers, and would she have gone back to his lair with him? He must have known she could be easily persuaded, but then why try to spike her drink?

"Sage?" Myles suggested.

"What?" Tuesday returned to their conversation.

"For Gilman House. You said you need an apology gift. Do they need sage? Do they have a supply?"

Tuesday thought for a moment. "Maybe. And we're going over the mountains; there's a couple of herb stands along the highway in Liberty Republic sometimes."

"Your note could say, 'I wish I'd been a little sager.' Because...sage...wise...You know?"

Tuesday shook her head, "Thanks Myles."

The Chihuly chandelier was gorgeous and gigantic. It lay spread out on the floor of the Museum of Glass like a glittering sea monster extending bright beckoning tentacles. The upper portion was at least five feet across and the numerous dangling pieces were all taller than Tuesday. Coleman knelt over the chandelier, gingerly dismantling it for transport.

"Looks like you've slain the Kraken," Tuesday greeted him.

"She was a worthy adversary," he answered, "but in the end, pride in her own beauty was her downfall." Tuesday knelt beside him and touched the smooth, cool glass silently. He continued, "She thought she was the prettiest one. That's why I chose to sell her."

"But she wasn't the prettiest?"

"If she hadn't thought so much of herself, she might have been. Pride clouds beauty."

"I'm going to pretend to understand." Tuesday started to wrap one delicate detached piece reminiscent of a six-foot sea urchin spike.

"Watch out you don't impale someone with that thing. Are we transporting art or a weapon?" Myles appeared, looking down at the glass spread out on the floor.

"Well, if it isn't Myles Whatever-your-last-name-is the pilot!" Coleman grinned. "Been awhile."

"How you doin', Coleman. Nice to see you again."

Tuesday broke in, "He doesn't need a last name. He runs a transport business and his name is Myles. MILES."

Myles ignored this amiably, "Oz came in with us, but he's glued to the cafe now. I think Elora's frying up some hash he's optimistic about."

"Can't blame him. I'm optimistic about breakfast, too," said Coleman, rising to his feet and stretching his back. "It's all in manageable pieces. Now we just need to protect it."

"That sounds so profound, even though I know you're just talking about the chandelier," Myles said.

"Am I?" asked Coleman absently.

With the chandelier safely nestled in the soft materials and secured in the truck bed, Tuesday opened the cab to let Oz hop in the back. He made it on his second attempt.

"Sore?" she asked the dog. "We certainly did more jogging than planned. Maybe we can get you a doggie massage later."

"I want to drive," Myles volunteered. "Precious cargo needs a gentle touch."

Tuesday pretended to be offended. "My touch is like cotton candy on a cloud!"

"That sounds...sticky," Myles said.

"Okay, get your asses on the road," Coleman joked and winked at

Tuesday. "And tell that Suit you're working for that he's lucky you picked up the job. Ask for a tip."

On the road Tuesday watched the scenery slip past—abandoned industrial buildings, swaths of burn scars from wildfires, and eventually a few restored cities. The drive between Tacoma and Bellingham never seemed to trigger the dream, or cause her pulse to quicken. It was only when trees whizzing past closed in on narrow curves that her heart raced.

"Category," Myles interrupted her thoughts. "Boys' names that are also verbs."

"Nick."

"Pierce."

"Lance. Why are these all verbs related to stabbing?" Tuesday asked.

"How about Pat then?" Myles suggested, "That sounds more benign."

"Rob. Not benign."

"Mark."

"Um. Wade."

"Niiice," Myles nodded and paused.

"Is that all you got?" Tuesday prompted.

"So," Myles started, " I don't want to *harry* you, but you were going to *grant* me the privilege of hearing about the recurring nightmare you've been *stew*ing over. *Will you*? Or were you *josh*ing?"

"Ugh, Ralph." Tuesday propped her elbow on the door panel of the truck and rested her head on her fist. She sighed, "It's been happening more often. I used to just get the same little snippet every couple of months. Now sometimes it's longer than a snippet, more like a scene from a movie, and it happens maybe once a week."

"But," Myles was eager, "What's it ABOUT? I knew you never wanted to talk about it, so I never asked."

"Yeah, I know I know," Tuesday said, "Don't rush me!"

"It's been seven years!"

44

Tuesday breathed deeply, "It's an accident. Everything is dark and swirling and I'm so angry I can't see a damn thing, but I'm gunning it anyway. Suddenly there's this dog—thing. Right in the middle of the road, just standing, staring with blank, shining eyes. I swerve and feel myself slam from side to side, rolling, listening to the crunching of metal and the screaming…That's the worst."

Myles fixed his eyes on the road. "It's not just a nightmare, is it?" More statement than question.

"No."Tuesday turned her gaze back out the window, "It's real."

"That's jacked up."

Back in Bellingham with the chandelier safely stowed in the airplane hangar and evening beginning to fall, Tuesday walked through town to clear her head with Oz at her side. Should she have told Myles more? Putting the images into words felt like bobbing for apples—attempting to capture thoughts that dodged and drifted. Voluntary waterboarding with a questionable reward. She didn't even tell him the worst parts. She did feel relief in finally having explained even a little of the vignette that was lodged so thoroughly in her psyche, but it also raised new anxieties. The dream was already coming more often. Tuesday sometimes could hang onto just a little more, could see more blood, could hear the rain pounding on the shattered windshield. Already when she woke, guilt clung to her like a hangover.

Tuesday intentionally skirted the block where the Whatcom County animal shelter, now boarded up, still stood. She felt the shelter drawing her closer, but she didn't want to see the building itself. That would trigger the nightmare for sure. The surrounding streets were not Bellingham's finest; Suits generally steered clear of the sector. A jungle of vegetation from medians and roundabouts spilled out of their containers to claim sidewalks and roads. Tuesday passed a building collapsed by the earthquake; cheatgrass, brambles, and shrubs had rendered it an accidental unruly botanical garden occupied by transients.

45

The VR junkies and other misfits didn't frighten Tuesday. She could easily visualize a trajectory that would land someone in the rubble of an abandoned building, or huddled in a thicket, blocking out the world with goggles. The loss of a satisfying career and happy home, loved ones succumbing to the pandemic, the present unbearable and the future even bleaker—free falling with no safety net. Tuesday's free fall was triggered by the loss of any hope of career or home, her own brush with death, and the death of the one person who truly mattered to her. It was not through strength of character, but through random chance that she and Oz were walking under the flickering streetlights en route to their tiny shipping container house, instead of sheltering in wreckage each night, starving, crazy, or worse.

"You're a good soul, Oz," Tuesday said.

A soft gray morning broke over the tiny house on Alabama Hill the following day while Tuesday stared at the wood slatted ceiling from the mattress of her loft. Long, straight line, swerve to the left, through a smear of pine tar, back to straight. She inhaled and focused on the sound of a robin's insistent call from the trees nearby. Sensing the tension in her muscles, she stretched her arms above her head and pointed her toes as she exhaled. She rolled onto her side and peered down at Oz, who raised his eyebrows at her, but did not lift his head. "I miss listening to frogs at night," Tuesday said. She turned to Oz, "When was the last time you heard a frog?" Oz didn't reply.

She swung down from the loft, landing lightly on her bare feet. "It's dry enough for outdoor yoga today I think." Oz watched her shred some cooked chicken for his breakfast, licking his lips. "I don't know how you can eat this in the morning," she said. "Lucky for me, I still have some pumpkin oat cakes. Thank you Myles." She smiled to herself as she watched the heating element glow in her toaster oven.

Still licking the last of the crumbs from her fingers and without changing out of her thin night tunic, Tuesday opened the door and followed Oz out. "Some mornings you need to kick some ass, and some mornings you just need to be zen," she said to no one. Oz had already loped away, half-heartedly chasing a squirrel. Tuesday took a clean throw blanket down from her drying line and laid it out on the clover, seating herself in lotus position. After a series of poses that caused just a glisten of sweat to shine on her skin, Tuesday returned to lotus position and counted her breaths. Suddenly she heard the screams. The world was a blur of spinning shadows and she felt herself thrown against the car door as the vehicle rolled. A trickle of blood reached her eye. Through the rain and the jagged spider-web cracks in the windshield, she made out a figure running away, holding something triumphantly in the air.

Tuesday gasped and snapped open her eyelids, her heart thundering in her chest. It had never happened when she was awake before. Tuesday slumped onto her back and draped her arm over her face. How was she supposed to carry on with any semblance of normalcy if flashbacks to a distorted death crept into her waking hours? A lump rose in her throat, but before the sob escaped, she sensed a shadow falling over her. With one arm still covering her face, she reached out blindly and immediately made contact with Oz's thick fur. She could hear him panting lightly as he stood over her. "Thanks for your concern," she said. "Just don't drool on me."

"Are you sure you want to drive over the mountains today?" Myles asked, as Tuesday threw her knapsack into the cab of the truck. "We could fly over if you wait a few days until I'm back from taking my client to Whistler."

"I'm sure," Tuesday asserted.

"All right then," Myles conceded. "We'll still head to Utah when I get back, like we planned?"

"Yup," Tuesday commenced checking the air pressure in the truck's tires.

"Thanks for talking to me," Myles said to her back.

47

She looked up at him from where she knelt, squinting from the brightness of the sky. "Yeah," she said. She was at a loss. Should she confess everything? Should she tell him about the horrific new development—that the dream is happening even when she's awake and that there's a jagged man running away and she can't remember what happens next?

"What does happen next?" she asked herself quietly.

"I don't know," Myles answered. "But if it made you feel better, you can talk more. To me. After everything we've been through, everything everyone's been through. Who can judge anyone else? Stones in glass houses or casting first stones or...I don't know. There's a saying about it."

"From down here you look like a damn angel, all backlit like that," Tuesday said.

Myles cocked his head and half-smiled, "You don't believe in angels."

"Damn right," she agreed.

Tuesday first stopped at Mr. Modi's fuel station where she filled the truck's tank and bottled a few extra gallons, just in case. "Gumption," said Mr. Modi, "I learned this word from my son yesterday." Tuesday sensed there was more to the topic.

"Oh?"

"Yes. You, Deliverer Miss, have gumption," he declared.

"All the Deliverers did," she deflected. "The canine ones especially." She looked at Oz, who ignored the compliment and poked around in the empty buckets and cleaning rags near Mr. Modi's counter.

"You brought medicine to places no one else would go. No fear. And even now you drive over the mountain passes alone: bad roads, bad weather, bad people. Gumption," he repeated.

"Unpredictable, for sure," Tuesday nodded, "but you can't let unpredictability stop you. You just need to be prepared."

"Ah, so you want three more gallons of fuel then?" Mr Modi winked.

"No, but that does remind me to charge my solar flashlight. Thanks."

It was true that the highways between Bellingham and the east side of the Cascade Mountains, formerly part of Washington State, were sometimes flooded, sometimes iced over, and sometimes buried under mud slides. And it was true that looters and mavericks roamed the countryside unchecked, but Tuesday was undaunted.

When unrest in Washington State had divided residents, and the west side chose to join Oregon and British Columbia to form the sovereign state of Cascadia, relations with former Eastern Washington remained civil, yet tense. Cascadians crossing to the eastern side of the mountains could expect to face questioning when entering Liberty Republic, and navigating the somewhat lawless land took expertise in the art of blustering. Tuesday didn't mind.

"We've reached cruising altitude," she told Oz, who sat in the passenger seat looking out at the stretch of empty road ahead of them. "I don't know where they've got the border kiosk set up this time, but I guess it doesn't matter to us, does it?" She scratched Oz under his red Deliverer collar.

Over the course of the next two hours, the landscape changed from a region rendered barren by blight to a coniferous forest at the foot of the mountain pass. Their pace slowed to accommodate the mud from melted snow and the potholes where erosion had caused the pavement to sink. Tuesday could feel gusts of wind pushing against the truck, and pine boughs from a previous storm still littered the highway. Concentrating on the road kept Tuesday's thoughts from wandering and she was relieved that the unsettling topics kept themselves sequestered in the glove box in the back of her mind where she'd shut them.

Nearing the peak of the pass, Tuesday scanned for potential places to pull over. "I know, pal," she said to Oz as she guided the truck to a stop in a patch of mud and moss, "It's not my favorite weather either, but we've got to be at high elevations to find the good stuff." She grabbed an empty canvas bag from the cab of the truck and went to the other side to let Oz out. "Why didn't I train you to sniff out truffles?" she mused as they made their way into the forest.

Returning to the truck an hour and a half later, the canvas bag now stuffed to the brim with mushrooms, Tuesday pulled herself into the driver's seat and rubbed her palms together to warm them. "Three pounds of alpine morels ought to be enough to get Gilman House to forgive us." She turned the key in the truck's ignition and then blew into her fists, "Worth the frostbite." She pulled the truck back onto the empty highway and said, "Category," to Oz. "Dogs I would rather go road-tripping with." Oz was silent.

"You're right," Tuesday agreed, "There aren't any."

Winding down the leeward side of the mountain pass, Tuesday felt the wind weakening and the foliage petered down from tall evergreens to low shrubs and brown grasses. In the distance she spotted a small blue booth, signaling a border security check and vehicle search. She waved and didn't even slow down. A short while later, a silver drone with a flashing light appeared in the rear-view mirror. "What's this about?" she murmured to herself. "I don't have to stop. They can scan my tags." The light on the drone flashed more insistently. "Fine," Tuesday hit the brake and brought the truck to the edge of the road. She pressed the button to roll the window down with one hand and pulled her Deliverer tags out from under her shirt with the other as the drone zipped over to the vehicle.

As the drone hovered just outside the driver's side window, Tuesday began, "Everything is in order; I have authority from the—"

A man's voice cut her off, "You're approaching a detour due to an avalanche ahead. It's passable in your vehicle, but you'll need help. One of our men is at the site to assist; just let him know the span of your axle and height of undercarriage when you arrive."

"Oh. Okay," Tuesday hardly had time to answer as the drone zipped away. "That's a pain," she said, pulling back onto the road, spitting gravel out from under the truck's tires.

Only ten minutes later, the site of the avalanche came into view on the horizon. "Not as bad as I was expecting," she said. Oz whined.

Just as the rocks became cumbersome to drive over, a man hopped out of an unmarked truck alongside the buried road. Boulders, slabs of slate and huge chunks of soil had spilled down a cliff face into a pile, but the profile was low, only a few feet higher than the truck itself. Tuesday couldn't see the damage on the other side of the blockage. Wearing a hardhat, jeans and heavy boots, the man picked his way over to Tuesday and Oz. He slapped his hand on the hood and called to her, "How high up are you?" without coming to the window. Tuesday shrugged exaggeratedly at him.

He disappeared under the vehicle and she saw the fur on Oz's neck raise slightly. A strange man under the truck made Tuesday feel inexplicably vulnerable. When he reappeared, the man pointed at the rock slide and called, "Over here!"

Tuesday crept behind him in the truck as he led her off the paved road and across a make-shift path of plywood, intended to smooth out the rough terrain. "Now square up!" he instructed, indicating that she should bring the truck perpendicular to the avalanche again. She could see the blockade was shorter here, and the slope to the top somewhat gentler. Boards had been placed strategically to create ramps and span gaps between some of the boulders. Oz snorted as the man pushed two of the boards closer together to match their tire-span. "Give it a go!" The slipshod ramp held as Tuesday inched the truck up over the rocks and found the most solid path to the top. When she could see the other side, she lined up the truck's tires with a similar haphazard ramp that eased their bumpy descent.

The man did not follow them over the avalanche to bid them a safe journey or accept any gratitude, which Tuesday would not have given anyway. "Did not like that," she admitted aloud.

Woodward Canyon Winery and Orchards lay in the desertous Walla

Walla Valley, balanced between a rift in the earth and a craggy cliff face. Much of Liberty Republic's once fertile land had been decimated through a combination of wildfires and subsequent pernicious frosts caused by lingering thick smoke obscuring the sun. Many plants that survived the fire and frost succumbed to the lab-engineered fungi intended to control weeds, which morphed into relentless blights. Somehow though, small anomalous plantations like Woodward Canyon had adapted and survived.

The sun had just begun to dip, sending pinks and oranges rippling through the sky when Tuesday turned onto the dirt lane leading to the homestead at Woodward Canyon. A willowy woman stepped onto the porch of the old farmhouse, waving with one hand and trying to keep her wild black curls out of her eyes with the other. Her flowing skirt was printed with bold purple hyacinths; the matching scarf fluttered around her shoulders in the wind.

Tuesday returned the wave as she jumped out of the truck, and as the dust from her tires cleared, she saw a little girl on a bicycle, pedaling furiously through the dusty cloud. "I almost caught you!" the girl shouted gleefully at Tuesday. Oz barked and ran a circle around her as she skidded to a stop.

"Filomena," called the lady from the porch, "Take Oz to go meet Calypso! She's with Uncle Damian in the orchards."

"C'mon, Oz!" the girl gestured to the dog to come along as if gesturing to another child. "You'll love our new puppy!" she sped off, her long black braid flying behind her.

"Fil is ten, going on twenty-three," Ismene Pantazis laughed. "Here, leave your bag and we'll take an evening walk before dinner. The vineyard is just gorgeous at sunset."

Ismene was right. Row upon row of orderly grape vines glowed in the setting sun's rays, and in the distance, the mountains kissed the sky gently. Ismene walked with one hand stretched out, absently brushing the leaves of grape vines as they strolled. Tuesday turned her face into the

52

wind and breathed in the sweet scent of fruits. "This place is delicious," she said as she exhaled.

"Yes, I think anyone can see why we stayed," Ismene agreed, "Especially once we knew this land could still produce. We had to stay." Tuesday nodded. She could hear Filomena whooping and the dogs barking excitedly as they romped. "It's lonely for Fil, of course," Ismene continued. "Now that she's older. The nearest children are a day's drive away at best, but a family moved into the old ruins of the dairy down the canyon so we've spent some time there helping them settle in and rebuild."

"And you finally let her get a dog," Tuesday noted.

Ismene nodded, "Yes, finally got over losing Luna, I guess, and Fil was so lonesome. Damian's always been more of a cat person." On cue, a black cat emerged from somewhere in the grape vines, his tail held high. "There's Voodoo now."

Just then Filomena came blazing down a row of the vineyard toward them, both dogs chasing her bicycle. As she zipped past, she shouted, "I'm hungry!" Instead of bolting in the opposite direction as expected, Voodoo the cat joined in the chase, following closely behind Calypso.

"Fil's not so subtle, is she?" Tuesday laughed.

"Not a lot of need for that around here."

The Woodward Canyon farmhouse stood two whitewashed stories high, with a rooftop that came to points above shutterless windows, and a verandah encircling its substantial girth. Inside the stately home colorful tapestries and thick woven rugs brought life to the spacious wooden rooms, which clearly were meant to house more residents than just the current little family of three. A bunting banner of fabric remnants hung over a huge stone fireplace, the work of Filomena, no doubt.

Ismene busied herself in the kitchen, putting Tuesday to work muddling some herbs. Filomena announced, "I'm going to make our salad!" and marched out the door with a basket.

"Her father would be so proud," Ismene said, watching Fil in the front garden from the window. "She'll be a better cook than I am by next week, and never a peep of a complaint about anything."

"Must have done something right," Tuesday said because it was something people say about child-rearing.

"Maybe," Ismene pondered, "but I don't think I can take credit. I'll give credit to the mountains and the sky and the soil in the fields for raising her."

"Oh, I can't believe I almost forgot!" Tuesday threw a hand in the air and started rummaging through her knapsack where she had left it on the wooden bench of the kitchen nook. "I've got our dessert!" She produced five full bars of dark chocolate, delicately wrapped in wax paper tied with twine.

"Oh. My. God." Ismene put her hand on her hip, still standing at the kitchen counter. "Did you read my mind? Our 2019 cabernet is just begging to be paired with a dark chocolate bar," she swooned. She lifted the folded corner of the wax paper on one of the bars and held it to her Grecian nose, eyes closed. "It's divine."

Tuesday smiled and downplayed the gift, "I hoped you would like it." She had painstakingly packed and carried it from a chocolatier, Vosges Haut-Chocolat, in Chicago, ensuring all the correct storage conditions to preserve it perfectly.

Filomena bounced back into the house through the front door. "Yard chard!" she held up her basket. "And some other stuff that doesn't rhyme. Does anything rhyme with radish?"

"Caddish," said Ismene.

"No, like, real words," Fil protested, peering at the chocolate bars on the table. "You should eat dinner before you have dessert."

Tuesday laughed and Ismene saluted, "Yes ma'am."

The farm table was spread with an array of dishes: baked yams, wheat buns with apricot preserves, and grapevine leaves stuffed with mint, dill, and rice. Ismene, Tuesday and Fil sat down to eat. Calypso and Oz each gnawed on a yam in separate corners. "Is Damian coming?" Tuesday asked, noting the extra place setting.

"He said he was almost done," Fil piped up. "When I saw him in the yard."

"Probably not," Ismene answered. "He's not usually one for socializing, you know. He'll stop in and then take a hot bath I'd bet."

Tuesday sensed a twinge of grief and guessed that Damian hadn't always been this way. In all the times she had made deliveries to and from Woodward Canyon, Damian had never dined with her.

"I'll be head winemaker someday," Fil informed Tuesday. "Just as good as Damian and my daddy."

Tuesday always felt awkward talking to children. "Oh," she replied.

Fil continued, "I used to want to be an astronaut when I grow up. Or maybe a meteorologist. But that was when I was nine."

"She's moved on," said Ismene.

"I can do them all," Fil said. "If I know the weather I'll be better at making wine, and I can blast off to the stars on vacation."

"Smart," said Tuesday.

"What did you want to be?" Fil asked Tuesday, smearing apricot preserve onto her bun.

"What did I want to be?" Tuesday hesitated.

"Yeah, because they didn't have Deliverers when you were a kid. You couldn't want to be that."

Ismene chimed in, "Did you always want to help people with your faithful fido at your side?"

What had Tuesday wanted to be? Safe with a stable home? Not responsible for someone's untimely death? A business major?

Fil chewed her bread and stared patiently at Tuesday.

Ismene saved her, "I used to want to be a fashion designer." She laughed, "Now I have my own line of farm fashion wear, as modeled by the lovely Filomena Pantazis!"

"A Pantazis in pants!" Fil stood and spun with her arms out.

"Or an event planner," Ismene said. "More realistically. I did that for a while. I organized your Aunt Alexia and Uncle Damian's wedding. It was gorgeous."

Filomena pointed her fork toward the wooden wall of the living room, "From the picture on the wall. Where Damian is so happy, and you are hugging your sister."

"Yes," Ismene said.

"I wish I had a sister," Fil said matter-of-factly, unaware of the tears welling in Ismene's eyes and the lump rising in Tuesday's throat.

"I wish you did too," Ismene said, letting a tear slide unabashedly down one cheek. "Sisters are the best people in the world."

Just as Tuesday thought she might have to flee the table, they heard the back door open and close gently. A slim man with a floppy hat in his hand leaned through the arched doorway, nodded at Tuesday and may or may not have whispered, "Hello," before disappearing.

Ismene stood up and started filling the empty plate from Damian's seat with food. "I'll take him his dinner," she smiled, the trace of the tear still bright on her face, "And I guess I'll save him at least one of the chocolate bars."

When Ismene headed up the creaking stairs, Tuesday realized she had been frozen, staring blankly through the past several minutes. "A dog trainer," she told Fil. "I wanted to be a dog trainer because, after sisters, dogs are the best people in the world."

After dinner, Fil took her allotted three squares of chocolate to her room, explaining, "I want to read to Calypso and Oz before bed. Oz hasn't heard my new story, and it's Calypso's favorite one so far."

"Don't share your chocolate with the dogs," Ismene said and then added to Tuesday, "I think it's been a year since Fil had any candy." She lit candles as they moved from the kitchen to the living room. Tuesday arranged herself on the sofa and Ismene handed her a woven afghan blanket and a glass of wine. "That was my first attempt at dying alpaca wool with beets," she nodded toward the blanket. "And in juxtaposition," she unfolded a second blanket and held it by the corners, letting it hang in front of her, revealing a cartoon dinosaur, "I got this on clearance at Target at least five years ago."

"Whatever keeps you warm," Tuesday said as Ismene wrapped herself in the dinosaur.

"At the time, my only choices were either dinosaurs or the Utah Jazz logo, and I don't even know what sport they played."

"I'm headed to Utah next week before going to California. I'll ask."

"Cheers," Ismene tilted her glass toward Tuesday and smiled warmly. After a sip she added, "Wine connoisseurs would describe this as velvety and opulent."

"YOU are a wine connoisseur," Tuesday reminded her. "How do you describe the chocolate?"

"Same," said Ismene, nibbling the corner of one chocolate square and rolling it around on her tongue, "Same. Maybe I'd like to be velvety and opulent myself."

Tuesday smiled at the thought, "If someone were describing me with wine adjectives, I don't think I would get such a positive description. I can imagine it: astringent and unbalanced..."

Ismene laughed, "How about: complexly structured with a lengthy dryness. Pair with dark chocolate."

"You're better at this than I am."

Upstairs in one of the spare rooms, Tuesday set her knapsack on the daybed and pulled back the simple cotton curtains. The darkness was too complete for her to see the vineyard or mountains, but she knew they were there. Anyone looking in would have been able to see her clearly illuminated by the lamp in the bedroom, the only light on in the farmhouse. But of course, there was no one to look.

In her dog walking days in college, she might have opened drawers to learn where people kept their valuables and secrets. Now she opened the drawer of a small vanity just out of curiosity. Empty. Tuesday slipped quietly down the hallway and pushed open the door to Fil's room very slightly. In the dimness, she could just make out the shine of Oz's eyes as he lifted his head. The shine triggered a flash of memory from the nightmare—the dog standing like a statue in the road, eyes like coins. She shook free of the phantom dog and whispered, "Hi," to Oz. He obligingly stood and followed Tuesday back to the spare room where he immediately curled up on a woven rug. Tuesday lay back on the bed and stared at the ceiling, imagining the wood grain of her own tiny loft. Long, straight line, swerve to the left, through a smear of pine tar, back to straight. She turned off the lamp and draped her arm down the side of the bed, finding she could just brush the tops of Oz's ears with her fingertips.

Four

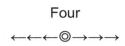

In the morning Tuesday peered out the still-open curtains into the fields. From the height of the house, looking down into the faraway vineyard, the figure of Damian slipped in and out of view among the grapevines, more ghost than real. Tuesday sat at the rustic vanity and took out her phone, which seemed like an affront to the simplicity of the whole homestead. She checked for GoferGoods messages or a word from Myles, but there was nothing.

Downstairs Tuesday found Ismene in the kitchen with the front door open. Calypso danced around her feet, hoping for scraps. The flowing drape of Ismene's floral satin robe gave her a stately air, despite still being in pajamas. "Hot tea is ready," she said, setting a steaming mug in front of Tuesday at the table. "But don't thank me, I only just came down here. Fil made it before she went out."

"You say it like she took the L-train to a high-rise office building for her job in HR."

"Well, who knows. She's very independent," Ismene said. "Though maybe not quite ready for a career and a mortgage."

On cue, Filomena came through the open door, her arms full of her morning's accomplishments, which she spread out on the table. "Caddish IS a word," she said.

"Good morning," said Ismene.

"I looked it up. You COULD have a caddish radish."

"Usually our vegetables aren't so...er, mischievous."

"I brought some stuff," Fil turned to the table. "More yard chard, teeny zucchinis, and bootleg eggs!"

Ismene took this in stride, sitting down at the table with her mug of tea, "Mmm. Will the poultry authorities arrest you for the bootleg eggs?"

"No, I asked the hens nicely. Bootleg is, like, illegal. The dictionary said."

"Tuesday might know a thing or two about bootleg eggs," Ismene pointed out.

Tuesday nodded, "Yeah, some people really might steal rare eggs. But not from your chickens. I made a delivery of endangered gyrfalcon eggs once."

"When that skunk got in the coop and ate eggs, those were bootleg eggs!" Fil spun one of the eggs on the table like a top. "Do you really have to go home today?" she asked Tuesday, and then added, "That makes me saddish."

"Do feel welcome to stay as long as you'd like," Ismene offered. "I know you're always on the go, but we're happy to have you anytime."

"Thanks, I'll take you up on that sometime, but I really should head out this morning," Tuesday said.

"Is there time to eat bootleg eggs first, and then play one more game with Oz before you go?' Filomena asked hopefully.

"Yes," Tuesday affirmed.

"That makes me glad-ish!"

"Just glad-*ish*? Not super glad?" Ismene teased.

"Ecstatic didn't rhyme."

After breakfast Filomena bounded out the front door with one fist in the air, the dogs trotting after her, "C'mon Deliverers, we've got to make a delivery of medicines to Chad!"

"The country or a person?" Ismene asked, but Fil was already too far away to hear.

"And I've got to make a delivery of wine to Cascadia," said Tuesday.

"Also important," Ismene said.

"I'll just drop off my stuff in the truck and pull up to the storage barn to get the wine crates," Tuesday said, shouldering her pack.

60

As Tuesday approached the truck where she had parked it along the dusty farm road, she could make out the shape of a small parachute floating down toward the hood of the truck, and heard the faint whine of a drone whizzing away. She was not expecting a drone drop. Without putting her knapsack down, she swiped the item from the hood of the truck. It was a disc the size of a small make-up compact, and it opened the same way, like a clam shell When Tuesday opened it, a tinkling song began to play, as if from a child's music box. The tune was familiar, though without the words, and ploddingly slow.

Alouette, gentille alouette

Alouette, je te plumerai...

She snapped the disc shut and spun around, as if the sender would be behind her, though of course, no one was. She couldn't help frantically scanning the fields within view—who could have sent this? Either the sound of blood rushing in her ears or the sound of the wind through the grape vines was deafening. *Think*, she told herself. Could this be a mistake? Intended for someone else? No, this was a message. Deliberately slowing her breathing, Tuesday slipped the disc into the pocket of her tunic, jumped into the truck and threw it into gear. Where was Oz?

Grinding to a halt on the dirt driveway near the wine storage barn, Tuesday hopped out of the truck and jogged to Ismene, who was now dressed in floral-print coveralls and black boots. "What's wrong?" she asked, reading concern on Tuesday's face.

"Were you expecting a drone drop? Something for Fil, or...?" She pulled out the musical disc and held it in her palm.

Ismene took the smooth disc and turned it over in her hand. "No. Should I get Damian?"

With Filomena, Oz, Calypso, and Voodoo the cat trailing behind him,

Damian joined Ismene and Tuesday at the kitchen table. The last thing Tuesday needed was a family intervention about this. Damian and Fil sat down, his expression serious, hers expectant.

Tuesday kept her voice from wavering and put on her best poker face. "I'd just like to know if anyone was expecting a drone drop containing this." She opened the disc and set it on the table. The tinkling song crawled out.

Alouette, gentille alouette

Alouette, je te plumerai...

"It's that earworm kids' song," Ismene mused. "It gets stuck in your head for days."

"It's slow. Why's it so...creepy?" Fil wondered.

Damian shook his head.

That confirmed it. "Okay, that's all I needed to know. It's meant for me. Thanks, and I really need to go now," she rushed on.

"Wait," said Damian quietly. Just the fact that he was speaking stopped Tuesday short. "Are you in danger?" he asked.

Tuesday stammered, "I-I don't... Probably not."

"I heard you talking in your sleep," he said, his eyes fixed on the table in front of him.

Ismene's eyes darted back and forth between Tuesday and Damian, "What does that have to do with..."

Damian continued, "You were afraid."

Tuesday's heart pounded. She needed this conversation to end. "It's not a big deal, stay calm."

"Everyone is calm," said Fil.

"Good," Tuesday reassured them, "That was just a nightmare. I get this dream sometimes. It's...nothing."

"You said, 'Take me away,'" Damian added.

"I did?"

He looked up at her, his dark eyes searching her face. "Yes." He looked at Ismene. "Maybe she needs to visit your grandmother." Then he addressed Tuesday, "You are going to California, is that right?"

"Yes," Tuesday answered hesitantly.

"You're safe with us. If you need to know more about yourself, and whatever danger you are facing—go see Kosmina." In the silence that followed, Damian stood and put on his hat. "Best of luck," he nodded to Tuesday as he walked back into the orchard, the cat gliding along behind him.

Tuesday turned to Ismene for an explanation. "What?"

"He's right," Ismene said, the realization registering on her face. "You'll be so close! You've got to meet Yia-yia."

"Your grandmother is still alive?" The impertinent question slipped out before Tuesday could stop it.

"I know, twenty-eight percent of the world is dead, and 100-year-old Yia-Yia pulls through."

"But why would I go—"

"Yia-youla knows things," Fil said. "Stuff that no one else knows. It's like magic but real."

Tuesday furrowed her brow, "Okay, I don't think that's going to help—"

"I know," Ismene broke in, "I don't buy into all that either—crystals and hocus pocus and chakras," she wiggled her fingers as if casting a spell. "But, I don't know." She shook her head. "You've heard of the Oracle of Delphi, right?" she asked.

"Yeah," Tuesday answered.

"Well," Ismene shrugged.

"Well."

On the road with a case of reds and a case of whites strapped tightly into the bed of the truck, Tuesday kept her foot firmly on the accelerator.

She used the open stretches of straight highway to make up for the time she'd lost, first at the leisurely breakfast of pita bread stuffed with scrambled eggs, and then the impromptu family discussion. An uneasy knot tightened in Tuesday's gut.

"It doesn't make any sense," she began, trying to put the pieces together. "Seeing the man running away in the dream is new." Oz dozed in the passenger seat. "I couldn't see him in the dream before, but he was always there." She let the thought hang for a moment. "Someone was there." Tuesday watched more closely than usual for drones whizzing above the potholed highway, but the air was as deserted as the road. Reality and dreamland swirled together in a fog when she tried to parse out the events of that night. "I crash. We roll. There's screaming." She couldn't bring herself to say *there's death*. "I know all that is real. Then what comes next? I say, 'take me away'?" Oz was no help, though he sat up and scratched his ear with a hind foot.

"And now a drone drops this...this—she searched for the right words to describe the eerie musical disc in her pocket. "What is it? The Ghost of Christmas Past? *Change your life, Ebeneezer*." She thought about calling Myles, still on his transport with the Suits at a ski resort, but reception wouldn't have carried the call, and what would she say anyway?

At the crest of a hill, as the boulders obscuring the road came into view, Tuesday remembered the avalanche. She swore under her breath, but was partly relieved to have something else to occupy her mind. Seeing no one on her side of the debris, she got out of the truck and surveyed the rocks, letting Oz join her to stretch his legs. She searched for the gentler slope where she'd come down before. Off to the side of the road, near the spot where she estimated they had made the descent, Tuesday found the boards of the ramp thrown into an untidy stack. "Cool," she muttered to herself sarcastically.

Within the space of half an hour, Tuesday had placed the planks onto the rocks in her best reconstruction of the ramp, hoping she had adequately covered all the pits to avoid getting a tire trapped or dislodging a boulder. Back in the cab, Oz whined and Tuesday answered uneasily, "I agree." After lining up the truck's tires with the ramp, they inched upward, with Tuesday jumping out twice to realign the boards. Eventually, they safely reached the top. "Halfway there," Tuesday sighed. She had hoped that at the peak of the avalanche she would see someone from the Liberty highway crew again, though she would have hated to ask for help from the brusque man she'd seen the day before.

Tuesday repeated the same ramp-building process descending the rock pile, carefully placing boards along the mildest slope and then creeping over them in the truck, the wine crates creaking in protest over the jarring terrain. When the truck was back on the main road, Tuesday checked the straps securing the crates once more before driving away. "Well that didn't make up for any lost time," she said.

"Back on track," she said to Oz as she pulled away from the aftermath of the avalanche, feeling triumphant. She watched the sides of the highway for the Liberty border kiosk among the grasses and sparse trees of the landscape. Border patrol relocated the pop-up booth regularly, sometimes more than once in a day. When she spotted it, she slowed, even though she knew she didn't need to stop. Rolling down her window as she approached, she started, "Hey!" and then caught herself, "Excuse me!"

One of the two attendants strode toward the truck shouting, "Scanner read the tags. You don't have to stop." He waved her on.

"I know," she spoke loudly to be heard across several yards. "You should know your guy at the avalanche site abandoned his post."

"We don't have a guy," the border attendant took a few steps closer, puzzled.

"The one who was supposed to help people cross? The drone said he'd be there?" The ends of her sentences raised up, along with the hairs on the back of her neck.

"No idea," he said curtly and tried to wave her on again.

"Really, you had a guy yesterday helping with a ramp, and a drone

65

that alerted me to the blockage," Tuesday insisted, louder than the distance between them required. The second attendant, a woman with her hair in a tight bun and a gun at her waist, came toward them.

"Listen," the man began, "One, I do not care who is or is not able to maneuver their vehicle over a road block. I do not. Liberty Republic does not." Tuesday pursed her lips. He continued, "Therefore, two: we would not use a drone to tell you anything about anyone at an avalanche. Sidebar, three: Liberty patrol drones don't have voice broadcast capability."

Tuesday's expression changed as the man talked. "No guy?"

"Imaginary guy. Imaginary drone."

The second attendant scolded him, "Show some respect. You read her tags." Then she said politely to Tuesday, "We are sorry for any inconvenience to you. And this dolt is correct. We don't man road obstructions or use vocal broadcasts from our drones. Have a pleasant journey—both of you," she nodded to Oz.

"Apologies, ma'am," the man mumbled to Tuesday, and tipped his hat to Oz, "Sir."

By the time Tuesday returned to Bellingham, night had fallen and as she passed the flickering lights of downtown, she considered stopping in at The Rabbit Hole. Or maybe checking for a nearby Chum. It had been a hell of a day. Instead, she turned down the drive toward Myles' trailer and Lake Whatcom. Passing up the turnoff to get to the trailer, Tuesday drove to an old city boat launch and parked the truck with its front tires touching the water. She jumped out of the cab and let the water lightly lap at the toes of her boots while she looked out across the expanse of the lake. It sparkled in the moonlight, a reflection of the starry sky.

In the passenger seat, Oz wagged his tail, antsy to enjoy a late-night beach romp. When Tuesday opened the door, Oz briefly looked down but the inch of water didn't stop him from jumping out of the cab onto the boat launch with a small splash. "Sorry pal, I parked like I was going off the deep end." She looked at the truck, which did indeed appear as if it were going to plunge into the lake, grill first. Tuesday picked up stones and tried to skip them across the water while Oz put his nose to the ground, snuffling through the sand and rocks. It was too dark for Tuesday to see how many skips she got with each throw, so she tried to listen for the percussive sounds of the stones bouncing on water like the high hat on a drum set.

"I forgot to eat," Tuesday said to Oz, when he gamboled up to her a while later. "And I think I've sunk enough stones to go home now."

Tuesday let herself and Oz into her tiny shipping container home and clicked on the stained-glass wall sconce—courtesy of Coleman, of course—that bathed the little room in yellow light. On the way to Alabama Hill from the lake, Tuesday had stopped for a midnight snack at a drive-up Mexican restaurant. She opened the paper bag and took out a bundle wrapped in wax paper. "No guac on yours," she said, setting a soft corn tortilla stuffed with rice in front of Oz. She picked at her own taco and perused GoferGoods briefly, snagging two easy jobs for the next day, before sighing and putting down her phone.

The sconce glowed warmly and cast a dramatic shadow onto Oz's official Deliverer vest hanging on the wall. Tuesday turned her attention to the vest and let her thoughts linger there, hoping it would steer her away from more unsettling places. She recognized the absurdity in this. She was more comfortable in the depths of a South American jungle facing a pit viper with her dog and a pack full of antibiotics than in the depths of her mind facing thoughts of family or ex-lovers.

That trip with the pit viper had been one of their first, well before there was a vaccine for the raging pandemic. She'd had to send Oz forward when she couldn't continue hacking her way through the thick tropical foliage. Tuesday had cued him remotely, giving commands through the device in his vest as he continued on his own. She had watched the progress of his journey in real-time, viewing footage from the vest camera on a tiny screen designed for Deliverers. Oz stumbled onto the sleeping viper so suddenly that Tuesday hadn't had time to react before the snake reared up, striking menacingly. From the camera's view, all Tuesday could see was the open mouth, fangs exposed, lunging toward the camera's tiny lens on Oz's chest. She couldn't tell whether Oz had backed up in time. "Freeze!" she had yelled. And then, with the viper still erect, hood flared, Tuesday wasn't able to control the tremble in her voice, "Oz, sneak back." The snake, precariously poised like a crystal goblet about to tip off the edge of a table, slowly shrank as Oz crept backwards. It wasn't until after Oz made the drop-off and returned to her that Tuesday knew for sure the viper had missed. Kneeling in the mud, surrounded by vines and unwitting insects, she slipped her fingers through the two holes in the vest just over Oz's heart, and choked back sobs of relief. Several kilometers closer to civilization, Myles had helicoptered them out.

Even now Oz occasionally wore his official Deliverer vest in addition to his distinctive red collar, but only when Tuesday got an alert from the World Disaster Relief Organization. Most of the surviving canine Deliverers were too elderly to take special assignments. Since Oz had been barely more than a puppy when they took their inaugural Delivery mission, Tuesday and Oz were still technically on active duty. WDRO assignments were rare now, and Oz hadn't worn the vest for several months.

Tuesday swallowed the last bite of her taco and gulp of hibiscus tea, trying to keep Oz and these small tasty pleasures at the forefront of her mind. She brushed her teeth and climbed the ladder to her bed, pausing to say goodnight to Oz on her way. She lay on her back, staring at the ceiling for a long time before falling asleep.

Two days later, after locating and delivering some lab-grown meat products as well as a pair of jewel encrusted Miu Miu heels, Tuesday Devlin's mind couldn't let go of the little musical clam shell disc from the drone, or its plodding tinkling song. *Alouette, gentille alouette.* She'd

68

turned down an under-the-table request to deliver ammunition, as these deals often came with just as many risks as delivering guns. *Alouette, je te plumerai.* When did Myles say he'd be back? Why hadn't he texted?

Tuesday put her hand in the pocket of her tunic and took the smooth disc in her hand, working her fingers absently around it while she and Oz walked through Western Washington University's campus. When they arrived at the administration building, Tuesday's tags triggered the sliding doors to open. She quickly realized something was amiss. "Practically deserted in here," she said, stopping in the middle of a hallway near a bank of cubicles. Only one desk was occupied. "Spring break, huh?" Tuesday was still talking more to herself.

"Yeah," said the young man sitting at the desk. "But aren't you the Deliverer?" he continued. "Sharon said she left you a message in her office."

"Thanks," Tuesday said, heading toward Sharon's office. Inside, Tuesday saw the flashing video note on Sharon's desk and pressed the button to play it. The image of Sharon's face with her dark-rimmed glasses and brunette bob popped up over the notepad, floating in the air.

"Oh it's YOU!" Sharon teased.

"It's me," Tuesday answered the recording dryly.

"Well, here I am on spring break and I don't have anything to *wine* about!" Hologram Sharon giggled. "And that's the problem!" She proceeded to detail her desired quantity and scheduling for the wine delivery while Tuesday sat in the desk-chair combo in the corner of the office.

When Sharon signed off, Tuesday looked at Oz, "Okay pal, that's settled now. But I can't focus. This musical thing is gonna burn a hole straight through my pocket while the song burns a hole in my brain." She put her head down on the desk. As it had done the previous time Tuesday flopped into the desk-chair combo, the wooden writing surface clattered to the floor. "Urgh," she uttered a frustrated sound while she reattached the desk to the chair. "I do have two cases of wine...," she reminded herself; but of course there was no reason to drink the top tier liquid gold she'd gotten from Ismene when The Rabbit Hole was so close.

On the walk to The Rabbit Hole she chewed on a piece of dried fruit leather and mulled over what Ismene had said about her ancient Greek grandmother. "Nonsense," she told herself, tossing a piece of the fruit leather to Oz in mid stride. Then added, "Baloney. Hooey. Poppycock," just because they were fun to say. "Right?" She looked to Oz for confirmation and received a doggy smile. "Right."

The longer she sat at the bar, the more agitated Tuesday began to feel. Gabe and Nick's antics did not cheer her as they usually did, and after a couple of drinks, when she still had not heard from Myles, she texted him, asking, *Are you home?* And added, *Wine is still in your truck.*
Yeah, got back this afternoon, he returned, and then was silent.

Tuesday soon found herself knocking on the door to Myles' trailer, and swinging it open before Myles completed his sentence, "Come on—" Tuesday was already through the door with Oz right behind her. "In," he finished. Oz play-bowed in greeting and Myles tousled the big dog's ears affectionately with one hand while balancing a platter in the other. Noticing Tuesday's expression, he asked, "What's up? Everything okay?"
Now that she was here, Tuesday didn't have the words, "I don't know. Weird stuff is happening and it's totally getting to me. I can't stop thinking about—" she stopped short, noticing Myles' table settings.
"Mox?" Myles guessed.
There was sparkling cider in the two glasses he'd set out, and the aroma in the air told Tuesday he was definitely baking a pie.
"What? Well, yes, but also—"
"Your dream? You said it was happening more."
She rushed on. "Yeah that, too. But also, I got a drone drop in the middle of nowhere and this weird message and a recommendation to see

a Greek oracle," she trailed off as a realization dawned on her. "Oh shit, you've got a date."

Myles opened his mouth as if to answer, but closed it again silently.

"Shit, shit, sorry. I'm totally barging in and you've got someone coming over and I'm being self-absorbed and weird," Tuesday cued Oz to follow her as she turned back to the door.

"Hold on, hold on," he interrupted. "This sounds important. I've got some time."

Tuesday hesitated. "Really? Because this is going to sound so bizarre, but...could we go for a walk to the Humane Society?"

Myles put down the platter he'd been holding and crossed his arms over his chest. "Tuesday Devlin, somehow you never cease to surprise me."

Tuesday hadn't been to the Humane Society building itself in many years, though of course it had stood there the whole time, right where it had been when she'd volunteered at the facility in college. She knew she needed to see it again, but the prospect made her insides turn to water. Myles did not pretend to understand why his presence was required. He simply accepted it, just as he'd accepted her silence about her past for so many years. While they walked he chose safer, yet still pertinent topics, "So you made it to Liberty and back. And got the extravagant wine. But you've still got to take some to Sharon before you put the rest in the hangar, right?"

"Right. And don't worry, I don't need you for the dropoff, so you don't have to try to interact with Sharon," Tuesday clarified.

"FAN-tastic," Myles approved. "What about getting sage for Gilman House?"

"I took advantage of altitude and weather on the way and I gathered a bunch of rare morels. That's a gift that will go much farther than herbs."

"Oh that's even better! You can make the note say, 'Sorry I didn't take the *morel* high ground last time...'"

"Gawd, Myles."

The front window of the animal shelter had been boarded up for ten years, since the first wave of the pandemic when there were no more pets left to adopt and it was too hazardous for potential adopters to visit anyway. Tuesday had helped clean out the last of the kennels and lock the doors with the director, who had optimistically hoped the closure would last only a month. The graffiti on the boarded windows read, "Woof!" and "I need a home."

Myles glanced at Tuesday as they stood on the cracked sidewalk, studying the building. He waited. It started to drizzle. "I recovered here," she said finally. "After the accident."

"You didn't go to the hospital?" Myles furrowed his brow.

"No. It was the same night as the earthquake. Even before that, hospitals were overwhelmed and setting up those emergency care quarantine tents in parking lots and sports fields all over. You know how it was." She squeezed her hand into a fist around a key in her tunic pocket.

"Right. Really dangerous just to go to the hospital at that time, I guess."

"I don't know how I ended up here," Tuesday said, considering approaching the door.

"Um…" Myles looked back at the street they had walked along.

"After the accident. I remember waking up here. But I have no memory of getting here." She took the key out of her pocket and showed it to Myles, holding it flat in her palm, "I kept the key."

He searched her expression. Tuesday hoped he couldn't see her trembling, hoped there were no tears in her eyes. When she spoke, her voice came out clear and strong, "I needed to come back here, and I need to go in." She stepped to the door and put the key in the lock.

"Does it still work?" Myles stayed on the sidewalk.

Tuesday felt the key turn, and the click of the dead bolt echoed in her mind like a gunshot. Taking the knob in her hand, she pushed hard on the door, and it gave in on her third thrust. It creaked open and she turned back to Myles. "I'm going in."

"I'll be here," he answered, putting his hands into the front pocket of his sweatshirt and leaning against the window ledge. "If you need me."

"Thanks," she stepped into the darkness inside.

A moment later she said, "Myles?"

"Yeah?" he called back.

"Um, it's really dark. Do you have your watch?"

He stepped through the threshold of the doorway, "Yes." A flick of his wrist lit up his watch like a flashlight. He aimed it at Tuesday, illuminating her pale face.

"What are we looking for?"

"Nothing. We're just...looking."

There was nothing remarkable about the lobby of the animal shelter in the dim light. Tuesday ran her hand along the cold counter top and looked at the walls. She could just make out the posters, their corners starting to curl, advertising doggy daycares and flea medications. There was even a small flyer promoting Tuesday's own dog training and walking services. It was all exactly as she remembered.

Behind the desk, through another swollen door that Tuesday forced open with a "whoomph," were the rows of small enclosures and socialization pens, all emptied of bedding, food bowls, and dog toys. Oz padded noiselessly into the kennels to inspect them, his nose to the floor, tail held high. At the end of the rows of kennels, Myles lifted his watch to shine on a door with a plaque that read, "Staff Break Room." A public service notice with a large red exclamation point blocked their view through the window into the room.

Tuesday knew precisely what was behind the door. Every piece of scant furniture, every mismatched knob on the cabinets, every crack in the paint. Stepping into the tiny room confirmed her memories. A cot stood against one wall, opposite a small kitchenette, several cupboards, and a microwave. Three spindly chairs ringed a table, which, Tuesday

73

knew even before she touched it, wobbled when weight was placed on the edge closest to the bed.

"Right here," she said. "I woke up here." Myles shined the light at the cot and Tuesday sat gingerly on it. "I opened my eyes, but I couldn't move. And right there," she pointed to the spot between the bed and the kitchen cupboard a few feet away, "was a dog, staring at me."

"One from the kennels?"

"No," Tuesday fixed her gaze on the spot. "Just a dog. Scraggly and old. I couldn't get out of the bed for days, and every time I opened my eyes, she was there, staring at me. I tried yelling at her to get her to leave, even threw things at her when I could finally move. She didn't care at all. So I started talking to her instead. I thought I would die here."

"But you didn't."

"I called her Fury. Like the Furies from mythology, but also because I was so angry. Every time I opened my eyes, I was so angry that I was still alive. That I was the one who lived."

Five

Back at her tiny house, Tuesday felt both triumphant about having returned to the animal shelter—the vault that harbored so much emotion—and anxious about what this foray might bring. After she and Oz left Myles to continue meal preparations for his date, before she could even see the porchlight of her tiny house by itself on the hill, Tuesday had already decided on her activity for the night. Inside, she pushed her throw rug askew with her boot and knelt on the floor, running her hands over the boards. Oz snuffled, pressing his nose into the rug, and then further hindered Tuesday's already fumbling hands by excitedly standing too close to her as she crouched.

"Buddy, I can't see what I'm doing when you're in my face." Her fingers found the latch and she pulled up a small hatch panel, revealing a storage cellar the size of a large camping cooler. The space contained only a few of her valuable items, including three glass bottles. Grasping a bottle by the neck and holding it up to the light, she affirmed, "Just enough."

Oz followed her the few steps to the kitchen where she set a lowball glass on the counter with a clink and filled it four fingers high. "None for you pal," she told him, then paused. "Hang on." She found apple juice in the mini fridge and poured some into a bowl, setting it in front of him. "You deserve a little something for this momentous occasion too."

She tipped her glass toward Oz and said, "Cheers," which reminded her of Mox and the toast they had shared just before getting thrown out of the bar. She sighed and poured another finger of whiskey into the glass.

"Facing my subconscious and dredging up memories from the muddy bottom of my mind is...*whiskey* business." Oz drank his apple juice.

"No? Didn't like that one?" she asked and then shrugged, "Myles would have laughed." The whiskey burned bewitchingly on the way down.

Tuesday awoke sharply, curled on the padded bench with her fists tucked under her chin. Somewhere in the tiny house, her phone buzzed with an alert. Oz was already sitting up, his tail wagging patiently. As she sat up, Tuesday pressed her fingers against her temples, knowing movement would make her head pound. "Is that what I think it is?" she asked Oz. Still massaging her temples, she found her phone by the whiskey bottle on the counter and read the alert. "Holo wouldn't come through," she said to the dog, "but I get the gist from the text translation. You've got a job to do, Oz."

One of the benefits of knowing where to get anything for anyone was that Tuesday always had a fully stocked medicine cabinet. Listening to the hiss of the shower as the water warmed, Tuesday swallowed a couple of pills for her head and rubbed her eyes. When she opened them, steam had fogged the mirror and her reflection was hazy. She looked into her own eyes, "Not too shabby for hung over, unshowered, and neurotic," she told her reflection. "Bedhead suits you."

In a pinch, Tuesday could close the door behind her with a click, bright-eyed and snappy, in seven minutes flat. Today she took an additional three minutes to put Oz into his red Deliverer vest, give him an extra helping of breakfast, and pack a small knapsack. "Ready?" she asked, and answered for him, "Ready. Transport will be here any minute. Not Myles this time," she added, disappointed. They would be riding with another WDRO transporter from Cascadia who had transported them once the year before, when she and Oz delivered seizure medications to a community fraught with volatile militia activity in rural Montana.

An emergency task from the WDRO was a welcome diversion from the ongoing melee in Tuesday's mind. On the brief helicopter ride south, she tried to clear her head and focus on the details of the message she'd received. A thirteen-year-old boy had gone missing while his family vacationed at Mount Rainier; he was last seen about 24 hours ago. Inclement weather had caused disruptions in the trail systems, and possibly trapped the boy. Though Oz was not a search and rescue dog, he was trained in scent work, and had once successfully recovered victims of a landslide. Tuesday watched the city of Tacoma slip by beneath the helicopter on its way to the mountain. Suburbs gave way to green belts and fields, and soon the helicopter descended onto the landing site where the search and rescue team awaited them.

The air was dry, and pleasantly chilled, as they approached the small cluster of anxious people. "Glad we brought your boots," she said to Oz as the remnants of snowfall crunched under Tuesday's footsteps. The search party included another dog and her handler, several experienced hikers, and a former ranger from the days when Mount Rainier was still a national park. The ranger, a stocky man about ten years older than Tuesday, extended his hand to her, "Pleasure to meet you ma'am. I'm Craig. And this is the family of the missing boy—the Vandenburgs." The couple and their teenage daughter stood together with their arms around one another. The father nodded to Tuesday, but said nothing. They looked like Suits, for sure. If not for their tear-stained faces, the family could have been an advertisement for a winter wonderland resort, or snowboarding lessons. Tuesday wondered whether she had provided Mr. Vandenburg's optometrist with those designer frames.

Craig handed her a button-sized object and continued. "Here's your tracker so we know where YOU are if you find him. We have articles of clothing from the subject for reference. The subject ran off during breakfast yesterday after an argument with his sister."

"It was so stupid," the teenage girl butted in, wiping her cheek with her gloved hand. "He called me ugly, so I broke his Lego thing and then he ran away!"

Mrs. Vandenburg added, "Oliver is usually very wilderness-savvy. We didn't worry until he'd been gone for five hours without checking in. That was unlike him."

Tuesday nodded grimly. "This is Oz. He'll do his best to find your brother." She spoke specifically to the girl, who clearly felt the weight of guilt in addition to grief.

The search party resumed once again, breaking up into teams and fanning out from the resort-like mountain cabin where the boy was last seen. Tuesday separated herself and Oz from the rest of the group so the scents of the other humans didn't interfere with his ability to detect the boy. They covered ground quickly as they loped along rocky terrain until narrow trails, new snowfall, and steep embankments slowed their progress. This far from civilization, the boy could easily have slipped off the trail and become tangled in foliage, buried under snow, or knocked unconscious. Oz paused near a boulder that partially blocked the trail, his nose to the ground. Tuesday took the opportunity to swallow another pill for her headache.

Suddenly Oz whined. He looked down the slope off the trail where patches of heather and black sedge peeked through the thin layer of snow cover. "You think he went down there?" Tuesday tucked her water bottle back into her knapsack and touched the dagger at her thigh. "We can hack our way through the heather to take a look if we can get down there," she mused. She tested a step off the trail and onto the steep slope. The pebbles immediately gave way and slid down the face of the mountain toward the subalpine growths below. Oz took two steps off the trail, his paws better able to take purchase on the side of the embankment. He turned toward Tuesday and whined again, his big brown eyes looking into her stormy ones. "All right then. Let's do our thing. Be careful, pal." She activated the device with camera and microphone capabilities in Oz's vest and secured a wilderness survival kit to it before cuing him: "Oz, go alone."

He turned and scampered down into the low shrubbery among the jutting rocks on the hillside. Tuesday jogged along the trail, searching for a gentler slope. Checking the monitor frequently, and treading carefully along the slick pathway, she made steady progress until she found a safer embankment to zigzag down after Oz. She scrambled across the steep terrain, grabbing onto the tough plants to keep from sliding. The tableau of the Vandenburg family standing at the helicopter landing site flashed in her mind. Mr. Vandenburg's furrowed brow, Mrs. Vandenburg clutching his arm tightly, and their daughter standing between them, hanging her head. Who would run away from that family? Son-of-a-Suit spoiled brat, that's who.

Just then she heard a sound and stopped to check the Oz-eye-view on her monitor. He was on a bluff, still steep, and heading toward a small fissure in the cliffs. "Oz, keep going!" she cheered. Even though she couldn't see his body language, the intensity of Oz's movements suggested that he was close to his target. Skidding down the hill took concentration and Tuesday lost track of time thinking about the Vandenburgs. Suddenly, she heard another sound. She looked carefully at the monitor. Someone who wasn't Oz whimpered.

"Oh thank God!" the whimperer sighed. "Thank God. Someone's here." Then louder, "I'm here!"

The boy must be below Oz, out of the camera's view, Tuesday realized. "You've got a Deliverer vest," the boy said to Oz. "Your trainer can hear me, right? Someone can hear me?"

"Oz," Tuesday spoke through the vest's device, "Three-sixty." As Oz turned in a slow circle to show Tuesday a panoramic view of the area, she said to the boy, "Yes, I can hear you. And that's Oz. There's a kit in his vest for you if you can reach him. Are you...in a hole?"

"Yeah." Tuesday heard sniffling as the boy pulled himself together. "I twisted my ankle, but then when I was trying to limp back, I slipped off the trail up there and rolled down." He sounded embarrassed.

"Did you get hurt rolling down?" she asked, and heard only a mumble in reply. "What?"

The boy answered louder, "Just my other ankle!"

"Oh bummer, TWO twisted ankles? So you can't reach Oz, can you? There's one of those little blankets in his vest, and some water. That's important."

"I can kinda stand on my left one a little...He's too tall."

"Oz," Tuesday cued, "Face right." He did. "Lay down." He did. "How

79

about now?"

"I think I can reach him." The boy sounded like he was struggling. "Are you coming?"

Tuesday had already started fumbling her way down in the direction where Oz and the boy were waiting.

"Yes, but if I go too fast I'll end up in that hole with you." She tried to sound encouraging, "You don't sound like you're doing too bad for someone who spent an entire day in a hole."

"I took a wilderness survival course," he said, trying to sound brave, but Tuesday still heard the tremor in his voice. She heard some scuffling and grunting before he said, "I got the kit, but can't reach the water."

"That's okay. Put the blanket on and I'll get you water when I get there. There's no room for Oz to jump in with you. I can see it's sort of tight down there. More of a fissure, or crevice than a hole, really." She could tell her rambling was not comforting him.

"They must be really worried if they brought a Deliverer to come for me," he said mournfully, the emergency blanket crinkling.

"They care about you. You shouldn't have run away." What was she doing? She wasn't anyone's mom.

He took the rebuke, but added, "I know, but I didn't mean to. First I just ran outside to sit in the hot tub gazebo."

Spoiled brat.

"And then I felt bad for calling my sister a name. I knew she'd hate it. I was being a d—" he stopped.

A hint of a smile crept into Tuesday's voice, "It's okay. I've heard swearing before."

"So then I went to pick some of these wild flowers she likes but that are really hard to find. I was going to bring her some."

Okay, just spoiled, maybe not a brat. "She broke your Legos, they told m-EEE!" rocks rolled out from under Tuesday's boot and she slid several sloping yards down before catching herself. "I'm fine," she said flatly before the boy could inquire. Brushing herself off, she resumed creeping

80

downward. "What'd you call her?"

"My sister?"

"Yeah. What name made her so upset?"

"Sasquatch."

Tuesday grabbed the roots of a scrub bush to keep from sliding again. "Meh. I've been called worse."

"Well...The boy she likes said he didn't want to go out with her because she was tall with crazy hair, soo..."

"Oh ouch. You're lucky she broke your Legos and not your legs, huh?"

"Dude, do you know how long those Lego ships take to build?"

Tuesday suddenly saw the bright red of Oz's vest around the edge of a jutting crag. "I see you. I'm almost there," she reassured him. When she reached them, Oz stood and looked down into the hole, which was a thin crack in the side of the mountain, about eight feet deep. She joined Oz at the edge and met the boy's gaze. What had they said his name was? Oliver?

"Hey," she greeted him.

"Hey," he said from the bottom of the fissure under the shiny thin blanket. "You sounded younger."

"Don't go there," warned Tuesday amiably. I've already been "ma'am-ed" twice this week."

When the whole team reconvened at the helicopter landing site, Craig and another of the searchers carried Oliver sitting up on a stretcher to his family. After water and some peanut oat bars, he appeared bright and surprisingly undamaged. The men set the stretcher on the uneven ground of the Vandenburg's acreage, and the boy's sister was first to reach him. She fell to her knees and tackled him with her hug, "I'm so glad you're okay!"

He hugged her back, "I'm sorry Bailey."

Tuesday's insides sloshed. What had he said? The phrase shot through her mind and ricocheted between her ears. *I'm sorry, Birdie.*

No: *Bailey*, he'd said. Not Birdie.

Craig interrupted her disquieting thoughts with a firm handshake, "We thank you, Ms. Devlin. And Oz, of course," he nodded deferentially to the dog.

"I can't express how deeply we appreciate this," Mr. Vandenburg said as he watched his wife embrace Oliver. His eyes were watery behind the designer frames. "We owe you," he sniffed and blinked, "everything."

Tuesday shifted her weight and brushed at the dirt on the side of her tunic, "No no, it was—I'm just glad he's okay," she said finally.

Mrs. Vandenburg, her dainty nose red-tipped from the chill and tears, took Tuesday's hand, "You're a godsend. We're eternally grateful."

"Oh," Tuesday deflected, "Oz loves working. Happy to help."

From her knees by the stretcher, Oliver's sister looked at Tuesday and said, "Thank you. I would never have forgiven myself."

"I know," Tuesday's heart ached, "You're welcome."

On the return helicopter ride, Tuesday's mind buzzed as the ground sped by beneath them. She felt the fatigue of a restless night and an intense morning, but the churning in her gut prevented her from relaxing. She thought about the ceiling above her lofted bed: long, straight line, swerve to the left, through a smear of pine tar, back to straight. Suddenly there were screams. She felt the sensation of being flung against the car door, saw the figure running away, barely visible through the shattered windshield. Tuesday gasped, immediately grateful that the loud thrumming of the helicopter masked the sound. Her throat started to close and she turned frantically to be sure Oz was still secure in the chopper with her. Of course, he was. She slowed her breathing—now was not the time to panic—not 2,300 feet in the air with a stranger. What triggered the memories this time? The movement of the helicopter in flight? She'd been on dozens of similar rides with no such reaction. The siblings reuniting? The echo of "I'm sorry, Birdie" rattling in her ears? Tuesday exhaled and pushed the thoughts to the compartment in the back of her mind. And she hoped that's where they would stay.

After landing in Bellingham, Tuesday found herself and Oz making their way to Myles' trailer. She often experienced mild disorientation after a quick job. Something about being yanked out of the days' plans and then dropped back into them made everything seem off-kilter. It was like jet-lag without the jetting. Now she had to deal with the additional unsettling nightmare without the night.

Oz had found Oliver speedily so there was still plenty of time to meet Sharon and deliver her bottles of wine as requested. In fact, Tuesday had time to complete some simple GoferGoods jobs, if her mental state would allow it.

Myles' truck was parked in front of the trailer, and Tuesday realized she should have texted to tell him she was on the way. Pointless, now that she and Oz were at the door. She knocked and when Myles opened the door she blurted, "Do you speak French?" At the same time Myles asked, "What dropped on you?"

They stared at each other for a silent moment. Myles leaned against the door frame and said, "I feel like our conversations used to be a lot less…"

"Crazy?" Tuesday suggested.

"I was going to say 'unpredictable.'"

"Yeah."

"Oz is wearing his vest. You got called to an emergency, huh?" They sat down in the captain's chairs inside the trailer.

"A lost kid on Mount Rainier. Oz found him, of course."

"Of course. That's quite a way to start the day. Especially after…I mean, you probably didn't have a very restful night."

"Is that your way of saying I look like hell? Because I'll have you know I looked fine before I rolled down the side of a mountain."

"You're getting dirt on my chair," Myles pointed out.

Tuesday's stomach growled audibly. "Oops. Okay so, I'm starving AND I look like hell. I packed Oz's lunch, but not mine." She was reminded of the previous night, "Oh shit, how was your date?"

Myles was already up and puttering in the kitchen. "Uneventful," he said into the fridge.

"I find that hard to believe," Tuesday answered. "With the culinary production you had going on in here."

He presented a tray of soft cheese, flatbread crackers and sliced vegetables, "It wasn't that fancy."

Tuesday spread some brie onto a cracker and asked, "How does it smell like fresh baked pie in here again?"

"I'm heating you a slice of blackberry cobbler. Okay, us. I'm heating *us*, "he put a finger in the air for emphasis, "*slices* of blackberry cobbler."

Tuesday smiled and poured water from the bottle in her knapsack for Oz, who had flopped onto the floor. When she sat back down in the captain's chair, Myles handed her a piece of cobbler with flaky pastry crust, glistening purple berries, and toasted brown sugar on top. "It's best served warm, while the filling is gooey," he said.

"This dessert in itself is an event," Tuesday said, letting the granules of sugar dissolve on her tongue. "It's DE-vine."

Myles took a bite of his blackberry delicacy, "*Bon appetit*! See? I do speak French." He continued, more seriously, "So I asked what came for you in the drone drop because I think I got something meant for you today."

"Oh?" Tuesday swallowed, "What makes you think it was for me?"

"It's just this photo," Myles unfolded a piece of paper from his pocket and handed it to her.

Even as she reached for the photo she could see precisely what it was. The note below the picture of a locket read, "Lost something valuable?" Her hands began to tremble.

"Is that your necklace?" Myles asked, putting a hand to his collarbone.

Instinctively, she mirrored the gesture and felt the bump of her locket where it always was, underneath the fabric of her tunic next to her Deliverer tags. "No," she swallowed again and cleared her throat. The photo, printed on regular printer paper, showed a close up of a locket that matched Tuesday's exactly, against what appeared to be a man's palm.

"You didn't lose yours?"

"No." She knew this locket, and the word hidden inside it. "The locket in the photo is bent, right there." She pointed to the picture, "Right where it hangs from the chain. Just a little." Her heart sped up under the hand at her throat and she could feel her breath coming faster.

"I guess someone found the one in the photo and thought it was yours?" Myles suggested incredulously.

"No," Tuesday shook her head in a daze. "No one could have found this."

"Someone did," he shrugged. "It's a coincidence that they would have known you have the same one though. I mean, that's weird, right?"

"You have no idea."

"There's a quote on the back," Myles told her. "Also strange."

Tuesday turned the paper over and read aloud, "If I had a world of my own, everything would be nonsense."

"I looked that up. It's a quote from the Mad Hatter," Myles said helpfully.

That part didn't make any sense to Tuesday. The necklace—that she recognized. But why a quote from the Mad Hatter? Her eyes had been glued to the photo; now she looked up at Myles intently, "Where were you when you got the drop? Why would the drone think you were me?"

"I did a quick transport this morning, so just in an industrial park up north. Ferndale area."

Tuesday stood up slowly with the paper in both hands, as a realization dawned on her. "Shit," she said under her breath, then louder, "Shit, shit, shit." Oz jumped to his feet as Tuesday flung open the trailer door and ran outside.

"What?" Myles was two steps behind. "What's wrong?"

Tuesday reached Myles' truck, dropped to the ground and rolled underneath it. "I know how they found me!" she called out. He knelt on one knee and peered under the truck at her. She was on her back, both hands feeling frantically around the truck's undercarriage. "There's gotta be something..." she growled angrily.

Oz joined Myles in staring at Tuesday under the truck. Myles put his hand on the dog's back and asked, "Do you know what she's doing?"

"AHA!" she exclaimed and rolled back out from under the truck. She held up a small object between her thumb and forefinger, absently slapping dirt off of her clothes with the other hand.

"What's that?"

She placed the metal object, about the size of a button, in Myles' palm, "Tracker."

He held the tracker up to the gray sky to inspect it. "Who's tracking me? How long has this been there?"

"Me," Tuesday interjected. "They're tracking me."

"When I crossed into Liberty, a man posing as highway maintenance patrol must have planted the tracker on the truck! That's how I got the drone drop at Ismene's. Then someone dropped this photo of the necklace on you, thinking it was me in the truck."

"I'm lost," Myles declared. "Like, Bermuda Triangle lost."

Tuesday snatched the tracker, hastily flung it to the ground at his feet and then stomped on it, grinding it into the dirt under the heel of her boot with a satisfying crunch.

"I'm not sure what's happening either," she stared at the mutilated bits of computer parts on the ground between them. "But I have to find out."

"I have *so* many questions."

"Someone is trying to get my attention. The dropped items, they're both...from my past, you could say," Tuesday put her hand on Oz, who had sat down almost on her feet.

"I'm guessing we're not talking about your high school bestie trying to reconnect," Myles crossed his arms. "What's the other item that dropped?"

"You know that French song they teach little kids for some reason?" Tuesday presented the disc from her tunic pocket and opened it. The tinkling song drifted eerily into the air.

Alouette, gentille alouette,

Alouette, je te plumerai.

Myles knit his eyebrows, "How is this from your past?"

"Not important," Tuesday asserted.

"Seems impor—"

She continued, "*Alouette* means lark in French. The song is about plucking a bird."

"Ew. That doubles the creepy factor."

Tuesday clicked the disc shut to silence the music. "Yeah."

"I think I'm still in Bermuda." He picked up the photograph of the necklace from the ground near the truck's tire where Tuesday had let it fall when she ducked under the vehicle. "So, if they knew the necklace wasn't yours, then—this note? '*Lost something valuable*'? It sounds like a threat now. What do they think is valuable?"

"Family," Tuesday said, staring into the distance over the choppy waters of the windblown lake.

"You always said you don't have a family," Myles watched her expression carefully.

"Everyone has a family."

Unsettled as she was, Tuesday decided she had time to complete a simple delivery from GoferGoods before her rendezvous with Sharon. After finishing her blackberry cobbler and saying goodbye to Myles, she returned to her shipping container home to change out of her muddy clothes and pull a comb through her hair. She planned to return to Myles' trailer for the wine that evening. As soon as she removed his red Deliverer vest, Oz rolled onto his back, wriggling and snorting.

"Celebration for a job well done?" Tuesday asked him. "Don't get too cozy; we're not staying." The GoferGoods job was a man's request for Disney paraphernalia as a gift for his girlfriend's birthday. Tuesday had a small stash of prints, toys, and collectibles in the hangar, and he'd chosen the fifteen-year anniversary figurine of *Frozen*'s Anna and Elsa as little girls, building a snowman together. Noting that the delivery location was adjacent to the fitness center for transient teens, Tuesday reminded herself to make a drop-off there too.

With the figurine wrapped in brown paper and tucked into her knapsack, she ventured out into Bellingham again, her head swimming with the events of the past several days. "Do you ever dream, Oz?" she asked the dog as they walked. "I mean, I see you twitch in your sleep I guess, but do you *dream*? What would a doggy nightmare be like? Can you dream of the past?" She derailed this train of thought abruptly. "A dog nightmare would probably be about a shortage of rabbits to chase, or no beef bones to chew." She stopped in surprise and looked down at Oz. "Dude. That's *now*. We're living in a dog's nightmare?" They started walking again at a quicker pace. "I'm sorry about that, buddy."

Tuesday and Oz reached their destination in front of a nursery, which had done booming business since the pandemic began ten years ago. Many people had converted their yards to sustenance farms and vegetable gardens, and even built greenhouses if they could afford it. But most people lacked a green thumb and anything beyond rudimentary knowledge of gardening, so the horticulture consulting business prospered. Tuesday had completed many assignments with help from the ladies at the nursery, delivering a rose bush for a Suit's fiftieth anniversary gift, transporting a delicate endangered orchid across the country, and once delivering a variety of pollinators in an attempt to revive a wetland in British Columbia. Two of the ladies, Marcy and Ginger, stood in the window of the nursery building, waving an enthusiastic greeting at Tuesday and Oz from afar. Tuesday waved back and faked a smile.

The leaves of a willow sapling poked through the wrought iron bars of the nursery fence and Tuesday rolled them between her fingers while she waited. A man in a rust-colored jacket that matched his wiry beard approached hurriedly, a little out of breath from the exertion. This was definitely her rendezvous from GoferGoods.

"I didn't like *Frozen Three* much," he said without introduction, which didn't bother Tuesday.

"I'm a *Lilo and Stitch* fan myself," she nodded.

"But she'll love this," he added. "She and her sister used to build snowmen and sing that song all the time when they were kids in Montana."

"This is perfect then," Tuesday agreed. "Though I still think the *Oliver and Company* poseable action figures are a great find."

"Maybe next birthday," he replied.

With the first item on her agenda accomplished, Tuesday walked the couple of blocks to Pure Bliss, a bakery that had also survived the pandemic and subsequent economic chaos. The afternoon sun waned and Tuesday knew it was late enough that she could negotiate for the day-old price on some of their stock. She had also thought ahead to wrap a blend of dried herbs into a packet as an offering. Inside the bakery, Tuesday said hello to the clerk rearranging various baked goods in the display case, and set the packet on the counter top. "I brought you an Italian herb blend. I know you'll be able to make something tasty with it."

"Ooh, yeah," the young woman said, "Laura will know just what to do with that. And we got a bag of garlic the other day; I smell Tuscan garlic bread in our future!"

"I'm sure it will smell and taste wonderful," Tuesday said. "What trays can I take off your hands this afternoon? These breakfast biscuits? And maybe these loaves of sweet bread are getting close to being second-day too?" The goods other bakeries might call "day-old" were labeled "second day" at Pure Bliss. The owner felt it was more optimistic—giving the goods a second chance to fulfill their purpose.

Just then, Laura, a curvy woman with thick brunette braids wrapped

89

around her head like a crown, came through the doors from the kitchen, wiping her hands on her apron. "Oh, Tuesday! How nice to see you!" Her cheeks were flushed and rosy from the heat of the ovens. Laura excelled at small talk, and Tuesday did her best to match the easy flow of her conversation.

While they talked, the woman at the counter opened a crinkled paper bag and pulled out two small cheese rolls. She placed one delicately on a ceramic plate and circled around to the customer side of the counter where she set it in front of Oz, who gulped it down in two bites. He watched eagerly as she then wrapped the second bun in a napkin and handed it to Tuesday. "For later," she winked conspiratorially. Laura began gathering an assortment of baked goods into a box.

Some minutes later, Tuesday and Oz exited the bakery with a dozen drop biscuits, fifteen butter rolls, and two loaves of Laura's special honey sweetened barley bread—a recipe from a medieval monastery. And in its own tiny box in her knapsack, Tuesday also carried one hockey puck-sized chocolate peanut butter cheesecake.

At the entrance to the old fitness center, Tuesday pushed the glass door open with her elbow, her arms full of bakery boxes. Several teenagers milled in the large common room, their attention focused elsewhere, to Tuesday's relief. Tucking the boxes next to a laptop on the gym's former check-in desk, she was able to duck back out the door without engaging in any chatter, already having depleted her reservoir of niceties for the day.

"Don't worry, I saved your cheese bun," Tuesday told Oz. "I wouldn't sacrifice your treat. Let's go find Myles."

On the way to the People's Market to meet Sharon, Tuesday and Myles each carried two bottles of Woodward Canyon wine in their backpacks, the bottles clinking lightly as they walked. "You didn't have to come," Tuesday told him again. "I can carry four bottles of wine."

"I know," Myles sounded as if he were reciting, "You're capable and independent." He continued lightly, "But I needed to go to the market anyway. And Sharon's not SO bad."

"She's an acquired taste, but she's always been a good client. All the way back when she was the registrar at Western and I used to get Xanax for her."

"Where did YOU get the Xanax?"

"Oh, you know, here and there," Tuesday responded casually.

"I don't like that Sharon's so bitter, but also bubbly. You're bitter, but at least you frown."

"I have an honest face."

"Hey," Myles brightened, "Let's go around to the backside entrance to the Market. I love passing the laundromat."

"Nothing weird about that," Tuesday answered. "I made you go to an abandoned animal shelter yesterday, so sure, why not?"

"They use the same detergent my mama did when we were kids. Reminds me of Saturday mornings with a week of clothes banging around in the washer while my brother and I watched cartoons, eating cereal straight from the box. That washing machine was so damn loud. Sounded like a drum set falling down stairs."

"The puppies in *101 Dalmatians* had both their parents," Tuesday pondered.

"You're such a great listener," Myles said amiably.

"Most Disney characters don't," Tuesday went on. "The dalmatians were such a wholesome family. Like yours."

"No one ever tried to make coats out of our skin, but if they did, my parents would have been right there for us. Barking. At old ladies. Or whatever the parent dogs in that movie did."

"Maybe it's because the adult dogs are the real protagonists. Did THEY have parents? Well, they still had both owners. That counts," she directed the last part to Oz.

Myles stopped on the sidewalk in front of the laundromat and inhaled deeply, "Ah, *Spongebob*, corn flakes, one ratty blanket for two of us plus Papa sometimes. He'd let us sprinkle frosted flakes into the regular corn flakes if we didn't fight."

Through the glare of the setting sun in the window, Tuesday could make out the shapes of a few people loading machines and folding their clothes. "All that from detergent. Huh."

"Scent is the sense most closely linked to memory," Myles explained. "I learned that from a Trivial Pursuit card."

"So what you're saying then, is that a dog's memory is 44 times better than a human's, because their sense of smell is 44 times more powerful."

"Yes, that must've been where I was going with that."

Inside the People's Market building, formerly the lower level of a small shopping mall, a rotating cast of entrepreneurs peddled their goods and services whenever they had enough product to sell and money to rent a week's space. Tuesday had learned to keep track of the availability of the best products; the goat's milk cosmetics booth only popped in about twice a year from Liberty, the leather-working man with his handbags, belts, and kid gloves appeared about quarterly, the traveling caramel and taffy company showed up only once a year in winter.

Today the usual array of soap makers, family farmers, and various creators of edible goods were sprinkled throughout, along with a booth selling bolts of fabric and a new merchant creating and selling made-on-demand 3D printed products.

"She's meeting us by the leather-working kiosk. Not sure where it is this time," Tuesday scanned the market's hubbub of activity, searching for the leather booth. "Must be in the other wing." She started making her way toward the opposite end of the building, "If we pass the jerky place, I'll pick up a few ounces. You said you needed to come here anyway. What do you need?"

"Berries and sugar for more desserts, if they've got 'em."

92

"She liked the cobbler then," Tuesday stated rather than asked.

"'Course she did," he smiled.

At the Be a Jerk booth, Tuesday purchased dried meat for Oz and some for herself, while the boisterous man hocking his goods bragged a little too loudly about how a famous Deliverer dog eats nothing but Be a Jerk brand jerky. "Well, honestly," Tuesday mumbled, "he'll eat just about anything you give him permission to..." But she accepted a couple of ounces free of charge on Oz's behalf.

They passed the berry farm's booth without stopping. Myles pointed out, "On second thought, if we're going to Utah tomorrow, it'll be a few days before I can bake anything. I'll skip those today and get them fresh next week."

Tuesday spotted Sharon at the leather-working booth, speaking to a man wearing a tool belt and holding a leather punch. Sharon braced one hand on her hip, the toes of her purple pumps just visible at the cuffs of a crisp black pin-striped pantsuit. A piece of scaled, beige leather luggage on wheels sat between them, its handle extended, as they talked.

As Tuesday, Myles, and Oz approached, Sharon squealed, "Ooh, the opportunity to test your workmanship has arrived!"

"The clasp is fully functional now, I assure you," the man said, turning back to his booth.

"Speaking of clasps," she said, acknowledging the three, "I shall clasp my hands together with joy if you've brought me my wine." She did not clasp her hands.

"I definitely have the wine, all the way from Liberty Republic," Tuesday and Myles placed their packs on the floor and began taking out the bottles. "But I couldn't come up with the Reese's peanut butter cups as fast as I expected."

"Ah well," Sharon smiled at Myles, "The eye candy will have to suffice for now then. Thank God you brought that. "Before Myles could respond, Sharon greeted Oz, who was sniffing her bag intently. "And of course she's brought you along, darling Toto," she put her arms around Oz in a way that was either to hug him, or possibly just to push him away from her leather bag.

"You strike me as more of a cat person," Myles noted.

"That's not what my cat thinks," said Sharon.

Tuesday cued Oz to back up from the bag so Sharon could put the bottles into it. She cleared her throat, "I did bring something in place of the Reese's for now."

"I don't really have a cat."

"Well, it's not for the cat," Tuesday said exasperatedly, rifling through her knapsack in search of the tiny box.

"I don't blame you, he's very difficult to shop for."

Tuesday shook her head and produced the cheesecake from her pack, presenting it to Sharon, "A personal peanut butter chocolate cheesecake, limited edition from Pure Bliss."

"Now I shall really clasp my hands in joy over this delectable no name morsel I didn't ask for!" She actually clasped her hands this time.

"Um..."

"The cat's lactose intolerant, so I'll have to eat it myself," Sharon patted Tuesday's hand as she took the cheesecake and placed the box into her leather bag. She straightened up and took off her dark-rimmed glasses, dangling them from the finger and thumb of one hand, her nails painted purple to match her shoes.

"*How* limited is this edition of cheesecake?"

"Oh, uh, mostly that's just a saying. This was the last one. I know they don't always have cocoa, and sometimes even if they have it they use the cocoa to make something else like their flourless cake or—"

"Mmm-Hmm," Sharon nodded, putting her hand out to stop Tuesday's rambling. "I'd like to be kept abreast of the future editions' publication."

"Sure thing," Tuesday agreed.

"All right, tell this one," she twinkled her fingers at Myles, "to turn off his charms. I'm flattered, but there's no time for philandering today. I told my cat I'd be home in time to watch the whole second season of *Real Housewives of Cascadia* tonight." She set her glasses back on the bridge of her nose, spun around and called, "*Au revoir!*" as her purple pumps tapped away with the leather bag rolling in tow behind her.

"I can't tell if she has a cat," said Myles.

"I can't tell if she wanted the cheesecake," Tuesday added.

They watched Sharon disappear into the bustle of shoppers.

"Bird person," suggested Myles. "Could be a bird person."

The man with the leather punch leaned into their conversation, "Not any type of animal person, judging by that rare pangolin leather bag she's got."

"Huh," said Tuesday.

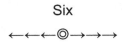

Six

Back in her shipping crate on top of Alabama Hill, Tuesday kicked off her boots, and Oz sprawled onto the braided throw rug on the floor. "I'm with you, pal," she affirmed, sinking onto the padded bench. With the distractions of her errands gone, thoughts of the mysterious drone drops barged to the forefront of her mind. She put her hand in her pocket and spun the smooth musical disc in her palm. "How has this week been a month long?" Her fingers slipped absently under the catch on the side of the disc and the music tinkled out, muffled by the material of her tunic. What message was she supposed to glean from this all-too familiar macabre tune? She let the song play though. "*Gentille alouette*," Tuesday murmured to herself. Then adding in frustration, louder, "*Je te plumerai!*"

Hoisting herself off the bench, Tuesday traded her tunic for her airy nightshirt and started water boiling on the single burner in her kitchenette. While she waited for the water to heat, she rinsed the empty whiskey bottle and tucked it into the corner by the door so she could take it to the distillery for a refill after their trip. From a little jar in the cupboard above the sink, she sprinkled some chamomile and lemon balm into her mug, reminding herself to pick more herbs from her garden in the morning. To calm herself while the herbs steeped in the steaming water, she sat cross-legged on the floor next to Oz, stretched her arms behind her back and interlaced her fingers, trying to release the pressure in her chest.

But the drone drops haunted her. What did the line from the Mad Hatter have to do with any of this? *Everything would be nonsense*. Who had the necklace, where had they gotten it, and how did they connect it to her? Who knew about its significance to her? There would be no way to stop the dream tonight. She could hear the echoes of the screams already. She lay down and put her head next to Oz's, squeezing her eyes shut.

After a few moments she lifted her head and Oz raised his eyebrows at her. "I'm fine," she told him, standing and taking the mug of hot tea in her hands. After a few sips, the warm liquid loosened the lump in her throat. She touched the locket at her neck and allowed herself to open it. She ran her fingers along the sparkling cursive word inside and whispered, "Angie."

After another night of troubled sleep, daybreak brought an unusually clear sky, under which Tuesday punched out her aggression on the speed bag hanging from the eaves. She despised the feeling of impending doom that the drone drops had stirred in her, especially because she felt its intrusion at her own tiny home, her retreat. She punched the bag harder. Oz chose not to chase squirrels, lolling lazily in the sunlight instead. When she finished, Tuesday slumped onto the porch near him. "I'll work out for the both of us today then," she said breathlessly. Her meticulous planning ensured there was no last-minute rush of packing or preparing for their trip to Salt Lake City, so she gathered some herbs from the garden to replenish her tea jar and pulled weeds from around her little weeping willow, both of which seemed serene and peaceful, juxtaposed with the turmoil of her thoughts.

She allowed herself the luxury of a few extra minutes in the hot shower before patting her hair dry and putting on her forest green leggings and sapphire blue tunic. Double-checking the contents of her knapsack and fastening Oz's to his back, she asked, "Are you ready, buddy? You always know when we're going to fly, don't you?" Oz bounced twice toward the door and then play-bowed. Tuesday smiled, "Okay, you're in a hurry, I see. Let's bring Myles some breakfast then." She grabbed a paper bag from her mini-fridge and closed the door behind her.

The uneasy buzz in her mind and stomach had subsided somewhat, but the musical disc and photo of the necklace felt like bricks in her pocket by the time Tuesday and Oz reached Myles' trailer. Remembering her recent erratic entrances to the trailer, including an interruption of date preparations, Tuesday knocked softly this time and waited for Myles to answer.

"Hey, I brought breakfast," she announced, handing him the bag.

"Morning," said Myles, peeking inside. "Um, this is not breakfast. This is ingredients."

"It can BECOME breakfast," she corrected. Myles unpacked half a dozen eggs, a bell pepper and an onion.

"And Oz doesn't get onions in his omelettes," Myles said, tossing one of the eggs in the air and catching it again. He had prepared the dog's meals frequently enough to know his share about canine nutrition. "*Omelette*," he repeated, now attempting to throw and catch two eggs at once. "That's French."

Tuesday could predict the direction of his thoughts, "Yes."

To the tune of the French children's ditty, he sang, "*Om-el-ett-a*," and glanced at Tuesday before continuing, "*gentille omelett-a. Omelett-a, je te plumera*i," He paused. "Hm, I guess translated that would mean…?"

"It means you're going to pluck the gentle omelette," she said flatly. "Instead of the lark. Don't drop breakfast on the floor."

Myles stopped juggling the eggs. "Why do they teach that to kids?"

"I guess even children enjoy torture if there's a catchy tune," Tuesday sighed.

During the final minutes before take-off, Tuesday strapped Oz into his seat and placed his noise canceling headpiece over his ears while Myles performed the preflight inspection on the Cessna 182. He always meticulously calculated for his trips, accounting for distance, speed, and cargo weight. If they packed light, the three of them could fly to Salt Lake City on one tank, which was far preferable to stopping over in Boise to refuel. Of course, Tuesday's tags could get them preferential treatment at the airport, and a discount on the fuel, but she didn't always like to play the Deliverer card, especially in cities where People United for Life and

98

Liberty had strongholds.

"Cleared for take-off!" Myles announced, hopping into the pilot's seat.

"Ready, Captain," Tuesday said, adjusting her seat belt in preparation for the ascent.

When they reached their cruising speed, a humble 150 miles per hour, the Cessna hummed loudly, but Tuesday liked the rumbling feeling of the machinery churning. Myles' voice crackled through her headset, "Welcome aboard; thanks for flying with Myles Air. The in-flight entertainment will be whatever you already downloaded onto your phone, as well as free dad jokes. Meal service is available at an additional cost, unless you are a dog, in which case, all food is free. If you are sitting in the co-pilot's seat, the price of your meal is to keep me company for the duration of our five-hour journey. Have a great flight."

"I brought my own lunch," Tuesday smiled in his direction, speaking into her headset, "So I owe you nothing."

"Fine, I'll talk to Oz then. What's that, Oz? You'd like to hear some dad jokes? Well, you're in for a real treat! I call them "sire jokes" when I tell them to dogs."

Tuesday swiped her hand in the air at him, "No, stop, stop. Of course I'll keep you company."

Myles used his commercial pilot voice again, "Ladies and gentle-dogs, there's been a slight delay with the dad jokes at air traffic control; they haven't been cleared for take-off. We apologize for any inconvenience."

"Thanks."

After a moment, Myles began, "Category."

Tuesday raised her eyebrows and waited expectantly.

"People who want to drop cryptically threatening items on Tuesday Devlin."

"I do *not* want to play that category."

"Unhappy client?"

"My clients are all happy," she insisted.

"Handsome ex who is jealous of my ability to grow facial hair?"

"What good is the ability if you always shave? And no, that's not Mox's style," Tuesday shook her head.

"You might be surprised at the effect my 5 o'clock shadow can have," Myles joked.

"Seen it," she said. It was indeed effective.

"Disgruntled People United for Life and Liberty operative making a statement?"

"Nah. PULL would want to do something more public and sensational, not just confuse and unsettle a random woman."

"You are not," Myles said pointedly, "a random woman."

"None of it makes sense. And really, maybe I'm just overreacting. The items themselves aren't threatening. A song and a photo. So what?"

"Yeah," Myles said musingly, "It seems like your puzzle is missing some pieces."

"I think we're missing the picture on the front of the box."

"Maybe so," Myles agreed. He snuck a glance at her, "But you have a better idea than I do."

She wanted to tell him. "I had a—" the words caught in Tuesday's throat.

Myles waited.

"Had a—" She diverted, "Rubik's Cube. When I was a kid. That's a puzzle where you don't need the picture."

Tuesday didn't doze during the flight, partly because she wanted to use the time to think, and partly because she worried that she might have another waking dream like she'd had in the helicopter the previous day. Was that only yesterday? She looked over at Myles, who was content to let her sit in silence after playing their game with categories including: items in the kitchen starting with "O," famous people with the initials "B.S."

100

and fad toys of the 2000's.

Shaking oven mitts, B.F. Skinner, and Bratz Dolls out of her head, Tuesday watched the ground underneath the plane drift lazily along. One hundred and fifty miles per hour felt so slow at 7,000 feet. She turned in her seat to check on Oz, who was also watching the scenery below, his doggy smile enhanced by the ear muffs. Maybe when their feet were on solid ground, when she wasn't talking through the headset, when he didn't have to keep his attention on a 2,000 pound piece of machinery hurtling through thin air, she would tell Myles. She could even pretend to be nonchalant about it. After all, Mox knew. No big deal. Right?

The descent toward Salt Lake City's landing strip showcased the beauty of the surroundings, as rolling green hills gave way to white-capped mountains under a sky dotted with puffy clouds. Great Salt Lake commanded the scene, an expanse of deep blue, surrounded by a moonscape of stagnant pools in varying colors.

Tuesday's Deliverer status ensured they encountered no snags getting cleared for landing or passing through customs, though on their way out of the terminal, Tuesday noticed a group of people she judged to be part of the PULL faction's rally. Two men in camo hats stood with a woman who wore a shirt emblazoned with a sequined logo of an arm flexing its bicep. Tuesday and Myles continued strolling past the other travelers in the make-shift airport, Tuesday keeping Oz heeled close to her. "You see the trio, two o'clock?" Myles asked quietly out of the side of his mouth.

"Packing," answered Tuesday. She could see the shape of a firearm tucked into one man's belt and the woman open-carried a Glock at her waist. "All bluster, I think, but they're giving some side-eye." When they were out of earshot, Tuesday stopped to pour Oz a drink of water from the bottle in her knapsack. "We'll just need to keep our wits about us for the next couple of days. Keep our cool and stay out of people's way."

"You must be talking to yourself. I never lose my cool."

Tuesday pressed her lips into a thin line. She did have a tendency to get into scuffles now and then, and certainly had more of an impulsive streak than Myles did. "Okay, you're right. *I* need to be cool," she conceded.

They'd planned their trip to maximize productivity. Tomorrow, Tuesday would visit the Hoyt factory to acquire a hunting bow for Representative Brogan, while Myles flew an executive to Texas. The following day, Myles would return to pick up Tuesday and Oz from Salt Lake City and return to Bellingham. If Tuesday could squeeze in a few GoferGoods deliveries or under the table jobs while she was in Salt Lake city, she'd make the most of her time here.

Without the truck, she'd considered renting a vehicle to travel through the city, but instead Tuesday had simply booked the only AirBNB with shuttle service. Again, her Deliverer cachet earned her preference and perks when booking stays at the location. Normally she chose small, out-of-the-way rooms on occasions when she didn't have close friends like Coleman or Ismene to stay with. This time, because of its proximity to the airport and Hoyt factory, Tuesday booked herself and Myles rooms in what was essentially a mansion.

"I'm definitely taking advantage of the sauna," Myles rubbed his hands together while they waited for their ride. "What are you looking forward to?"

"Um," Tuesday felt distracted, "How about no one tracking me, no one drone-dropping on me, and not having to watch my back all the time?"

"I would have guessed the room service."

"Sorry," Tuesday shook her head. I am looking forward to that. I've just got a lot on my mind."

"Yeah. You're right. I can imagine you're having a lot of...turbulence," he finished.

"I'm not an aircraft, but that's a pretty accurate statement. I'll be fine. And yes, room service will be amazing. Someone can deliver something to me for a change," she tried to smile.

"That's the spirit," Myles nodded as their shuttle approached.

"Oh God, is that a limo?"

"Hot damn," said Myles.

"So much for laying low," said Tuesday as the sleek vehicle pulled to a stop in front of them.

"I had one of my connections set this up," Tuesday explained, "so I didn't really get all the details..."

"Above board or below board connection?" Myles asked, not really expecting an answer as he slid into one of the velvety seats.

"What's the fuel efficiency on this thing?" Tuesday wondered as she helped Oz get situated in the limousine.

"I don't think that's what you're supposed to be thinking about when you ride in this," Myles opened a compartment in the console and discovered a stash of candy. "Hell-LO!" Myles chose a Milky Way bar.

"Aaagh! Tuesday snatched up one of the packets, "It's a Reese's peanut butter cup! Save it for Sharon!"

"It's electric," said the chauffeur, as the window between the driver's seat and the passenger seats rolled down. "Newest battery tech can take this thing 500 miles on one charge,"

"Cool," Myles nodded, closing the candy compartment with a click. The sound reminded Tuesday of how she pretended to clamp uncomfortable thoughts into the glove compartment in the back of her mind. *Thump-click.*

"Where the hell did they get Reese's?" The limo pulled away from the curb. The trio from PULL watched them pass and subtly made the PULL rallying sign, a movement as if doing a bicep curl.

Myles watched them out of the rear window, as they shrank into the distance. He took a bite of the Milky Way, "Someone should tell them that's the damn baking soda logo."

Their chauffeur, a young man who seemed barely out of his teens, left the privacy shield rolled down as they drove through Salt Lake City, and provided a running narrative of the scenery. The city was not new to Tuesday, but hearing locals' perspectives on a town was always useful in her line of work, so she listened attentively.

"This church on the left was one of the ones that just barricaded themselves all in there during the pandemic," he said, adding simply, "No one survived. On the next street though, there's a place that locked down and did really well. They dug a tunnel system connecting themselves to supplies and water. That was key. Ooh, now on the corner here you'll see our new sorbet shop—I recommend Peachy Keen." Like most places in North America, present-day Salt Lake City was an amalgam of condemned buildings and rubble butting up against posh homes and thriving businesses.

Posh did not begin to describe the first impression of their accommodations as the limo approached and the sun set over the Utah mountains. An iron gate swung open to allow them access after the young chauffeur looked into a retinal scanner.

"I bet you'd love to chase rabbits in that yard, Oz," Myles said to the dog, who hung his big silvery head out the window. A pristinely manicured expanse of grass stretched out before them as they approached the estate building.

"He'd have more luck finding wildlife in the forested south property," the chauffeur noted.

"Of course. The forested south property," Myles repeated.

"I won't really let him chase rabbits, if you have any," Tuesday assured the chauffeur, knowing dogs were probably not part of the usual clientele at the mansion.

"Oh, I don't care," the chauffeur shook his head, "And there's no rabbits anyway. You can chase all the squirrels you want though. My parents own the place." The limo eased to a stop in front of the entrance, which was a set of grand steps leading up to double doors inset with plates of opaque glass. The chauffeur, who was also apparently the bellhop and concierge, and had never introduced himself, got out of the vehicle and offered, "Should I help with your bags? You're packed a lot lighter than most visitors."

"We're good," Tuesday waved him off as she and Myles each slung their knapsacks onto their backs.

Inside the building the chauffeur, now playing desk clerk, welcomed them into the front room, an open hall furnished with oversized leather couches, brass-riveted ottomans, and plush white area rugs carefully placed over polished hardwood floors.

The chauffeur slipped behind a small kiosk near the front door and pointed to a glass-fronted cabinet behind him. "You get an access bracelet while you're here. Which one do you want?" An array of bracelets ranging from bangles to bejeweled to understated circles of silver hung in the cabinet. "We'll program it to get you into all the common spaces and your room, plus entry to the property. People usually want one that matches their outfit."

Tuesday looked down at her clothes. Good thing she'd put on her best leggings that morning.

Myles held his arms out to the sides, "I think anything goes with cargo pants and a hoodie. The black leather strap will do fine." The chauffeur ran Myles' choice under a scanner and handed it to him, then raised his eyebrows at Tuesday.

"Um. The blue jade beads, thanks," she said.

While he activated Tuesday's bracelet, Myles inquired, "So, with the rally nearby—" Tuesday shot him a look, but he continued, "Were you all booked up this week?"

"Nah," the chauffeur shrugged. "They all seemed to want to stay closer to the action, I guess."

"More likely couldn't afford to stay at an estate the size of an 18-hole golf course," Tuesday muttered to herself.

"Your room is this way, c'mon," the young man said to Myles, heading through the main lobby and down a long corridor. Tuesday watched them

105

leave and then let Oz explore the room while they waited, taking in the lavishness of the manor. If she looked up, she could see the ceiling, three stories high, with its crystal chandelier dangling in the center. Each of the two upper floors had balconies overlooking the room where Tuesday stood, and she imagined a chase scene from an action movie being played out there, the hero and villain leaping off the balconies to land on the leather couches below. She reminded herself that no one was chasing her. She'd destroyed the tracker from the truck, and this was probably the most secure location in the whole city. Still, her fingers danced on the dagger at her thigh.

When the chauffeur returned, he crossed to the opposite corridor, announcing, "Okay, your place is up the stairs." Tuesday had asked for the smallest, most out of the way room in the estate. She got what appeared to be an opulent attic. After climbing three sets of stairs, passing two landings, one with a VR entertainment center and one with a pool table, they reached a narrow hallway with only two doors.

"Just wave your hand in front of the sensor like this," the young man put his own bracelet up to the panel on the door and it clicked open. "*Ta-da*! Your bathroom is down the hall though. Old building. Info's posted on the wall there for room service or whatever."

"Great, thanks," Tuesday said as he tromped back down the stairs. "Wow," she said to Oz. "This is the humblest room? Okay."

The attic room was small, but dramatic. The wall opposite the door consisted entirely of one enormous window, so it appeared that if she walked in the door and just kept going, she would fall right out of the room, three stories down onto the landscaping below. Swaths of heavy purple velour framed the window and a vintage claw-foot tub had been upcycled into an upholstered couch, overlooking the estate's trees and forest beyond. The wall adjacent to the tub was covered floor to ceiling with golden damask-patterned wallpaper, accented by a variety of intricate but empty frames, as if someone had gone through the trouble of laboriously carving and constructing the frames, only to decide that no painting was worth displaying in them. Across the room stood a queen-sized bed against a brick wall, adorned with a giant mirror.

"Don't touch anything," she said, but then added, "Aw, look—they brought this up here for you!" She patted a cushy dog bed on the floor against the brick wall. "Ooh, the chimney must run up through here, this wall is toasty. And you can have one of my throw pillows. Or two. I probably don't need all five." She sat on the bed for a moment, but felt out of place and moved to the floor near Oz instead.

Dude, she texted to Myles. *We're fancy now.*

Lobby in 5? He replied.

"Do you have a throne? I swear the armchair in my room is for royalty," Myles said when Tuesday arrived in the lobby, "And my minibar is not even mini. It's a maxie-bar."

"No throne in my room," she smiled, "Actually, there's not even the other kind of throne. I have to go down the hall to use the bathroom."

"Well, you're welcome to come sit on my throne," Myles offered, then retracted, "I meant the armchair. Never mind."

Tuesday shook her head, "Let's go out to the back; I want to let Oz run around a while." She headed toward French doors leading out onto a verandah. Oz trotted down the steps and began cavorting through the rose bushes, while Myles seated himself on a long porch swing. Tuesday did not sit with him. Swaying on porch swings at sunset was not something she and Myles did. She leaned on the railing and watched Oz's antics, lost in thought.

After a few minutes, Myles joined her at the railing. "You know my mama's dog, that I've told you about before?"

"Tink, right?" Tuesday answered.

"Yeah. Tinkerbell was one of those Yorkies, weighed maybe all of five pounds. My mama had so many names for that dog. Stinkerbell if she was being naughty, Tinkle-bell if she had to pee. Bella-donna, Tinker-toy, Dinky-bell. Mama carried Tink around in a bag—she was one of those dogs. Mama loved that dog so much."

Tuesday waited, sensing that this was going somewhere.

After a pause, Myles continued, "So why then, name a dog you hate?"

Ah, there it was. Myles was dancing around asking her to talk about Fury, the dog she woke up to after the accident. Tuesday kept her gaze on Oz in the garden, "Because that mean old ugly bitch was the only thing in my 23 years that hadn't left me."

"She was mean?"

"Oh yeah," said Tuesday, emphasizing the *Oh*. "Well, not to me. I don't know why not—maybe the peanut butter and coffee creamer I fed her from the staff room cupboards after she wouldn't leave and I was well enough to walk. But mean as hell to anyone else we encountered. We lived out of the Humane Society, on our own, just sort of skulking around, trying to stay alive. You know what the early days after the quake were like."

"You lived at the Humane Society? During the height of the pandemic, when everyone was scared shitless. During the unburying of the dead from the quake and then the reburying in the mass graves, and the pillaging..."

"It sounds stupid probably, but yeah. For months, even after I'd recovered. The place had cleaning supplies to try to disinfect everything so I wouldn't catch the virus, plus it had a bed, and it was secure; no one knew I was there. No place better to lay low while the world tore itself apart."

"No one...missed you?" Myles asked carefully.

For a fraction of a second, Tuesday felt her stomach lurch and saw the shattered windshield, spattered with blood. She squeezed the railing tighter, her knuckles turning white.

"No."

"I guess it was different for me during that early time of the sickness. I had people."

"Yeah, but having people is its own kind of hard. More to lose,"

108

Tuesday said.

Myles nodded slowly, "I had a lot to lose. But I didn't lose everybody." He was silent for a few moments before asking, "What happened to her?"

"Fury barely left my side for three years. Until she died. About two months after Oz was born. Just walked out and never came back, like animals sometimes do. I don't know when she found time to get knocked up in the first place. I'd say she was a figment of my imagination if I didn't have Oz as proof she was real. He was the only puppy."

Tuesday inhaled quickly and released her hold on the railing, "Anyway, whatever," she said uselessly, backing away toward the French doors to the mansion's lobby. "Let's get something to eat." She whistled for Oz, "C'mon pal."

Myles lingered for a moment at the railing, "Anyway whatever, indeed."

Back inside the open hall, Tuesday stood in the middle of the room, feeling as if she shouldn't have her boots on the pristine white carpet. "There's gotta be a good shinery nearby, or—Oh! Remember the Paradise twins from that Westminster dog show job we did a couple years ago?" Tuesday asked when Myles walked in.

"Could not possibly forget," he said matter-of-factly.

"They opened a cocktail bar here in Salt Lake called Shifting Tides," Tuesday elaborated. "I'm sure it's wildly popular, knowing them."

"I don't know if going to the new hot spot in town counts as laying low, and I've got to get an early start tomorrow," Myles tried to negotiate. "My room has a fantastic sound system. We could put on some music and—" he put his hand on his chest and inhaled with ironic audibility, "Maybe they would deliver pizza here!"

Tuesday toed the rug with her boot. "I don't know. I feel...restless. Maybe I just need to go for a walk."

"Do you want company?"

"You don't need to protect me; I can take care of myself," Tuesday reminded him again.

"I'm not saying you can't. Maybe I'm the one who needs YOU to protect ME. I get the feeling they're not used to seeing brothers too often around here," Myles pointed out.

Tuesday half-smiled, "I know you don't need me. And thanks, but I think Oz and I will just go. Gotta stop at my room first though." She started toward the stairs, "Enjoy the music and room service!"

After going up two flights of stairs, Tuesday stopped on the landing and quietly passed the pool table to peek over the railing down into the lobby. Instead of heading to his room, Myles was still standing in the middle of the lobby, his hands on his hips, looking at the polished wood floor.

Waving her wrist in front of the door to her attic room, Tuesday waited for the click and then turned the knob, letting Oz in first. "Let's be smart and bring the flashlight," she said, fishing the small solar light out of her pack. A vibration from her phone in her pocket alerted her to a message, "Probably Myles raving about the room service menu," she said to Oz. But it wasn't. The icon for Chum, the singles app she sometimes perused, was illuminated next to a man's photo. He was brown-eyed with a dimpled chin, about five years younger than Tuesday. His voice message played while she looked at the photo,"Hi there. Looks like you're in town, and I'm eager to meet someone NOT from Utah, you know? You look like fun." To learn anything more, she would have to interact. An intriguing thought. When she put her phone back in her pocket, her fingers brushed the little musical token and then she felt for the photo of the locket, finding it folded up right where she'd tucked it.

"Ready?" she asked Oz. "Let's go see what Salt Lake City has to offer."

The sun had completed its descent behind the mountains and while Tuesday mulled over the possibility of a night out, she took the opportunity to explore the mansion's grounds. To navigate through the garden and back lot, Tuesday needed her solar flashlight. She hugged the fence line as they traipsed through the forested acreage, her boots sinking into the thick moss. Oz stopped to sniff the trees and pee on ferns. Eventually Tuesday shined her light at a gate in the fence, just large enough for a person to walk through.

"What's out there?" She aimed the beam through the fence, but couldn't make out anything beyond. Oz stood in front of the gate and wagged his tail, excited to be exploring in the dark. Tuesday lifted the latch and walked slowly, illuminating their immediate surroundings as they went. "Huh," she said. "Not as interesting as I'd hoped." The light caught a gleaming object ahead of her for just a moment. When she got there, she realized it was a faucet. Not just a faucet, but an entire cracked kitchen sink, laying on the ground. Next to the sink she could see a pile of rags, or maybe t-shirts, half buried in months or years of filth. Rotting plywood boards, scrap metal, a couch cushion, pieces of cracked plaster and concrete blocks.

"Oh nice," she said sarcastically. "We went sightseeing and found the garbage dump." Oz was just as impressed with the garbage pile as he'd been with the forest. He stuck his head into the broken frame of a cabinet and pawed through decaying cardboard. Tuesday sighed. When her phone buzzed again, she switched the flashlight off, leaving herself and Oz in darkness. The easy smile of the man from Chum lit up the night air around them as his message played, "I'm Conner. Just thought I'd try again. I'm usually not so persistent, I promise." He laughed, "I see a dog in your photo. Mine's named Mindy. Send me a Cast if you want to chat."

Tuesday put her phone back in her pocket and plunged the world into darkness again. She could hear Oz pawing and snorting as he investigated their findings. Anything useful had been scavenged long ago, so Tuesday had seen no glass, tires, intact appliances, or usable construction site scraps. But there was also no stench of food decomposing, since no one dared throw out food these days. Moving toward the direction of Oz's activities, Tuesday shuffled a few feet before tripping on something.

She took her flashlight out and shined it at the vestiges of a toy box, now smashed and sunk into the mud like a shipwreck. Half a teddy bear, the stuffing long gone, lay with grass sprouting up through it, and remnants of something bright pink and plastic were sprinkled around like seedlings. Tuesday touched the outline of the musical disc through her tunic and then sat down on a stack of two cinder blocks. She stopped herself from reaching to touch the locket at her throat and sighed.

"Shut up, brain," she said to herself. A scuffling and snorting told her Oz had returned to her side. "Wanna talk to a guy named Conner?" Oz had no opinion. Tuesday balanced her flashlight on something that may have once been patio furniture and pointed it at herself while she sat on the cinder blocks.

Casting in the Chum app sent a notification to another party to invite them to video chat, and Tuesday touched the button before she could second-guess her decision. After a few seconds of babbling brook noises, the handsome face appeared, complete with chin dimple.

"Hello, Conner," Tuesday said.

"Hi, I'm glad you Cast. Your profile got me hooked." Tuesday knew her profile was extremely sparse.

"Hooked? I wonder how many times that joke's been used on Chum."

"You're right, that wasn't funny," he apologized.

Tuesday backtracked, "Oh no, that's not what I meant, I just—It was just an observation…"

Conner broke in, "I'm always awkward on these Casts. I'm more charming in person. I, wait—where are you? It's so dark."

Tuesday was unabashed. She looked around, "I guess I'm at a dump. There's a lot of debris anyway."

"Well, Salt Lake has better nighttime hangouts than that!" Conner laughed. "I know some great spots. Let's meet up."

She briefly entertained the idea of a rendezvous with this stranger in a tropical cocktail bar. "I dunno. I'm pretty comfortable here with my cold concrete slabs and rusted out car parts."

112

"I can't see anything around you. You look like you're about to tell a ghost story, lit up like that. Where are you staying? I assume not the dump?"

"Just a place close to where I'm doing some business," she said elusively. Their banter continued for a few minutes longer; Tuesday carefully avoided divulging any details about herself, her business, or her whereabouts. Conner was good-natured and quick to laugh, even if a little awkward.

Eventually he nudged again, "So, how long are you in town for? You've gotta let me show you someplace better than a trash pile."

"I'm here another night. Maybe tomorrow. There's a place I want to check out."

"Okay," Conner seemed pleased. "Just let me know. Have a good night."

"It's been 'reel,'" Tuesday finished, ending the Cast.

Back in the extravagant AirBNB, Tuesday and Oz climbed the stairs quietly. From the wall to wall window in her attic room, she could see the starlit sky above the treetops, swirling in navy and black. Kicking off her boots, Tuesday caught a glimpse of herself in the mirrored wall by the bed and paused to assess her reflection. Her eyes had rings beneath them, and the belt around her tunic was starting to show its age. But her tunic accented the blue in her eyes, and her unkempt sandy brunette hair could pass for carefree bohemian waves.

"I dunno. Do we want to meet someone?" She realized her excuse for going on a walk had been to find food and she had forgotten that task completely. Remembering the chauffeur's instructions, she scanned the code on the wall with her phone to peruse the room service menu.

While she waited for her order, Tuesday thumbed through GoferGoods app for jobs. She considered contacting some of her more secretive clients to set up deliveries, but ended up laying on her back on the bed's fluffy down comforter. Instead of shoving her unsettling thoughts to the glove compartment in her mind, she let the tsunami of them take over for a few minutes. Who would be sending these strange items, like clues to lead her to something? Why the mysterious Mad Hatter quote? It must have been the same person who sent both drone drops, but who would know the effect these things would have on her? Whoever it was didn't know her whereabouts because they'd had to track her. The man from Liberty who had placed it on Myles' truck must have been a hired henchman. Why would someone be dredging up pieces of her past now? Was it to be sure she never had peace, to be sure she never forgave herself? She was already doing a fine job of that without help. And winding through all of those thoughts, tangling itself among them, floated Mox's words: *I'm sorry, Birdie.*

A quiet tapping on the door thrust Tuesday back into the present. When she opened the door, a small bamboo tray, neatly arranged with her order, had been placed on the hardwood in the corridor. Tuesday had chosen an array of appetizers for herself, and an order of hash browns with cheese for Oz.

"Ooh, those probably aren't real bacon bits on your hash browns, but they're very realistic!" she said, setting the plate in front of Oz, who licked his lips. Sipping her apple cider from a fluted glass, Tuesday assessed her tray: a cup of honied granola, two deviled eggs, two skewers of roasted vegetables glazed with an orange sauce, four herbed meatballs, and several airy meringue cookies.

She untied a ribbon from around her cloth napkin and helped herself to a puffy meringue cookie. "No reason not to eat dessert first, right?"

Despite the elegantly prepared foods, Tuesday ate with a feeling of impending dread. She needed rest, but knew that sleep would bring nightmares, which had only become more intense and more perplexing. Instead of waiting for the dream to take over her psyche, Tuesday tried recounting what she thought she knew. She saw the accident play in her mind as if she were there again. She swerved to miss that ghostly dog-thing in the road, the car rolled with the sounds of crunching metal amid the screams. She saw the torn body beside her, and was gripped by panicked grief. Horrified. She glimpsed the figure running away, with something held high in the air, but her view was fragmented by the broken glass and driving rain. What came next? This thought process almost caused Tuesday's delectable meal to come back up.

"That's enough of that," she said, throwing her napkin against the wall. She then took off her socks and threw them at the wall as well, followed by her belt and tunic, all of them falling harmlessly to the floor. She sat on the bed and buried her face in her hands. Oz, who had long since finished his hash browns, watched Tuesday's tantrum from his position curled up in the dog bed. She looked at him from between her fingers, "I think I'm done now."

Tuesday set the service tray back in the hallway, peeled off her leggings and slipped between the bed's silk sheets. Maybe she would tell Myles when he came back.

Seven

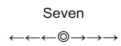

When she heard Oz pawing at the door to their room in the early morning, Tuesday had already been laying in bed awake for some time, staring out the floor to ceiling window as the dawn light crescendoed. She propped herself up on her elbows and turned to Oz, "You're right, up and at 'em. Hang on."

Tuesday left Oz in the room while she performed a truncated version of her morning routine in the bathroom down the hall. She wanted to savor the steaming shower, with the streams of water shooting down to dance on her skin, but didn't want to keep Oz waiting. She pulled a brush through her hair and left it down around her shoulders to dry in the thirsty Utah air. Wrapped in the robe she'd found on a hook by the shower, Tuesday padded back to her room in bare feet, grateful that she'd remembered to take the access chip bracelet with her to the bathroom. "That would have been an embarrassing morning," she mumbled as she reentered the room, noticing the food service tray had been picked up sometime while she had been gone.

"Just gotta get decent before we can go," she assured Oz while she sifted through her knapsack. She put on the same outfit she'd thrown at the wall in frustration the night before, adding a muslin pouch onto her belt so she didn't need to bring her pack, and then left without looking in the mirror.

While Oz stretched his legs in the greenery behind the mansion, Tuesday seated herself on the wood deck of the verandah and tried lotus position, but quickly found that she was unable to relax. With the potential for other AirBNB guests or employees to wander by, the best she could do was sit cross-legged and breathe deeply, eyes open. Probably for the best anyway, to be sure to avoid any waking flashbacks.

Her appointment at the Hoyt factory was still several hours away, which gave Tuesday's mind too much freedom. She decided to head into the city to search for potential business opportunities. In the lobby, Tuesday approached the kiosk where the young man had given her and Myles their access bracelets. A brass service bell sat on the table, but as she reached for it, the young man emerged from one of the hallways, chewing on a bite of the muffin still in his hand. "Mornin'" he said. "I'm starting breakfast orders if you want something. I've got oatmeal on the stove, and could make some eggs." He popped the last bite of muffin into his mouth, "Sorry, there's no more muffins," he said with his hand over his mouth.

"Thanks, but I already had my heart set on getting around the city this morning. I'll grab a bite in town."

"We have scooters for guests. You wanna check one out?" he asked, swallowing the muffin. "There's even one with a sidecar," he nodded toward Oz.

"Hell yes."

Zipping through the streets on a cherry red scooter with a large silver dog in the sidecar wasn't the most effective way to lay low, but Tuesday didn't care. Usually she enjoyed walking to clear her mind, but she also enjoyed the increased efficiency of having a vehicle and, business advantages aside, she liked to feel the wind on her face and watch Oz's ears flap in the wind. A few pedestrians meandered the Salt Lake City streets in pairs or small groups, but Tuesday gave a wide berth to the main events of the PULL rally happening at Uber Stadium.

Just to see what it looked like, Tuesday and Oz puttered up to Shifting Tides, the bar her friends the Paradise twins owned. It was closed, of course, this early in the morning. Even from the outside Tuesday could see that Shifting Tides invoked an atmosphere that would transport their patrons to a convincing tropical South Pacific locale. Tuesday slowed to a stop to better view the entrance to the venue. There was no front

117

window to give a glimpse of the interior, but the exterior was painted with a mural showcasing huge tropical flowers in blues, purples and reds, and tall broad-leaved trees. Real wicker torches were set into the wall, which also featured live vines that climbed through the painted scene and framed a door covered by a full-length painting of the Paradise twins themselves. Tuesday envisioned herself with a cocktail in hand, swaying to music along with the trees dancing in the breeze. Yes, she would visit Shifting Tides later that evening.

Tuesday scootered off, leaving the festive exterior of Shifting Tides behind her, turning her mind to matters of business. Next she would try her luck at connecting with a tech guru she'd met through a secretive job for the Cascadia government, who had relocated to Utah. It had been a long time, but she was confident this connection had not forgotten her. Soon she and Oz were parked in front of an electronics repair shop with a neon "open" sign. The shop was a jumble of electronic devices and appliances, cell phones, computers, smart coffee makers, and remote controlled toys, some torn apart with their guts exposed, clearly works in progress, others displayed in glass cases, ready for sale. Tuesday pushed open the door and, seeing no one inside, called, "Hello? Watts?"

A tall lanky man with round-framed glasses appeared from a door at the back of the store, answering, "Tuesday Devlin! I almost didn't believe the feed from my security cam, but it IS you! What brings you to Salt Lake? I don't suppose you traveled this far just to let me fix your VR goggles?"

"No, you're right," she smiled. "I'm here on business at the Hoyt factory, but thought I'd pay a visit. See what the infamous Jay Watson has been up to." A Roomba bumped her foot and Oz began following the machine curiously as it maneuvered through the other electronics around the room.

"Shhh, I'm not infamous. No one knows I had any part in that operation, remember?" Watts said affably.

"So how have you been? In fact, how are you doing specifically this week, with the world's premiere anti-science idiots swarming your city?"

"I did have a little trouble the first day they started coming into town. I look too much like a science-loving nerd I guess." He pushed his glasses farther up on his nose ironically. "But I offered to switch out a cracked screen on one of their phones and gave another one a battery booster for his van, and I've been lucky since then."

"That doesn't sound lucky; that sounds like you paid a tax to be left alone," Tuesday said.

"Meh. I'd rather be three parsecs away from PULL, for sure, but I can handle them for a couple of weeks."

"I'm sure you can," she agreed. "I have to say, this isn't quite what I'd envisioned for you," Tuesday looked around at the disemboweled computers. "This is kids' stuff, compared to what I know you can do, Mr. My-computer-is-faster-than-the-FBI's. And you hate interacting with people, so running a store at all doesn't seem like your cup of tea."

"My cup of tea is Earl Grey, hot. But you're right. This is a front. The military-grade stuff, covert operations, and proprietary hack projects are in the back," he nodded his head toward the door he'd come through with no hint of irony this time.

"Ohhh," Tuesday responded. "That makes way more sense."

After some more casual banter and an actual cup of tea, Tuesday left Jay Watts and his business with the muslin pouch on her belt now carrying several high-value commodities including yet-to-be-released memory cards, storage devices, and video cards. Anyone from Suits to die-hard VR junkies would salivate at the sophistication of these tiny pieces of technology, so there was no question of an available market.

"Success," Tuesday said, buckling Oz into the scooter's sidecar again.

A short distance farther into the city, the population seemed even more sparse. Maybe residents were joining in the week's rally at the stadium district, or maybe they were hiding out until the ordeal was over. As Tuesday navigated toward the Hoyt factory compound, she noticed evidence of flooding, though whether it was from the Great Salt Lake itself, increased storm front activity, or from snow pack melts, she couldn't be sure. The uneven streets and occasional obstructions from fallen streetlamps or stop signs slowed her progress enough that she had time to glance down a side street and see a man dressed in medical scrubs trying to make his way to a door through a group of bystanders. The narrow backstreet was lined with several vacant storefronts across from a strip club. Tuesday brought the scooter to a stop and unbuckled Oz, keeping him heeled close as she watched the event unfold. The man in scrubs gestured with exasperation toward one of the storefront doors as the group began jeering and pushing him. He quickly lost his footing and covered his head as he fell onto the pavement among them.

Tuesday strode over to the group and shouted, "Hey!" She braced her elbow on her hip and dangled the scooter helmet from her fingers casually. The six men and two women turned to look at her. One man curled his bicep at Tuesday. Several of the others displayed the People for Life and Liberty logo on their clothing.

The man on the ground did not attempt to stand or uncover his head, but turned slightly to observe this interaction. Tuesday had their attention. "Look, I don't really care what happens to Doc McStuffins there, but I happen to know the owner of that club," she inclined her head toward the strip joint across the street, "and he doesn't like fighting in his alley. That's a security camera right there," she pointed at the light fixtures outside the club. "And if you beat the shit out of this guy, your asses won't get past the door when you come back later for post-rally spankings." One of the women laughed at her male friends, "Ooooh, you better listen to her!" Two of the aggressors backed away from the man on the ground.

Tuesday added, "And he's a big shot around here, he'll make sure no one sells you any weed either."

Three more backed up and they let the man in scrubs stand up and scurry into the building he'd been entering when they intercepted him.

One man in a tan camo jacket with a PULL patch on the shoulder crossed his arms and demanded, "Who the hell are you and why should I believe you?"

She was committed now: "I work there." Tuesday turned toward the gaudy exterior of the strip club, its door painted neon pink. *Please be unlocked,* she thought to herself, knowing that her cover would be blown if the door didn't open.

She overheard their remarks as she walked away, but did not divert from her beeline toward the club.

"You workin' tonight, honey?"

"She's a Deliverer—did you see the collar on that dog?"

The door knob turned, and thankfully, the door pushed open. Tuesday closed the door behind Oz and released a breath she didn't realize she'd been holding.

From just inside the door, Tuesday could see a woman sitting at the club's bar, a notebook and laptop on the counter beside her. "Hello," she greeted Tuesday with interest. She wore a fitted silk fuchsia blouse and clinging gray trousers that stopped in time to show off her strappy spike heels. Auburn waves cascaded around her shoulders and accented the color of the gloss on her heart-shaped lips.

"Hi." Tuesday was smitten.

The woman stood, balancing a pen between her slender fingers. "What brings you here today?" she asked with an authentic smile.

Tuesday walked toward the velvet voice, "I just broke up a...scuffle in the alley outside."

"Oh, is everything all right? There's been some tension this week," the woman took Tuesday's hand and squeezed, the series of thin bangled bracelets on her arm tinging musically. "I'm Celeste. I'm the owner of this club. Do sit down." Tuesday allowed Celeste to guide her by the elbow to a barstool.

"Nice to meet you," Tuesday said, noting the classic orchestral music floating through the club.

"And who is your gorgeous companion?" Celeste held her hands out to Oz, unafraid of marring her pristine appearance with dog fur or drool. Oz gratefully accepted scratches from her French-tipped nails.

"This is Oz."

"Short for Ozymandius, like the poem? 'Look on my works, ye mighty, and despair'?" Celeste quoted.

"Um, I didn't do great in Lit class," Tuesday replied.

Celeste laughed, "It's not my favorite sonnet anyway." She returned to the matter at hand, "What was going on outside?"

"Some of the PULL supporters were harassing a man trying to go into a place across the street from here," Tuesday left out the part about pretending to work at the strip club.

"Thank you for putting a stop to that," Celeste nodded. "They've been setting up a new women's clinic in the vacant building across the alley. I hoped there wouldn't be any trouble from the PULL enthusiasts, but..."

Just then the main lights in the club dimmed, and the spotlights snapped on above a stage with poles and a long runway. A mocha-skinned being dressed only in a pair of spandex boy-shorts glided onto the stage, every limb a ripple of lithe muscle. Tuesday watched entranced as the being began dancing to the orchestral music, a marrying of ballet and erotic rhythms.

"That's Trinity," Celeste said admiringly.

"Beautiful," Tuesday said without looking away from the stage.

"We pride ourselves on artistry here," Celeste agreed. "Trinity is also the bookkeeper for the women's clinic across the street. Or will be when it opens. That's why I know about the on-goings over there."

Trinity continued dancing, now incorporating an aerial display using the drapes of fabric that hung down from the ceiling alongside the poles. "I see," said Tuesday.

"And another of my dancers, Marissa, she's one of their nurses. Things were going so well, but just before they were able to open last month, the database systems failed and then there were compatibility issues—" Celeste stopped herself, "Never mind, I'm just rambling now."

"Tech issues?" An idea dawned on Tuesday.

"Back to you though. You used to be a Deliverer, I see," Celeste put her hand over her heart, either out of emotion, or to show she'd noticed the tags Tuesday wore. "We owe such a debt to you for all your service," she said earnestly, adding, "and to you," looking at Oz.

Tuesday's eyes were glued to Trinity's feats of athleticism, "Actually, maybe there's another way I can help."

Half an hour later, Tuesday had connected Trinity and Marissa with Jay Watson, who could ensure the women's clinic received a cutting edge database system and IT support. In exchange, Tuesday received a makeover. She exited the club in a slim-fitting leather jacket, cherry red to match her scooter and helmet, over a sleeveless black top with a neckline designed to intrigue. Her eyes smoldered with Sultry Steel shadow lined with an ebony cat's eye, and Trinity insisted the Russet Obsession lipstick would bring out the natural highlights in Tuesday's simply styled waves. Even Oz's silver coat had been brushed to a glossy shine. Tuesday felt formal enough for a stuffy lunch, and sexy enough for Shifting Tides. She mounted the scooter and revved the engine, pleased with this transformation.

"Let's ride," she said to Oz.

Because of her expertise in archery equipment, Tuesday had visited the Hoyt Archery compound twice before, though never for such a high-profile client. In her head, she sometimes referred to the conglomerate as the "Hoity Toity Hoyt Factory." On her first authorized visit, she'd had to prove herself worthy by dropping comments like, "My client is in need of a cam optimized for her shorter draw cycle, and of course, she'll expect the shock pod dampening system." Tuesday had also fielded some snide remarks about Katniss Everdeen and "you know nothing, Jon Snow." But she quickly won the respect of the Hoyt executives when they realized she had buying power from wealthy clients in addition to her intimate knowledge of hunting bows.

By now, Tuesday's reputation preceded her, and she required no introduction at the secondary compound gate. She'd already scootered past the first security check-in without stopping, since the scanners picked up the Deliverer tags around her neck. Dismounting the scooter and unbuckling Oz in the midst of a cloud of road dust, Tuesday paid little attention to the bumbling guard who offered to valet park her vehicle.

"I can park it somewhere out of the dust and nearer to the training range—or nearer to the R and D department, or—"

"Here is fine," she took off her helmet and shook out her sandy hair, now bouncy and gleaming. Handing him the helmet and keys, she added playfully, "And I charge by the minute for joyrides."

Her liaison for the afternoon, a tall Black man with a chevroned tie, strutted stiffly out from the Hoyt main building to meet Tuesday..

"Welcome, Ms. Devlin," he greeted her, "I hope your journey has been pleasant. Let me escort you to our buyer's lounge for some refreshments before we get started."

"Of course, Mr. Fletcher," she replied. "Though let's hold off on the stronger refreshments until after we've settled things."

When they arrived in the third floor lounge overlooking an extensive green practice range, Mr. Fletcher waved away the server bringing the tray of aperitifs. "Just the tapas at the moment," he requested. The lounge was staged with small oak tables, barrel chairs, and a scattering of cocktail tables spaced around a central bar, all surrounded by windows for viewing the activities at the compound. Already renowned in their field, Hoyt Archery took full advantage of the disruption in meat supply chains and the munitions shortages after the pandemic. The corporation absorbed its competitors and many of the arrow and bow string manufacturers, quickly dominating a now lucrative industry.

124

Tuesday and Mr. Fletcher stood at one of the cocktail tables, watching two archers on the range below, as a second server brought a tray of crudite and charcuterie. Mr. Fletcher stopped the server, "Excuse me, Ethan, please bring another tray of the elk bresaola and prosciutto for our friend." Oz had positioned himself under the cocktail table, relaxed, but alert in the new surroundings.

"Very much appreciated," Tuesday thanked Mr. Fletcher.

"We can't very well woo you without wooing Oz too, can we?" he admitted, careful to show he remembered the dog's name.

"You've got me nailed down," Tuesday agreed. "But I'm pretty well won over for this transaction. I'll still need to do the full inspection and watch the trials, but I expect we'll be able to meet Representative Brogan's requests. From what I understand, you've nearly perfected your newest hyper cam and split-cable system and are just waiting for the right moment to release it."

Mr. Fletcher smiled, "So much about archery is waiting for the right moment to release."

Only after a thorough tour of the facility, including Hoyt's boot camp for archery instruction and their beehive paddock for making string wax, did Tuesday, Oz, and Mr. Fletcher arrive at the research and development department to inspect and test Representative Brogan's bow. They entered a sterile lab reminiscent of a hospital, where a woman led them to a table with Tuesday's items laid out. Tuesday ran her fingers along the bow as she examined it, then balanced the piece in her hands, feeling the potential energy bound up in the curved carbon. "I'd like to see it in action," she told them.

"That's what I'm here for," a sturdily-built man tipped his camo hat to her. "I'm Jim. I'll be your stand-in for Mr. Brogan today," he said with a twitch of his mustache. Being smaller in stature than Brogan, Tuesday couldn't reliably judge the bow with precision, so Jim would demonstrate instead.

They chose a target on the compound's range and Tuesday noted the direction of sun and wind. She first asked Jim to nock the arrow, and then stood apart from him, watching as he drew back. With her eyes steady on the mechanisms, she asked him to shoot and watched the bow's reaction to the release. The arrow whispered through the air and sunk solidly into the target across the range. Brilliant.

"Nock again please," Tuesday said, stepping very close to Jim this time.

"Nock, nock," he said as he fitted another arrow.

"Who's there?" Tuesday asked, eyeing the bow's stabilizer closely.

Jim drew back a second time, with Tuesday close beside him, "Goddamn, I can't believe I never thought of that."

Jim let the second arrow fly soundlessly. After several more shots and several more angles of view, she was satisfied that Brogan's money would be well-spent.

"Pack up that beautiful piece of art—it has a journey to make," she said, shaking Mr. Fletcher's hand.

Sometime later, after promises to keep in touch and a toast to future business deals, Tuesday strapped Oz into the sidecar and swung her leg over the seat of the scooter. With the bow tenderly arranged in its carrying case, and the various accoutrements stowed in the under-seat storage, Tuesday waved goodbye, accelerating through the security gates toward the main road.

With her mission complete, Tuesday let her mind wander with the winding Salt Lake City lanes on her way back to the AirBNB. She had surreptitiously transferred the little musical disc from her tunic pocket to the pocket of the leather jacket when Trinity had convinced her to keep the jacket. "It's been just miserable in my dressing room closet, pining away for someone with your complexion to wear it," Trinity had declared. The photo of the locket was in her pocket too, and Tuesday found herself picturing the inside of the locket, imagining what it felt like to run her fingers over the word inscribed there in tight cursive. The Mad Hatter's quote scrawled on the photo troubled her. Who would want everything to be nonsense? Who could possibly know the significance of these seemingly unrelated trinkets, and why did this person choose to remain in the shadows?

The Utah sun began to set in resplendent shades of pink and orange as Tuesday puttered into the mansion's garage. Feeling like a warrior returning with the spoils of war, she slung the bow on her back. Instinctively, she touched her thigh, her pocket, and her chest to check for her dagger, the items from the drones, and her locket around her neck. All accounted for.

Inside the first floor of the magnificent home turned AirBNB, Tuesday searched for the young man who seemed to be the sole employee. She peeked into the kitchen and then into a ritzy entertainment lounge before finally finding him exiting a spacious linen closet. "Oh good, there you are," she said.

"Looking for me?" he answered, closing the closet with a stack of towels balanced on one arm. "Or maybe hunting for me?" he pointed at the bow on her back.

"Good one," Tuesday approved. "Yes, I wanted to tell you I'd like to keep the key to the scooter in case I need it later tonight." Myles wouldn't return until the following day, which left her and Oz to themselves for another evening.

"Sure thing. I won't sign it back in yet. Do you need me to watch your dog while you're out?"

"Nope," she shook her head. "He goes where I go." Tuesday thanked the young man and crossed the house to the staircase leading up to her room. Oz, still energetic after the day's events, ran up the stairs ahead of her to wait on the landing, looking back down at her.

"Okay, I hear you," Tuesday acknowledged. Then added with a British accent, "After we pop in at our suite, I'll let you frolic in the courtyard, so long as you mind not to get your paws soiled, dear." The British accent suddenly reminded her of Mox and she no longer enjoyed her joke.

Stepping into the lavish little room, Tuesday deposited the bow on the bed and caught a glimpse of herself in the mirror along the wall. She flipped her hair over one shoulder, stood up straighter, and put her hands on her hips, inspecting her appearance. Kind of a sexy badass with the leather jacket and sultry eyes. She crossed her arms and nodded slowly. "You wanna go meet someone?" she wasn't sure if she was asking herself or the dog.

While Oz romped in the yard behind the manor, Tuesday perched on the porch swing where Myles had sat the night before. She tucked one foot underneath her and used the toe of her other foot to push the swing into a gentle sway. A bird twittered from somewhere deep in the forested acreage where she and Oz had explored and stumbled upon the dump. Is that what she wanted to do for another night? Spend time alone at a trash heap? Try to choke down another meal while her mind ran on a treadmill that kept her ruminating over unsettling puzzles and reliving ancient pain? No, it was less like a treadmill and more like one of those teacup rides at a carnival—the teacup spinning, plus the giant arm attachment spinning, all the scenery whipped up together into a slurry. A Mad Hatter's tea cup party.

Tuesday ran her fingers through her hair and shook her head to free herself of her anxious thoughts. She twisted a lock of her hair around her fingers. No sense wasting her make-over. Conner from Chum had been easy to talk to and a pleasant enough diversion from the tense mood in the Salt Lake City air. She took out her phone and arranged to meet him at Shifting Tides.

As a chill crept into the evening, Tuesday was glad for her red leather jacket covering her exposed shoulders while she rode toward the city. In the sidecar, Oz stuck his snout into the air to smell the world as it passed, his tongue hanging out of his doggy smile. In front of the vibrant mural

128

she'd seen earlier in the day at Shifting Tides, Tuesday chose a parking spot for the scooter and unbuckled Oz, who extended his front legs in a deep stretch. "Ooh, big stretch!" Tuesday said, extending her arms also, "I hope you're not too tired to meet a new friend!"

The wicker torches set into the mural wall glowed with battery-operated lights, illuminating the flowers and vines, as well as the painting of the Paradise twins on the door. The dimly lit interior was as elaborately decorated as the exterior, with spiraling vines climbing the walls and rafters, and lush mosses hanging in clumps from potted trees. Airy and Paisley Paradise had rejected the grimacing totem faces and scantily dressed native women sometimes portrayed in tropical themed bars. Instead, they choose to celebrate the distinct cultures, flora and fauna of the South Pacific. Intricately painted maps of Fiji, Micronesia, and Polynesia graced the walls amid live ferns. A sound track of calling birds and crashing waves told patrons they were entering another land.

Tuesday seated herself on a tall wooden stool at the bar, scanned the room briefly for Conner, and then, not finding him, turned her attention to admire a wall of booze. An ebony-haired pixie of a person appeared behind the bar with a floral headpiece that matched the hibiscus and orange blossoms on her dress.

Her mirthful eyes grew even wider when she saw Tuesday. "Oh my God!" she threw one arm up; the other held a bottle of rum. "Is it really you? It's so good to see you!"

Airy Paradise scurried around to the other side of the bar to embrace Tuesday, bringing the bottle of rum with her. "Good to see you too," Tuesday agreed, accepting the hug.

"Paisley! Tuesday is here!" squealed Airy, which brought a second ebony-haired pixie bursting out from the door behind the bar, a neat arrangement of tiny purple orchids tucked behind her ear.

When she saw Tuesday, Paisley threw her arms up and cried, "Oh my God!" Even in three-inch leopard print heels, Paisley and Airy Paradise barely cleared five feet tall.

"Ringo, Archer, come say hi to Oz!" Airy called. She welcomed Oz in a high-pitched voice, "It's so good to see you too, sir!"

"Paisley went back behind the bar and opened the door for Ringo and Archer, two shiba inus wearing Hawaiian print bow-ties on their collars. The small red dogs, reminiscent of foxes, bounded out to greet Oz with wags of their arched curly tails.

"This place is amazing! The plants, the paintings—they're so beautiful and...accurate!" Tuesday gushed. "It's like you took the tacky out of tiki!"

Airy and Paisley beamed.

"I'm so glad you think so!" Airy said excitedly. "That's how we picked the name. We're shifting the tides of tropical bars!"

"Tasteful and tasty—that's us!" agreed Paisley.

Tuesday was suddenly sorry she'd agreed to meet Conner at all. She would have a much better time catching up with the Paradise twins than awkwardly getting to know a stranger, even if he was handsome. Relieved that she'd arrived early, Tuesday admitted, "It's so wonderful to see you guys! I want to know everything that's going on, but also I have a date on his way."

"Ooh!" said Airy.

"Ohh! said Paisley.

"He's just a Chum though. Nothing special. Should I tell him not to come?" she reached into the small muslin bag for her phone.

"No no, he can come!" said Airy.

"I don't know, does he like dogs?" Paisley asked. "That's the most important criteria."

"Of course it is," Tuesday laughed. "He did mention that he owned a dog."

"Okay then," Paisley agreed.

"But we still want veto power if he shows up and we don't like him," Airy added.

"I always liked Myles," Paisley said, setting her elbows on the bar and cupping her chin in her hands. "So handsome and nice. And a PILOT."

Airy raised up the bottle of rum that she still held by the neck. "I'll make us drinks! I'm working on a new recipe. It's got crushed pineapple in it and we'll serve it in coconut shells!"

"That sounds a-maze-ing," Tuesday was delighted. "Where do you even *get* pineapple around here?"

"A Westminster friend from Georgia brought us a case last week," Paisley explained, setting a half coconut shell filled with the cocktail on a stand in front of Tuesday. She sipped it through her bamboo straw and felt the bright tang of pineapple on her tongue.

"We made our own elderflower liqueur for this one," Airy bragged. Tuesday savored her drink until in the bottom of her coconut shell cup she found a wheel of fresh pineapple. Picking it apart with her fingers, she relished each bite. The Paradise twins chattered rapidly with her, still muddling herbs and pouring drinks for patrons. Conner was late, but Tuesday didn't care. It would only be a minor bruise to her ego and waste of a makeover if he stood her up.

When a man in dark jeans and a tan t-shirt entered the bar, Tuesday recognized Conner immediately. He stood in the entryway, his eyes skipping around the venue looking for her. Before she flagged him down, Tuesday turned to the Paradise twins and pointed at Conner wordlessly. Airy stage whispered, "He's cuuute!" bouncing lightly on her toes and tapping the palms of her hands together in silent applause. Paisley twisted her ruby lips to the side in a contemplative expression, then shrugged and held her arms out, miming an airplane. Myles was cuter.

Tuesday caught Conner's attention with a low wave and Oz stood up when he approached. He gave a nervous smile, "Hi, sorry I'm late. I got a little lost. I'm Conner."

"I know," said Tuesday, amiably. "Not your usual stomping grounds, huh?"

"This place is new," he concurred. "What are you drinking?"

131

"It's a concoction the lovely Paradise twins invented. Or it was. I'm already a cocktail ahead of you."

"I'd better catch up then," Conner said, lifting a finger at Paisley, "Two more of whatever this is!"

"She didn't tell me what it was called," Tuesday noted while Airy started to make the drinks. "Do you like pineapple?"

"Sure, I guess," he answered. "I'm more of a bread and potatoes kind of guy."

"No potatoes here," Paisley said, adding the bamboo straws to their coconut cups.

Airy popped into the conversation, "But we DO have our specialty sweet soda bread with dried mango!"

"No thanks," Conner dismissed her.

"Maybe later," said Tuesday.

Their conversation flowed more easily in person than over Chum, and Conner's chin dimple was just as cute. Tuesday slowed down on her second drink, which Airy had informed her was titled King of the Ring, as in dog show ring, as well as pineapple ring. Conner sipped slowly in between telling stories of his days playing high school baseball and his job as a welder. Maybe that explained the well-toned biceps.

"I'll be right back," Conner said, trying to touch her thigh seductively as he stood up, but instead giving her more of an awkward buddy-pat on the knee. Tuesday chewed the end of her bamboo straw and twirled it between her forefinger and thumb, letting her mind wander while she waited for him to return. Conner wasn't the most suave guy, but he was trying, and she was only in town for tonight. She put her hand into the pocket of her leather jacket and her hand brushed the musical disc. Looking down at Oz, she said, "Do we keep trying to forget and have fun, or do we abandon ship and go back to overthinking?"

"Overthinking," said Paisley, eavesdropping on Tuesdays' comment.

"Fun," voted Airy.

"Oh jeez, didn't know you guys were so close," Tuesday laughed. "I'll give him one more drink and see where it goes." She sucked the last of her King of the Ring through the straw, making a slurping noise while the twins laughed.

Conner returned and said, "Ah, I see you're in need of another drink!"

"Don't worry, Paisley's got another on the way," Tuesday stopped him from ordering her another. "And anyway, you're just barely finishing your first!" She nodded toward his coconut cup with the pineapple ring and remainder of the cocktail still at the bottom.

"You're right, I'm behind," he said. "Tell you what, when yours comes, we'll toast and I'll finish this one off."

"Deal," Tuesday smiled.

"Oh hey, here's a video you gotta see," Conner fished in his pocket for his phone and then handed it to Tuesday, tapping it to start the playback as Paisley set Tuesday's drink in front of her.

"It takes a little bit, but watch closely," Conner turned away briefly while Tuesday watched a video of some brush rustling gently in an evening breeze.

"Wait, where is this?" she asked, noticing the foliage was not reminiscent of the Salt Lake plants she'd seen. She watched as a coyote suddenly slunk out of the shrubs and trotted away, followed by two pups.

"Just a little ways away from my place," he said.

"Huh." Tuesday looked up from the video and handed him back the phone. "Cool. Doesn't look like Utah. Cute puppies."

"Okay, here," Conner held his cup in the air and pushed Tuesday's drink toward her. She held her cup up as well, raising an eyebrow in expectation. "To..." he paused. "I'm not good at speeches. To tonight!"

"To tonight," Tuesday agreed, locking eyes with him while their coconut cups tapped together. Conner made a show of taking a deep breath and sucking up the rest of his King of the Ring while Tuesday

133

laughed and took a daintier sip.

She ran her tongue across her teeth, "This one tastes different," she noted.

"The other girl made the last one. They must do it different," he said. "Or she didn't stir it maybe. Stir and try again."

As Tuesday stirred and sipped again, her head began to feel heavy. The long days were taking their toll on her. She looked down at Oz, who sat up, alert. For just a moment, she worried that she would have another flashback, that she would experience the horrific crash again and panic here in the bar. She slowly turned to Conner; he looked like he was underwater.

"Ready to go?" he asked, reaching to caress her thigh.

Tuesday struggled to make sense of her clumsy thoughts. Yes, she was ready to go. But something was too familiar: her looking down, him turning away, an almost imperceptible flick of his hand.

"Bastard," she muttered.

In the same instant, Conner asked, "What?" and Tuesday stood, flashing her dagger out fast enough to catch him on the forearm before he pulled back. "Whoa, hey," he held out his hands to calm Tuesday, his arm starting to ooze blood.

At the commotion, both twins rushed over, Airy with her hands on the sides of her head, shrieking, "What is *happening*?"

Tuesday stood in a crouched stance, one arm outstretched with her dagger, trying to hang onto consciousness. "Mother fucker...spiked...my...drink," she spat. She felt the dagger slip from her hand and the Paradise twins became dozens of pixies swarming Conner, jumping on his back, kicking his shins, punching him in the stomach, biting him; they were everywhere. The floor came up and slammed Tuesday in the head.

The room went dark, but Tuesday could hear Ringo and Archer barking and Paisley and Airy screeching as they assailed Conner.

"I wasted pineapple on you!"

"Who wears a t-shirt on a first date?!"

"You didn't even say 'please' when you ordered!"

And the last thing Tuesday thought before succumbing to the blackness was: *I've got to find Mox.*

Eight

Tuesday's eyes fluttered open. The rafters of a ceiling loomed far above her. The room was dim and the wall next to her was paneled with dark wood. Where was she? Her heart seized for a moment: where was Oz? But when she tried to roll over, she discovered his large furry form laying next to her, and he raised his head as she propped herself up on her elbows. She rubbed her bleary eyes, forcing them to take in her surroundings.

Both Paradise twins came into focus sitting on little wooden chairs beside the bed where Tuesday and Oz lay. Their make-up, flowered dresses, and victory-curled hairdos were still immaculate.

"Hey," said Paisley softly, touching Tuesday's arm, "You can relax. It's all fine."

Airy giggled quietly, "But what a weird way to wake up, with us staring and hovering over you!"

Tuesday put an arm around Oz and sat up. "I'm so goddamn glad to wake up to you guys though!" she sighed. The fog began to clear from Tuesday's mind, and she half-smiled, "Did you guys...kick Conner's ass?"

"We tried to detain him, but he made it outside," began Paisley calmly.

"Detain?" Tuesday was almost laughing, "It sounded like you were beating the bejeezus out of him!"

"There may have been some of that," she nodded. "But we lost him."

Tuesday gingerly pressed on the side of her head where she'd hit the floor. She'd get a goose egg for sure. She rested her head against the wood panel wall next to the bed. "Are we still at the bar?" she asked, finally noticing the tropical ambiance in the room. She could hear the bar's soundtrack of waves and bird calls. "What time is it?"

"Yeah, this is the upstairs of Shifting Tides," Airy assured her, "Totally safe. You weren't out very long. Just a couple of hours."

"Seems like he dosed you with a mix of Vitamin K and that new one, Blix, based on how fast you went down and then came back around," Paisley said knowingly. Tuesday looked at her quizzically.

Airy shrugged, "Mom was a doctor."

After lingering a while in the good graces of the Paradise twins, Tuesday felt she had recovered enough to scooter back to the AirBNB. She and Oz said their goodbyes to Paisley, Airy, Ringo, and Archer with hugs and promises to keep in touch. "I owe you guys," Tuesday said.

"No," said Airy, "Friendship is free."

Now under the darkness of a midnight sky, the Salt Lake City streets were even more deserted, and the flickering street lights illuminated peeling billboards and crumbling buildings. Approaching the mansion, the shoddy streets turned into new pavement, and recently constructed or renovated structures. Sprinkled among the ruins were a pearly hotel, a furniture store, and a payday loan shop that Tuesday felt sure must be a front for arms deals. Just before the AirBNB mansion, the suburban landscape seemed almost untouched by the devastating pandemic. The earthquake that had shaken the Northwest and Bellingham was too far from Utah to have done any damage here, but clearly they'd suffered their share of natural disasters over the ensuing decade. Bellingham. Thank God Myles would be here to take them back home tomorrow. Well, today really, since dawn was not far off.

Tuesday returned the scooter to the garage, and crept up the flights of stairs with Oz to their attic room. To ensure the long day didn't take a toll on Oz, Tuesday gave him some of the jerky from her knapsack and turned the lights down. He curled up on the doggy bed with a grunt and a snort. She knew she should be concerned about the toll the day would take on herself, too. She sat on the bed staring stonily at the wall. Tuesday was sure the drugs had worn off completely, but she teetered on the edge of a bizarre soporific panic. Her flight or fight instinct had kicked in at full throttle, but she felt thwarted, too. She had nothing to fight against and nowhere to fly to. So she chose the third option: sleep. And the dream began.

Trees raced past in the darkness. She felt queasy as the road curved ahead and her foot stomped the accelerator. Angie screamed, "Slow down! Stop! Stop!" Suddenly the ghostly canine with coins for eyes appeared and the car wrenched off the road, rolling, crunching, and Angie still screaming. Until she wasn't. Silence. And the figure running away while Angie's blood dripped on everything—how was it on everything? The windshield, her necklace, the glove compartment, the ceiling...everything.

The silence after the screams haunted Tuesday as much as the screams themselves. She opened her eyes to the echoes of silence in the room, her heart pounding. She tried to hang on to the fragments of the dream, but they slithered away. What happens next? Without moving, she thought of her own wood grain above the lofted bed in her tiny house. Long, straight line, swerve to the left, through a smear of pine tar, back to straight. Breathe. Suddenly, the words *I'm sorry, Birdie* shot into her mind and quivered there, like an arrow sunk into its target.

Tuesday had to get up. Myles would arrive soon, assuming he'd completed all his transports on time as planned. She realized she'd slept with Representative Brogan's bow on the bed beside her. "I guess no one would mess with me while I'm in bed with that beast of a weapon," she said. Oz yawned and rubbed his face against the fluffy sides of his bed. Tuesday glanced at her reflection in the giant mirror, surprised to see her gaze returned by a polished-looking woman. Though most of the lipstick had worn off, Tuesday's smokey eyes and liner remained, her hair was charmingly ruffled, and the concealer under her eyes hid the circles she knew were there. "Huh," she said approvingly. She turned to inspect the lump on her head, her souvenir of the previous night; fortunately her hair covered it completely.

"You always wake up looking handsome," she told Oz, lowering herself to the floor to sit with him. She hugged him and then searched for her phone to see if Myles had texted. In her coat pocket she found her phone, along with the musical disc and photo of the necklace. *If I had a world of my own, everything would be nonsense.* Everything did seem like nonsense to Tuesday. Her world was becoming the Mad Hatter's world. But someone must know how to put these pieces together. "Dammit, Mox," she muttered.

Up early enough to snag a carrot muffin this time, Tuesday shared it with Oz on the verandah as the sun rose into a cloudless sky. The chauffeur popped his head out of the French doors, "Shuttle leaves in five minutes!"

"Okay," she answered without looking up from her muffin.

"Or whenever you want, actually," he rescinded. "You're the only passenger."

"Five is great."

After dropping Tuesday and Oz off at the make-shift airport, the chauffeur waved his hand out the window, calling, "See ya!" Tuesday watched him leave and then declared to Oz, "Time to find Myles and get our asses airborne!" She couldn't get out of Salt Lake City fast enough. With her Deliverer tags, Tuesday swept past security and onto the tarmac where she could see the Cessna parked in the distance and Myles with his preflight checklist. As she and Oz began crossing the fields toward him, Tuesday noticed another small plane on an adjacent runway with a group of people milling near it, loading their luggage. She squinted in the morning sun—three of the passengers were the PULL supporters who had sneered at them when they'd arrived in Salt Lake City. Tuesday recognized the fourth passenger as he boarded; he wore a baseball hat,

139

tan t-shirt and dark jeans, now with the addition of sunglasses. She didn't need to be close enough to see the chin dimple to know it was Conner. Anger boiled up from the pit of her stomach and Tuesday yelled, "Come face me, goddamn you!" knowing he would never hear her with the noise of the wind and the plane's engine.

Standing helplessly in the sun's glare in the middle of a tarmac, at least a quarter of a mile away, Tuesday watched the plane taxi for takeoff. Aware that there was no chance in the universe of hitting the plane, Tuesday picked up a fist-sized rock and hurled it as hard as she could in the plane's direction. Brogan's compound bow, tucked into its case, couldn't hit a target at more than 1,000 feet, even if there was time to set up the shot. Tuesday searched for more rocks and ended up throwing two more stones and a stick at nothing. "Son of a bitch wasn't even from Salt Lake City," she said finally, breathing heavily from exertion and anger. Oz panted and looked at her as if trying to read her for clues. She looked back at him. What now? Just go home and pretend life is normal? Life with nightmares and riddles and strangers hunting her down? No. It was time to do something.

Myles was too far away to have noticed Tuesday's temper tantrum. He continued dutifully performing his preflight checks on the Cessna 182. She watched him for a moment, composing herself, and then sent Oz racing ahead across the airfield to greet him. Oz play-bowed and ran circles around Myles while Tuesday closed the distance between them. A steady wind sent leaves and debris skipping over the tarmac and Tuesday brushed her hair away from her eyes. She was as happy to see Myles as Oz was.

From where he knelt giving Oz a belly rub, Myles looked up and said, "You look nice."

"Thank you for not sounding surprised," Tuesday answered earnestly.

"I'm not," he shrugged.

"I need to find Mox," Tuesday announced. Before Myles could react, she added, "Unrelated. That's not why I look nice." Fortuitous, but unrelated. "I look nice because of an empowered strip club."

"I have," Myles sat down onto the ground from his crouched position, "so many questions." He shook his head. "Last time you had a run-in with Mox, it went over like the Hindenburg, by all accounts."

"Exactly. That's why I have to find him. I need an explanation."

"Okay," Myles agreed. "If we're in a hurry, let's get this pretty lady purring," he nodded toward the plane, but didn't stand up.

Tuesday reached into her pocket and pulled out a Milky Way bar. "Here. They refill the candy compartment in the limo shuttle." She handed him the candy bar, "And I snagged another Reese's peanut butter cup for Sharon, too."

"Sweet!" Myles drew out the "ee's."

"And I got some video and memory cards with capacity you wouldn't believe," she took the muslin pouch from her pocket and started to attach it to her belt.

Myles whistled. "Damn. What else is in those magic coat pockets?"

Tuesday pulled out the photo of the locket and unfolded it. She stared at it for a moment. "I used to have a sister," she said, looking down at Myles to gauge his reaction.

He met her gaze and nodded slowly, letting this new information soak in.

Touching the locket at her throat, Tuesday said, "This is her necklace." She turned the photo toward Myles. "The one in this photo is mine."

After a moment Myles asked, "Where is yours?"

"I have no idea," Tuesday shook her head. "But I'm going to find out."

"I'm in," Myles said seriously," shielding his eyes from the bright sky as he looked up at her. "This time you're the one who looks like an angel."

"Do you believe in angels?" she asked.

"I might."

In the air, with the Great Salt Lake disappearing into the horizon behind them, Tuesday and Myles settled into silence. Oz dozed in the back seat. Though it seemed like mundane information, Tuesday felt as if she had divulged an ancient secret—dug up a mummy's tomb and disturbed its slumber. Seven years of friendship and she never once mentioned her sister to Myles. Tuesday had told him she had no family, which was technically true, if a little disingenuous. She never mentioned how, when she and Angie bounced from foster home to foster home as children, Angie was Tuesday's anchor. Her ability to smile, laugh, and soothe was only amplified by her unwavering faith in Tuesday as an older sister. Their myriad guardians always loved Angie. It was Tuesday who was trouble. Tuesday had never mentioned to Myles that when she got in a fight with a foster mom and ran away, she lived in a shed behind a duplex in the neighborhood so she could still meet Angie to walk her to school every morning. She had never mentioned how Angie forgave every angry outburst and begged foster families not to kick Tuesday out of their houses. Even as a teenager, Angie retained a childlike buoyant optimism. "You can get us through this, too," she would say, "As long as we're together."

Tuesday still didn't say any of this to Myles now, as they soared above what was left of farmlands and skyscrapers. He would piece everything together before long. Then he would know that Angie was dead, and that Tuesday had killed her. He would know that Angie's screams were the ones that visited Tuesday in the night. He would know that Tuesday was guilty of having killed the only person who had never given up on her.

She glanced across the cockpit at Myles. He had graciously not asked any questions. Tears pricked at the corners of Tuesday's eyes and she felt a familiar lump rising in her throat. Instead of allowing herself the luxury of crying, she cleared her throat and said into her headset, "Category."

Receiving her message that all was well, Myles sat up taller in the pilot's seat and half-smiled, "Bring it."

"Songs with single word titles starting with the letter H."

"So specific!" Myles complained. Then threw out, "*Hello*, by Adele."

"*Human*, The Killers."

"*Havana*, Camila Cabello."

"*Holiday*, either Lil Nas X or Weezer."

"I'd take a Havana holiday," Myles said. "There are lots of songs called *Home*."

"*Hologram*, by Pandemic Panthers," Tuesday supplied.

"*Happy*."

"*Halo*," Tuesday let that one hang in the air for a moment.

Myles broke the silence, "*Hypnotist* by Drake."

The song title reminded Tuesday of Ismene and Damien's suggestion about her dreams. "Have you ever been to a psychic? Or like, a...soothsayer? Or what do you call those people who read palms and auras or whatever?" she asked.

"Oh sure, all the time," Myles said. "Because that's a totally normal thing to do in 300 B.C., where I'm from."

"Stop it," Tuesday said, smirking. "You know what I mean, right?" "Prophets, tea leaf readers...okay, yes I know what you mean and no, I've never been to one. I once knew a pig that predicted World Series winners though."

Tuesday ignored this. "Ismene gave me a...recommendation."

"For a psychic? You don't believe in that bullshit. There are so many frauds who claim to talk to the dead now, taking advantage of everyone who's lost someone in the pandemic."

Tuesday nodded. "I do trust Ismene though. And she didn't say she was psychic. Just that she's...a seer, maybe."

"Well," said Myles, "you could go see 'er, maybe."

Tuesday made a noncommittal sound, "Go see yer seer," and then added, "Hindsight,' that new Blue Ivy song."

"Hellraiser, Ozzy Osbourne," Myles responded, and dove directly into a dicier subject, "So why exactly do we need to find Mox?"

"He knows something." Tuesday decided only minimal details were necessary, "I was assaulted at Shifting Tides last night."

"Whoa!" Myles started to react.

"Everything is fine," Tuesday assured him, "but there were too many coincidences for Mox not to be involved somehow."

"And you think he knows something about these drone drops that will help?" Myles asked.

"Help! by the Beatles," Tuesday added as a side note. "Yes, I think so."

"Then an equally important question: *where* do we find Mox? Usually we just stumble across him."

"Yeah…" Tuesday pondered. "He stays somewhere on Antique Row in Tacoma. That's where we'll have to start."

"Okay," Myles reluctantly agreed. "I just wish he wasn't so…"

"Caddish," Tuesday finished for him.

"Exactly."

Sitting motionless in the copilot's seat for the next five hours was agonizing for Tuesday. Her mind was reeling and she wanted to make her body race along with her thoughts. She was impatient to take steps to get closer to answers—metaphorical steps and physical steps. She was full of nervous energy that made her feel like she could run a marathon, but on the Cessna 182, there was nothing to do except tap her toe and drum her fingers on her own knee. Landing in Bellingham brought a wave of relief, and soon they were on the road, Tuesday in the driver's seat of Myles' truck, headed toward Tacoma and Justin Mox.

By the time Tuesday parked haphazardly on top of a curb in Tacoma's old theater district, their shadows stretched out on the pavement under the setting sun. Though virtually none of the shops on Antique Row operated as antiques businesses anymore, many of them still functioned as related businesses—furniture repair, thrift stores, construction businesses.

Remnants of the antique dealers created an atmosphere of dilapidated delight on the street. A neon sign over one storefront read, "Trash and Treasure," with the "sure" flickering erratically. Life-sized paintings of ladies from the 1950's, their slender hands holding bottles of soda, decorated the window of another building. On the sidewalk someone had propped the grill from a classic car against a dumpster, and it grinned widely at passersby.

No one was passing by. The street was empty as Tuesday, Myles, and Oz made their way down it, peeking into storefronts, searching for activity. "This place looks open," Tuesday said as they approached a textile dealer with rolls of fabric stacked in the window. Inside, huge carpets hung from the high ceiling amidst bolts of fabric and an industrial sewing machine. A bell dinged to announce their entrance, and a figure batted her way out from behind a rack of hanging tapestries in response. "Yes?" asked the woman, dressed in folds of beige fabric, as if not wanting to outshine her merchandise, "Can I help you?"

Tuesday got straight to the point, "We're looking for a man named Mox who lives around here. Do you know him?"

"About yae high," Myles added, holding his hand level with his own head, "Blonde and caddish."

The woman rolled her eyes, "Never heard of him." She turned away from them, flicked on a vacuum cleaner and began running the long tubular attachment across one of the hanging rugs.

Unfazed, Tuesday tapped the woman on the shoulder. The woman turned to face Tuesday, but did not turn off the roaring vacuum. "I know someone who can fix your sewing machine!" Tuesday yelled over the sound and pointed at the heavy-framed machine at the back of the shop.

The woman flipped off the vacuum, "Come again?"

"I know someone who can fix your sewing machine. For cheap. He's local."

"How do you know my machine is broken?" the woman asked

145

suspiciously.

"It's dusty. You haven't used it in a long time. And it's a cylinder-bed machine, so you've been doing your bulky stuff by hand. That must be a pain. Here, I'll just bump you the number and you can call if you want. Say Tuesday Devlin sent you." She held out her phone.

The woman raised her chin haughtily, but pulled her phone out from under some of the folds in her voluminous skirt and tapped Tuesday's phone. The woman turned away and spoke over her shoulder before flipping the vacuum on again, "He lives over the lighting repair place a block up."

Outside the building marked "End of the Tunnel Lighting," Tuesday looked for a staircase or doorway in the adjacent alleys. "Should I tell my brother to expect a call from a crabby tapestry lady?" Myles asked, backpedaling off the sidewalk to view the upper level of the building more easily.

"Probably," Tuesday answered. "I think the entrance must be through the shop. I don't see a way to get in from out here."

The interior of the whole lighting shop was ablaze with glittering chandeliers, candelabras, and brass fixtures. Frosted mirrors on the walls enhanced the effect of floating through a starry galaxy. "Wow," said Myles, "I think I need more light in my life. Ooh, this one is a lamppost. Narnia style." He hoisted onto his shoulder and followed Tuesday to the counter where a scruffy man in a scarf was sorting light bulbs by shaking them next to his ear.

"We need to see Justin Mox," Tuesday interrupted, impatient now that she was closing in on him. "He lives here, doesn't he?"

The man rubbed his goateed chin, "Mmm," he pondered, "No."

"Dad," a small girl piped up from the floor near the counter. She wore a headband that sparkled along with the lamps. She sat criss-cross next to several tiny lampshades, stacked up like a snowman, with a face drawn on the top one. Oz sniffed the lampshade doll while the girl

146

reached out to touch him. "This dog is one of those ones, Dad. Like the one who brought Uncle Ed his medicine." She held up her toy for Oz to inspect more closely. "You have to let them go up. They can go anywhere."

Tuesday, whose Deliverer tags could not be concealed in her new low-cut top, dangled the tags from her fingers silently. The little girl had done all the necessary talking.

"Let them up, Lucy," the man nodded agreeably.

Myles set his lamppost down, "I'll be back for this," he said to the shopkeeper as they followed Lucy to the back of the shop.

Lucy produced a ring of keys and unlocked a door at the back of the shop. Pointing up a steep stairwell, she said, "Mr. Mox's door is up there." She patted Oz on the head, "So nice to meet you."

At the top step in front of a heavy black door, Tuesday swung her foot to kick the door instead of knock. In the same instant, the door opened and her boot connected directly with Justin Mox's shin. He doubled over, "Christ, what the bloody hell?" Oz licked Mox's face exuberantly. Mox dropped the duffle bag he'd been carrying, "Is that how you always say 'Good evening'?" he asked Tuesday.

"I should've aimed higher," she retorted.

Mox acknowledged Oz with a tousling of his ears before straightening up, "Well, I'd invite you fine folks in for a cupp-a, but I was just on my way out."

"Where to?" Tuesday asked, toeing the bag. "Weekend getaway?"

"Yeah, the Maldives are beautiful this time of year," he said dryly.

"Bring a snorkel," called Myles matter-of-factly from a few stairs down, "They're under the ocean now."

"Oh good, you've brought Skipper," Mox saluted down the stairwell at Myles.

"You know his name is Myles," Tuesday was ready to be angry at anything.

"Ah, well that's the problem then. We use the metric system where I'm from."

Tuesday took a step closer and tapped her finger on Mox's chest, "Tell me what you know."

He crossed his arms, "What I *don't* know, is what you're talking about." Oz wiggled around Mox and trotted into the room behind him. Tuesday pushed past Mox, following Oz inside Mox's apartment.

"Please do come in," Mox said with mock cordiality, "Make yourselves at home."

Myles shrugged and then raised his eyebrows at Mox as he brushed past him, following Tuesday.

"Bloody hell," Mox muttered as he stepped back inside and closed the door behind them all.

The location of Mox's studio above Antique Row clearly influenced the decor. An ornate brass headboard hung on one wall next to a wooden steering wheel from the helm of a ship. A giant world map, the edges curling with age, hung on the opposite wall. A trunk served as a coffee table in front of two wing-backed armchairs. "You only have two chairs?" Tuesday said agitatedly.

"I wasn't expecting company," Mox retorted in exasperation.

Oz found an oversized blue and green striped cushion on the floor in front of a grandfather clock and dug at it before curling up contentedly.

"I'll just be in this corner with the elephant," Myles said, lingering by the door.

Mox squared his shoulders and stepped closer to Tuesday, "Tell me why you're here, or you can bloody leave."

"I'm 'bloody here' because someone pulled the exact stunt on me last night in Salt Lake City that you tried at Gilman House," Tuesday hissed. "Tell me why."

"Sounds like someone hired a hit on you. A Deliverer-napping," Mox said as if he were just deducing this.

"Well, you failed. And who would want to kidnap me?" Tuesday demanded.

Mox spoke evenly, "*I* did not fail. I didn't take the job. If I'd wanted to kidnap you, you'd be kidnapped."

"Then what the hell were you doing? And how do you know all this?"

"*I* was orchestrating a valuable learning experience," he said. "And we've spent enough time running in the same circles to know I can't reveal sources. That's a death sentence."

"A learning experience?" Tuesday fumed, raising her voice, "I'm supposed to believe you tried to drug me as a *warning*?" She clenched her fists.

Instead of backing up, Mox stepped even closer. He growled, "You remembered to draw your bloody dagger, didn't you?" He touched the weapon strapped to her thigh.

She batted his hand away. He was right. She had noticed the sleight-of-hand Conner used to try to spike her drink just in time because it was familiar. "That's ridiculous; you're trying to cover your tracks. If you knew someone was going to try to kidnap me, why not just tell me?"

"Right," he said, "How do you suppose it would've gone over if I'd said, 'Listen, dearie—details are nebulous, but remember to watch your back'?"

"Hindenburg," said Myles from the doorway.

"Exactly," agreed Mox, "You'd never have listened. I'd be up to my arse in flunkies trying to put my head on a stake because I snitched on their boss, who is barking mad. Sorry, Oz," he added to the dog.

Tuesday shook her head, "I can't believe I'm having this conversation." She walked in a circle around one of the wing-back chairs. "I don't know whether to believe you, and now I'm too pissed to care. Who is barking mad and ordered the hit? If you can't tell me who's after me or why, I'm not letting you out of my sight. Good thing your bag is packed. You're coming with us." Tuesday picked up Mox's bag from where he'd dropped it by the door and swung it over her shoulder.

"C'mon, Oz," she said, opening the door for the dog, who stood and shook out his coat. Mox started to protest, but Tuesday was adamant. "I'm serious, Mox. My life isn't a game for you, or anyone, to play with. Until I figure out what the hell is going on, you go where I go."

"And just where do I have the pleasure of accompanying you?" he asked angrily.

"California," she answered, as she headed back down to the lighting shop. Mox and Myles locked glares, "But not until tomorrow. So Bellingham first."

Mox exaggeratedly held the door for Myles and gestured for him to proceed. "I guess you've got yourself a new road trip buddy," Mox said with sarcastic cheer.

"Hallelujah," Myles said flatly as he followed Tuesday out.

"By Leonard Cohen!" she called up the stairwell.

Walking back to the truck with his new lamppost in tow, Myles listed logistical issues with the new arrangement. "We'll have to recalculate the fuel stops. I didn't account for a third person's weight. And where is he sleeping tonight? We're still getting dinner from that grilled cheese truck on the way home, right?"

"Sure. We have to eat, even if we've got this rat following us everywhere."

"I'm being held against my will, if you remember," Mox said.

"Can he ride in the truck bed? Because I just had the cab detailed and slug slime is impossible to get out of the seat covers," Myles said as they reached the vehicle.

"If you actually wanted information from me, I would expect you'd be a bit kinder," Mox said, taking his bag back from Tuesday. "Honey catches more flies and all that."

"You're right," Tuesday's voice dripped with sarcasm, "I'll remember to be sweeter to people who try to have me kidnapped. And you ARE much more like an insect than a rat."

A tone sounded above them and all three looked skyward to see a packet floating down and a drone whizzing away.

Tuesday snatched the drone drop out of the air before it landed next to the truck, her heart pumping with a combination of panic and fury. It was a box about the size of a Rubik's cube, covered in brown paper. "What do you want?" she yelled after the drone. Then to Myles, "How did they find us now?" She dropped and rolled under the truck, her hands searching the undercarriage.

Myles knelt and stuck his head under the truck, "What's in the box though?"

Tuesday popped back up, "I don't see anything under here. Where else could it be?" She patted herself down and then spun Myles around, looking inside of the hood on his sweatshirt.

"What the bloody hell," Mox said in subdued bewilderment.

Tuesday turned to him, "It's you." Mox held out his hands in confusion as Tuesday opened Mox's leather jacket and ran her hands over the material. She turned up his collar and he raised an eyebrow as she pawed in a circle around his belt. "Nothing," she said when she was finished.

"Someone," Mox turned his collar down, "is going to have to explain."

Tuesday continued to examine the sides and tires of the truck, "I've gotten two, now three, mysterious drone drops with...weird, creepy things inside. Someone is trying to tell me something, or maybe just make me crazy."

"Bingo on option two, I'd say," Mox commented.

"We found a tracker on the truck once," Myles interjected, "So that's how the drones found her before."

"Well, it's obviously rubbish to think I'm the one wearing a tracker," Mox defended. "I didn't know you were going to be barging in and taking me hostage today. I couldn't possibly have known to be wearing one."

"He's right," Myles conceded.

151

"How do you know this drop isn't just some tampons or something you ordered?" Mox asked.

Tuesday made a frustrated sound and started tearing off the paper. "Oh God," she said, mystified. "What in the name of..." She held up a small plastic baggie containing a lock of golden blonde hair, twisted into a neat ring.

"Is that," Myles started.

"...human hair?" Mox finished. "That is, indeed, a 'weird creepy thing.'"

"So weird," echoed Myles.

"So creepy," said Tuesday, taking a slip of torn paper out of the box. Dread welled up inside her, "There's a note."

All three leaned in to look at a photograph of the back of a woman's blonde head. On the other side of the photo, scrawled in bold black marker, read the words: "Angelica Ingall. Not resting. Not in peace."

"This can't be—" Mox touched the baggie, "I mean, Angie..."

Tuesday whirled away from them, "You don't know anything about Angie!"

"You said you used to have a sister. Is this her?" Myles asked delicately, "I thought maybe she was—had passed on."

"She is. She did," Tuesday fumbled. "I saw her." She sank to the pavement and leaned against the tire of the truck, burying her face in Oz's shoulder.

Mox opened his mouth and closed it again without saying anything.

Myles took the note and the hair from Tuesday, "She was blonde?" he asked.

"Very," answered Mox.

Myles looked at him in surprise and continued, "'Not resting.' The note implies that your sister's not really dead. Is that possible?"

Tuesday was crying now, no longer caring that Myles and Mox were witnessing her breakdown.

"Could the person in this photo be her?" Myles prodded gently.

Tuesday tried to focus on the torn scrap with the image on it. The only thing discernible was the hair, maybe the shape of the head. Tuesday put her hands on her temples and shook her own head in disbelief, "I don't...I mean, how could it be?"

Mox filled in, "I didn't spend a lot of time gazing at the back of the girl's head, but I'll be damned if that's not her." He dropped to one knee next to Tuesday, "Birdie, I think Angie is alive."

Trying to come to grips with this, Tuesday looked between Mox and Myles, their edges blurred from her tears. "If 'not resting,' means she's not dead," Tuesday felt a familiar strength awakening and starting to flow through her veins, "then 'not in peace,' means she's in danger."

She pressed her lips together in determination and swallowed hard, "Look, I don't have an explanation, but if Angie is alive, I'm going to find her."

"I'm in," Myles didn't have to say. Tuesday nodded at him gratefully.

Mox stared at her silently, a crease between his eyebrows.

Tuesday took a deep breath and moved to hug Oz once more. She stood up and then stopped suddenly. "What's this?" she twisted Oz's collar around, her fingers working at a small object. As the realization struck her, Tuesday swore furiously. She pried the button-sized object free of the dog's collar and held it out in her palm for the two men to see. "The tracker was on Oz."

Nine

On the road back to Bellingham, Tuesday wanted to tell Myles to drive faster, but she knew speeding on the freeway would not bring her any closer to discovering the truth about Angie. She had not stopped staring at the ragged photo since she'd smashed the tracker and they'd left Antique Row behind them. Ten years might not change the back of a person's head much. Could this really be Angie? Could the sister who drew flowers on Tuesday's hands with colored markers and curled against her in the dark during windstorms really be alive? Tuesday wanted desperately, wildly, for Angie to be alive. How would it be possible? Her memories of that night were ensconced in the fog of a dream, but she knew, had known, that she'd seen her sister's corpse in the passenger seat. The sight of Angie, lifeless, with her ear and half the skin of her face torn loose and dangling, blazed like a perpetual bonfire in Tuesday's brain. But what happened next? If only her nightmares would give her a glimpse of what followed, maybe there would be an explanation.

"I'm going to see the Oracle of Delphi," Tuesday announced, breaking the silence in the vehicle.

"Is that the Greek place next to the grilled cheese truck?" Myles asked.

"No, I mean the old Greek seer. Kosmina," Tuesday said.

"I thought we were going to California. Now we're going to Greece?" Mox was perplexed.

"She's in California; I'll go before we give the bow and chandelier to Representative Brogan."

"Oh, I have an idea then," Mox said brightly, "We can just go ask a Magic-8 Ball where Angie is instead! It will be just as useful, without all the fuss."

"You don't get to weigh in on this," Tuesday brushed him off. "My sister, my rules."

"My Lord, you're stubborn."

"Listen," Myles broke in, "We'll do whatever it takes to figure this out. There's no harm in visiting an old lady if there's a chance she can help. In the meantime, we can think about cracking the case with the clues we have."

"Thanks, Nancy Drew," said Mox.

The evening air in Bellingham hung still and heavy when Myles slowed the truck to a halt near the airplane hangar. Mox unfolded himself from the back of the cab, "It's a tight fit back there, but at least I get to sit with the dog. He's the best of you lot anyway." Oz jumped out after him and began his usual patrol of the perimeter of the hangar, investigating the scent of birds or squirrels.

"Dinner time, Oz," Tuesday called him into the hangar. "We'll play outside more later," she promised.

Though the Cessna itself took up much of the space in the hangar, a section of it was reserved for a variety of storage options: large bins, a small plastic shed, a free-standing bank of cupboards. It also included a wine barrel table, a couple of dining room chairs, as well as an air mattress, and of course, a dog bed.

Myles doled out the sandwiches they'd picked up from the grilled cheese truck. "With spinach and tomato for the lady," he handed Tuesday a wax paper bag. "With sauerkraut for yours truly," he put his own meal on the barrel table. "With ground turkey for the canine," he let Tuesday serve Oz. "And for our reptilian friend: with curry sauce." He tossed a packet to Mox. "Fries are first come, first serve," he took a sweet potato fry from the bag and set the rest on the barrel.

Tuesday placed Oz's sandwich on its wax paper on the floor with a few fries. He made short work wolfing it down and licked his chops, watching Mox to see if any further treats might be forthcoming. Myles

155

slipped a few more fries into the bag with his sandwich, explaining, "I told my nephew I'd help him with his math tonight. I've gotta call before his bedtime." He left the hangar, closing the door gently behind him.

"A little late for a tutoring session, isn't it?" Mox noted.

"I think he might be politely allowing some breathing room," Tuesday answered mildly. Or was he calling his date from a few nights ago? Tuesday seated herself on a chest that she knew contained a dozen bottles of Woodward Canyon wine. Mox sat on the floor, leaning against a bin of miscellaneous designer accessories. Oz curled up beside him.

"So, Angelica Ingall, "Mox pondered. "Angelica Ingall. It's a little on the nose, isn't it?"

"Her name? Because her name means 'angel angel'?"

Mox tapped his nose.

"It fit her though, didn't it? You knew her." Tuesday felt like she was dipping her toe into the sea before a tsunami. "She was angelic. Never a bad word about anyone. Even our guardians who were terrible, or the principals who expelled me." She looked up from her sandwich to meet Mox's gaze. "Even you." Her former self, the one Mox had known so intimately, was reflected back when she looked into his eyes. She hated and loved it. He didn't say anything.

"Justin," Tuesday tested out using his first name, "The day you broke up with me and I found out you turned me in for cheating was the day Angie died. I know you didn't know that." Mox still said nothing, but the crease between his eyebrows returned. Damn those eyebrows.

"She mattered more to me than anything," Tuesday pressed. "You *did* know that."

"Yes."

"So if she's alive, I need you to tell me what you know about the hit someone put on me. If there's a connection, I need to find it. I need to find Angie."

Mox ran his hands through his short blonde hair and inhaled deeply,

156

"All right," he agreed. "The source of the job was a man called Ben Hatter, who goes by The Mad Hatter. He masterminds one of the biggest drug dealing operations around, plus he's got his fingers in every other dubious activity you can think of—mafia business, gang wars, human smuggling"

"Okay," Tuesday blinked in disbelief. "And what does Ben Hatter have to do with that guy, Conner, in Salt Lake?"

Mox shook his head, "The PULL operative was just a convenient willing participant who took the job. He wasn't a mastermind. Hatter knew he could find someone shady mixed up in that organization. Someone who would have a grudge against a girl and her hero vaccine-delivering dog."

"That explains Conner's motive I guess, but why does this Mad Hatter want to kidnap me?" Tuesday was flummoxed. "What does he have against me? Or Angie, if that's really her in the picture?"

"I really don't know," Mox sounded sincere.

"Why is he called The Mad Hatter?"

"Because he's completely cracked. Not an exaggeration—he's certifiably insane. He's the drug lord who other drug lords are afraid of."

She tried to make sense of all this information. "All that devious activity seems like a lot for someone crazy to manage," Tuesday pointed out. "I guess we're not talking ax-wielding horror movie crazy."

"He's more a Moriarty-meets-the-Joker kind of crazy, I'd say," Mox shrugged. "Calculating but entirely unstable. Excellent qualities in a drug lord, really."

"How do you know him?" Tuesday asked bluntly.

"Probably a little obsessive-Gollum-My-Precious crazy thrown in too," Mox rubbed his dimpled chin.

"Tell me how you know him," Tuesday demanded.

Mox gave in. "I know *of* him. I have since you and I were in university at Western."

"How?" Tuesday enunciated slowly.

"You and I were mixed up in some unsavory things," Mox said carefully. "I was mixed up in some nasty things. Hatter was mixed up in some downright sinister things. He and I had some...business associates in common. That's all. He was just dealing in small time stuff then— prescription drugs, maybe a little cooking meth and pimping on the side— but heading toward bigger game. Fast."

"I see," Tuesday watched Oz breathing deeply and twitching in his sleep next to Mox. Tuesday brought her knees to her chest and rested her chin on them, letting the silence settle. "Mercury, wasn't it?" she asked, watching Oz's ears flick as he dreamed. "That made hatters crazy? Back in the days when there were hatters."

"Yes. But Ben Hatter ran a drug lab for years, even before he was a head honcho of a big network of dealers. Speculation is that his particular brand of crazy was caused by exposure to a cocktail of chemicals from cooking meth, and God knows what else, out of an old manufacturing plant. Knocked him clean off his rocker."

"Crazy enough to send weird relics of the past to a person he doesn't know and try to kidnap her." Tuesday was pensive.

"Apparently," Mox answered. "Listen, it's not that I care all that much, but you need to know what you're up against. Hatter is unstable, but powerful: that's dangerous. He's a cruel killer. And he's looking for you."

"You knew of him in college. So he's from Bellingham then?" she asked.

"That's where you crashed into him with your car, isn't it?" Mox replied.

The punch landed hard. Tuesday felt heat rising to her cheeks.

They sat in silence again until Mox ventured, "What dropped from the other drones? You said you had two more."

Tuesday reached into her pocket for the items. "First this little music box," she held up the clam-shell disc, but didn't open it. "And then this photo," she held out the image of the locket to Mox.

He cocked his head to the side, examining the photo. "It's your

158

necklace, eh?" he asked.

"Sort of. Angie and I each had a necklace with our name inside, remember?"

"I remember."

"I have one," she held up the locket that hung with her Deliverer tags. "This is the other one in the photo." She didn't say that the one around her neck bore Angie's name inside, or that she didn't know where her own had gone after the accident.

"Hm," Mox contemplated. "And what's that gadget?" He indicated toward the disc.

Tuesday clicked it open and let the song float into the air between them.

Alouette, gentille alouette,

Alouette, je te plumerai.

Tuesday snapped the compact shut after the first two lines. She didn't need to explain the significance to him.

Mox nodded in comprehension, "Blimey. All in all, I'd expect you to be absolutely unglued. I mean, more than you are."He scratched Oz between the ears.

"Thanks," she said sarcastically. "That's what I aim for: surprisingly glued together."

"You always did put on a brave face, no matter what," Mox said.

"Thanks," she said without the sarcasm this time.

"Not a compliment," he clarified. "Just truth."

More silence.

"Listen," Tuesday started, "You're scummy, and sketchy, and shady—"

"Love where this is going so far," Mox interrupted.

"But I guess if you've told me everything you know, then it's not helpful for me to watch your every move. You can sleep on the cot here in the hangar if you want though."

"Ah, I'm released from indentured servitude then? Yes, I promise I've told you what I know."

"Your promises are worthless," Tuesday stood up and nudged Oz. "C'mon pal, I said we'd have some play time before bed tonight." Oz eagerly bounded out the door of the hangar. "Goodnight," she said, allowing herself to look over her shoulder at Mox's handsome features once more before closing the hangar door behind her.

Outside she could see Myles at his free-standing punching bag, the one he'd used to teach her to box before she had her own bag at her tiny house. Tuesday suspected Myles was listening to music using earbuds too small to be seen in the dim light, and he didn't turn around when she approached him from behind. He'd taken off his sweatshirt and she admired his broad shoulders as he threw punches at the bag, light on his feet, despite his boots. Oz trotted into Myles' view, alerting him to Tuesday's presence. He turned and took out his earbuds, sweat starting to glisten at his temples.

"Are you getting pumped for going to the fighting arena in California, or are you pretending this bag is someone we know?" Tuesday asked, putting her arm around the hanging punching bag as if it were a person.

"Pumped," he answered. "I've always wanted to meet UFF fighters. I hope Proximo is there. Also, it's probably not healthy to pretend your punching bag is someone you know."

"Oh damn, I've been doing it wrong," Tuesday said innocently.

"But I mean, if I did pretend it was someone we know..." Myles threw a combination of right jabs, followed by a left hook and a roundhouse kick.

"Well, I said he could leave," Tuesday responded. "He told me everything he knows, I think."

Myles hit the bag with an uppercut. "I'll have to trust you on that one. I can't read the guy. You know him best."

"'All you ever learned from love, was how to shoot somebody who outdrew ya,'" Tuesday said, looking up at Bellingham's nighttime sky.

"Sounds lonely," Myles observed, pulling his sweatshirt on over his head.

"Smart man, Leonard Cohen." Tuesday called for Oz and then turned to Myles, "We're gonna head up Alabama Hill to the house for a few hours of...well, hopefully rest. See you tomorrow."

"I prefer the line about 'her beauty in the moonlight overthrew ya,'" Myles said.

In the moonlight at her tiny house, Tuesday sat under the wispy boughs of her weeping willow, watching Oz roam until he came to curl up by her side. "Tired already?" She sighed. "I don't blame you. It's a lot to take in—learning you might have a living sister and a deranged enemy both in the same day."

Inside the house Oz drank thirstily from his bowl, and Tuesday added a little pressed carrot juice to the water. "Gotta get your vitamins." She took a swig herself. Exhausted as she was, she wasn't ready to put her head down onto the pillow in her loft yet. The nightmare wouldn't be kept at bay tonight. It would either seep slowly and insidiously into her consciousness, or slam into her dreams, all synapses firing, like a sensory grenade.

Tuesday took all three items from the pocket of her red leather coat: the musical disc, the photo of the locket, and the strands of hair attached to the photo of the back of Angie's head. She set them in a row on the padded bench next to her. Two photos and a song. She dared to let her heart soar, just for a moment, with the thought that her little sister, now thirty years old, still had a corporeal form. With feet that touched the earth, blonde hair that blew in the wind, and eyes that danced with light. One day maybe Tuesday could hear Angie's laughter in the air, instead of her screams in the night.

But Tuesday had reached a dead end, now knowing that Angie was alive somewhere, in a room with someone close enough to snip a lock of hair and take photos of the necklace against his hand and of the back of Angie's head with just a sliver of her neck and left ear peeking through her hair. Except Angie didn't have a left ear. It was the most gruesome of

161

the images that flashed unbidden in Tuesday's mind. Angie's ear and the side of her face, ripped loose by something stabbing through the roof as the car rolled over and over. Tuesday brought the photograph closer to her face and squinted. The photo was too unfocused—or Tuesday's eyes were too blurred from unshed tears—but she thought she could just make out a thin bolt of a scar behind the ear.

Tuesday tucked all three items into her muslin pouch but then couldn't figure out what to do with it. Leaving the pouch unceremoniously on the bench or counter didn't feel right, and the safe under the floorboards seemed melodramatic. The objects were cryptically threatening, and they made Tuesday feel cornered. She stood and paced the length of her shipping container home a few times. Maybe she shouldn't view the items as threats. Maybe they were arrows, directing her to something long lost. If she could follow these puzzling breadcrumbs, she would find Angie. Yes, that was it. Tuesday slipped into her nightshirt, leaving the outfit she had shed on the bench for the morning. She climbed into the loft, taking the objects in the muslin pouch with her, and setting it next to her pillow. These puzzle pieces were precious connections to a sister she hoped to see again.

The night did not go as Tuesday expected. She awoke staring at the wood grain ceiling above her, in the precise position she had been in when she fell asleep a few hours before. She hadn't dreamed. Somehow, Tuesday found this unsettling, though she was glad to have gotten rest. She peeked down from the loft to look at Oz, his triangular gray head tucked under his tail, his sides rising and falling peacefully. Quietly placing her feet on the rungs instead of jumping down, Tuesday tiptoed into the kitchen and started water boiling for tea. Oz stirred in his bed under the loft.

"Morning," Tuesday said. "Ready for another day?"

Oz snorted and stretched.

"Let's make ourselves presentable for our trip, shall we?" Tuesday let her dandelion tea steep while she stepped onto the stone floor of her shower and felt the water run down her face.

A few minutes later, she stood in the doorway of the tiny home, sipping her tea and looking out over the view of Bellingham while Oz dug at a molehill in the yard. Tuesday mentally checked off her to-do and to-pack lists for their trip to California, the foreign feeling of butterflies fluttering in her stomach. Oz came to the stoop of the house and looked up at her, his tail arched high. "I'm not used to preflight jitters," she admitted to him. "Probably this will all lead to nothing," she said, to herself more than the dog. "We know hope is a four-letter word."

With her knapsack on her back and Oz at her side, Tuesday arrived at the hangar, thinking belatedly to text Myles to let him know she was on the way.

Here already, she texted.

Us too, Myles replied moments later. Us? Tuesday let herself into the hangar to discover Justin Mox and Myles sitting at the wine barrel table, each with a Mason jar of juice, sharing a stack of oatcakes.

She stopped in the doorway. "I didn't expect you to be here still," she said, her tone inadvertently sour.

"Good morning to you, as well. I slept on the cot, per your invitation," Mox replied. "I was knackered."

"We get it, you're British," said Myles. He continued to Tuesday, "Oatcakes and preserves to get us started. Load up."

"And I can see you've brought your own honey," Mox added, "You're always all sweetness in the morning."

Myles shook his head and stood up, "You can have the seat. I've got to do some last-minute checks." He crossed the hangar, leaving Tuesday and Mox in silence again.

"So, I was thinking," Mox began, "I've got some business that would be much easier to attend to if I were in the Republic of California, and I shouldn't pass up a free ride leaving this morning."

Tuesday was taken aback. "What? Now you *want* to come? That's—as you would say—'bloody suspicious.'"

"I'm shady if I don't want to come with you and suspicious if I do? There's some logic for you."

"Weren't you going somewhere? The Maldives?" she reminded him.

Mox played on his earlier sarcastic dodge, "I hear they're underwater. Trip canceled"

Tuesday threw her arms up, "Fine. Just don't slow us down." She started walking toward the Cessna and Myles.

Mox threw his arms up as well, "You're welcome."

"It's going to be a really tight squeeze to make it to Buchanan Field for refueling with the chandelier and an extra passenger," Myles reminded Tuesday when she explained Mox would be joining them after all.

"But you can do it, right?" she asked.

"Yeah," he said a little reluctantly. Trip canceled." That'll give us an extra hundred miles of range."

"Great," Tuesday said, not feeling great. She changed the subject. "Are you still excited to go to the arena? I was just confirming all our arrangements."

He nodded. "I'm stoked! I was debating though," he pointed to the logo on his sweatshirt, "Is it too much to wear my UFF fan shirt to the arena?"

"Um…"

"Or should I go more upscale fancy? I have a nice polo…"

He looked great in the polo. Tuesday stopped him, "I think it doesn't matter what you wear. Everyone will like you."

"UFF pride shirt it is, then," Myles confirmed. "They don't have to know my boxers match the shirt."

"Your underwear matches your shirt? You're wearing…*boxing boxers*?"

"Maybe," said Myles, ducking into the cockpit, leaving Tuesday

164

shaking her head.

With the chandelier painstakingly padded and protected, the hunting bow strapped tightly in its case, and all passengers seated and wearing their headsets, the Cessna took to the air, leaving Bellingham's skyline behind. Oz, his ear protectors cupping his head, watched the scenery below with his tongue hanging out the side of his mouth.

"You are now free to move about the cabin," Myles announced in his fake pilot voice. "Just kidding, nobody do that please," he added in his normal voice. "It's really small in here."

Tuesday felt the muscles in her jaw relax just slightly as she touched the muslin pouch at her waist. The items were connections, clues to finding Angie. But who had put the tracker on Oz? They'd been in contact with so many people in the past few days, and apparently this Mad Hatter had his tentacles extended from Liberty Republic to Salt Lake City, and who knows where else. She wanted to turn to check on Oz, but she was keenly aware of Mox's proximity; if she turned around, they would be eye-to-eye. Tuesday needed to prepare for that.

Instead, she spoke through the headset, "How's Oz doing? Is he scratching at his ear protection?"

"He's right chuffed, I'd say," Mox's voice registered in Tuesday's ears. "Maybe because he has a headpiece to block out that annoying, shrill sound I keep hearing in my headset—ah wait, that's just your voice."

Tuesday couldn't resist turning around now, her icy stare meeting his grin. "Stuff it," she ordered, irked to see Oz turn from the window briefly to lick Mox's face. What did Oz see in that guy anyway? Dogs wouldn't be swayed by piercing blue eyes and muscular forearms.

"Oops," Myles broke in over the headset channel. "Looks like your microphone isn't working right, Mox. I guess you'll be listening to annoying shrill sounds but unable to respond for the duration of the flight." Tuesday laughed.

After about three hours of the flight, during which Tuesday and Myles were lost in thought and Mox dozed, or pretended to, Tuesday sensed stirring in the backseat. Mox was rifling through his bag, which he had pulled onto his lap. Oz tried to shove his nose into the contents. Momentarily, Mox produced a container of what appeared to be trail mix. He tapped the container, and then tapped his headset.

"Myles," said Tuesday, still facing backwards, "Mox will trade trail mix in exchange for microphone privileges. What do we think?"

"I don't know," Myles was amused, "What does he put in his trail mix? Is it good, or is there, like, shredded coconut in it?"

Tuesday played along, "Hm. Looks pretty good. No coconut, plenty of peanuts, and—" now she was sincere, "Ooh, there's gummy bears. Turn his mic on!"

Mox's British accent crackled over the communication channel, "Wonderful. And as a token of my gratitude—" he handed Tuesday two soft snickerdoodle cookies the size of her palm.

Myles took one from her, elated, "With real cinnamon? Okay, I give. He's not so bad."

"Well played," Tuesday said, taking a bite.

The stopover at Buchanan Field was uneventful, with a little time to stretch, eat, and pee, but nothing more. Tuesday would have liked to stay and hike in the lush wildlife preserve or visit Mount Diablo nearby, but that was in a previous time, before she had a sister to find and an enemy to confront. Not to mention a chandelier to deliver. Tuesday found herself looking to the air, scanning for rogue drones, though she knew none would be at an airfield. When the Cessna rose again over the mountain, heading toward Los Angeles, Tuesday felt she was one step closer, but to what?

The rough landing at Fullerton Airport was expected; the runways there had sunken unevenly after a series of earthquakes, and the small

Republic of California airports (those that still functioned as such) were out-competed for funding by the larger LAX and San Diego airports. But Tuesday preferred the less crowded facility, even if it was a little bumpy. Fullerton's current director had been a coordinator for the World Disaster Relief Organization and had orchestrated many of Tuesday's vaccine drop offs during her years with Oz as a Deliverer. Even if he was too busy to say hello, the coordinator would ensure a smooth visit.

"Now what's the plan?" Mox asked, as they crossed the landing strip with their bags.

"The goods and plane stay locked in the AirplaneBNB storage hangar here until tomorrow. Now we pick up our vehicle, find our accommodations, and make the delivery in the morning," Tuesday outlined.

"You didn't mention food," Myles pointed out. "I'm going to need food."

"Don't worry, that should be all taken care of too," she assured him. "Oh and look, there's our car."

Mox was incredulous, "That?"

Myles wasted no time, "I'm driving!" he proclaimed.

Tuesday opened the door of the sporty sapphire custom Mercedes AMG-2000. "Until yesterday he was going to lend us the Porsche, but whatever model he has is only a two-seater, so we get the Mercedes instead."

"Who exactly is 'he'?" Myles asked.

"You know that lost kid Oz and I found on Mount Rainier the other day? His family, the Vandenburgs, offered to help us out."

Mox stood outside the low-slung vehicle while Tuesday situated Oz. "I just spent all day folded like an origami frog in the back of an airplane. Isn't it someone else's turn to sit in the kiddie seats?"

"I'll sit in back," Tuesday climbed in next to Oz, "and let's put the top down."

Myles revved the engine, "Where to?"

"Right, so I was saying about the Vandenburgs—they happen to have a second beach house in Long Beach and apparently—"

Mox cut her off, "A second beach house?"

"Yeah, their first beach home is in Cascadia, but the second beach house is here, and apparently they own a line of resort rentals," she explained. "So that's where we're headed for the night."

"I'll be damned," Mox approved. "Do you always travel this way? Because when I ran across you in Germany you—"

Tuesday stopped him, "Let's not bring up old times, hm? And no, I don't always travel like this. I mean, I'm just as happy to spend the night at a Motel 6. You know me." She winced at accidentally letting that last part slip out, but didn't correct herself.

Already speeding toward Long Beach, Myles persisted, "So Daddy Warbucks is providing meals then?"

"At least some, yes," Tuesday confirmed. "Even Oz's food. Actually, especially Oz's food, from what I understand." She patted Oz's side and rolled down his window to allow him the luxury of hanging his head out into the warm California evening air.

Southern California's landscape bore evidence of the devastation the pandemic wrought on the region's population. An especially verdant strain of the sickness had struck early and hard, smothering the economy along with the people. But despite being quick to succumb and slow to rebuild, the Republic of California still boasted some highlights. The beaches, now uncrowded, were one of those highlights, and a small but growing tourism industry was recovering.

"Should I keep going?" Myles asked. "We're practically on the beach, and I don't think Mr. Vandenburg will like it if we get sand up in the chassis."

"No one likes sand in their chassis," Mox said.

"Yes," Tuesday replied from the back of the convertible. "Our place is right on the beach. But there will be a paved drive and someone comes to detail the car every couple of days."

168

"Of course they do," said Myles.

"It's these here," Tuesday said a minute later, "Numbers eleven through thirteen." Myles stopped the Mercedes behind a row of identical bungalows, narrowly spaced facing the ocean. Each structure sat on a foundation raised above the sand, with steps leading to a deck ringed by a railing. Large windows peered out toward the ocean and grass roofs capped slatted walls. "He asked if we wanted a cabin for four, but I said we wanted the separate accommodations, even if they're small."

"Bless you," said Mox. "I choose thirteen, at the end."

"Eleven," Myles said.

"Okay," Tuesday shrugged.

The interior of bungalow twelve juxtaposed modesty with extravagance. The bed was twin-sized, but covered in silk sheets; the kitchen was hardly bigger than the one in Tuesday's tiny shipping container home, but the pans were cast iron and the mini fridge stocked with top-shelf booze.

A Holo message blinked from a disc near the fridge and when she pushed the button, Mr. Vandenburg's face hovered in the air. "Welcome, Ms. Devlin and company! I hope everything is to your liking. I've had the fridges stocked for both human and canine palettes. Enjoy your stay, and again, I can't thank you enough." His image disappeared and a crystal candy dish on the counter caught Tuesday's eye.

"Another one!" Tuesday cheered, grabbing a Reese's peanut butter cup for Sharon from the dish. She tucked it into her knapsack. "Thanks, Mr. Vandenburg," then to no one, "All right, Long Beach, we're here. Now what?" Oz barked at the door.

From the slim deck surrounding her bungalow, Tuesday could see and hear the activities on the porches of Myles to her left and Mox to her right. She unlaced her boots and discarded them on the deck before

169

descending the steps to feel the cool sand on her bare feet. Oz dashed and bounded in the lapping waves and Tuesday felt the urge to join him.

Mox leaned on the railing of his bungalow, staring at the sea, but Myles came down his steps a few feet from her. "Beautiful evening," he said, looking up at the stars.

"It's perfect for a nighttime jog," Tuesday said, heading for the sturdier sand closer to the tide. "Oz has some energy to burn, and I'm all jittery too. We'll be back soon."

Even on the more solid wet sand, each step required extra effort, and Tuesday found herself worn out after half an hour. She'd seen only one couple enjoying the warm breeze and moonlit dunes, but a few lights glowed in beach houses similar to hers, signaling occupancy. Saddled with a torrent of determination to unleash, and nowhere to direct it, Tuesday jogged with the hope of exhausting her mind as well as her body.

By the time she returned to the strip of beach at their bungalows, Myles had settled himself in the sand among some tufts of seagrass, his legs stretched out in front of him, propped up on his elbows. Tuesday put her hands on her hips, still panting from the exertion of jogging in the sand. Myles was watching Mox, who had wandered toward the surf, leaving his jacket in the sand nearby.

"Do you trust him?" Myles asked bluntly, his eyes still focused toward the sea.

Tuesday took a moment to respond between gasps, "I don't know."

"Because he got a Holo while I was sitting here by his coat," Myles continued. "It was a bot, so it automatically played. It asked if he'd like to reschedule the trip to Salt Lake City that he'd canceled"

As the information sunk in, Tuesday's blood boiled. "What the hell?"

"I've been sitting here for ten minutes trying to think of *good* reasons why Justin Mox might have been going to Utah."

"That's big of you," Tuesday said, already marching toward Mox, who was walking the beach with his hands in the pockets of his black cargo pants. It was impossible to stalk angrily through soft sand. She started

170

yelling over the roar of the ocean before she reached him, "Maldives, my ass!"

Mox, unfazed, replied loudly, "I sense a storm coming!"

Tuesday had to stand close to be heard and she was now short of breath from anger in addition to the exercise. "Damn right I'm stormy," she said. "So sorry you had to cancel your trip to Salt Lake City!"

"Ah, That's what our knickers are in a knot about."

"My knickers are not knotty—knotted, not...my knickers—Never mind!"

"Not wearing naughty knickers, eh? Shame," Mox said calmly.

"Just cut the bullshit and tell me why you were going to Utah!" Tuesday shouted, "Because otherwise, I'll have to fill in the blank myself. Are you working for Ben Hatter? Were you going to help drug me? Kidnap me? *Kill* me? What?" The wind whipped through her hair and she tasted salt from the sea on her lips. She stepped closer so she could be heard over the crashing waves. "What am I supposed to believe? You just happened to be going to Salt Lake?"

"Believe?" Mox said. "You can believe whatever you bloody well want to, but that won't make it the truth."

"So give me the truth then," she demanded.

"I was going to Utah because I was worried about you."

For a moment Tuesday was dumbfounded.

"Yes, Bir—," he stopped just short of using the old nickname. He took a breath, "Yes. But you'll recall, as I was leaving, you appeared at my door and kicked me in the shins. Safe and sound."

"Worried?"

"That's the truth. Believe what you want." Mox started toward his bungalow.

"We're not done!" Tuesday shouted to his back.

"We're done," he called out, "because I have nothing more to say, and you hate arguing without your shoes on!"

He was right; she did.

Stomping through the sand, Tuesday couldn't keep up with Mox, and she watched him pick up his jacket, nod goodnight to Myles and Oz, and then close the door of his bungalow behind him. Myles was standing as she approached him, brushing the sand from his clothes. Oz still panted lightly from jogging.

"What did he—"

"It's so hard to be mad on sand!" Tuesday fumed.

The expression of concern on Myles' face turned into a grin, "Never thought about it."

Tuesday almost laughed. "Well, it's true. And he said he was worried about me."

Myles cocked his head thoughtfully, "I'd believe that," he admitted, sounding surprised.

"Really?" Tuesday was incredulous.

"Because if he really was worried and wanted to help, he'd go about it all wrong. Just like that."

Tuesday contemplated this, nodding, "Maybe being worried is out of character, but being shady about it is *in* character?"

"Maybe."

Tuesday touched the pouch on her belt to be sure of its presence, and then put her hand on Oz's furry neck.

After a moment Myles ventured, "So I get the connection with the hair and the locket."

Surprised by the change of subject, Tuesday waited for more.

"But the song? *Gentille alouette*. It's creepy that it's about killing a bird, and it's a damn bizarre thing to drop on someone. But how is it related to you?"

She took the disc from her pouch, opened it, and let the first two lines drift eerily in the night.

Alouette, gentille alouette,
Alouette, je te plumerai

She closed the disc, but kept it cupped in her palm, "Alouette is my real name." She searched Myles' face for a reaction. "I'm the lark."

Ten

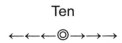

A low tide rendered the California beach wide and meandering in the glow of the early morning sun. Tuesday was already awake, sitting on the stoop of her bungalow watching the wind sweep through the grassy dunes, when the first rays warmed her shoulders. She had discovered a yoga mat rolled up in a corner near Oz's bed, and spread it on the wooden deck beside her. She waited for her mug of coffee to cool and for the sun to rise higher in the sky before she settled into her first position. Beginning with lotus, she moved deliberately through a series of poses, balancing on a fine line of freeing herself from a hurricane of thoughts, and avoiding falling into a waking nightmare again.

After half an hour, Tuesday took cat's pose, on all fours, her back curling and uncurling. With her eyes fixed on the deck near her mat, she noticed the wood grain was reminiscent of her ceiling in the tiny home on Alabama Hill. She focused on it, as she often did at home. Long, straight line, swerve to the left, through a smear of pine tar, back to straight.

"Ugh, blech" she sputtered as Oz interrupted with a sloppy lick and wet nose-bump. "You aren't very good at yoga," she wiped her cheek.

"I bet he's great at downward-facing dog," Myles' voice carried from his balcony to hers. He knew better than to ask how she'd slept. "Do I smell real coffee?"

"Yeah, no synthetic stuff here. You've probably got some too."

"I'm more interested in the eggs and bread," Myles informed her. "My spice rack has cinnamon, so I'm thinking there's French toast in our future."

"Not too far into the future, I hope," Tuesday said, taking a sip of her coffee. "It's early, but I want to head out soon."

"Our appointment with Brogan isn't until this afternoon though," Myles

174

responded with a puzzled look.

"I know." Tuesday paused, "But I'm going to visit Kosmina this morning."

"The seer?" Myles asked, and then without waiting for an answer added, "Okay. French toast is on the way. Hop over whenever." He gestured to the railing, suggesting facetiously that Tuesday should jump from her deck to his.

"Right," Tuesday smiled and scoffed, "Just put down a cushion to soften the crash landing. I'll be over after a shower."

Inside her bungalow, Tuesday realized that the shower was outdoors. A screen at the back of the living space slid open to reveal a back deck, complete with a rather airy shower stall. Wrapping herself in a towel and grabbing a bar of soap from the bathroom, she stepped into the stall where she would be concealed from her neck down and her calves up. Then she threw her towel over one of the stall's bamboo panels and felt the water rinse the gritty sand from her skin. Wetting her hair, she gingerly worked the soap around the healing bruise near her left temple where she'd hit the floor at Shifting Tides. Dammit, Justin Mox. Was he really telling the truth about everything? Or anything? He was deceitful and a liability, yet, Tuesday found herself reluctantly grateful for his presence. After all, he was the only person left in her life who had known Angie. And now what? Could she really be so lucky as to find her sister, the person she held most dear? Or would she find Angie only to lose her at the hands of The Mad Hatter? How did that madman fit into this picture at all? To find Angie—to uncover the truth—Tuesday would have to track down a maniac. And she had nowhere to start. Yes, now was the time to see the seer.

Tuesday turned off the water and wrapped herself in the fluffy towel again. She peeked at the balconies to either side of her own before slipping out of the shower stall and back inside her beach bungalow. "You're going to need a bath too, after all this beach time," she said to Oz, who was reclining on the bare floor.

Even in the early morning, Tuesday didn't need her red leather jacket as she stepped out onto her front deck again in her black sleeveless top and leggings.

"Going to visit the fortune teller, after all, eh?" Mox's voice startled Tuesday, but she tried not to show it.

She didn't turn to look at him on his balcony; instead she pretended to concentrate on lacing up her boots and attaching the muslin pouch to her belt. "She's not a fortune teller. And unless you have some more information to share, I don't have a lot of other leads. I'm at a dead end."

"Interesting choice of words."

"Well, it won't hurt to talk to an old lady. I need to find Angie and The Mad Hatter, and figure out what happened the night she—I thought she died."

"You were with her though," Mox said carefully. "At a party that night."

"How do you know? After that day, I didn't talk to you for years!"

"I read your texts."

"You read...my texts?" Tuesday asked, more confused than angry.

"That day. You forgot your phone when you stormed out the final time we talked. Remember?"

She remembered. "When you broke up with me. I *forgot* my phone, or you took it?" she pressed.

"Doesn't really matter after a decade, does it?" he said without emotion. "And of course I read your texts. I always did. Emails too."

"You're a monster," Tuesday said simply, giving up on being angry. "So, yes then you know I was with Angie the day I found out you were a deplorable human being. We went to a party later. But I don't really know what happened that night." Tuesday didn't know why she was still talking. "All I can remember is what happens in the nightmares I keep having."

Mox remained silent.

"So if this seer can help me make sense of Angie's death, or life, then

I'm going to see her. Maybe she can help me unlock and empty the box in my head that's full of unanswered questions."

"You know enough: you were reckless; you caused an accident," Mox was insistent. "Some boxes are best left unopened."

"Go to hell," was all Tuesday could think to say. She turned to Myles' balcony at the sound of his door opening. "How's breakfast coming?" she asked him, as if she and Mox had not just been having an incredibly weighty conversation.

"Almost ready," Myles reported. "Hop on over." He held out his arms as if to catch her.

"I might make the leap, but Oz isn't as young as he used to be," she said with a smile. "We'll just use the stairs." She glanced over her shoulder as she walked to Myles' bungalow, but Mox had already disappeared.

Breakfast was a brief, though tasty affair, after which Myles insisted on taking a plate of French toast to Mox. "To deny someone this nirvana would be a sin," he said. Tuesday left the two men to navigate the morning how they pleased.

According to the address Ismene Pantazis had given Tuesday, Ismene's mysterious Greek grandmother lived at the Winds of Change Casino, at an address followed by the parenthetical stipulation: "Limitless Sky Elite Poker Room." A set of three sample-sized bottles of alcohol from the beach house mini bar accompanied Tuesday and Oz on the drive, nestled in a paper box. "Never hurts to bring a little offering," she said.

Having fully charged the Mercedes overnight at the bungalows, Tuesday didn't bother plugging it in after she parked in the former casino's parking structure. The seven-story casino building itself still appeared glitzy and inviting, though ten years ago it had shut down in response to the deadly pandemic and then had been briefly reborn as a hospital unit, including one entire floor used as a morgue. In its current life, the Winds of Change Casino had diversified its enterprises. Two

177

floors continued to operate as a casino, but another floor housed flashing arcade-style slot machines that had been converted into virtual reality kiosks. The casino's buffet room was a shinery, an unregulated dispenser of homemade brews to patrons who couldn't afford or didn't want to eat and drink at the licensed restaurant on the fourth floor. The Winds of Change Casino's adjacent hotel resort easily transformed into a community of apartments, yet this did not seem to be where Ismene's yia-yia resided.

When Tuesday entered the foyer with its banks of elevators, a bot announced, "Deliverer detected," and she watched the numbered lights track the elevator's journey toward her. From the crude signage in the parking garage, Tuesday couldn't tell which parts of the casino were operating as what businesses. "Seems like you need to already know where you're going to get around in here," she said to Oz as she eyed the elevator control panel. "I guess we'll start at one."

Tuesday and Oz wandered through the largely empty casino floors where there was no one at the slot machines, and players occupied only one poker table. The shinery hadn't opened for the day yet, but the beauty salon beside it had a stylist and customer inside. More activity buzzed on the virtual reality floor, where Tuesday passed row upon row of VR machines, many of them in use, and observed people standing to stretch or snack in between trips. Another section of the casino seemed to be a vast dance floor, though no galas or Zumba classes were in progress. In front of the funeral services business on the fifth floor, Tuesday began to feel aggravated at what had begun as curious exploring. She would have to ask for directions.

"Hi," she announced her presence impatiently as she peeked just inside the door of the funeral home. "I'm looking—"

"Have you lost a loved one?" the attendant at the desk asked in a voice that sounded like an advertisement. "I'm Beatrice. You've come to the right place."

"No, no," Tuesday stopped her. "I'm in the wrong place. Can you tell me where the Limitless Sky Elite Poker Room is? I figured it's probably just...up."

"Seventh floor," Beatrice cooed pleasantly. "And please keep us in mind for any post-existence needs, either yours or those of a loved one."

"Nope," Tuesday said almost inaudibly, backing out of the office space.

The carpeting on the seventh floor blazed in a kaleidoscope of purple, red, and electric blue that reminded Tuesday of the background to one of her school photos from the 90's. "Don't look down, you'll fall into another time," she said. Following an arrow on a plaque adhered to the casino wall, Tuesday made her way to the end of a short hallway where a sign reading, "Limitless Sky Elite Poker Room," hung above a set of unassuming double doors. "Must've been where the big spenders played," she ascertained. She took a deep breath and rapped on the door, straightening her shirt and adjusting her braid, as if meeting a date.

"Who is it?" croaked a small warm voice from within.

"It's Tuesday Devlin, your granddaughter's friend," she answered.

"What's in the box?" asked the voice curiously.

Tuesday's eyes darted quickly around the hallway. "It's for you," she answered uncertainly. "If you're Kosmina, that is. It's ouzo. And brandy. And coffee liqueur." That was the kicker. Real coffee was hard enough to come by; coffee liqueur was a luxury only enjoyed by Suits like the Vandenburgs.

The door swung open, revealing a woman with a face like a smiling shrunken apple, and a nest of tight gray curlicues crowning her head. She wore a black tracksuit with a neon pink racing stripe bearing the name and logo of the casino. Teardrop pearls hung from her ears and an array of clunky rings adorned her wrinkled hands.

Kosmina spoke with a hint of a Greek accent, "Welcome. Please, come in." The elderly woman's walk was deeply stooped, but there was energy in her steps as she led Tuesday into the room that at one time would have been the stage for high stakes poker games. "And don't have

179

such a confused face," Kosmina assured Tuesday, "I knew you were holding a box because of the security camera in the hallway."

Tuesday smiled nervously, "Oh, of course."

"And I saw the dog, so I knew already you should come in. I see he has a happy tail, and it is always good luck to have a happy dog in a home."

"I like to think so," said Tuesday, admiring the decor in Kosmina's quarters.

Kosmina had subdivided the large hexagonal room with decorative screens depicting Grecian isles and Athenian ruins. Deep blue walls were zealously spattered with flecks of gold paint. In the center of the room a column of glass as big around as an oak tree stretched from the floor to the ceiling. It must have previously been an aquarium, adding ambiance during poker tournaments, but in these times, keeping tropical fish as an extravagant centerpiece for a room was absurd. Instead, Kosmina had filled the column with seashells of all kinds: oyster shells, abalone, cockle shells, and conches, in no particular arrangement.

Kosmina brought a coffee pot out from behind a screen and urged Tuesday to sit in a dining room chair at a table set for two. "Sit, sit." Kosmina poured without asking Tuesday how she took her coffee.

"Thank you," Tuesday said, unsure how to proceed. "I like your decor. And you've got a great view," she inclined her head toward a panoramic window overlooking the city.

"Yes, it's lovely," Kosmina answered pleasantly as she drew sparkling drapes closed over the window, blocking the morning light and dimming the room. The sequined curtain, now swaying from the movement, gave Tuesday the feeling of being underwater. "When people began to be sick, I told myself I would go home to Greece to die," Kosmina said matter-of-factly. "But then no planes are flying or boats are going, and instead I came here to the California beach to die." She shrugged. "And then I didn't."

"I see," said Tuesday.

"It's not Greece, but it is the sea." Kosmina opened the miniature bottle of coffee liqueur and split it evenly between Tuesday's mug of coffee and her own. "There now," Kosmina said, seating herself across the table from Tuesday. She looked at Oz where he had settled near the shimmering curtain. "What is his name?" she asked Tuesday.

"Oz."

"He is your familiar?"

"My...what?"

"Your familiar," Kosmina repeated.

"That's like a, um, a Patronus or something, right?" Tuesday tried.

"Mmm," thought Kosmina, "A bit. Your familiar is something embodying your essence. It is the inside of you on the outside. You know what I mean?"

"I guess so."

Kosmina leaned forward in her chair, her cloudy eyes meeting Tuesday's gaze. "Do you have a familiar?"

Tuesday thought only briefly before asserting, "Yes. I used to, I guess."

"What has happened to it?"

Tuesday shifted in her seat, "Dead. Disappeared, at least."

Kosmina shook her head. "A familiar does not die. When it is lost, it will simply come back to you transformed. As you have transformed." Tuesday knit her eyebrows. Kosmina sat back and continued, "My familiar was a pretty pink stone I found on the beach as a little girl. I carried it everywhere, in my pocket, sometimes in my mouth even, just to feel the shape of it under my tongue or against my teeth. Pretty, and strong. Then it came back to me as a pearl in a bracelet—a gift from my husband. It was buried in rubble along with my home in the earthquake, but has come back as an opal." She drummed her fingers on the table to draw Tuesday's attention to one of the rings she wore. "It is softer now, and full of light."

Tuesday didn't know what to say, but this didn't bother Kosmina. She sipped her coffee and urged Tuesday, "Drink, drink. No sense saving a

181

delight that will grow cold."

Tuesday started to raise her mug to her lips, and Kosmina held up her mug as if to toast. "*Opa!*" she said conspiratorially.

"Doesn't that mean 'grandpa'?"

Kosmina put her mug back down. "In German, dear. We are in Greece. Here 'opa' is a celebration of life." She lifted the mug again, prompting the younger woman.

"I can drink to that. *Opa!*" Tuesday approved as they clinked mugs.

"Now then," Kosmina was ready to proceed. "What's in the other box?"

"Pardon?"

"The box in your head," Kosmina tapped her temple. "Ismene sent you here for a reason. Tell me what is on your mind," she said invitingly.

Tuesday cleared her throat uneasily, "I really would like to find someone. Or find out If she's even alive...Is that the sort of thing you can...do?" Was it rude to ask a clairvoyant what she knew or how she knew things?

"Do?" Kosmina took a sip of her coffee.

"Yes," Tuesday began, "Ismene said you are a...seer? Of sorts?" Asking the question felt akin to looking up someone's skirt.

"No, no, dear. You are the eye," Kosmina said pleasantly. "I am only the spectacles. The lens, if you like."

"Okay," said Tuesday, considering this.

"What have you already seen?" Kosmina asked. "Something has made you come here, to see more. Tell me about this."

Tuesday's stomach lurched; it took seven years for her to tell Myles about her nightmares, and now she was going to disclose everything to a stranger. But this ancient, wrinkled, mystical person might be her only chance to find Angie. Tuesday forged ahead, "I have this recurring dream—a nightmare, really. It used to happen only occasionally, but it's been more and more frequent, and now it's coming to me almost every night, and sometimes even in the day."

182

"That is not a nightmare, girl," the old lady said. "That is a vision. Describe it to me."

"Well, it's sort of chopped up and blurry, but it's a memory. I know some of the things that happened that night, but others are just a fog or totally black."

"Start from the beginning," Kosmina told Tuesday gently, "And come, let's be comfortable." She led Tuesday to a velvety blue loveseat along with her mug of coffee, still pleasantly warm. Scooting a matching armchair closer to Tuesday, Kosmina folded her hands together, her rings glinting in the light dancing off of the undulating curtain.

Tuesday had never explained the whole dream to anyone, had barely even allowed herself to try to fit the pieces together. She started with the details leading up to the dream. "I remember that my sister, Angie, was with me at a party. We weren't supposed to be having gatherings, because of the pandemic, but it was college and we were stupid. *I* was anyway. I convinced her to come with me. She wasn't even old enough to drink, so she didn't. That's how she was."

Realizing she'd been talking into her mug, Tuesday looked up to read Kosmina's expression, to see if there was judgement there yet. The old lady merely blinked interestedly. She waited for Tuesday to continue.

"She came with me because she was worried. About me, what I might do." Tuesday took a deep breath. "My boyfriend had betrayed me and left me that day. I was so furious and hurt."

Kosmina let the silence hang heavy in the air for a minute before speaking, "You loved the boy very much." It wasn't a question.

"Yes."

Kosmina relaxed in her chair, hands still folded on her lap, and Tuesday couldn't tell anymore whether her delicate wrinkled eyelids were open or closed. "But he is not the one who is lost."

"No."

"You love your sister very much," again Kosmina was not asking a question.

"She mattered more to me than anything," answered Tuesday. "When things were hard, and when we couldn't trust anyone else, we always had each other. She's been gone for ten years."

"Have you brought anything of hers with you? Or something that reminds you of her?

Touching the locket near her heart, Tuesday said, "This was her necklace. We had matching ones with our names inside. We wore them all the time. That's part of my blacked-out memory though. When I woke up I was wearing hers and I've never taken it off since."

"Good," Kosmina said softly, "A very strong connection. We can use this." Tuesday didn't ask what for, and didn't look up at Kosmina, but she could hear the little Greek woman breathing deeply.

"I do not sense any love in the energy here with us," Kosmina pondered.

Angie didn't love her? Tuesday started to panic. If Angie were alive, of course she would be angry after Tuesday's recklessness had nearly killed her. Is that why Angie never tried to find her? She didn't love her anymore? Tuesday had spent ten years feeling the weight of crushing guilt for having killed Angie, and now—now that Angie might be alive—Tuesday would have to live knowing that she'd destroyed the one relationship she treasured. Her throat started to close and she concentrated on staring into her coffee mug to keep from sobbing. "So that means," Tuesday said shakily, "wherever she is, she doesn't love me?"

"I think it means her presence is not here with us," Kosmina answered. "Because her spirit still inhabits a form. I think it means your sister is alive."

Tuesday's emotions cartwheeled wildly. According to the seer, Angie was alive! Tuesday should have been overjoyed, and for a moment, hope welled up inside her, but she didn't reward herself with any relief from the burden of guilt. Maybe she hadn't killed Angie, but she had killed her sister's love for her.

Tuesday was suddenly exhausted. She hung her head and almost didn't notice when Kosmina rose to light incense and returned to the

184

armchair. "We become weary of the work, digging up bones of the past. We must take such great care—dusting off each piece and connecting them all together again, just so. But it is not only the old bones and memories that are delicate. We are the brittle ones."

A tear dropped into Tuesday's coffee and Kosmina reached out to Tuesday's mug, helping her bring it to her lips, "Here, more of this will help."

"Nothing can help," Tuesday murmured, but sipped more of the coffee anyway.

"Rest your eyes if you like," Kosmina suggested quietly. Tuesday felt herself slumping toward the arm of the loveseat as Kosmina took her mug of coffee from her slack fingers. "Everything you need to know is already with you. We will just gently brush away the dust."

"Okay," Tuesday agreed, her cheek resting on the blue velvet as she felt herself plummeting into the past.

Tuesday burst into her nightmare. The car's tires grinding on the wet pavement, her foot heavy on the pedal. The forest on either side of the narrow road blurred. She heard Angie's high-pitched scream, "Slow down, you're going too fast! Stop, stop!" And then just screaming. Tuesday knew the silent statuesque canine with pupil-less eyes would appear in the road, but she couldn't turn away. Then suddenly it was there, eyes reflecting in the headlights, and she felt herself jerk the steering wheel. Her head slammed against the window, and Angie's screams crescendoed until the vehicle tumbled over an embankment. Then Tuesday felt Angie's silence. For the first time, Tuesday could see clearly, though she could still feel the blood trickling into her eyes. She couldn't stop her head from turning to look at Angie. She knew what she would see—Angie's limp figure, blood everywhere, her grotesque ear hanging loosely. Through the fractured windshield, Tuesday saw something else that had remained hidden in her subconscious: another car. In their vehicle's wild rolling, they had hit another car. She watched as a frantic figure stumbled out of the other vehicle, and braced himself over the hood. Even in the dark, through the rain, and through the unearthly halo of the headlights, she saw sobs wracking his body. Then he ran, holding something above him—his phone. He was holding up his phone to get reception. As the man ran away, her crushed car door was suddenly pried open. She couldn't move but she could see in lucid detail. What she saw was Justin Mox's panicked face. "I'm sorry, Birdie," he said softly, reaching for her.

Gasping, Tuesday burst back into the Limitless Sky Elite Poker Room. Her eyes snapped open and she shot up to a sitting position, her chest heaving. Oz stood by the loveseat, his snout resting on the cushion next to her. She reached for him and tried to steady herself. They were back in California. There were no smashed vehicles here; no bodies, no blood. She took slow, intentional breaths. As her grip on reality tightened, Tuesday became aware of Kosmina, humming while she poured two glasses of water. "Ah, you've returned," she said, handing Tuesday one of the glasses.

"Oh my God," was all Tuesday could say.

"Yes, that is why we must do these things gently," Kosmina agreed. "How are you feeling?"

"Shocked," she answered honestly. "Not everything makes sense yet, but I could see more. I could...think. Instead of just letting it all happen."

"Mm," Kosmina nodded. "Sometimes when you brush away the cobwebs, you don't like what you see underneath."

"Yeah," Tuesday agreed breathlessly, her strength and wits returning.

"Now listen," Kosmina cautioned, "your mind will dwell in this place for some time. More will be revealed. Your soul and psyche will not be easily released from these things. But you have begun."

Outside the Limitless Sky Elite Poker Room, after profuse thanks to Kosmina, Tuesday found the kaleidoscope of colored carpet in the hallway dizzying. She felt like it should be dusk, though it wasn't even midday. "Here we are," she said to Oz, "Once again, on our way to ask Mox what the hell is going on."

Buckling herself into the Mercedes AMG-2000, Tuesday glanced at Oz, secured in the back. "Keep it together, okay?" she told him. Pulling out of the parking garage, the incongruous sun clashed with the shadowy figures of her memories and her tempestuous emotions. There was another car. In all of her nightmares, she had never seen another car. It was only just recently that she sometimes saw the man running away from the scene. And it was just today she realized he was not leaving with a triumphant fist in the air. He was holding up his phone to get reception and running to call an ambulance. And just today she saw Justin Mox pry open the door and reach for her. *I'm sorry, Birdie*, he had said. But even in this new lucid version, aided by Kosmina's guidance, Tuesday still saw Angie dead. What had really happened next?

Several blocks before the Vandenburgs' beach bungalows, Tuesday steered to the side of the road and parked near the former boardwalk, facing the ocean. She thought of the wood grain on the ceiling of her tiny house. Long, straight line, swerve to the left, through a smear of pine tar, back to straight. Her emotions spun like a roulette wheel. She wanted to be angry at Mox. Ten years of bumping into each other after the accident and he'd never once let on that he had been at the gruesome scene. What did he know and why hadn't he told her? But the timbre of his voice and the concern on his face when he'd pried open the car door drained her wrath away. Now the sight of the other car, a grim spectacle of imploded metal and plastic, lingered vividly in Tuesday's mind. She had caused even more harm than she realized, and the deep remorse she had wallowed in for a decade should have been even deeper. Despite all of that, knowing her angelic sister was still alive should be pure joy. But If Angie was alive, where had she been all this time? A canyon of fear hollowed out Tuesday's joy. Tuesday's actions had severed her connection with Angie. Even Angie's generous, forgiving nature could not overcome what Tuesday had done to her.

Tuesday arrived back at the beach bungalows steeled for a confrontation. But either the soft white sand under her boots, or the sight of Oz galloping to greet Myles and Mox in their bare feet on the beach washed away her desire for a fight. The two men were standing next to one another, facing the sea, as Tuesday stepped in line with them. She felt oddly composed, staring with them into the rolling blue ocean, and letting the fringes of the waves lap at her feet.

"We saw a whale," Myles said toward the ocean.

"Right there," Mox pointed at a spot in the calm water beyond the outgoing tide.

"Huh," Tuesday said. "I guess we've all seen some amazing stuff this morning."

After a pause, Myles said, "I'm too excited about visiting the arena this afternoon. I'm gonna go hook up the trailer to the car. Whenever you're ready." He started up the beach toward the row of little houses.

Tuesday turned to Mox and they locked eyes for a moment, each searching the other's face for a clue. "I don't know where to start," she said almost kindly.

"Maybe don't then," he suggested without irony.

"Later," she agreed, still reading his expression. Tuesday felt her defenses floating out to sea with the waves as he brushed a loose strand of her hair out of her eyes. He touched her cheek, just as he had in her dream, before she'd been wrenched back to reality. She put her hand on his and held it there.

After a moment Tuesday dropped her hand and glanced furtively toward Myles' bungalow where she saw the door closing behind him. "We'd better get going," she said to Mox, and left him standing in the sand.

Tuesday knocked on Myles' door, though it was slightly ajar. "Hey," she said, peeking inside.

"Hey," he answered, coming from the bedroom still pulling his sweatshirt on over his head. He ran his hand through his short black hair and sat on a chair in his breakfast nook while he put on his shoes. "So did you get some answers?" he asked her.

She leaned on the door frame, "Some," she replied, "And also more questions. Kosmina said I might still see more as time goes on. I don't really know how these things work."

Myles nodded, "How do you feel?"

"Like a tiny ship in a big ocean."

"An ocean of emotion?" Myles rhymed his question.

"Yes, and I'm just going to ride the tide," she said with a half-smile. Then she added, "I see you've got your UFF shirt on, so we just need the trailer and we're ready?"

"What do you see in him?" Myles asked abruptly.

Tuesday thought for a moment. "Myself."

Eleven

After the small trailer was hitched to the Mercedes, Mox and Myles briefly debated who should drive to the Schwinn Ultimate Fighting Forever Arena. Myles won, arguing, "We've got delicate cargo. You'd have to be so careful, it wouldn't be any fun to drive anyway."

Tuesday gladly relegated herself to the backseat again, collecting her thoughts wedged between Oz and the case containing Representative Brogan's hunting bow. The Chihuly chandelier, still separated into pieces and protected in the wooden crate, was secured to the trailer. Their progress was slow over the uneven backstreets, but picked up when they reached the smooth highway. Southern California's cityscape still bore the scars of trauma, like all the places Tuesday had traveled in the past decade. Here, natural disasters had impeded recovery after the initial blow, when nearly seventy percent of Californians perished from the sickness itself. Wildfires raged unchecked, feeding on the invasive grasses that allowed flames to rip through landscapes and devour cities. Then there had been the series of earthquakes and tsunamis along the coast. Despite these misfortunes, the current condition of California gave Tuesday a flicker of hope, with some businesses miraculously surviving, and others under construction, forged from the ashes of destruction.

Tuesday imagined the roulette wheel in her mind slowing to a stop, the ball bouncing irregularly through the tumult of her emotions. She willed the ball to land in the "poised and determined" slot. Yes, that would do for now. As interesting as a delivery to an elected official at a professional sports arena would be, Tuesday felt eager to get the job done. She wanted to direct all her energy toward finding Angie. She was relieved when the arena came into view.

Schwinn Arena's pre-pandemic purpose had been as a sports venue for some of California's major league teams, but Tuesday couldn't remember which ones. After serving as a shelter for Californians displaced by the pandemic, the venue had returned to its roots in athletic entertainment as the premier training and events center for Ultimate Fighting Forever. The UFF was born through the ascent of competitive mixed martial arts in a time when the infrastructure for organized team sports had largely imploded. UFF Fighters came from a variety of backgrounds: some had been professionals in other sports before the pandemic, some came from careers such as mining, iron-working, personal training, or logging. Others became fighters as a means to avoid starvation, since some Suits would sponsor a tenacious young person willing to take a punch. Fighters' expertise ranged widely, from boxing to ju jitsu to street brawling.

Today the arena parking lot, designed to accommodate masses of game attendees, was sparsely occupied by vehicles belonging to fighters, trainers, and arena staff. Several makeshift fighting rings had been constructed for the amateur fighters and exhibition leagues in the spacious lots. Tuesday's Deliverer tags allowed them to drive the Mercedes directly into the dome of the main arena.

With no matches in progress, Schwinn Arena was staged for practice and training; several fighters sparred on the periphery, their managers and trainers nearby. The main stage, ringed with bleachers and luxury box seats, stood empty except for an arena attendant cleaning the mats.

"I can just drive in?" Myles asked uncertainly.

"Sure," answered Tuesday, "There's a vehicle entrance onto the arena floor. We'll just act like we know what we're doing. Park by the section labeled "VIP" under the UFF banner there."

Myles followed instructions, "Don't mind us—just a couple people and a dog in a Mercedes with a monstrous chandelier at a fighting ring. Nothing unusual here."

"Okay, so we might draw a little attention," Tuesday conceded. "But at least this way Jeff Brogan can't miss us." She pulled on her red leather jacket before exiting the vehicle behind Mox and Myles. Oz shook out his fur and glanced around the arena, his soft brown eyes taking in the new surroundings. Tuesday surveyed the venue. Though designed to hold thousands of spectators, the arena hadn't seen a crowd like that for a sporting event in many years. Tuesday tried to picture the stands full of raucous, cheering fans. An arena official wearing a shirt with a UFF logo approached them, wearing a quizzical expression. Before he could begin, Tuesday presented her hand to him, "I'm Tuesday Devlin. Representative Brogan is expecting us."

The official raised an eyebrow at the car parked conspicuously next to the UFF main stage, and cleared his throat. "Yes, Mr. Brogan is expecting you," he said. "Right this way."

"I'll stay here," Mox interjected, leaning against the Mercedes, "Not that interested in politics or punching."

"Very well," answered the attendant mildly.

Representative Jeff Brogan, former TV personality, outspoken podcaster, and avid mixed martial arts fan, loomed large on the UFF scene. Through his leadership, determination, and generous funding, he had built the UFF during grim, turbulent times. Combined with his celebrity status, this earned him a devoted post-pandemic political following, and eventually a position as a lawmaker in the Republic of California.

The arena attendant led Tuesday, Myles, and Oz to a section of seating where an enclosed balcony protruded out toward the main stage. At the sliding door to the booth, the attendant started to wave his security badge at the sensor panel, but the door opened automatically before he had a chance. He looked at Tuesday, who tapped her Deliverer tags, which were more prominent against the neckline on her smart black top than tucked inside her tunic.

"Representative Brogan, your guests have arrived," the official announced.

192

Seated in one of the captain's chairs overlooking the arena, Representative Brogan swiveled to greet them. Now in his mid-sixties, the heavy-set man's biceps were still well-defined, and his dark hair, though sprinkled with gray, was thick. His broad hands were folded over the beginnings of a paunch stomach. "Welcome!" he said casually. "Right on time! Punctuality is a feat these days," he approved.

"Nice to meet you, Representative Brogan," Tuesday said. "I'm Tuesday Devlin, and this is Myles and Oz."

Brogan sized up the three, and asked, "You a big UFF fan, Myles?"

"Absolutely, sir," Myles affirmed, putting his hand on the UFF logo on his shirt reverently.

"You fight at all?"

"I used to box a little, but nothing serious," Myles answered.

"He's being humble," Tuesday said. "He has a few titles under his belt from what I hear."

Myles brushed this off, "High school was a long time ago."

Brogan nodded, "Who's your favorite fighter?"

"I'm a Proximo Bro, all the way," Myles smiled.

"Hey, hey, then you're in luck! He's on deck for sparring in the ring." Brogan indicated for the attendant to join their conversation. "Take this gentleman," he pointed at Myles, "get him suited up, and tell Hays he can sit out. Proximo will have a guest partner for his training warm up today."

"Seriously?" Myles asked excitedly.

Brogan held his arms out and broke into a wide grin, "When a dream-come-true falls into your lap, don't question it!"

"No more questions," Myles promised quickly, then turned to the arena attendant, who led him out toward the arena floor.

Alone with Tuesday and Oz in the balcony box, Jeff Brogan took a moment to assess his visitors. "Not your typical Gofers," he said candidly.

"Lucky for you," Tuesday responded. "You wouldn't use GoferGoods anyway," she added blithely.

Brogan chuckled, "You got that right. Now, the custom bow is an accomplishment by itself," he said admiringly, "But a genuine Chihuly?" He whistled admiringly. "That's something."

"You're welcome, and you certainly made it worth my time," Tuesday answered graciously. She peered out the window of the balcony onto the arena activities below. A tattooed man with a shaved head entered the main ring, stretching his arms and dancing lightly on the balls of his feet.

"That must be Proximo Aponte, there?" Tuesday pointed to the man.

Brogan stood and joined her at the window. He was shorter than Tuesday had expected. "Yeah, that's Proximo," Brogan was pleased. "Not a bad choice for a favorite. He's going to be one of the best. Scouts discovered him in an encampment of refugees from Venezuela."

Myles had already been fitted for shin guards and headgear. He adjusted his gloves as Tuesday watched him approach Proximo Aponte. The two men's conversation was inaudible from the balcony, but Tuesday knew whatever Myles said would be perfect. Proximo grinned broadly and gave Myles a friendly fist bump. As they began throwing light jabs, testing one another's defenses, Tuesday's attention was drawn to Mox, still near the Mercedes parked by the ring. A barrel-chested man in a cowboy hat stood close to him, speaking in what Tuesday imagined to be hushed tones.

"Who is that?" Tuesday's tone was more insistent than she'd intended.

"Who?" Brogan asked, "Oh, in the hat, talking to your compatriot there? That's Bob Weaver. He used to be Bob 'The Weevil' Weaver, back when he wrestled."

"What does he do now?" Tuesday couldn't help being immediately suspicious. She shouldn't have left Mox alone.

"Risk assessment consultant," Brogan answered and then burst out, "Whoa!" Tuesday followed his line of sight fast enough to see a man with Proximo's entourage knock over a folding chair and send a water bottle sailing through the air. It hit the mesh cage surrounding the center ring and bounced harmlessly to the floor. "There goes Hays blowing a gasket!

194

Should have expected that."

"Why? What's he upset about?"

"That's Proximo's usual warm-up partner, Gideon Hays. He's pissed to be replaced, even for just one workout."

"He's pretty fired up," said Tuesday, her eyes back on Myles. Myles and Proximo were engaging in more energetic combat now. Watching Myles move so swiftly and precisely was riveting.

"Hays isn't good enough for the pro circuit," Brogan continued while Hays stalked away from the ring. "Maybe someday—if he can get his mental game together. For now he just does some minor league and exhibition rounds, but he thinks a lot of himself."

"He's gotta be good to spar with the best though, right?" Tuesday said, trying to give the tantrum-thrower the benefit of the doubt.

"Oh he's good. But it takes more than that. It takes self-control. It takes discipline. Maturity. And he better get it quick because he's not getting any younger. There's a reason you don't see guys past the age of thirty-five out there!"

"So you need a young body and an old brain for this sport," Tuesday observed.

Representative Brogan laughed, "Exactly, Tuesday Devlin! Exactly."

Tuesday returned her attention to Mox and his covert conversation with Bob Weaver. What were they talking about?

Before she could ask about Weaver the Weevil again, Brogan changed the subject, "How about you? Do you fight too?"

"Oh no," Tuesday shook her head. "I mean, I've definitely been in my share of scuffles, and Myles taught me a *lot*, but...I think I'd be a Hays type. Too hot-headed."

"Oh yeah?"

"Yeah," she affirmed. "Seems likely." Tuesday watched Weaver tip his hat and walk away from Mox, his barrel-chest leading the way.

"Well, I don't know if you follow the UFF buzz," Brogan began.

Tuesday definitely did not follow the UFF buzz. "But since we debuted doubles matches a couple years ago, they've been such a success that we've got a plan in the works to roll out *mixed* doubles matches. It's gonna be ground-breaking! Really blow everyone away."

"Men and women fighting together?" Tuesday was incredulous.

"Yes, each team will be a duo of a male and a female fighter. First rounds will be the two women fighting each other; second rounds will be the two men fighting each other, and third rounds will be all four: two on two action!"

"Exciting," Tuesday commented, though her mind was elsewhere. Myles had struck Proximo squarely on the jaw, hard enough that the larger man stopped momentarily and shook his head playfully, as if he had something in his ear.

Jeff Brogan chuckled again, "That was a damn fine right hook!" Myles took a kick to the thigh that made Tuesday wince, but Brogan added, "No no, that looked bad, but your guy can take a leg kick like that and stay standing—and look at that defensive posture—" Brogan sounded like a commentator announcing a match for a roaring crowd. "Myles is going to have a hard time staying out of Proximo's reach; the Venezuelan's got at least a couple inches more wingspan. But oh, did you see that dodge and then a surprise combo starting with the left—Proximo wasn't expecting that!"

Tuesday suddenly understood the draw of the sport, feeling a thrill rush through her as Myles landed another punch.

"Tables are turning now though," Brogan continued, as the pro fighter drove hard at Myles with a combination of jabs followed by a roundhouse kick. "Yup, here it comes. We knew Aponte was going easy on the newbie, and after that last hit he took (which was SO beautiful) he's gotta come back and show that he was just playing around."

When Myles surrendered amiably with a knee to the mat, Proximo raised his hands in the air and cheered, seemingly for Myles, rather than his own victory. He helped Myles back to his feet and hugged him, slapping his back enthusiastically. Myles took off his protective headgear, beaming and unfazed.

"Excellent showing," Representative Brogan applauded, though no one except Tuesday and Oz could hear him. Proximo and Myles both turned to the balcony and waved. Tuesday waved back. Oz wagged his tail. "Now," Brogan concluded, "Let's go see the toys you brought me."

Back on the arena floor, Jeff Brogan led the way to Mox and the Mercedes, where Tuesday showed the congressman the dismantled chandelier. She pried open the wooden crate, displaying the twisted spires of colored glass stowed in the nest of packing materials. "All the pieces are cataloged, and certified," Tuesday used her professional tone, reserved for important, formal transactions. "And here's the care manual and instructions for assembly."

"My wife is going to go through the roof when she sees this! I'll have my guys install it this evening while Jess is at Pilates, so she'll come home, open the door and BOOM! Genuine Chihuly hanging over her head in the foyer! We're making dreams come true today!" Brogan's exuberance was contagious.

"I'm so glad it'll make her happy," Tuesday said. She scanned the arena for the man in the cowboy hat. Instead, Gideon Hays caught her eye. He was still fuming, his voice raised and movements exaggerated while he spoke with a woman in a matching hot pink sports bra and sweatpants. Her blonde hair pulled up into a high ponytail and the flip-flops on her feet reminded Tuesday of a genie. The genie petted Hays' arm to soothe him while a knee-high bug-eyed dog circled them, yapping furiously.

Tuesday couldn't make out any of their conversation except when the genie shrieked, "Stop it, Banzai!" to the dog.

"Now how about that Hoyt bow you brought me?" Brogan continued, and Tuesday turned her attention back to him. "I'm looking to beat my personal best and take down a buck at 250 meters!"

Tuesday presented the bow and its paraphernalia, explaining, "It's all custom made to your specifications with state-of-the-art technology. If you don't make your shots, it's not the bow's fault!"

Brogan whistled lightly in admiration as he ran his fingers along the trigger mechanism. "Bee-u-tee-ful!" he affirmed. "All right then," he pointed at Tuesday, "Bring your trailer around to the parking lot to transfer the chandelier. I've got a van waiting." He held up the bow and started walking away, adding, "And I want to test this gorgeous piece of work."

"Meet you out there," Tuesday responded, wondering what Brogan planned to shoot in the arena parking lot.

Myles appeared behind them, still jubilant from his sparring match. "Pinch me," he said, extending his arm to Tuesday.

"I would have thought the punches to the face would have been convincing enough proof that you're awake," Mox cut in.

Tuesday rolled her eyes at Mox and said to Myles, "That was quite a show you put on. Brogan was impressed anyway. And it seems like you cozied up pretty quickly to your idol, Proximo."

"He was so *nice*!" Myles gushed.

"Aside from the face-punching, which we've already mentioned," Mox added.

"And we do seem to have royally pissed off that guy," Tuesday nodded toward Gideon. Oz stood at alert, watching Gideon, Banzai, the genie, and the small group of various attendants near them. Tuesday put her hand on Oz's furry neck, "Let's steer clear of what's going on there."

"What IS going on there?" Myles asked.

"Basically, that ass-hat is all salty that you do his job better than he does," Tuesday summarized.

Myles shrugged, "Tough luck."

"Hey," Tuesday turned suddenly to Mox. "Who were you talking to? In the cowboy hat?"

"He's a very well-connected bookie," Mox answered.

"Brogan said he was a risk assessment consultant," Tuesday

countered.

"Euphemism," said Mox. He stepped closer and lowered his voice, "Listen, I think he knows something. Something that could help with your...whatever this is. Quest."

"He knows something that could help find Angie?" Tuesday felt her pulse quicken. She needed a lead.

"Let's just get the chandelier transferred and then talk," she said as she strode toward the arena exit with Oz while Myles revved the Mercedes' engine. She looked over her shoulder to see Mox standing with his chiseled chin cupped thoughtfully in one hand, his piercing blue eyes watching her leave.

Outside of the arena, Myles pulled the Mercedes parallel with a van parked adjacent to one of the exhibition rings where a handful of arena staff and fighters milled about their business. As Tuesday came closer, she spotted Bob Weaver in his conspicuous hat, propping himself against the wall of the ring while he chatted with another man. The scene reminded her of an Old West watering trough complete with horses and cowboys. What might Weaver know? Something about the Mad Hatter? About the drone drops? A bookie could be connected to all manner of dubious business. No surprise that Mox found the slimiest character in the arena to schmooze with.

Tuesday walked directly toward Bob Weaver and inserted herself into his conversation. "Hi, I'm Tuesday Devlin, big fan of The Weevil," she had almost said "weasel," but caught herself.

"Bob Weaver, Miss," he said, tipping his hat to her. Miss—not Ma'am. Maybe he wasn't so slimy. He looked older closer up, in his late fifties, with crinkles around his eyes.

"What do you do in these parts?" Tuesday couldn't help the southern twist that crept into her question.

"Risk assessment consultant," he said, sizing her up.

"Is that as exciting as it sounds?" she asked without sarcasm. The lanky man Bob had been talking to laughed, "Sure is!"

"She didn't ask you, Sticks," Weaver said. Tuesday wondered whether the name Sticks was because of the man's long skinny legs, or maybe short for a surname like Stickney or Stickley. Or maybe because his hair looked like a pile of small twigs.

"Sticks is right," Bob supplied. "I love considering the odds. You can make anything risky."

"And he does!" Sticks joked.

Tuesday was trying to figure out what information Weaver might have and how to get it from him, when they were interrupted by Representative Brogan on the other side of the ring.

"What's two hundred yards away?" he asked loudly, holding his new bow above his head. "That sandwich board?" he pointed across the parking lot to a sandwich board with a red arrow painted on it.

"Now see our esteemed Congressman over there? Boasting?" Bob went on. "People want to analyze something like that and make their 'risk assessment.' In fact…," he trailed off, took out his phone and typed quickly for several moments. When he looked up, he smiled at Tuesday, his teeth pearly white, "I'm giving a chance for all present to make a risk assessment on this shenanigan right now."

She watched the bystanders take out their phones and contemplate Brogan's situation. Weaver winked at Tuesday as she realized what was happening.

"So you'll take bets on whether Brogan can hit the sign." Tuesday clarified.

"People will bet based on how much they trust Brogan's skills, how much they trust that fancy bow, and some people won't trust Brogan or the equipment, and they'll just bet on themselves."

"How would they do that?"

"They might bet that the sign is really only one hundred and eight-six yards away."

"Huh."

The gamblers evaluated the risk. Tuesday heard someone ask, "You ever shot that bow before, Boss?" and someone else called over, "That sign's a lot smaller than an elk!"

Bob continued, "Everyone alive already beat the odds of living through a pandemic, but the aftermath we're in now—well, you know. All bets are off. People are desperate to beat the odds with a risk they can control."

"And you're here to capitalize on desperation," Tuesday said with a wistful sarcasm.

"Well, aren't you a gooseberry," Bob replied with a smirk. Tuesday raised an eyebrow. "Looks sweet, but tastes sour," he explained.

"Ah," she accepted the appraisal. "And what are you?" she asked.

Weaver sucked his teeth for a moment, before answering, "Cheese."

"Old and smelly?" Tuesday guessed.

"Precisely, Gooseberry," he smiled, "but people like it anyway."

Just then Jeff Brogan declared good-naturedly, "I need complete silence!" The crowd was now hushed as Weaver whispered, "Wagers closed," while he orchestrated the betting system from his phone.

Gideon Hays and the lady in pink had joined the crowd outside the arena, and Tuesday heard them shout at Banzai to quit yapping. Tuesday watched Brogan draw back on the Hoyt, and she realized she was holding her breath. She glanced at Myles and Mox, standing near the chandelier now loaded into Brogan's van, their eyes fixed on Brogan and his bow.

He let the arrow fly. It cut noiselessly through the air and sank into the red lettering on the sandwich board sign. Cheers of delight and dismay erupted from the crowd.

"Nice shot," Tuesday said to no one in particular. Weaver turned his attention to his administrative duties and Sticks left to congratulate Brogan. Banzai resumed barking. The genie, who Tuesday presumed to be Gideon's girlfriend, snapped a leash onto Banzai and spoke

201

animatedly with Gideon, both their tempers visibly rising.

Tuesday didn't notice Myles until he was beside her.

"Now Brogan just has to skin and quarter it, and that sandwich board will feed his family for weeks," he said, as Brogan approached them, glowing.

"Woo-wee, that was nirvana and Mardi Gras mixed up together!" he proclaimed. "Heaven in an adrenaline rush!"

Tuesday was pleased, "I knew it would be. And the Chihuly is all repacked in your van, ready to go."

"Wonderful! Oh, but since you're the expert, you'll be available in case there's trouble with the installation tonight," Brogan said without a question mark.

"Don't worry, we're not leaving town until tomorrow," Tuesday assured him. "You can contact me with any questions at all."

"Let's do one better. How about you come to my place for drinks during the installation. Enjoy a mini garden party; ensure that everything goes smoothly. Then you'll see the look on Jess's face."

"I think that can be arranged," Tuesday agreed.

"It's settled. We'll see you this evening—bring your friends," he gestured to Mox and Myles, "and any California voters you're familiar with." Brogan laughed, but Tuesday got the impression this part was not a joke. As he walked away, Jeff Brogan added, "And of course, dogs are welcome!"

Mox joined Tuesday and Oz as Brogan strutted away. "Did we just get invited to drinks at the congressman's house?" he asked.

Tuesday nodded, "And we accepted." She sensed Oz tensing beside her. He stood motionless with his ears pricked, and his weight balanced as if on springs while he watched Banzai, Gideon, and the genie's agitation increase. "Yeah, that's raising my hackles too," she told Oz.

Tuesday turned to Mox, intending to grill him about Bob Weaver and his potential leads, when Banzai shot away from Gideon with the leash trailing behind him. He was snarling now, charging straight for Oz.

Tuesday's reaction was stupid. Before she could think, she found herself on her knees, hugging Oz to shield him with her body. Myles was smarter. He sprinted toward Banzai and stomped on the end of the trailing leash, stopping Banzai short before he reached Tuesday and Oz. In an instant, the genie was beside Banzai, fussing over him, "Oh my God, are you okay, Baby?" she cooed. Then she whirled to Myles, "Stay away from my dog!"

Myles blinked blandly. "I would love to."

"Claudia, grab him," Gideon ordered the genie, gesturing to the dog, who was tugging at the end of the leash to get at Oz. Banzai was awkwardly large to pick up, but Claudia made a show of it, gathering him in her arms. "I could kick all your asses!" she announced as she stomped away. Tuesday's stomach flipped a somersault when Claudia passed her and Oz.

Gideon Hays stepped toward Myles, "Watch yourself," he growled.

Myles didn't back away, "Seems like you might need to watch your dog," he suggested. "And your lady friend."

Gideon made a guttural sound and launched a loogie that landed in a quivering gluey wad by Myles' shoe. A cloud darkened Myles' expression, but he said nothing. To Tuesday's surprise, it was Mox who said, "Oh, hell no."

Then too many things happened all at once. Gideon shoved Myles, who stayed on his feet until Claudia jumped onto his back from behind. Tuesday charged Gideon, surprising him and slamming him to the ground. Mox took Claudia by the waist and flung her off of Myles. In an instant, all parties were back on their feet, crouched in defensive positions, and breathing heavily with adrenaline.

Still poised for action, Myles shouted authoritatively, "Wait! I am one hundred percent ready to throw down today. But we are going to do this right!" A crowd formed a circle around the commotion. "We use regulation rules. I know who you are, Hays. You're better than a parking lot brawl."

Tuesday thought this exceedingly generous of Myles.

"You got it," Gideon sneered. "Ring's right here."

Spectators called out from the crowd, cheering and heckling.

"We want to see Claudia!" a fan called out.

"Mixed doubles!" another man in the crowd yelled. This incited more cheers.

"You can't all fight! That's three on two!" This was a fair point.

"Make the pretty one sit out!" someone suggested. Tuesday shrugged and dropped her fists, starting to back away from the others.

"No, not her! The pretty one! The Brit!" A titter rippled through the crowd. Mox smiled and bowed low as he backed away to the sidelines. Tuesday and Myles were going to fight Gideon and Claudia.

Myles started directing the action, calling into the crowd, "We need three exhibition judges and a ref! Who out there is qualified?"

An idea struck Tuesday, and while Myles quickly organized the fight, she grabbed Mox by the arm. "Bet Bob Weaver on this," she insisted quietly.

"What?"

"Make a deal with him to get the information he has on Ben Hatter and Angie," she whispered urgently.

"Ah," Mox's slow smile reminded Tuesday of scheming with him in college. "In need of my negotiation skills now, are we?"

"Yes, I need this," she said seriously.

"Desperation looks good on you, Birdie."

"Hurry!" Tuesday hissed.

Mox slipped into the crowd and Tuesday turned her attention to the ring where a match was being hastily arranged. Sticks and two other men seated themselves at a narrow table, ready to judge. A third man, an ogre with tree trunks for legs, stood in the center of the ring, presumably as the referee. Representative Brogan and Proximo Aponte stood together a few rows back in the crowd. The gravity of what she had just agreed to began to dawn on Tuesday. Sure, she had been in plenty of fights, starting from when she was a teenager, and of course everyone had had to do a little dueling to scrape by during the pandemic. But this was a proper fight, with rules, against opponents who were experienced in combat. And she had just wagered on what might be her last connection to her sister.

She jogged to where Myles was claiming their corner of the ring. "Myles, what are we doing?" she cried.

"Claudia's not a real fighter," he told her. "She's like Gideon—just a warm up and sparring partner. She's the B string." He looked Tuesday squarely in the eye, "You're the A string."

"We'll have to fight separately and then together, right?" Tuesday's mind raced to construct a strategy. "I don't know anything about their styles. What do I do?"

"Claudia's a wrestler. Do your best to stay on your feet and hit her as hard as you can."

"Okay, okay, I can do that," Tuesday said, assuring herself.

"Think back to what I taught you."

With Angie at stake, she could do this.

"And Gideon? What do I do when we all fight at the same time?"

"He's a striker and so am I. Do what you can to stay away from his fists. Kick him, duck, dodge, go for knees—anything to keep away from his hands."

Tuesday took a moment to picture the calming wood grain ceiling of her shipping container home: long, straight line, swerve to the left, through a smear of pine tar, back to straight.

"Ladies!" the referee called Tuesday and Claudia to the center of the ring. It was all happening too fast.

Tuesday whipped off her boots and left them next to Myles and Oz in her corner, "You got this," Myles assured her as she handed him the dagger from its holster on her thigh. Oz wagged his tail encouragingly.

Tuesday's opponent stood in the center of the ring, still in her pink sweatpants and sports bra. Claudia resembled a genie even more now, with bare feet and her hair wrapped in a bun. As Tuesday tapped fists with Claudia, the referee began the countdown to fight.

Tuesday spotted Mox and Weaver standing in the front row of the crowd, as close as they could get to the action. "Well, Mate," she heard Mox say, "It doesn't look good. FedEx Barbie here won't be able to stay on her feet."

"Three! Two!" announced the referee. Mox's comment boiled white-hot in Tuesday's stomach. She wouldn't be able to stay on her feet?

"And her friend, Sky Uber?" continued Mox, "Well, he's nothing but a spineless windbag."

Spineless windbag? The wrath rocketed up into her fists. Tuesday couldn't hear Weaver's response as the referee shouted, "One! Fight!"

With one explosive swing, all of Tuesday's anger connected with Claudia's jaw. The genie wilted limply to the mat. Tuesday stared in shock at the form in front of her, a motionless pile of neon pink sweats. Tuesday covered her mouth in disbelief with the same hand she'd just used to knockout Claudia. She turned to lock eyes with Myles, his expression mirroring her bewilderment. Then Myles threw his hands in the air. The crowd roared.

Gideon and the referee helped Claudia up as she re-entered the world dizzily. Amid the shouting and chanting, Tuesday heard Myles call out, "That's it, you did it!" and he waved her over to him. She shook Claudia's floppy hand and waved politely to the crowd before meeting Myles in their corner.

"Okay, I know you're good," Myles raised his voice delightedly over the ruckus, "But where the hell did that come from?"

Tuesday shook her head, "I don't know! I can't believe it—" She spun to look at Justin Mox where he stood by the edge of the ring. He shot her a smug smile and applauded approvingly. Tuesday knew he couldn't hear her, but she yelled, "Fedex Barbie stayed on her feet, didn't she?" Son of

206

a bitch.

Tuesday didn't have time to collect her thoughts before the referee called Myles and Gideon to the center of the ring. She couldn't think of anything encouraging to say to Myles so she repeated his own words to him. "You're the A string," she told him. He was her best chance to get a lead on finding Angie.

"Thanks," Myles answered with a half-smile before he bounded into the ring to meet his opponent. Gideon Hays tapped Myles' fist with disdain at the referee's command. Both combatants were shirtless; the veins on Gideon's biceps already bulged. Myles had put on a good show sparring with Proximo Aponte, which was indeed impressive. But it was just sparring—this was real. Would Myles be too exhausted after already engaging in a match with a pro today? Tuesday glanced at Mox, who looked markedly more serious than he had before Tuesday's round with Claudia. He was watching Claudia's entourage tend to her while Banzai pulled against his leash, barking furiously in Oz's direction.

The referee began his countdown. The next five minutes were an eternity. As the referee declared, "Fight!" the noise of the crowd welled up in Tuesday's ears. Gideon charged instantly and Myles backed away, dodging and blocking until Gideon's breath came in frustrated huffs. When Gideon dropped his hands almost imperceptibly, Myles took his chance. He made solid contact with two jabs and a hook before Gideon could get his hands back up. Tuesday watched as Myles repeated this method several times: Gideon drove in hard; Myles danced and took glancing blows until Gideon's own anger tired him and Myles could take advantage. Both men stayed on their feet, though Gideon tried twice to throw Myles to the mat. Each time, Myles pushed him hard against the caged wall encircling the ring.

Gideon blew his cheeks out, puffing with rage and exhaustion. Myles looked fatigued, but calm. Tuesday's own fists were balled up hanging at her sides. With Gideon's energy flagging, his position grew sloppier.

207

Myles landed a roundhouse kick to Gideon's thorax that made the whole crowd groan. Gideon returned with a vengeful uppercut followed by a hook; both landed squarely and made Tuesday's teeth hurt. A gash had opened over Myles' eye. How much longer could he fend off this angry ox?

Gideon threw his body at Myles, slamming him against the cage wall. Was he trying to take Myles to the ground? They were both strikers, Myles had said, but surely Gideon would have the upper hand on the mat. Experience plus the size advantage would leave Myles helpless if he went down. Myles slipped lithely away from Gideon and hooked his arm under Gideon's to reverse their stances, pressing Gideon into the cage wall and planting a knee hard into his stomach. Tuesday saw the hate rising in Gideon's glare. He drove wildly at Myles twice more, each time swinging punches that would end the match if they connected. Cheek-shattering, knockout blows. Myles blocked each one. In the instant it took Gideon to recover his balance from the force of his efforts, Myles charged with a burst of jabs that left Gideon reeling.

At the edge of the ring, Tuesday gripped the thick fur of Oz's' neck. *Fall, fall!* But Gideon didn't. When Myles wiped the trickle of blood out of his eye with the inside of his elbow, Gideon seized the chance to throw his hulk onto Myles once more, and this time, they both fell to the mat, with the larger man straddled on top. Tuesday's heart jumped into her throat.

Suddenly the blast of the referee's whistle called time. Time! Myles had finished the round! A split second after the whistle, Gideon threw one last punch, aimed precisely at the cut above Myles' eye.

The referee hollered and hauled Gideon off of Myles. Relief washed over Tuesday as Myles bounced easily to his feet, and she stopped herself from running to him in the ring. Just staying conscious for an entire round against Gideon was nothing short of incredible, but it was up to the judges to decide the winner. The crowd buzzed, anxiously awaiting the judges' decision. After an agonizing minute, the three men at the judges' table thrust their scorecards in the air: one vote for Gideon, two votes for Myles. Tuesday whooped and this time let herself rush into the ring. The crowd erupted into cheers and cries of surprise. How had this amateur held his own with Gideon Hays?

Gideon turned his back without a sportsmanlike fist tap with Myles. Tuesday saw Gideon push through the spectators, cussing out the judges, and she saw him distinctly shoulder-check Mox on his way past.

Tuesday turned excitedly to Myles, "That was amazing! I mean, I didn't doubt you, but that guy's practically a pro!"

Myles put a hand to his eye, "I just let him beat himself."

Tuesday's mind raced, "We won two rounds! Does that mean we don't have to fight the last one? Because, holy shit, I don't think I can survive like you did."

Myles looked at the blood on his fingers coolly. "No, we don't automatically get a win. The final round is worth double, so every match has all three rounds."

"Wait," Tuesday realized, suddenly angry, "Gideon hit you after the whistle. Doesn't that disqualify him or something? Why didn't the ref care?"

"It should be a disqualification, but it happens. It's impossible to prove it was intentional, so fighters get away with that all the time."

"Ugh, now I want to punch him more than ever!" Tuesday said, her hands on her hips.

"Claudia's the real question," Myles explained. "After a knockout, fighters have to agree to get an anti-inflammatory and stimulant injection to keep going. Saves the brain cells, and probably law-suits. But they can also forfeit instead."

"They don't seem like the forfeiting type," Tuesday observed. Already a commotion had developed around Gideon and Claudia. They were yelling at an official with a med kit. Banzai barked and snapped, taking cues from his owners' tempers.

"No," Myles agreed. "They don't. Let's get something to fix my eye.

They've got a med kit in our corner."

"I'll be right there," Tuesday said, letting Myles and Oz leave the center of the ring. She whirled to where Mox still stood near the cage wall. "What's wrong with you?" she yelled over the din on her way to him.

"Don't come over here!" Mox warned.

"Did you see that action? Who are you calling spineless now?" she fumed.

"Get out of here, the match isn't over! I can't be seen talking to you if I've got skin in the game!"

He was right, but she couldn't resist asking with indignation, "Did you bet *against* us?"

"No," Mox hissed. "You needed a fire lit under your ass! Your heart wasn't in the fight and you were going to get pulverized."

Tuesday balked. Would she have thrown such a forceful blow if she hadn't been seething at Mox?

"Go!" Mox instructed.

Now completely unsure what to be irate about, Tuesday returned to the corner where Myles held gauze to his eyebrow. Tuesday took a roll of medical tape out of the kit beside him. She tore off a piece of the tape, which he pressed firmly over the cut. "That'll hold for now," he said, wiggling his eyebrows up and down.

Tuesday was wrapped in her own thoughts of Mox and the wager, but seeing the strip of tape and dried blood on Myles' face stirred something in her. "Are you okay?" she asked earnestly. "Because that was brutal, and we're about to do it again. It's okay to not be okay."

Myles smiled, "That sounds like something I would say."

"Well, you're right." Tuesday realized she might actually believe it. "You don't always have to be fine."

"I'm really fine," Myles assured her. "And I'll tell you when I'm not," he said pointedly. "But right now, I feel like I could kick that Goliath's ass a dozen more times."

"Let's just do it once," Tuesday said, putting her arm around Oz. He whined and his soft brown eyes were wide. "Oz is getting unsettled," Tuesday said. "I don't want him to stand here by himself while we both fight. He'll be worried."

"Take him to Mox," Myles suggested.

"Good idea," Tuesday agreed. "But I can't talk to Mox right now, so I'll have to just send Oz over on his own before the next round."

"You can't talk to him?" Myles questioned, and then observed, "I think they're about to call us up. Looks like Claudia agreed to get that shot after all." Banzai continued to make a ruckus, but the rest of the commotion in their corner had died down.

Tuesday nodded and directed Oz, "Oz, go alone. Find Mox." She pointed to Justin Mox, who was watching Team Hays intently.

The big silver dog trotted across the ring toward Mox in the front row on the other side. As he crossed the center, a blazing brown bug-eyed blur came snarling into the ring and plowed into Oz, knocking him off of his paws. A confused cry rose up from the crowd. Tuesday watched in horror as Oz and Banzai transformed into a ball of flying fur and flashing teeth. Banzai latched onto Oz's neck and shook. Oz threw Banzai off and then leaped at him, rolling the smaller dog onto his back with his throat exposed. Tuesday felt rather than heard Oz's deep growl as he stared into Banzai's eyes. *Oh God, don't kill him!* Tuesday's body finally responded and she dashed to the center of the ring. Before she reached the dogs, Oz released Banzai and barked sharply twice. Banzai heeded this warning and slunk out of the ring with his tail tucked, perhaps realizing his life had graciously been spared. The crowd went wild.

Tuesday knelt next to Oz, still absorbing the events of the past two minutes as Myles joined her in the ring. "It's okay now, pal," she said, more for herself than for the dog. Her hands shook as she examined him, "I think most of this blood is from his ear," she said, gingerly palpating under Oz's fur for wounds. "And this spot here on his neck—it's a shallow cut, but it's long."

Suddenly Claudia was in the ring with Gideon on her heels. "I told you to stay away from my dog!" she shrieked, shoving Tuesday with both hands. The crowd still rumbled with surprise and disbelief. Out of the corner of her eye, Tuesday saw the referee and Proximo Aponte rushing toward them. Gideon Hays swung his foot back, winding up to kick Oz, when Mox appeared suddenly behind him. With one swift sweep, Mox kicked Gideon's leg out from under him, toppling him heavily onto the floor. Claudia emitted an enraged screech and swung wildly at Tuesday, who ducked easily. And then the only punch Claudia had thrown all day connected hard with the referee's nose.

The crowd exploded. Proximo pushed Gideon Hays away from the center of the ring, telling him to get a hold of himself, and two of the judges already had placed themselves in front of Claudia, blocking her from further combat. The referee, blood oozing from his nose, yelled, "Disqualified! Team Hays forfeits round three!"

Tuesday turned to Myles amid the commotion, shouting, even though he was only inches away, "They're disqualified? Then that means—!"

"We won!"

The referee held Tuesday and Myles' hands in the air, declaring, "Match goes to Team Deliverers!"

As the tumult died down, Tuesday collected her thoughts. Gideon, Claudia, and Banzai were dragged away by their entourages. Bob Weaver looked positively radiant; the match had been a bookie's dream.

While Tuesday used their med kit to clean up Oz's injuries, Proximo Aponte congratulated Myles congenially. "That was the most surprising fight I've seen in years, man," he said, shaking Myles' hand. "If ESPN was still a thing, *Sportscenter* would be all over this! What a show!"

Tuesday pocketed some of the supplies from the med kit, realizing that her own hand, the one she'd used to knock out Claudia, hurt like hell. Now that Oz was patched up and the match was over, where was Mox?

She owed him a thank-you for saving Oz from Gideon with that leg sweep. And they'd earned their information from Weaver. Hadn't they? What had Mox bet on?

"Let's find Mox," Tuesday said to Myles after he'd said goodbye to Proximo. "I had him bet on our fight to get information from the guy in the cowboy hat. He said the bookie knows something that will help us."

"He bet on us?"

"I'm not sure what he bet on, honestly," Tuesday confessed. "I just trusted him."

"Dangerous," Myles noted.

"Yeah," Tuesday said pensively. "It felt right at the time. Here he comes," she pointed to Mox on his way to their corner.

Mox knelt beside Oz, asking, "How's the old boy? Didn't take too much of a beating, I hope?" Oz wagged his tail.

Tuesday softened at his concern for the dog, "No, fortunately. I think we took care of the worst wounds, for now anyway."

Mox straightened up, "Well, good. We've got to go collect our winnings from Weaver."

"What exactly did you win?" asked Myles.

"I made three wagers for three pieces of information," Mox said vaguely. "I won all three."

"One piece of information for each round we won?" Tuesday guessed.

"No. I didn't wager on your round."

"Wait, so…?"

"First, I bet that Kilometers here would win his round—he did. Second, I bet that the congressman and Proximo Aponte would both bet on him—they did." He addressed Myles, "Well done, Mate. You made those blokes very happy."

"And third?" asked Tuesday.

"Third, I made a bet that Oz wouldn't kill that lousy excuse for a canine."

213

"You bet that Oz wouldn't kill Banzai? But how did you know he would attack Oz again?" Tuesday asked. "That seems risky."

"It was all risky; that's the point!" Mox replied. "But I saw Gideon lose the leash on purpose the first time to let his dog attack."

"So you couldn't bet on me, but you bet on Oz?" Tuesday wanted to be angry.

"Yes. You're a complete bloody wildcard, but I'd bet my life on that dog," Mox said.

Tuesday didn't disagree. She would bet her life on Oz too. "Fine, let's just talk to the Weevil."

"Proximo bet on ME?" Myles said, mostly to himself as they headed toward the cluster of people surrounding Bob Weaver.

When the last of the gamblers finished marveling over the match and wandered away from the bookie, Tuesday, Oz, Myles, and Mox approached Bob Weaver. He tipped his hat to them. "Congratulations, Team Gooseberry. That was a match to remember! And a gold mine to boot. People love to bet on fights with an underdog. Although," he looked at Mox, "you're the only one who made a bet involving an actual dog today."

"Turned out in our favor, as expected," Mox said confidently.

"Usually in a dog fight, people will bet on which dog will kill the other—" Bob said.

"Not on which dog will show gentlemanly restraint?" Mox smirked.

"That was a first," Bob agreed.

"So, you have useful information as our reward?" Tuesday pressed.

Weaver nodded, "I'll give you three tidbits. He crossed his arms, "First, Mad Ben Hatter's fiancée died in a car crash ten years ago."

Tuesday turned to ice.

"Second—"

Tuesday didn't want to hear what was second.

"Hatter thought he found the culprit who caused the accident, but he got the wrong gal."

Tuesday gripped the fur on Oz's neck to stay upright. The Mad Hatter thought Angie was to blame for the accident. How long had a maniac been stalking innocent, warmhearted Angie, because of Tuesday's carelessness?

"Third, Ms. Devlin, now he thinks you're responsible for killing his fiancée, and he'll do anything he can to get revenge."

Tuesday felt a hand on her elbow, and for a moment she wasn't sure whether it was Myles or Mox; she wasn't even sure her feet were still on the ground. "Thank you," she breathed.

"And one more thing—a freebie because you made me a boatload today, and because I like you, Gooseberry."

Tuesday gulped. She couldn't take one more thing.

"Someone was assigned to put this," Weaver held up a device the size of a button, "somehow onto you." He placed the tracker in Tuesday's hand and closed her fist around it. She knew she was staring dumbly.

"Who was going to put the tracker on?" Myles demanded. "Who here is working for The Mad Hatter?"

Bob Weaver shook his head slowly, "I gave you the information I owed you, plus more." He shrugged. "No one here works for Hatter, so don't go on a witch hunt. This was just a grunt taking a well-paying gig he didn't understand. Now, if you don't mind, I'll kindly take my leave here to go celebrate this fortuitous occasion. Even if you do mind." He tipped his hat again and sauntered away.

Tuesday barely saw him leave. She stared dazedly at the tracker in her palm. Instead of smashing it, as she had the first two devices she'd found, Tuesday suddenly saw that it was more precious than diamonds.

"Okay, that was a lot to take in," Myles acknowledged gently, looking into Tuesday's unfocused gaze.

"Yeah," Tuesday managed.

"We got what Weaver promised us—" Myles started.

215

"What I won for us," Mox corrected.

"Yeah," Myles furrowed his brow. "What did you bet anyway? I mean, what if you'd lost any of those wagers?"

"I bet the Mercedes."

Twelve

Tuesday sat in the late afternoon sun on the dunes in front of her beach bungalow. She listened to the breeze sweeping through the coarse sea grass and ran her fingers through the silky sand. They'd driven back to their cabins mostly in silence, at Tuesday's request. She had been sure Weaver's information would send her spiraling into her nightmare—what had Kosmina called it? Her vision. But as she watched the fledgling California cityscape pass outside the window of the Mercedes, she had only seen snippets of the vision. Snapshots flashing through her mind: the man running away from the scene of the crash, the battered vehicle, Angie's bloodied face, and Mox reaching for her. *I'm sorry, Birdie.* She needed to talk to Mox, but didn't want to confront him while she teetered on the edge of unraveling. And Tuesday needed to have this conversation privately, not with Myles sitting inches away, steering the sports car calmly.

While Oz cavorted along the incoming tide in the distance, Tuesday inspected the items she had laid out on her red leather jacket on the beach in front of her. *Alouette, gentille alouette, Alouette, je te plumerai* Tuesday hummed the tune to herself, barely audible above the sound of the wind in her ears. *Lark, gentle lark, Lark, I will pluck you.* The musical disc was a clear message that Hatter knew who she was and who she had been. The photo of the necklace was proof that he knew what she cherished, with the quote that warned of his aim to create chaos and ruin her world. Then there was the photo of the back of Angie's head and the lock of her platinum hair. "Not resting, not in peace." The words wormed into Tuesday's stomach and made her feel sick. Angie was alive, but in danger—being tortured? Who takes a photo of the back of someone's head? Or cuts off locks of their hair? An unscrupulous drug lord maybe. Someone unbalanced, unstable, unhinged. But then, hadn't she also been those things after she had lost Angie?

217

The last item Tuesday had set in front of her was the tracker. She held it up toward the sky between her thumb and forefinger, "Come and get me," she whispered.

As she closed her fist around the tracker, a shadow fell across the sand and she turned to find Justin Mox hovering behind her, his hands in his pockets. He had changed into a crisp button-down shirt in anticipation of Representative Brogan's garden party. The shirt reminded her of his favorite one in college, the one he'd worn when they snuck into weddings at the Bellingham country club.

Tuesday faced the sea again, "Have a seat," she offered without hospitality.

Mox sat beside her, eyeing the collection of objects on her jacket. "I take it we're due for a conversation," he said.

"Yes." Her heartbeat quickened at the thought of the question, but she made herself voice it, "Why were you there?"

"Where?"

"We can drop the pretenses. I think you know where," she said evenly.

"At the accident?"

"Yes," she confirmed.

"What do you remember?" he asked.

"After I visited Kosmina, my dream—my memories—are getting clearer. The fog is lifting. You were there."

"I told you I read your texts," he reminded her. "I knew you were at that party. I always knew where you were."

"So you, what? Skulked around outside the party, waiting for us to leave?" she asked.

"You know how I love skulking," Mox answered dryly.

"And you followed us?"

"Yes."

"You saw the accident then," Tuesday pressed.

"Yes," he said, softer this time.

"You," she choked on the words, "saw her. After."

"Yes." He paused. "I pulled you out of the car."

Tuesday saw a flash of Mox's concerned eyes looking into her own while blood trickled down her face. "Then what?" she asked quietly.

"Then you asked me to take you away," he said kindly, as if telling a small child a bedtime story. "And I did. You had the key to the animal shelter, so I brought you there. And then I left."

Tuesday heard the echo of her own voice ringing in her ears. *Take me away.* Yes, she had said that. And he had granted her request.

Just then Oz came bounding up and skidded to a stop before prancing in happy circles, spraying Tuesday and Mox with sand.

"Ah, well the old boy's right," Mox said, standing and shaking the sand from his clothes. "We'd better get going if we want to make ourselves presentable for a party at a congressman's mansion. And by 'we,'" he added, "I mean the two of you. I'm already all rigged out," He gestured to his outfit and smiled his slow smile. He did look great, which was even more agitating.

"Don't be so British; nobody says 'rigged out.'" Tuesday looked at Oz, covered in sand and wet with ocean spray. The sea air had rendered her own hair a voluminous tumbleweed, and her skin was tacky with dried sweat and salt. "But yes, we're going to get cleaned up," she said. "Not because you said to. Just because a cool shower sounds like heaven right now."

Inside the beach bungalow, Tuesday surveyed her clothing choices. The snazzy black top, which had served her well through the day's unexpectedly active events, would pass for garden party attire. The red leather jacket was classic. She looked at her leggings, "Way too casual, but I don't suppose we can do anything about that, can we?" she said to Oz. She rifled through her knapsack, hoping she had miraculously left her only summer dress rumpled at the bottom of the bag somehow, though she knew she hadn't. No luck. "Let's clean you up first—you take forever to blow dry." She glanced around the beach house briefly until her eyes landed on the thin strip of blue fabric holding the curtains open. She removed it from the curtain and held it up to Oz's neck. "Perfect."

Tuesday brought soap, a towel, a hair brush, and the strip of fabric through the doors leading to the outdoor shower.

"Fair warning," Myles' voice carried over from his balcony next door. "There's a brother in his birthday suit out here." Myles was showering in his outdoor shower stall.

Tuesday feigned nonchalance and turned her back toward Myles' balcony. "Oz needs a bath before we go schmooze with big-wigs." She pulled her shower's extension arm down and started spraying Oz, lathering his fur with soap. Working carefully around the wounds on his ear and neck, she rinsed the soap out of his fur while she tried to keep her mind in the present. "So what are you wearing?" she asked Myles, still in his shower stall.

"I just said—?"

"No, I mean," she stumbled, "to the party. What are you wearing to Representative Brogan's? He said 'mini garden party.' That can't be too fancy, right?"

"I have a feeling our standards of fancy and Brogan's are not the same," Myles pointed out. "I brought a polo, so that'll do."

"The teal one?" Tuesday knew which polo he meant. It would more than do.

"Yeah," Myles answered, turning off his shower. "What are you wearing?" he asked. "Not right now."

"Actually, I *am* wearing what I've got on right now," Tuesday answered, rubbing Oz with the plush towel. "It's all I've got."

"Your new jacket is nice," Myles said helpfully.

Tuesday could hear shuffling noises that indicated he was toweling himself off. "Yeah…" she trailed off. "I'm using my curtain tie-back as a bow-tie for Oz, so at least one of us will look classy." She dared to peek over her shoulder toward Myles. Speaking of classy. He smoothed his

220

teal polo shirt over his chest and slid his belt through the loops of his cargo pants.

"Hold on," Myles said, as Tuesday finished tying Oz's bow. He ducked into his bungalow while Tuesday considered how to proceed with her own shower next.

"Here," Myles popped back onto his balcony with a length of black cloth in his hands. "Catch," he said, wadding the cloth into a ball so it would carry to Tuesday's bungalow when he threw it.

She caught it and unwadded it, "What is this?"

"It's the table runner from my dining set in here. I think it's silk." He shrugged, "Just a thought," and then disappeared inside.

Tuesday held up the black silk by its corners. "Huh."

With the layers of salt and sweat washed down the drain, and the fluffy towel wrapped around her, Tuesday felt refreshed, though still on edge from the information Bob Weaver had provided. Somewhere, Angie was being punished for Tuesday's sins. She desperately wanted to take action, but there was nothing to do except wait.

She tamed her hair into a simple braid and then ran her hands over the silk cloth Myles had thrown her. It wrapped around her waist twice, and if secured with a safety pin from the Vandenburgs' kitchen drawer, it transformed into a sleek silk skirt. She strapped her holster to her bare thigh beneath her unconventional new skirt and slipped the dagger in. Adding her black low-cut top and red leather jacket, she didn't need a mirror to know she rivaled Mox and Myles' sex appeal.

"Category," started Myles, as they drove toward Representative Brogan's estate.

Tuesday bristled at the idea of Mox joining in their private game, but the Mercedes was too small to exclude him.

"Things you would see at a celebrity-turned-congressman's party. Starting with the letter M," he finished.

221

"Myles, Mox, and myself," Tuesday said.

"Marble," Myles suggested. "Tiles, or maybe a statue or something."

"Moguls," Tuesday ventured.

Mox caught on to the game and interjected, "Microalgae served at the buffet. He seems like that type."

"Maids," offered Myles.

"Like the kind who clean, or like maidens?" asked Tuesday.

"Why would there be maidens?" Mox scoffed, "We're not visiting King Arthur's court."

"If we were, I'd say that Merlin would be there," Myles said.

"And minstrels," Tuesday added.

"Merlin is a myth and minstrels are medieval," said Mox flippantly, "but today we can count on seeing a millionaire, at least," Mox said. "And this Mercedes."

Tuesday touched the muslin pouch she had tucked into the pocket of her jacket. Mad Hatter starts with M...now where would he be?

The unmanicured border of towering foliage surrounding his estate illustrated Jeff Brogan perfectly. Brazenly unpolished, Brogan spent money on what was important and ignored the rest. A beautiful spacious home with grounds to roam was important. Landscaping was not.

"I think this garden party was impromptu, so I don't think we can expect anything too extravagant," Tuesday said, as they stepped out of the sleek sports car. A valet, whose very presence contradicted Tuesday's thought, took the keys and said, "Most everyone's out back. Head inside and go all the way through the foyer."

From the driveway, Tuesday could see a figure casually seated on the grandiose front steps, his phone in one hand, and a stemmed cocktail glass balanced in the other. He wore a suit jacket with khakis, and even though a ball cap partially obscured his face, Tuesday recognized him. He was Francisco Cruz, stage name Frisko, who had been a prominent comedian and illusionist back when L.A. could support an entertainer. Tuesday nodded to him in greeting as she passed; Myles and Mox were equally subdued in acknowledging him.

The double doors beyond Frisko were propped open, providing a view of the activities in the foyer, where two men and a woman concentrated on bringing the Chihuly glass sculpture back to life. The entryway's vaulted ceilings were two stories high and embellished with crown molding, an atmosphere worthy of displaying the chandelier. Beyond the foyer, through another set of open French doors, the garden was aglow with the spark of a nearly descended California sun. Careful to pick their way past the ladders and tools for the glass installation, they passed a buffet table adjacent to the open doors. A man with a trumpet on a strap hanging over one shoulder filled a plate with appetizers.

As they passed, Myles elbowed Tuesday and Mox simultaneously. "Microalgae!" he whispered excitedly. Tuesday stifled a laugh. As they stepped onto the back terrace, they were met first by two brindle, snub-nosed, snuffling boxers, one with a ball in its mouth. After official dog greeting customs, one boxer play-bowed to Oz and then charged away. Oz accepted the invitation for a game of chase and bounded after the boxers into the garden. "Garden" did not adequately describe the plot of land behind the Brogan estate. Fields of grasses stretched across several untamed acres, scattered with mole hills, low shrubs, and decaying stumps. Three targets for archery practice stood in the distance; otherwise, no particular attention had been paid to altering the meadow. Closer to the home itself, a patio featured a hefty barbecue grill, brick oven, and fryer, positioned as if they were a band about to belt out their first number of the evening. An outdoor kitchen with refrigerator and cupboards would have seemed imposing in any normal yard, but was balanced by the broad openness of the adjacent field.

"I see you've met the boxer bosses, Sugar and Pacquiao!" Jeff Brogan stood from his lawn chair and opened his arms wide. "They run the place, and don't let anyone tell you otherwise!" A few patio chairs, arranged randomly near the grill, contained evidence of other guests: drinkware, a jacket, a pair of sensible ladies' shoes. The occupant of one chair, facing away from them, raised her Mason jar in the air and agreed, "He's right!" She turned and smiled over her shoulder, a dazzling, red-lipped Hollywood smile.

"That's Tess," Brogan's introductions were brief. "Tess, meet Tuesday, Myles, Mox, and," he waved toward the meadow, "somewhere out there, Oz."

"Hello!" said Tess brightly over her shoulder.

"You probably saw Frisko and Cliff inside." Ah, Cliff Carlisle, the jazz musician—that must be the man with the portable trumpet.

"And Doctor Darika is around here somewhere," Brogan continued.

Tess stopped him, "She hates it when you call her that."

"Well, she's a doctor, isn't she?" Brogan protested, and it's either her, or," he pointed to the shoes set neatly under a patio chair, "Or Cinderella is here."

"You're the Deliverers, right?" Tess asked, this time turning slightly in her chair.

"I am," answered Tuesday, "and this—," she started to brag about Myles' piloting skills, but Tess turned back toward the field, raised her glass again, and said, "I'm watching a Deliverer dog frolic in the sunset!"

Brogan moved on. "Have they made any progress in there with the Chihuly?" he asked, leading Tuesday back into the foyer.

"Looks great so far," Tuesday assured him. "They're just working on the first set of spires."

"Help yourselves," Brogan gestured toward the buffet table while he craned his neck to watch the installation above them. Myles and Mox needed no further encouragement.

"The naan and curry sauce smell delicious," said Myles politely.

"Darika made them," Brogan said. "And if you can take the heat, try the ghost pepper dip. The fire will hit you like a left hook from Proximo

Aponte!" In his own home, Jeff Brogan had dialed down the intensity of his politician persona, though an element of celebrity game show host and podcaster remained. He turned to Tuesday, "Do you think they'll be done installing by eight? Jess will be on her way."

"As long as they follow the diagrams." Tuesday put her boot on the bottom rung of a ladder and briefly considered climbing up for a closer look, but then remembered her miniskirt and decided to keep her feet on the ground.

"If Jess stops at the fruit stand on the way home then we've got until eight-fifteen," Brogan mused. "Ooh, I'll text her that we need apples for the chutney!" He grinned at his own cleverness. "Here," he stepped to the buffet table and poured Tuesday a snifter of clear liquid from a glass bottle. "Frisko makes better booze than any shinery." He handed her the glass. So that's what a comic magician does after a pandemic destroys much of society.

Tuesday pressed the cool glass of her drink against the back of her hand, which still throbbed from the force of slugging Claudia that afternoon. "I'll give these guys another half an hour to keep working and I'll check in again," she promised.

In the meantime, Tuesday tried to relax. The moonshine helped. She borrowed Jess's hunting bow so she and Jeff Brogan could shoot at the practice targets in the last of the day's light. Myles and Cliff took turns throwing a Frisbee for the dogs. Three more guests joined the party and Mox mingled easily with the lovely Tess. Doctor Darika, apparently a doctor of biology, reappeared, having had no luck searching the nearby bog for frogs.

By eight o'clock, with just a little guidance from Tuesday, the chandelier was assembled, its spirals and multicolored discs glinting radiantly. Brogan's guests gathered in the foyer beneath it in anticipation of his wife's arrival. Jess Brogan, a towering, willowy beauty, dropped her gym bag on the floor of the foyer when she laid eyes on the masterpiece hanging from the ceiling, and her guests cheered, "Happy anniversary!"

225

Her hands flew to her mouth and she squealed, "Oh my God, Jeffy! It's unbelievable!" She held her arms out to her husband and cocked her head to the side, "You outdid yourself, baby."

After the climactic reveal, the party returned to its easy rhythm. Mox played pool with Doctor Darika, who turned out to be a billiards shark. The dogs enjoyed dinners of dried elk jerky, while the humans sampled the array of juicy fruits and dipping sauces. Tuesday and Frisko salsa danced under the chandelier to music piped into the foyer. Jess and Tess were a coordinated pair of stunning, honey-haired enchantresses, giggling and whispering to one another like sisters sharing secrets. Tuesday's stomach flipped a somersault at the thought of sisters, and she tried to push her emotions into the compartment in the back of her head with a swig of Frisko's moonshine.

Tuesday gracefully left Frisko and moved to the patio. She didn't feel much like flirting, but she smiled to herself, knowing Frisko watched her walk away. He didn't know her skirt was just a table runner held up with a safety pin. On the patio, Tuesday chose a reclining chair and invited Oz to sit with her. Jeff Brogan emerged from the house and checked the progress on a batch of sea salt encrusted potato skins baking in the brick oven before joining Tuesday. "The look on her face was worth every penny," he said. "She loves it, and there's no way she'll be able to top that gift in a million years! Couldn't have done it without you." He continued, "I heard you were the only one who could get your hands on something like that."

Tuesday felt almost as awkward accepting gratitude from her clients as she did accepting gratitude for delivering vaccines. "Happy to be of service," she replied.

"I've never had a Deliverer on my podcast—that would be an amazing interview!" Brogan ran with the idea, "People would love to hear what it was like. Risking life and limb, and canine companion, all as a sacrifice for the greater good. That's some compelling, heart-warming shit." Brogan plowed ahead, "And what did you do before you were a Deliverer?

226

How did you get where you are today? Listeners eat that stuff up."

"Oh, my story isn't all that interesting," Tuesday deflected. "In my line of work, it doesn't pay to talk too much. Sensitive clients and accounts, you know. Myles would be really great to interview though."

"Listen, have you ever thought about a career change?" Brogan's tone reminded Tuesday suddenly that he was a politician.

"Oh, that knockout against Claudia was a complete fluke. I'd be garbage in the ring—"

"No," he interrupted with his palm out like a traffic cop, "Not as a fighter. We're looking for an au pair for my youngest daughter—"

Tuesday burst out laughing and couldn't stop.

"I'm serious!" Brogan was affably adamant, "We were thinking of an au pair who spoke Mandarin, but I think it's a job that would really play to your strengths!"

"I don't know the first thing about taking care of children," Tuesday said when she was able to speak.

"You don't have to! You were a child once; that's good enough. I want my daughter to have an example like you—smart, scrappy, doesn't take shit, but knows how to drop an opponent with one blow—that's something to aspire to!"

Tuesday shook her head in bewildered amusement.

Across the patio, Cliff Carlisle began to play a soulful rendition of "Taps" that made Tuesday suddenly wish she were going home to her own lofted bed in Bellingham tonight. She was starting to wonder where Mox and Myles were when they came through the French doors with the siren Tess gliding along between them.

Just then Tuesday became aware of a whirring sound from overhead.

"Someone expecting a drop?" asked Cliff mildly.

Tuesday lept into action. She grabbed Jess's bow from the stone patio and let an arrow fly. It struck the body of the drone with a crunch and sent the machine spiraling to the ground.

"Whoa, hey, what's going on?" Brogan shouted as Tuesday dashed into the field after the fallen drone.

"Is she nuts?" asked Tess.

"What if that was a trooper?" Cliff said, "The fine for messing with one of those is huge!"

Mox and Myles ran into the field after Tuesday as she rustled through the grasses. "Where is it, where is it? Where *is it*?" Tuesday fumed.

"It's gotta be close," said Myles, searching through the brush. "It looked like it landed right around here."

Oz barked at a shrub nearby. "I think the old boy found it," said Mox.

Tuesday rushed to Oz and picked up the drone with the box it had been assigned to drop. "I can't see out here in the dark," she said, hurrying toward the brightly lit patio.

"Again," Brogan started, as the other guests loitered nearby, "What is going on?"

"I'm sort of...being followed," Tuesday didn't have time to explain. She turned the drone over in her hands and inspected it closely, "Dammit. It's unmarked. I was hoping for some kind of clue. Where is that asshole?"

"What did it bring this time?" Myles asked.

Tuesday's heart pounded and she tried to keep her hands from trembling as she tore the brown paper from the unassuming box.

Tuesday held up the contents of the box, dangling the item from her fingers.

"Is that a..." Myles tilted his head quizzically.

"Wing," Mox finished.

It was indeed a wing.

"From a real bird?" Myles asked, examining the set of preserved bones and nondescript grey-beige feathers. "Very weird."

"Very creepy," Mox scowled.

"*Alouette*," sang Tuesday quietly. "It's a lark."

"Who would send you taxidermy bird pieces?" Jeff Brogan asked, stepping closer to inspect it.

"Someone with a vendetta," Tuesday answered. Attached to the lark's wing was a faded square of cardstock. "There's a tag. It looks old. It says 'Archer's Lark, National Wildlife Property Repository.'"

"There's something written on the back," Myles turned the cardstock over.

"This writing is newer; the ink hasn't faded," Tuesday observed, feeling breathless, despite standing still. "It says, 'Off with her head!'"

"Another *Alice in Wonderland* quote. It's from Ben Hatter for sure," Mox said.

"It's a threat, but whose head is he talking about?" Myles asked. "Yours? Angie's?"

"Either way, we have to stop him," Tuesday asserted.

"But we still don't know where he is. The drone is unmarked," Mox said.

"The National Repository," Tuesday said as feeling returned to her numb body, "is outside of Denver. Or at least, what used to be the Repository is there." She looked up at Mox and Myles. "We're going to Colorado. Now. Before anyone has time to do anything with anyone's head."

"You know I'm in," Myles promised, "But the Cessna can only hold three plus Oz. We won't have enough space if we find her." He glanced pointedly at Mox.

"And we might need to make a quick getaway," Tuesday considered.

"I'm bloody well not staying here," Mox insisted. "You dragged me this far—I'm not jumping ship now!"

Myles was calculating, "We'll have to find a different fuel stop after that nuclear plant melted down near Phoenix. It'll take an extra stop to get around that disaster."

"I don't know what's going on," piped up Brogan, who had been taking in their conversation silently, "But I think I can help. I've got a jet that'll get you to Colorado and back without refueling. Seats seven people." He nodded toward Oz, "Or dogs."

"Really?" Tuesday was dumbfounded.

Brogan turned to Myles, "Can you fly a Gulfstream G100?"

"Yes, sir!" Myles replied.

"Good," said Brogan, heading inside the house. "I'll arrange for you to take her from the airport in the morning."

Tuesday stared at the delicate lark's wing in her hand, "We're coming for you, Angie."

"That was a fantastic shot, by the way," Myles held up the remains of the smashed drone. "You're an archer's lark for sure."

As they unloaded themselves from the Mercedes at the beach bungalows under the starry ocean sky, Tuesday requested, "Can we regroup in the morning? I want to talk all this through." She rubbed her temples.

"It's been a long day," Myles agreed. He touched the cut above his eye and his hand came back with a drop of blood.

"Shouldn't have spent the evening waggling your eyebrows at the ladies," Mox chided. "See you all in the morning, if I still feel like it," he said, heading toward his beach house.

Tuesday watched Mox walk away with his head low and his hands in his pockets before she turned to Myles, "I brought some of the first aid supplies from the arena kit. Let's patch you up."

Seated on the steps of Myles' bungalow, Tuesday assessed their supplies.

"Just glue me back together," Myles said amiably, holding up a tube of superglue.

"I didn't know they did that for real," she commented, already opening the tube. "Close your eyes and hold still." Concentrating on the tube of glue poised near his eye, Tuesday touched her hand to Myles' cheek without thinking. An unexpected spark zipped through her and she drew her breath in sharply.

"Well?" Myles asked, his eyes still closed. "What do you think?"

Tuesday landed back on earth. "It looks good," she managed. She paused, her face close to his, contemplating his jawline and smooth mocha skin.

"Alouette is a pretty name," he said. "Does anyone still call you that?"

"Don't move,' Tuesday said softly, still studying Myles' features. "No. No one calls me that anymore. Hatter must be the only one. Angie used to call me Al."

"We'll find Hatter," Myles assured her.

Tuesday drew back and inspected her work. "Look at me," she asked. Myles opened his eyes and Tuesday met his gaze for a moment before turning her eyes to his brow bone.

"Does it hurt?" she asked.

"Not as much as you'd think," Myles said. "Not even Mox calls you Alouette?"

"He always called me Birdie. Because larks are birds, and in England at least, ladies are birds...It was kind of sweet." Tuesday didn't want to talk about Mox with Myles. She looked away and began unrolling some medical tape, wrapping it around her own sore hand.

"Don't you think Ben Hatter must be in contact with someone who knows your real name?" Myles asked.

"It seems like it, doesn't it?" Tuesday agreed. She anticipated his next question, "But I don't think it's Mox."

"No?"

"No. I can't quite explain why. I mean, I know he's done some really terrible things and there's no reason to trust him, but..." Tuesday sighed. "Something tells me he's being honest about not working for the Mad Hatter."

"Okay," Myles shrugged. "I don't trust him. But I trust you."

Thirteen

Now the dream is clearer. The edges less fogged and the sequence less fragmented. Tuesday feels her foot heavy on the pedal, feels her body being tossed against the side of the vehicle as it rolls, and hears Angie's screams, all with sickening clarity. She wills herself to stay in the vision. She knows what will happen. How many times has she seen these horrors? Her head turns, she sees Angie's blood on everything, sees her sister's ear and skin torn loose, dangling. She watches through the rain droplets on the shattered windshield as a desperate man runs away into the darkness. *That's who I'm looking for*, Tuesday tells herself. Then the car door wrenches open, and she looks straight into Justin Mox's striking blue eyes. *I'm sorry, Birdie*, he says. She feels his hand touch her face. She hears her own voice pleading, *Take me away*. Justin leans over her. *Stay*, Tuesday orders herself, *watch*. His hands deftly lift Angie's locket from around her blood-spattered neck. Tuesday watches him remove her own locket and replace it with Angie's. She feels herself being lifted, and Mox lays her gently on the muddy ground. He goes back to the car. *Lift your head! Watch!* she begs herself. Her body is limp and numb. It doesn't move. Justin is back, his arms around her again. She feels herself floating with her head against his chest, and the world is black.

Tuesday's eyes snapped open and she couldn't tell if the roaring in her ears was the sound of the stormy sea, or her own blood racing through her veins. She rolled over and glanced at Oz, still curled contentedly in his doggy bed. What time was it? Too early to barge in on Mox with more questions? Why did he switch the necklaces? And why did he go back to the car? Tuesday found herself wondering why he was so determined to join her and Myles in Colorado for what was obviously a dangerous undertaking. He'd even warned against the cruelty of Ben

233

Hatter. What did Mox have invested in this?

Tuesday pulled a chair up to the window of the bungalow and sat down, tucking her knees up to her chin as she watched the ocean. For that matter, what did Myles have invested in this? She and Myles were business associates. Was it really fair to put him in the way of a deranged criminal for her own agenda? She needed Myles, of course. He was the one who would fly her another step closer to finding Angie.

The realization was still sinking in: today she would be one step closer to her sister. Her living, breathing sister. But what would Angie think, seeing Tuesday after all this time? After Tuesday had nearly killed her? Wouldn't Angie have tried to find her...if she still cared? Maybe Angie couldn't forgive her because Tuesday was unforgivable. After all, even if she hadn't killed Angie, she'd killed *someone*. Tuesday had to make sure it was herself, not Angie, who faced consequences for that life. She touched the locket at her neck, and came around full circle to where her treadmill of thoughts had begun. Why had Mox traded their necklaces?

When the first hints of light streaked the early morning sky, Tuesday readied herself for the day. She changed into her leggings and slipped her dagger into its holster. She put on her favorite tunic, the one that matched her eyes. She braided her hair as she watched Oz bounding in the beach grasses on the dunes. Tuesday closed her eyes and felt the wind rippling her tunic and the sun kissing her cheeks. She imagined the ceiling of her tiny home. Long, straight line, swerve to the left, through a smear of pine tar, back to straight.

She needed to talk to Mox. Oz wagged his tail delightedly as Tuesday rapped on the door to Mox's bungalow. After some audible shuffling, Mox opened the door, still dressed in his clothes from the previous night, now with his shirt unbuttoned and untucked.

"I want to know the rest of the story," Tuesday said calmly but firmly.

He leaned against the door frame, "Ah, it's you. I was thinking I hadn't ordered any room service. Unless you ARE here for a...service."

Tuesday ignored his suggestive tone, "Why did you switch the lockets?" she asked.

"It sounds like you're figuring out the story on your own," Mox replied.

"I'm remembering more, like Kosmina said I would. Eventually I'll remember everything, so here's your chance to explain yourself, " Tuesday told him. She was adamant, "Why did you switch the lockets?"

His eyes met hers as he lifted her locket from her neck pensively. She let him, and felt the back of his hand against her collarbone.

"It was special to you. To both of you. The one nice thing you'd had since childhood—a sisterly bond and all that," he said, still holding the locket around her neck.

"So, it was just sentimental?" Tuesday pressed him. "You just thought I'd want to have it? Then why switch them? Why not just take Angie's and give it to me?"

"Is it that hard to believe I might have a heart?" Mox sounded offended.

Tuesday almost bought it. Almost. "And what else did you do?"

"I've done a lot of things, Birdie," he answered, releasing the necklace.

"After you pulled me out of the car, you went back to it. Why?"

He stepped back and frowned. "I was protecting you," he said defensively.

"From what?" Tuesday was indignant. She wanted to believe him. He had saved her, brought her to a safe place when her world was crumbling.

"Consequences."

"Consequences for what?" Tuesday's eyes narrowed.

"Well, if you remember, back when there were enforceable laws and a marginally useful court system, deadly crashes due to reckless driving were kind of a big deal."

"I was driving recklessly because I was upset! I was devastated about YOU!" she accused.

Mox turned away and walked back into his bungalow, leaving Tuesday in the doorway.

"That's not what I came to talk about," Tuesday said to his back. "You don't get to always walk away!"

Mox sat down in an armchair and replied, "I didn't get very far, did I?" Oz followed Mox inside and flopped down at his feet.

Tuesday could still see them from the doorway, Mox leaning forward with his elbows on his knees, Oz looking up at him. For the first time, it occurred to Tuesday that it must have been jarring for Mox. Witnessing the accident, seeing Angie limp and bloody, and then suddenly learning she was alive somewhere in Colorado. His head must be spinning too.

Tuesday tried a different tactic. More gently, she said, "I'm just trying to understand what happened that night. You're the only one who can help me." She realized the truth in her words as soon as they left her lips.

After a few moments Mox said, "I went back to the car to move her body into the driver's seat." He looked up at Tuesday to gauge her reaction. She didn't move. "I switched the necklaces, so she wore the one with your name. I moved the body—her—I moved her to the driver's seat so it looked like she'd been driving.

"So that Angie would be punished for what I did." Tuesday took the photo out of her pocket and looked at the back of the blonde woman's head.

"I thought she was dead," Mox answered flatly. He stood up and took a step toward Tuesday. "I didn't know that a literal shaking of the earth would signal the end of society as we knew it. In the end, no one cared who was driving."

"Someone cared." The image of Ben Hatter, bent over the mangled hood of his car, flashed through Tuesday's mind. She dropped her eyes to the photo and her hands began to shake.

Mox crossed the room again. She felt his hand on her elbow, pulling her ever so slightly toward him, and she wanted to press her cheek against his chest. Oz rose and scampered past them out the door. Tuesday turned and saw Myles at the bottom of the bungalow steps, Oz greeting him joyfully. She felt Mox's grip on her elbow tighten, his eyes

236

now fixed over her shoulder, glaring at Myles.

Tuesday broke the silence and pulled away from Mox as she headed down the stairs toward Myles, "I think Oz is ready for breakfast. I've got the ingredients for pancakes at my place. That'd be good, right?" Tuesday said clumsily. How long had Myles been standing there?

"Your pancakes are like Frisbees," Mox said from his deck as he watched them leave.

"No need to *flip* out," Myles quipped.

The knot in Tuesday's stomach loosened at the joke. "I think that pancake pun fell *flat*," Tuesday made a point to smile at him.

"In that case, if you have mushrooms and eggs, we can make an omelette. Breakfast of champignons," Myles continued.

Tuesday shook her head, "Okay, I can't compete with that."

"You mean you can't *beat* my egg pun?"

"No matter how hard I fried."

Standing at the burner in her kitchen with Myles seated on a barstool across from her, Tuesday flipped her second batch of pancakes. She tried to set aside her anxiety about how the day might unfold. "Maybe Mox is right," Tuesday admitted, frowning at the pancakes on their plates.

Myles took a bite. "They are a little...sturdy," he agreed.

"Sturdy!" Tuesday laughed. "That's not a compliment! But you're right. They're like hubcaps."

It was Myles' turn to laugh.

"How's your eye?" Tuesday asked, remembering the surprising spark she felt between them the night before when she tended to his cut.

He raised his eyebrow, testing the superglue holding the gash closed. "Doesn't hurt as much as my hands." Even with the protective gloves, his hands had gotten badly bruised. Tuesday felt a pang of guilt—she had benefited from her friend placing himself in harm's way, and she was doing it again by having Myles accompany her on this crusade to

237

Colorado to confront The Mad Hatter.

Myles put his hands on the counter top and extended his fingers. "I met a superstar, partied with a congressman, and saw a UFF referee get punched in the face," he listed. "Worth it."

Tuesday flexed her own fingers and placed her sore hand on the counter, not quite touching his. "I don't know if Oz thought it was worth it," she said. "Poor guy didn't know what he was walking into."

"That *was* a surprise twist," Myles said. "Who would have guessed Oz would get attacked by a Hellhound?"

"I guess Mox did," said Tuesday. Risking Oz's safety was nothing new. It was his destiny from the day Tuesday found him curled up next to his mom, grizzled old Fury. Tuesday looked at Oz, who had retreated to his dog bed to gnaw on a pancake. The big silver dog was an extension of Tuesday herself; asking him to put himself in danger was the same as putting her own neck on the line. He would do anything for Angie because Tuesday would do anything for Angie.

Tuesday poked thoughtfully at the sizzling batter with the spatula. "If Angie was alive all this time," she jumped topics, "why didn't she ever try to find me?" In a mumble she added, "Maybe Angie hates me."

"She doesn't," Myles said. "You know how I know? Hatter sent you a photo of her necklace, the one that means so much to you. If she kept the locket all this time, it must mean something to her too."

Tuesday let this sink in. "Yeah. Thanks."

"Besides, from what you've said, she doesn't seem like a person who hated anyone."

"No, she didn't," Tuesday agreed. "Or didn't before. Ten years can change things."

"I wish I had known her too," Myles said, glancing toward Mox's bungalow.

"Now you will," Tuesday realized.

Myles smiled and picked up a plate of pancakes, "I'm going to take this to our friend across the pond before we get going. I'll leave one so

238

you and Oz can play fetch."

On the beach in front of the row of bungalows, Tuesday stood with Myles and Mox, her insides quivering with anticipation. "Are we ready?" she asked, feeling like a quarterback in a huddle.

"Tell me again where we're going exactly?" Myles asked. "A repository?"

Tuesday nodded. "I know it's strange, but I'm sure it's where we need to go. The tag on the lark's wing said it was from the National Wildlife Property Repository. The Repository is the old building where confiscated items like elephant ivory carvings, python skin purses, or endangered coral bits would be sent when they were seized by authorities."

"Back when there were authorities," Myles deduced.

"Right. The whole U.S. used to send stuff there. It's a huge collection in a warehouse, plus some office space. But I imagine it hasn't operated since the pandemic and the government collapse," Tuesday reasoned.

"How do we get there?" asked Mox pragmatically.

"I've got an AirplaneBNB reserved for once we land in Denver, so we can leave Brogan's plane in a hangar. But then," she pulled her Deliverer tags from under her tunic, "I think I might have to play the Deliverer card to get us a vehicle to drive to the Repository. It's out somewhere on a wildlife preserve."

"Leave it to the Yanks to hoard a stockpile of useless curiosities in the middle of nowhere for no reason," Mox said.

"Wait," Myles interjected, "What's Hatter thinking here? I mean, why is he hanging out at the Repository anyway?"

"They might be useless, but a lot of the items in the Repository are worth a shit-ton of cash to the right buyer," Tuesday explained. "Maybe he's been using the building as a kind of home base? It used to have top-notch security to protect all the confiscated goods. And maybe he could sell some of the stuff to make money. It's probably kind of a sweet deal."

239

"And that's on top of whatever he's making running his drugs all over the continent," Mox pointed out.

"From drug dealing to wildlife trafficking—this villain does it all!" Myles said.

Tuesday held up the button-sized tracker. "Now that we know where we're going, I don't need this anymore. We don't want Hatter to know we're headed for him." She paused. "I want to crush this dramatically on the ground, but we're standing on sand," she confessed.

Mox took the tracker and pinched it between his fingers until there was an audible crack. He placed it back in her hand. "There."

"That *was* dramatic," Myles approved.

In the cockpit of Representative Brogan's private Gulfstream G100 jet, Myles rubbed his hands together enthusiastically. "I get to fly a jet AND meet your sister today."

He was so confident. "Yeah," Tuesday tried to smile back. "Good day. I'll get Oz settled."

The Gulfstream carried seven passengers in relative luxury compared to the Cessna 182. The cabin was well insulated, so Oz didn't need his ear protection, and once they were in the air he could even get up to stretch his legs.

Tuesday secured Oz into a seat facing Mox, who asked, "He won't get air-sick facing backwards, will he? Maybe let the dog be the co-pilot for once. Then you could take advantage of the posh accommodations back here."

Tuesday interpreted this as a request for her to join Mox in the cabin of the plane, rather than fly in the cockpit with Myles. "I'll switch with you halfway if you want," she told him, dodging the invitation. A frown crossed his face and he turned his gaze out the window sulkily.

Once the jet was airborne, Tuesday instinctively touched first the locket around her neck, then the dagger at her thigh, and lastly the muslin pouch in her pocket, which held the items dropped from the drones.

"Category," Myles began.

Tuesday welcomed the distraction, "Shoot."

"Animals that can anagram to another word," he proposed. "I've got: lion loin."

Tuesday smirked, "Okay: Dog god!"

"Of course," Myles nodded. "How about...wasp swap."

"Umm... Wolf flow," Tuesday said proudly.

"Trout tutor."

"What? You didn't think of that just now!" Tuesday accused jokingly, then added, "Caiman maniac."

"Oh, come on!" Myles protested with admiration, "YOU studied!"

"How could I? You just made up the category!" she laughed.

"Is that what you do in your free time?" Myles asked, "Just sit around and think of ways to surprise me?"

"No, it just comes naturally," Tuesday replied.

Tuesday watched wispy clouds pass lazily beneath the plane. Five hundred miles per hour never felt so slow. Her thoughts drifted. Had Mox's invitation to join him in the back of the plane been more than a simple request for company? His expression had suggested something more serious. "I'm going to check on Oz," Tuesday said to Myles. In the spacious aircraft, Tuesday could stand and walk from the cockpit through a door to the cabin. As she expected, Oz was sprawling contentedly near Mox's feet, enjoying freedom from his seat belt while the plane was in the air. He looked up and thumped his tail on the floor when he saw Tuesday settle into the seat across from Mox.

"Time for the in-flight entertainment already?" Mox asked drily.

"Never mind, just thought you might want to talk," she said, uncrossing her legs as if to leave.

"Wait."

She sat back in the seat, crossed her arms, and raised her eyebrows expectantly at him.

Tension hovered at the corners of Mox's eyes. "Let me talk to The Mad Hatter before we do anything dangerous. I've done business with some of his acquaintances. Maybe I can negotiate with him."

"No." Her voice was firm. "My actions put Angie in danger. Even if you did try to frame her. This is my fight."

"You always hated asking for help. Or taking it when it was offered. Let me talk to him. I might be able to get the Ingall girls out of this mess."

"That's not who I am anymore," she said as an aside. "And no, you can't."

After a brooding silence Mox said, "There's something more I have to tell you."

Tuesday eyed him warily, "I'm listening." Oz sat up and yawned.

"I'm telling you this now before you remember it for yourself. In the interest of full disclosure," Mox informed her.

"Just get on with it," Tuesday was impatient.

"I drugged you," Mox dropped the statement like a grenade and waited for the explosion.

Tuesday shook her head, "No you didn't. You tried, but—"

"Not at Gilman House," he interrupted. "Not when I was warning you. On the night of the accident. After I brought you to the shelter."

Tuesday was dumbfounded. "What? No, you—why?" she stammered.

Mox leaned forward and for a fleeting moment Tuesday thought he was reaching to take her hand, but instead he pressed his fist on the table between them for emphasis. "It was for the best."

"For the *best*?" Tuesday sneered, "How the fuck could that be for the best?"

"You were in pain; we couldn't go to a hospital," Mox reminded her defensively.

"Let me get this straight," Tuesday steamed, "You broke up with me, stalked me when I left a party, watched me crash my car, framed my sister for the crime, and then for some ludicrous reason, carried me away to safety and drugged me?" Her voice rose as she listed each item. "And you did this all in one night! Who *are* you?"

"You know me," he said without guile. "I'm Justin Mox. And you loved me."

Tuesday was not ready to be appeased. "I never knew what really happened that night, and I was plagued by nightmares for a decade because you *drugged* me?"

"I can't have known that's what would happen," Mox shrugged unapologetically. "I had to do *something*."

"You didn't have—" Tuesday protested.

"I didn't want you to remember!" Mox burst out.

The shout silenced her.

"I didn't want you to remember because you're not a killer," he continued quietly. "You're not a killer, and I didn't want you to feel like one for the rest of your life. Birdie, I did what I thought was best for you. Let me negotiate with Hatter. I want to earn your trust again."

Tuesday met his eyes and braced herself on the table as she stood. "I can never trust you." Anguish flickered in his expression before he set his jaw and his gaze turned stony. She turned her back and walked down the aisle of the plane toward the cockpit.

Gusting winds jostled the plane on their descent into Denver, and Tuesday tried not to interpret the rough landing as a harbinger of events to come.

"Taxi into hangar B-4, right here," she instructed Myles. "I'll check in and see about getting a vehicle at the desk inside," she said as the plane glided to a halt.

Mox popped his head into the cockpit, brandishing a pistol in one hand, "So do you—"

"Aaagh!" Tuesday ducked.

"Whoa!" Myles shouted.

Mox dropped his hands to his sides and rolled his eyes, "A little jumpy, are we, mates? I just want to discuss the situation of our...accoutrements, if you will."

Tuesday sat back up and adjusted her tunic. "I don't do firearms," she reminded him.

"Well, I do," Mox replied. "And I'd advise you to change your tune. I only have one piece with me," he wagged the pistol lightly, "as I haven't been back to my flat since the day you lot coerced me into joining your traveling circus. Otherwise I'd have provided arms for this operation." He nodded to Myles, "How about you? What'd you fancy? Handgun? A-K? Musket?"

"I'm best with a nine millimeter, but I don't—" Myles started.

"Wonderful, I know just where to get you one," Mox cut him off and bowed out of the cockpit.

"Wait, hang on," said Tuesday as all three of them plus Oz descended onto the tarmac. "We don't need guns! Especially not from your shady business connections. Let me get us a car, and we'll come up with a plan."

"While you do that, I'll get us some grub from the kiosks and food trucks over there," Myles inclined his head toward the main building of the airport.

"I'm in for some nosh as well," Mox chimed in.

"So *British*!" Myles shook his head.

"See you back at the plane," Tuesday said, heading toward an annex labeled "Rentals."

"What do you want us to get for you?" Myles asked.

"You know what I like," she answered over her shoulder.

"I certainly do," Mox replied lewdly.

Without turning around, Tuesday threw her hands up to signal her irritation as she walked away with Oz trotting at her heels.

"Welcome to the Independent Nation of Denver!" chirped a young woman at the desk when Tuesday reached the annex. The woman's agile fingers tapped away at a small screen, and her black hair, coming loose from her low ponytail, concealed her eyes. When she looked up at Tuesday, her expression did not match her cheerful tone. Her name tag read, "Gabriella."

"Thanks," Tuesday said uneasily. "We just parked in our hangar and I was hoping to get a vehicle for our stay." She held up her Deliverer tags, watching the woman's face carefully.

"Oh wow, it sure is getting smoky in here!" the woman declared.

Tuesday glanced around. It wasn't. "I don't—" she started, but stopped when the woman dashed from behind the desk and pulled the fire alarm. The shrill siren rang out through the small rental annex. Oz spun in circles, opening and closing his jaws, his bark inaudible over the alarm.

Baffled, Tuesday covered her ears, but Gabriella was already next to her, pulling Tuesday's hand down. Fear registered in the woman's wide, dark eyes. "This place is bugged," Gabriella nearly shouted into Tuesday's ear to be heard. "The Mad Hatter knows you are here! He told me to tell him when a Deliverer arrived. I sent him the message as soon as I saw you with the dog outside." Gabriella squeezed Tuesday's arm, "I didn't want to! You are heroes!" She was nearly crying. "He threatened my family!" She gestured toward the wall of rental car keys behind her, "Take what you need and go!"

"Will you be safe?" Tuesday shouted over the piercing alarm.

"I will be safer if you go!" she pleaded.

"Thank you! Tuesday yelled. She grabbed a key from the wall and exited the annex as quickly as she could without drawing any more attention than the fire alarm already had.

"Holy shit, Oz, that was not what I expected," Tuesday said as they jogged back to the Gulfstream parked in the hangar. "Let's hope Myles and Mox get back here quick."

When Myles stepped into the plane with two paper sacks, Tuesday announced, "Oh thank God you're back. He knows we're here."

"Who? Hatter? How?" Myles fired off.

"One of the staff was an informant. She told him when we checked in," Tuesday explained hurriedly.

"Wait, where's Mox?" Tuesday peeked around Myles to look outside the plane.

"He said he was going to find you," Myles answered, scanning the tarmac with Tuesday. "I'm guessing he didn't."

Tuesday's stomach dropped. "Shit."

"Snake."

"Sneak."

Fourteen

Mox was gone.

Tuesday paced the length of the Gulfstream jet with her fists clenched. "Hatter knows we're in Denver, but he probably knows a hell of a lot more than that if Mox took off and double-crossed us.

"Maybe Mox isn't doing anything devious. He could be out getting us guns," Myles suggested. "He seemed to know where to get some."

"Or," Tuesday suggested, feigning composure, "he could be out getting chummy with someone who's holding my sister captive and wants to kill me."

"Okay, so how long do we wait?" Myles asked. Tuesday turned to face him. How long could Angie wait?

"We can't." Tuesday answered. "You didn't see the girl at the rental desk. She was terrified of Hatter! It's not safe to hang around the airport, and Mox is a lost cause." Tuesday grabbed her knapsack from the cockpit and then held up the key she'd snagged off of the rental car wall, "Let's find out what this goes to and get out of here."

After hastily dressing Oz in his red vest and stashing the solar flashlight in Myles' cargo pants, all three exited the hangar warily. "The rental car lot's just on the other side of the annex," Tuesday pointed, casting guarded glances around the open airfield as they crossed.

"It says 28 on it," Tuesday read the tag on the key, "So, I think we just get to drive whatever car is parked in spot 28."

"I'm hoping for a Porsche, since we didn't get to drive Mr. Vandenburg's," Myles said, hurrying to keep up with Tuesday's brisk stride.

"We can't drive a Porsche onto a nature preserve probably. I mean, we'd better hope for a Rover or something. What if the roads are rough?"

"Ooh, yeah, a Rover!"

When they arrived at spot 28, Tuesday twisted her mouth to the side. "Um. Well…"

"A *Prius*?" Myles was nonplussed.

"Just get in."

While they navigated toward the Repository in the Prius, Tuesday gulped down some baked apple and zucchini bread from the airport food trucks. Myles and Oz shared a bag of tater tots with concerned expressions.

"What does it say about the people we hang out with," Myles knit his brow further, "when the *best* thing we think Mox might be doing is illegally acquiring firearms?"

Tuesday sighed. She had started to believe Mox. She had started to believe that his deceit, his withholding and bestowing of information, might actually stem from good intentions. Bastard.

She tried not to feel defeated. "So what if Mox bailed? We don't need him anyway, right? We just need to get to the Repository, find Angie and get the hell out of Denver."

"Right," Myles fed a piece of apple to Oz. "So how do we get inside the building? I'm guessing we won't knock on the Repository door and ask if Angie can come out to play."

The image of 7-year-old Angie on a park swing set, her blonde hair sailing behind her, sprang into Tuesday's mind. "We'll have to break in somehow," she responded, chewing her baked apple hastily, as if eating faster would get them to their destination more quickly. "And then maybe evade Hatter until we can find Angie. It's a pretty extensive storage site."

"Good thing you brought Oz's vest!" Myles perked up.

"Yes," Tuesday nodded, catching a glimpse of Oz in his vest through the rear-view mirror. "He can be our scout."

"Let me make sure I understand the plan," Myles cleared his throat. "We're going to break into a lunatic drug lord's hideout unarmed, and depend on a dog to guide us to rescue a captive who is also your long-lost, supposedly dead sister."

"About sums it up, yeah."

"I'm in."

Steady, dependable Myles. Tuesday smiled at him, but felt the pang of guilt for placing him in harm's way again. "We won't be totally unarmed," she tried to sound optimistic. "You just beat up a UFF fighter yesterday."

"I did, didn't I?" Myles beamed. "Still, I'd feel better if you had a bow. Or maybe Mox was right." He held up his hands in response to Tuesday's scowl. "Just *maybe* we should have brought some heat."

'We don't need guns," Tuesday took a deep breath. "We need a miracle."

Beyond the rusted out gates of the wildlife preserve, the Prius bounced along the rough dirt roads toward the National Wildlife Property Repository. Without knowing how far-reaching Ben Hatter's surveillance might be, Tuesday was hesitant to approach the compound in the vehicle. She wrestled the Prius to the side of the road. Myles looked at the navigation on his phone, "Still another mile into the preserve before we reach the compound."

Tuesday took a deep breath, "Okay. We'll go on foot from here in an hour or so when the sun starts to go down."

Waiting for the cover of darkness to launch their operation was smart, but it was agony. Oz panted nervously in the backseat, while Tuesday stared into the broad meadows and sparse forest out the windshield. Myles rolled his window down to listen to the birds singing in the twilight.

"Are there larks here?" he asked.

"Horned larks live in Colorado, so yeah, maybe," Tuesday said absently. "Not Archer's larks like the one from the drone drop though—those are from Africa. As a kid I learned a little about larks. It's my namesake, after all," she shrugged. "Or it was. When I was Alouette."

"What's in a name…"

Tuesday didn't finish the quote for him. "Just another few minutes, you think?" she asked, leaning forward for a better view of the sunset.

"Yeah," Myles agreed. After a pause he asked, "How do you feel?"

"Butterflies," admitted Tuesday. "You?"

He put his hand on his stomach. "I think I've got a school of eels."

"Well, you look calm as a clam," she said without mirth.

Myles turned to Tuesday. "Hey, I don't know how all this is going to end up," he said earnestly. "But I'm glad we're doing it together."

The right words didn't come to Tuesday's tongue. She managed an awkward half-smile and a nod she hoped came across as grateful. She had never been good at intimate conversation.

After a few moments she said, "Let's do this." Her heart began to race and she didn't know whether it was in anticipation of seeing her sister, in fear of facing Ben Hatter, or because Myles had just put his hand over hers. As natural as if he did it every day. Tuesday's whole body felt electrified.

Myles gave her hand a squeeze and got out of the car.

In her red leather jacket, next to Oz in his red Deliverer vest, Tuesday wondered if they blazed like neon signs in the low evening light. Too late to do anything about it now, as they tromped through the tall grasses. Even in spring, Denver temperatures could fall below freezing, so going without a coat wasn't an option for Tuesday, and even though Oz was hardy enough, the technology in his vest was a necessity.

Myles handed Tuesday the flashlight. "I've got my watch if I need a light," he murmured.

Tuesday kept her voice low, "Thanks. I think we're close now. That must be one of the Repository buildings just beyond the bluff." A looming warehouse and two small storage buildings with garage doors were barely visible in the distance.

"What's the plan?" he brought his voice to a whisper as they drew nearer. "Should we start with the outbuildings, or the main big one there?"

Tuesday pointed to the smaller structure. "Let's clear that little one first. Lights off." She clicked the flashlight off and the darkness swallowed them. A soft glow from the massive warehouse across the compound provided just enough light for Tuesday to make out Oz's shape, close at her side.

"I'll wait here and cover you where I can see the main building," Myles suggested. "You and Oz circle this building and meet me back here."

"Okay," she agreed, "We'll clear the perimeter and be back."

She didn't see any security equipment on the first storage building, but approached cautiously and aimed the beam of her flashlight through the window. She scanned the room slowly, aware that shining the light could draw attention, hoping it was worth the risk. The interior was mostly empty, and the contents mostly junk. An old dining room table, an overturned armchair, a stack of wood palettes, a pile of textiles. Nothing useful.

Tuesday and Oz continued their sweep of the exterior of the building and returned to where Myles was waiting. Except he wasn't.

Myles was gone.

"Myles!" Tuesday hissed. She crouched next to Oz, and whirled the beam of her flashlight around. "Where are you? Myles!" Silence. "Myles!"

She clung to Oz's neck and waited. The next five minutes were an eternity of her own rattling breath and her blood roaring in her ears. Nothing happened. What could have made Myles abandon his post? Another five minutes. Nothing. Oz whined. Tuesday stood shakily and kept her hand on Oz's neck as they circled the building a second time, hugging the walls for cover. No sign of Myles. She squeezed her eyes shut and suppressed a whimper. She would have to go on without him.

Tuesday crept to the second building, treading lightly so the gravel didn't crunch under her boots. Oz's footsteps were silent. She turned on her flashlight. The click sounded like a gunshot. She aimed the beam

251

through a window in the second outbuilding. A headless doll, crumbling ceiling tiles, empty liquor bottles. An overcoat hanging on a floor lamp like a skeleton doorman. Tuesday couldn't aim her flashlight far enough through the small window to see much else. But she could see that the roll-up garage-style door was several inches ajar. Someone had been here recently.

"Oz, sneak," Tuesday whispered to the dog, who put his belly to the ground and wriggled under the garage door. Tuesday followed, scraping her small frame along the concrete floor. She stayed flat on the cold cement, listening. Oz, undaunted by the darkness, began to sniff the array of objects in the room. Tuesday shined her light across the space, illuminating a broken granite slab, a dead squirrel, a taxidermy grizzly bear head hanging at a slant from one wall. In the center of the room, several items sat on the remnants of a table saw.

Stepping delicately around jigsaw puzzle pieces spewed over the floor, and more empty liquor bottles, Tuesday approached the table saw. Her light flashed over a vase filled with grime, a single dead stalk of a flower, and an odd metal teapot with the lid sealed. There was also a digital projector, pointed at a blank wall. She reached for the power button on the projector. It would be risky.

Oz yelped.

"Oz!" Tuesday whispered hoarsely. Her heart thundered. "Where are you?"

Relief washed over her when she saw a sliver of Oz's fur as he passed under the window on his way to her. She shined her light at him. He squinted in the bright beam, his mouth stretched in an anxious smile. "What's wrong?" Tuesday's flashlight fell on a smear of blood behind him. Two smears. Three. A trail. "Are you bleeding?" she braced the flashlight under one arm and checked Oz's paws. The pad of one of his front paws was wet with blood, a shard of glass jutting out from the pink center. "Oz, freeze." She would need something to wrap his paw after she pulled out the glass. Tuesday hurriedly rifled through a nearby cardboard box. Old electronics, books, a pair of women's heels. A scarf.

Tuesday held the length of gauzy fabric, forgetting her surroundings. For a moment, she was back at a department store, running her fingers along the thin material that felt like dragonfly wings. "I love the pattern," Angie was saying.

"It's not worth twenty bucks," Tuesday heard herself say. The following week she'd stolen the scarf for Angie's birthday.

Choking on the memory, Tuesday snapped back to the dingy garage, Oz's bloody paw, the projector. She dug into the box—were these items all Angie's?—until she found a pair of mittens.

"This is gonna hurt," she warned herself as much as Oz. He yelped again when she pulled out the glass. Tuesday felt his body quivering as she wrapped his paw in a strip from the scarf and pulled the mitten over it. "That's the best I can do," she apologized.

Then Tuesday returned to the saw table and flicked the projector's power button. The machine whirred quietly and Tuesday felt exposed when it threw a bright ray of white onto the opposite wall. Not exactly stealthy.

The projector played a slide show.

In her dreams—visions—Tuesday had never seen Ben Hatter's face. Now she saw what must have been The Mad Hatter a decade ago with a young woman. His expression was smug, his head cocked to the side, looking askance at the camera. The girl, her arms slung around Hatter's neck, smiled with unabashed affection. The following slides showed the couple in similar poses, like an old-fashioned photo booth. Her kissing him on the cheek in one photo, then laughing in the next, then sticking her tongue out in the next. Then a photo of the girl holding a wheat-colored puppy up to Hatter, and his face scrunched into the universal good-natured grimace all humans make when licked on the cheek by a puppy. In the next photo, Hatter and the puppy pressed their foreheads together playfully. *That's not who he is anymore,* Tuesday told herself. *Focus on finding Angie!*

The slideshow carried on, showing images of the woman in a tight pink dress and spike heels, then in a tank top lounging on a porch somewhere. Then in a bikini giving a come-hither look to the camera.

Tuesday wanted the slides to stop. This was the young woman she had killed. A vibrant girl with a trusting smile, who may have been a lot like Angie. She wanted to puke.

Abruptly the images weren't of Hatter and a beautiful woman anymore. There was a map of a Colorado town, then of the outside of a crumbling apartment complex. Then a photo of a jumbled crowd where Tuesday couldn't make anyone out, followed by a blurred image of the same scene from an odd angle, zoomed in on the back of a blonde woman's head. The next slide was fuzzy, but unmistakable—it was Angie with a man's arm draped around her. Her head was turned to the side to aim one ear at the man, revealing a purple scar running from her ear to her jaw. Next was a shot of Angie from behind, walking down the street alone, wearing the gauzy scarf. How long had Hatter been stalking her sister?

Tuesday snapped the projector off, blinking as her eyes adjusted to the darkness again. She focused on one of the garage walls as the remnants of the bright photos floated through her vision. Something on the wall caught her eye. Strokes of paint maybe? She shined her flashlight at the wall and read, in erratic dripping letters, "WE'RE ALL MAD HERE." An angry splatter of paint after the phrase showed where the painter had thrown the brush at the wall. Tuesday spun slowly, shining her light on the remaining walls, illuminating, "Mad, Mad, MAD," painted crazily over and over, in thick red, purple, and black.

Hatter was mad, by all definitions.

She couldn't stand any more. Tuesday flattened herself against the grit of the floor and edged under the door, with Oz close behind her. She circled the building once, whispering desperately, "Myles?" No answer. The brick of dread in her stomach grew heavier. She darted toward the large warehouse in the center of the compound.

From a clump of brush near the building, Tuesday surveyed the entrances and exits. She would have to risk a noisy forced entry through the window nearest the front door. It was the lowest, and hopefully easiest to climb though. She selected a hefty rock and wrapped it in a piece of canvas from a debris pile to dampen the sound of what she was about to do. Raising the rock above her head, she smashed it into the glass, until cracks spider-webbed out from the center of the window pane. After knocking the shattered glass from the frame, Tuesday dragged a rickety wooden palette and a cinder block to the window to give Oz a platform to jump from. "Careful of your paw," she cringed, and then tumbled inside after him.

Tuesday would have landed heavily in the lobby of the Repository, but a huge bag of bird feathers broke her fall. Feather boas snaked out of the bag onto the floor all around her. Oz was already patrolling the room intently, favoring his injured foot. The rest of the warehouse must be beyond the barely visible entrance at the back of the lobby. Peeking through the double doors, Tuesday decided it would be safer for Oz to go in alone. The night vision technology in his vest's camera would give her a better view and would be less conspicuous than her flashlight.

Taking the small monitor from her pocket with her hands trembling, she hugged Oz tightly and whispered, "Oz, go alone."

He did.

In ghostly black and white, Tuesday viewed the vast warehouse from Oz's perspective. The space was the size of a department store, with rows and rows of shelving units, some ten or twelve feet tall. Some shelves were overturned and some areas looked as if they'd been ransacked. The place was full of bizarre items, grotesque curiosities people had attempted to smuggle.

"Oz, three-sixty," Tuesday cued. Oz turned in a slow circle. A rattlesnake, reared back with fangs out, shocked Tuesday before she realized it was dead and preserved. "Jesus" Tuesday swore, her heart

255

racing. A snarling lion came into view, then a wolverine, then just the head of a wildebeest, all of them stuffed, with dead eyes, shining like coins in the night.

Then a gargantuan stump of an elephant's foot appeared, attached to a slab of wood and converted into an end table. Then an overturned basket with dozens of rabbits' feet spilling out onto the floor, and a partially reconstructed skeleton labeled "Jaguar." Tuesday was reminded of Kosmina, the Greek seer, and her warning about taking great care when unearthing the bones of the past.

"Oz, stay," Tuesday cued him, when he rounded the corner of a shelving unit. Through the camera's lens, she saw several steel tables with Bunsen burners, beakers, sinks, and an assortment of containers and tubes strewn about. A drug lab. Or part of one, at least.

Tuesday watched as Oz passed dozens of pairs of boots made from reptile skins, then racks of fur coats and fur rugs, and then a taxidermy ostrich head and swooping neck, and a bin of what appeared to be embalmed tiger embryos. Oz picked his way through an array of dried sea creatures, brittle seahorses, urchins, sea stars, and corals until Tuesday saw something swaying in the air near him.

"Oz, freeze," she directed, squinting at her screen. Suspended above Oz was the head from the doll Tuesday had seen in the garage. A fish hook was jammed in its mouth. The head spun lazily, dangling from...twine? Hair? What was on the wall behind the doll's head? "Oz, move left," she cued.

A huge rectangle made of interlaced antlers hung on the wall, framing something. A painting? No. A giant flat-screen TV. Then Tuesday's monitor went black as Oz picked up a moose antler from the floor. "Oz, cut it out!" she hissed. "You're blocking my view with that thing!" The big dog began to gnaw on one of the antler's points. Just as Tuesday started to cue Oz to get back to searching, a high-pitched giggle rose up throughout the building.

Oz stood up, alert, and let the antler clatter to the floor. Tuesday saw

Angie on the huge flat-screen TV. The view was of the back of Angie's head, just like in the photo that had dropped with the lock of hair, but the camera was zoomed out. Angie was sitting at a school desk, her head hanging with her chin against her chest. Her shoulders shook as if she was crying. Who was laughing? The room on the screen wasn't one she'd seen at the Repository so far. Tuesday racked her brain from her position in the lobby. Was Angie somewhere else?

A giant face appeared on the screen. It was the same face from the slide show, The Mad Hatter, ten years older, his eyes and cheeks hollowed out, his skin sallow.

"Thank you for accepting my invitation," he said cordially. "So glad you could make it! But I'm afraid I've given you the wrong address." Tuesday realized she wasn't breathing. She stood up from the bag of feather boas in the lobby, fear blooming in her gut. The Mad Hatter was live on the screen, talking to her. All her hair stood on end.

Suddenly Oz was barking. A deep, snarling, viscous bark. Tuesday burst through the lobby's double doors into the dark warehouse, shining her light frantically across the ghoulish curiosities. "Oz!" she called. The view from his vest camera had gone black and the audio cut out. She could still hear commotion at the back of the warehouse, and she stumbled toward it, now screaming, "Oz!" When she reached the dangling doll's head and the screen on the wall, she whipped the beam of her flashlight wildly.

Oz was gone.

"Where are you? Where is Oz?" she demanded of Ben Hatter's looming face on the screen. He steepled his fingers and set his pointed chin on their tips coolly.

"There is much to learn," he said, nodding in agreement. He wore a top hat and had the pelt of a dead hare draped around his shoulders, holes gouged where the eyes would be. The Mad Hatter was so close to the camera, Tuesday couldn't see the room behind him. Where was he?

"Where is Oz?"

"You didn't bring any wine, so I assumed he was a house-warming gift. A little stuffing and he'll go nicely with the rest of the decor."

Enraged, Tuesday yelled, "I'm here for my sister!" The screen flickered to Angie for a fraction of a second, then back to The Mad Hatter. He smiled. He was teasing Tuesday. Fury overtook her. She bolted to the steel tables she'd seen through Oz's vest. With a sweep of her arm she sent beakers, test tubes, and canisters from one table crashing to the floor. "I can destroy something you care about too!" Tuesday sneered, grinding the shattered glass under her boot.

"That's no way to behave at a tea party," Hatter's face remained composed. "Besides, I brew my tea in a new kitchen now," he chuckled.

Kitchen? What was he talking about? "Shut up with your riddles and tell me where you are and what you want!"

"I want her back!" Hatter howled, his voice ringing out in the warehouse. A vein bulged on his forehead. "Back!" he spat. He was breathing hard.

"That's impossible," Tuesday retorted.

"Then instead, you'll have to read the writing on the wall," The Mad Hatter growled.

Instantly, the lights in the warehouse flipped on, and the whole space glared bright white. Near the doll's head dangling by a fishhook, the words, "Off with her head!" screamed at Tuesday in dripping red paint.

"Off! With! Her! Head!" The Mad Hatter roared, and the echoes rang in Tuesday's ears, even as the screen went black.

Tuesday's legs turned to rubber and she sank to her knees. The Mad Hatter wasn't here, and neither was Angie. Myles was missing. And now even Oz was gone. For a minute, under the fluorescent lights, kneeling on the fragile bits of angelfish skeletons and sand dollars, Tuesday cried. A tear landed on the wooden floor, and as she brushed it away, the lines in the wood grain reminded her of her tiny house in Bellingham. Long, straight line, swerve to the left, through a smear of pine tar, back to straight.

Think! she ordered herself. What had Hatter said that might be clues? What could she use against him if he cared about nothing more than revenge? An idea struck her. She pulled out the monitor connected to Oz's vest. The camera's video and audio were useless, but whatever had happened to Oz hadn't affected the vest's GPS. She would be able to track him. Oz was a blip on the screen, speeding away from the Repository.

"Tuesday, go alone," she commanded herself. Then she sprinted through the Repository, vaulted out the window she'd come through, and ran back to the open garage door to the small storage building. She rolled under the door, swiped the strange sealed teapot from the table by the projector, and tore into the night.

When she reached the Prius where they had left it, Tuesday's breath came in fast pants and her elbow and chin were scraped from tripping on a tree root. She tried shouting once more, "Myles! Myles?" But there was no response, and she had no time to wait. Oz needed her.

First dashing through the foliage, then bouncing along the dirt roads of the wildlife preserve in the little car, Tuesday lost ground. But when her tires reached pavement, she started to close in on Oz and whatever vehicle he was being transported in. Tuesday concentrated on following the blip, but couldn't stop playing the reel of fearful thoughts in the back of her mind. She'd seen Angie. Her sister was alive! But for how much longer, being held captive by Hatter? When she caught up with Oz, would she find Angie there too? Tuesday didn't have time to dwell on how she had ended up alone in this ridiculous, unlikely crusade. She'd half expected Mox to turn on her, but Myles abandoning her really stung. It had been his own suggestion for them to separate. Why would he leave her vulnerable instead of cover her while she searched? Was he upset that she hadn't been able to respond to his sentiments in the car? She should have told him she was grateful he was with her. She'd missed her chance.

Oz's blip stopped moving. Tuesday's thoughts shifted gears. She would need an action plan for when she caught up to that blip. She had her dagger and the teapot, but no real firepower if it were to come to an altercation. Stealth would be her ally on this mission. But Hatter's technology was first-rate, if their interaction at the Repository was any indication. And hadn't he said he'd sent her the wrong address? As if he was intending to draw her to him all along. Maybe she was following Oz into a trap. Tuesday didn't have time to consider her options more thoroughly as she pulled over to the side of the road. The GPS showed she was close to Oz; she would have to go on foot again. Before she stepped out of the car, she texted Myles, just in case.

Where are you??!! she couldn't convey her urgency with enough punctuation.

Why did you leave me? Myles texted back. The question hit Tuesday in the gut. He must've just gotten reception again. From his perspective, she had abandoned him; not the other way around.

Where are YOU? Myles continued. *I saw someone across the compound and trailed him. Didn't lead anywhere.*

There wasn't time to chew Myles out for deviating from the plan. Tuesday typed agitatedly as she jogged toward the blip. *Oz is gone. I followed the GPS in his vest.*

Why did you leave me? Myles texted again.

Myles had chosen the tense moment in the car to throw out an unexpectedly intimate comment, and now he was getting pissy? Was it because she hadn't reacted the way he wanted? Tuesday felt defensive, but answered, *Are you OK?*

Doesn't seem like you care if I'm OK.

Tuesday had no response. She'd ignored his sincere remarks and then left him stranded. But what had he been thinking, leaving her at the Repository outbuilding like that? Tuesday growled under her breath.

Where are you? Myles asked again.

Tuesday shrank behind a bushy hedge to assess her surroundings

260

when the GPS showed she was within several hundred yards of Oz.

I think I'm at a school, she texted, *Someone must have brought Oz here somehow. Just call me!*

Oz's blip on her screen disappeared. Never in the seven years that Oz had been wearing that vest, had the GPS ever failed. "God damn it all to hell," Tuesday muttered to herself. Her only method of tracking Oz was gone. She had to act quickly.

The school appeared to have been abandoned mid-renovation. One wing of the building was pristine, as if newly constructed, while another was only scaffolding, three stories of flooring and beams. A school like this would have security cameras at all the entrances, and probably even in the hallways. Is this what The Mad Hatter meant when he said "there is much to learn"? That he was at a school? And the new kitchen he'd mentioned—schools had kitchens and cafeterias. Hatter must be using this school as headquarters for his operation.

Tuesday took her chances, crossing the school yard toward the unfinished side of the building, carrying her flashlight and the teapot in her knapsack. She moved in a stooped jog, her arms covering her head— in case Hatter had snipers watching from the windows of the upper floors. If she could climb to the second floor and get to where the new construction met the old, she might be able to avoid security cameras and alarms on her way in. Aided by adrenaline, Tuesday hoisted herself into the skeleton of the school, clamoring up the scaffolding and exposed beams.

As she was attempting to heave herself onto the floorboards of the next level, her phone vibrated in her pocket. "Now you call?" she stage-whispered, rolling herself successfully onto the open air of the second floor. She whipped her phone out, but it was too late. Myles had hung up.

Tuesday army-crawled across the fifty feet to the doors leading into the finished portion of the school. There was no time to think. She had to find Oz before the dog-nappers moved him. *Please find us, Myles*, she thought to herself, frustrated. Tuesday took a deep breath and yanked the school's door open. The inside of the school looked as she expected, a long, white-tiled corridor lined by classroom doors. She didn't try the light switch as she crept along the edge of the dim hallway.

Her pocket vibrated.

I'll meet you at the school. came Myles' reply a moment later. Tuesday was relieved. Whatever damage she had done was not irreparable. She could focus on Oz and Angie.

Hurry! she answered.

Tuesday continued down the corridor, following signs labeled "Cafeteria" illuminated by diffuse moonlight. An abandoned school's industrial kitchen would be the ideal location for cooking meth and other drug cocktails. That's where she would start her search. When Tuesday came to the cafeteria entrance, a thick odor of ammonia, like rotting eggs, hung in the air. She dared to peer through the clear acrylic windows that were set into the swinging doors. Hydroponic lights nourished a few rows of leafy plants in what was once the salad bar—just a basic weed-growing operation, and not even an extensive one. Along the opposite wall, where she could imagine a line of teenagers sliding their trays along the counter, were metallic vats warming on burners amidst a maze of tubes. Hundreds of plastic bottles, gas cans, and glass beakers covered the floor behind the counter where the food servers would have stood to dole out sloppy joes. This was The Mad Hatter's kitchen.

Tuesday eased one of the swinging doors open very slightly. She heard a snap behind her and a small canister flew over her and cracked into the door, just an inch from her ear, then tink-tinked onto the floor.

Booby trap.

Tuesday bolted away from the canister. The explosion rocked the hallway, rattling the classroom doors and ceiling tiles.

Gasping for breath, Tuesday paused to look over her shoulder. The grenade had been more of a make-shift flash-bang than an explosive. All her limbs were intact. Her hair wasn't even singed.

A slow, jingling tune floated out of the school's intercom system.

Alouette, gentille alouette,

Alouette, je te plumerai.

"So much for stealth," Tuesday muttered. The song bored into her skull. She looked up at the plaque on the door of the alcove where she had paused. Her heart lifted just a little when she read the word, "Security." That seemed promising.

The door was unlocked. "Not very secure…," she noted, stepping into a room to find exactly what she'd hoped for. It was just like in the movies. A small room containing only a desk, a control panel, and a bank of monitors, each featuring the live feed from a different security camera. There were too many monitors for Tuesday to take in all at once. She set her knapsack down, stepped back and scanned for humans—Hatter and Angie must be somewhere in the building. For a second, Tuesday thought she spotted Hatter on one screen, but when she leaned in, it was only a fur coat and fedora on a health class mannequin.

Then she saw Oz.

He lay motionless on the floor of a vandalized office. Next to Oz's body stood a taxidermy wolf, no doubt lifted from the Repository, with its head twisted, the stuffing yanked from its chest, and its eyes plucked out. The abomination was wearing Oz's red Deliverer vest. Leaning closer to Oz's image, Tuesday pleaded, "Please be alive." She willed the big dog's silver rib cage to rise and fall. "Please, please, be alive."

He took a breath.

Tuesday released hers, "Oh, thank God."

She needed to find that room. The bottom corner of the screen read, "Counseling."

"Good boy, Oz," Tuesday whispered to the monitor. This gave her an idea. Could she speak through this security system somehow? She fussed with the control panel briefly. Yes, yes, she could.

"Oz!" her voice was urgent. She watched his ribs rise and fall again. "Oz!" she repeated. His ears twitched. "Wake up! Wake up!" Oz rolled

263

upright, his head wobbling. This was good. This was very good. She would have to find the counselor's office. Unless.

If the door had a handle that could be pushed or pressed, Oz could free himself. She watched him try to stand up, his back end staggering until he sat back down on it. "Take your time, buddy," she encouraged him. Except time was something they had very little of.

While she waited for Oz to recover, Tuesday scanned the other monitors.

Then Tuesday saw her.

From behind, seated in a classroom desk, just as she had been when Hatter had flashed her image to taunt Tuesday at the Repository, and just as she had been when Hatter took her picture and cut a lock of her hair to drop from the drone. It was Angie. Tuesday reached out to brush the screen with her finger tips, then noticed the number "321" labeling the feed from the camera. Room 321.

"I'm coming, Angie," she whispered.

She realized if she could talk to Oz through the security system, then she could talk to Angie. She could speak to her sister for the first time in ten years.

She switched her speaker output to room 321.

"Angie!" Tuesday's hushed tone came out choked and desperate. "It's me! Alouette! Your sister!"

Angie didn't move.

Tuesday tried again, still softly, "Angie, I'm here! I'm coming to get you!"

Angie cocked her head and then rested her chin on her chest without responding.

Why wasn't she answering?

Alouette floated into the security office from the intercom and slithered into Tuesday's mind. *Alouette, gentille alouette.* She wanted to put her head down on the security desk and plug her ears.

Her phone buzzed in her pocket.

I'm here. Myles announced. *Meet me at the south entrance.*

That would be on the complete opposite end of the building, two floors down from where Hatter was holding Angie. Tuesday looked back at Oz in the counseling office. Where was that room?

Oz was standing now, shaking himself off as if he had just emerged out of Lake Whatcom after a swim near Myles' trailer.

"Oz," Tuesday instructed firmly, "Find Myles!" Oz moved off screen. Tuesday heard the recoil of a metal handle being pawed at. And then Oz was gone.

Then she instructed herself. "Find Myles."

Tuesday advanced down the hallway warily, sweeping the corridor with the beam of her flashlight, searching for booby traps—what did a booby trap look like? She passed the open shaft of an elevator, a janitor's closet, and more classrooms before discovering the staircase. On the first floor, fluorescent light seeped out from under several of the closed doors. Hatter must have been here recently. He might be here still. If she could just get safely down this hallway, Myles would be on the other side of the door.

With her dagger drawn, she rushed down the hallway to the school's entrance, and pressed herself into the corner by the main doors when she got there. She held her breath, waiting for someone to jump out from one of the occupied rooms. No one did.

In one swift movement, she shoved the door open wide to let Myles in, keeping watch down the hallway behind her. She whirled around to face Myles, "Quick—!"

It wasn't Myles.

The last thing Tuesday saw was The Mad Hatter, his lip curled into a sneer, swinging a hefty textbook at her head.

Fifteen

Tuesday didn't lose consciousness completely. She couldn't see anything, but she was vaguely aware of being dragged. She felt herself unceremoniously dumped into a chair, one of the student seat-desk combinations. She heard the *zzzzt* of a zip-tie and felt her wrists slap together, cinched to the metal bar under the desk that connected the chair to the writing surface.

She couldn't stop herself from pitching forward, smacking her nose on the desk. The haunting children's song danced through her head.

Alouette, gentille alouette,

Alouette, je te plumerai.

It wasn't in her head. Someone was singing. Wet drops slid from her nose onto the desk and Tuesday tasted blood. The pain focused her.

The Mad Hatter was singing. He was singing and puttering around the room, as if cooking a meal or dusting knick-knacks. He switched to English and made up his own tune, "I will pluck your head, I will pluck your beak," he chanted. Tuesday's eyes fluttered. She pretended to be unconscious.

Tuesday could feel him coming close, leaning over her. One of the long ears of the dead hare pelt he wore brushed her shoulders.

"I will pluck your eyes, I will pluck your neck."

She opened one eye and tried to take in her surroundings through the slit. They were in a classroom, so they were still at the school. Still close to Angie. Did she still have her dagger?

"I will pluck your wings," The Mad Hatter finished.

"I don't even have any wings, so fuck you," Tuesday mumbled into the desk. Keep him talking. She had to buy time until she could think clearly.

"Ah, no wings, and yet she has risen!" He sounded joyful. Then he slammed his fist down near Tuesday's nose, jarring her throbbing head.

He wore an engagement band on his ring finger. "Serena's the one with wings," Hatter smeared his fist into the blood that had leaked onto the desk from Tuesday's nose. "You gave them to her."

"Maybe she's better off than she would have been with you," Tuesday shot back drowsily. Why did this school desk seem so familiar?

The Mad Hatter was seething, "Serena was the best thing to ever happen to me. I'd have done anything for her."

"Trite," commented Tuesday. She considered trying to raise her head.

Hatter circled her. "I was going to change. Stop dealing, and make something of myself. For her."

"Instead you terrorize innocent women and kill people. Serena would be so proud."

Hatter wrapped Tuesday's braid around his wrist and yanked her upright in the chair. "Don't. Say. Her. Name." He released her braid. "Name," he said, contemplatively. "I made a name for myself." He sounded pleasant now, "YOU made a name for yourself."

Tuesday looked at the bizarre figure who had hunted her down and captured her. The Mad Hatter's whole wardrobe appeared to have come from the Wildlife Repository. In addition to the felt top hat and dead hare pelt, he wore a purple leather vest over a collared shirt. He was disturbingly thin. A pair of crocodile skin pants, meant to be skin-tight, hung loosely from his hips. He looked like he was either going to twist up a balloon animal at a child's party, or pistol-whip someone with the handgun tucked into his belt. Nut-job.

He continued pleasantly, "Name that tune," and began to hum. *Alouette.*

"Asshole."

"Call me names," he nodded and rambled on. "Put your name in the hat," he set his top hat lightly on Tuesday's head. "To take your chances."

He perched himself on the desk next to Tuesday and assessed her, "Common name. Dog. Scientific name. *Canis lupus familiaris. Familiaris...*" Hatter trailed off absently. "Familiar. You're familiar with

Canis lupus familiaris."

Oz. Tuesday's heart lifted. She remembered Oz, running free somewhere in the building.

Hatter opened his arms as if surprised, "And now here you are, *Canis deliverus* without your *familiaris.*"

Tuesday caught another glimpse of the pistol in his Hatter's red leather belt. Was that Mox's gun?

Hatter continued, "You've been abandoned. Surrendered at the pound." He shook his head and clicked his tongue, "Unwanted."

It was Tuesday's turn to seethe. "Oz wouldn't have left if you hadn't stolen him," she realized she sounded childish.

"Oz might be loyal as a dog, but the pilot..." Hatter shrugged and let Tuesday fill in the blank. She didn't want to. Where *was* Myles? Why had Hatter met her at the door instead? Her vision blurred.

"Myles wouldn't work for you," retorted Tuesday weakly.

"Would you put money where your mouth is? I did. That's all it took."

Tuesday struggled to grasp this. The GPS in Oz's vest had failed the moment Tuesday told Myles she was using it to track him. Could Hatter really have paid Myles off? Clearly someone who knew her had been helping Hatter, but it couldn't be Myles...could it?

"Don't believe me? When pigs fly, you think? He was just a fly on the wall, flying under your radar?" Hatter taunted.

"He wouldn't!"

"Wouldn't hurt a fly?" Hatter asked. "Would you bet your life on that?"

Tuesday was silent. After all this time, would Myles have turned on her? Had they been nothing more than business associates all along? Myles had plenty of opportunities to put the tracker on his truck and even on Oz. His texts had led her straight to Hatter. Had he been extra kind lately so she wouldn't be suspicious? Where was Myles now, right now when she needed him?

"Because you already did bet your life," The Mad Hatter concluded. "And now you have no one. No fly-boy, no pretty boy, no good boy

268

familiaris. Now you're like me."

His insults were hitting home. Tuesday looked down to avoid Hatter's wild stare. Suddenly Tuesday realized why she recognized the desk she was sitting in. It was the precise model of desk that Sharon, the former registrar who loved wine and Reese's candy, had in her office in Bellingham. Tuesday began to feel more lucid.

Hatter prattled on, "You have no one. And I'm going to make you, Alouette Ingall, watch your sister die. Just like I watched Serena."

Tuesday began to fidget under the desk, careful not to let Hatter see her movements.

"In *Alice in Wonderland*," Tuesday started, "The Mad Hatter is just a joke." She wanted to deflate him, "He isn't scary at all."

"But I am," Hatter whispered in her ear. Tuesday twisted her head away and kicked at him. The desk blocked her knee and she connected only weakly with Hatter's shin. The jostling helped, and Tuesday felt the screw she'd been working at come loose and fall into her still zip-tied hands.

"What else do you remember from the book?" Hatter asked. "Why is a raven like a writing desk?"

"I hated lit class," Tuesday growled. She stealthily inched her hands to grasp the edge of the desk, which was now separated from the chair.

Hatter leaned over her and repeated the quote, enunciating each syllable, "Why is a raven like a writing desk?"

In one swift motion, Tuesday stood up and hurled the top of the desk at him, screaming, "They both can fly!" The wood whomped heavily into his chest and threw him into a bank of cabinets. Using both her tied hands, Tuesday grabbed the gun and her dagger from his belt, and fled blindly down the school corridor.

The hallways all looked the same. The Mad Hatter could have brought her to any wing on any floor. She had only managed to surprise Hatter and knock him down, not knock him out. He would be close behind her.

269

As she ran, Tuesday scanned the dark halls for any clue about her location. If she could get back to the security room with the cameras, maybe she could find Oz.

Through the darkness Tuesday made out the frame of an elevator shaft. With her hands still bound together and holding the pistol, she balanced herself on the horizontal metal slats lining the shaft and climbed them like a ladder until her feet were out of view. Her heart pounded. She heard footsteps tapping toward her, and saw an agitated flashlight beam sweep through the elevator shaft below. Any moment now, Hatter would aim the flashlight up, see her, and that would be the end of her. Or she would have to shoot him—if she could even fire the gun with her hands bound together.

Suddenly, Tuesday heard barking. Distant, but unmistakable. Oz was still free! Hatter's footsteps dashed away down the hall. Tuesday waited an excruciating two minutes before climbing carefully down the slats and slipping into the hallway. She needed to find Oz before Hatter did. When she had helped him free himself from the counseling office, Tuesday had instructed Oz to find Myles. Her heart pounded in her chest and her breath was ragged. What if Oz *did* find Myles? What if Myles—?

There was no time to follow this train of thought. She needed to find a safe place to work at removing the zip-ties from her wrists. At the end of the corridor, Tuesday saw a weak light coming through the windows of one of the classrooms. She crept to the window and peeked inside. It was a history classroom, with maps and a globe. Someone was tied to a desk, exactly as Tuesday had been before she'd taken the desk apart and escaped. Even in the dim light, she recognized the silhouette of Justin Mox.

Tuesday fumbled with the door, her hands still clumsily holding the pistol. She slammed the door shut behind her when she finally entered. "What the fuck is happening?" she demanded of Mox.

"How the bloody hell are you alive?" He looked shocked. "And HERE?"

He threw his head back in relief, "I have never been so happy to see an angry armed woman."

"What's going on?" Tuesday repeated. "I thought you snuck off to help Hatter."

"No!" Mox defended. "I snuck off to get guns! Hatter's lackeys ambushed me!"

Tuesday wanted to believe him. "Oh yeah? I guess your negotiation skills aren't as brilliant as you thought, judging by your predicament," she said, setting the gun down and positioning her dagger to cut the zip-ties from her wrists.

"I gave him too much credit," Mox said quickly. "He's impossible to reason with. We have to get out of here."

While Tuesday tried to cut the zip-tie off her wrists, she thought aloud, "Someone has been feeding him info, and if it's not you..." She didn't finish her sentence. She didn't want to believe that it was Myles.

"I see you snagged my piece back from Hatter somehow," Mox nodded toward the pistol. "Not so opposed to firearms now, are you? Wait," he said, suddenly distressed. "Where's Oz?"

"Hatter nabbed him at the Repository, but now he's loose here somewhere. I've got to find him!" She made a frustrated sound as she dropped the dagger for a third time.

"You're a klutz trying to use that thing on yourself," Mox chided. "Cut me free first," he inclined his head toward his hands, zip-tied to the metal bar connecting the desk and chair. "Then I can properly use the dagger to cut you free."

"Right, I should just free you while MY hands are still tied together?"

"Fine, then bring me the dagger," Mox suggested. "I'll hold it for you so you can free yourself first. Then decide if you want to free me."

Tuesday considered this. Hatter was probably headed toward her right now, and she needed help. Oz was roaming the school hallways alone somewhere. God only knew where Myles was. And Angie was in room 321, tied to a chair, waiting to die.

271

Wordlessly, Tuesday placed the dagger in Mox's bound hands. He held it steady, and when the zip-tie snapped, he let her take the dagger back. She spun it deftly in her fingers. "Now why should I free you?" she asked.

"Because I just helped you free yourself," he answered.

"Not good enough."

"Because I will help you save your sister," Mox vowed.

"Why would you do that?" Tuesday grilled him.

Without a beat, Mox replied simply, "Because I love you."

Tuesday was speechless for a moment. Then she argued, "No, you don't."

"I always have," he said. "I never stopped."

Instead of being touched by this admission, Tuesday felt defensive. "You certainly didn't act like you loved me! You turned me in to the dean for cheating!" It all seemed so stupid now. "I would have been expelled if the world hadn't exploded that night. And then you broke up with me! I don't know shit about love, but I know that was NOT IT."

"I can explain," Mox said urgently.

"Better make it quick," Tuesday warned, "Or I'll leave you here with Hatter."

"Look, you only knew half of the schemes I was involved in back then. I was getting in over my head, and I was dragging you down with me. You'd have ended up indebted to a mob boss, jumped by gangs, or in prison. Or worse."

Tuesday furrowed her brow. There wasn't time to think all this through.

"I had to let you go so you didn't become what I was. What I am." His eyes implored her to understand.

"Why not just tell me that then?" she asked.

"That I was breaking up with you to save you from a life you didn't deserve? You'd never have listened." She knew he was right. "You're stubborn as an ox, and as loyal as your dogs." He added, "That's a

272

compliment."

Tuesday glanced out the window of the history classroom into the hall. She weighed her options. "So, then you rescued me from a car wreck, and left me drugged at the Humane Society." She hovered in front of him. "And then you completely disappeared!" she added accusingly.

"You said yourself that you were devastated and I was to blame. I didn't fancy hanging around waiting for you to wake up to claw my eyes out."

"So you just never came back." Tuesday shrugged angrily.

"I didn't say that."

Tuesday waited, puzzled.

"I may have...checked in," Mox admitted. "Occasionally."

She narrowed her eyes. "What does that mean?"

"I...stopped by. At the shelter, just at first. To make sure you had what you needed. Always on the sly, of course."

"You spied on me," Tuesday stated flatly. "Wait, did you say 'dogs'? Loyal as my dogs?" she asked, "Plural?"

Mox didn't try to dodge. "You had the meanest, ugliest mongrel of a bitch for a couple years."

Tuesday realized he was telling the truth. "You knew Fury."

"The dog and I ran into each other a few times while I was…"

"Skulking," Tuesday finished, but there was no bite in her voice.

Mox knew the dog who had kept Tuesday sane when she had no one, and who had later given birth to Oz. If he knew Fury, then he really had come back to check on her. He really loved her all those years.

"Coward," she said, but sank to her knees next to him. Tuesday wanted to make sure she understood, "You spent a decade crossing paths with me every couple of years, always pretending you didn't love me." Tuesday poised her dagger to cut his wrists free. "Why bother telling me now?"

He locked his eyes on hers. "Because your life is at stake."

She popped her dagger through the zip-tie, "Yours is too."

Mox stood up from the desk, rubbing his wrists, and asked, "Where's the Eagle Scout?"

Tuesday holstered her dagger and swiped up the pistol again. "I don't know," she admitted and rushed on, "I followed his text to find him, but when I got to the meeting place, Hatter was there instead!"

"You don't think he—?" Mox was interrupted by a blast that rocked the building. "What the holy hell was that?!" He didn't bother with hushed tones.

"Shit. Hatter's got this place booby-trapped." Tuesday looked down the corridor in the direction of the reverberating explosion. The ceiling panels still quivered. "I set off a flash-bang earlier, but this sounded more serious. Let's go!"

Mox grabbed her arm. "Don't run *toward* the explosion!"

"Oz could be over there!"

Tuesday didn't have to say more. They ran toward the blast together.

Brandishing the pistol instead of a flashlight, Tuesday almost tumbled into a giant hole in the floor. It was impossible to tell whether the chasm was caused by demolition from the school's abandoned renovation, a meth cooking endeavor gone awry, or one of Hatter's own booby traps.

"We'll never make it over," she said, peering into the gaping void. "And neither would Oz, if he's on the other side." She thought she saw the glinting of a pupil-less eye deep in the open hole.

Mox shushed her, "Listen. What's that thumping?"

A rhythmic banging was emanating from one of the classrooms. Tuesday and Mox crept toward the sound and away from the pit.

A breath of light shined out from under one of the doors. "It's coming from that room," Tuesday whispered.

"It doesn't have windows," Mox warned. "Who knows what's in there?"

She couldn't see Mox's face well enough to read his expression. The rhythmic pounding changed. *Thump, thump thump. Bang, bang, bang. Thump, thump, thump.* Was that Morse code?

274

"It's Myles!" Tuesday said too loudly, trying to burst in the door. "It's got to be!"

The door was locked. "Back up!" she ordered Mox.

"Whoa!" was all Mox had time to yell before Tuesday shot the doorknob off. She kicked the door open to reveal Myles, bound to a chair, just as Mox had been. A bandana gagged him. He had scooted his chair across the room from the other seats to kick a metal filing cabinet, banging out S.O.S. with the loudest noise he could make.

"See?" said Mox as he and Tuesday stumbled into the room. "He wasn't working with Hatter after all!"

"Myles!" Tuesday dropped the gun and hurried to him, drawing her dagger. How had she doubted him? She hastily cut through the bandana to ungag him.

As soon as he was able, Myles sputtered, "You thought I was—!"

Just then Hatter flew into the room and fired a revolver wildly into the ceiling.

"Stop!" Tuesday shouted. "Stop! I'm the one you want! Don't shoot them!"

The Mad Hatter looked absurd in his purple leather vest, and crocodile-skin pants, with rabbit pelt around his neck, but somehow his obliviousness to his comical appearance was more terrifying. He'd lost his top hat in the pursuit. "Yes, it's you who should suffer," Hatter agreed amiably. "Your suffering will be more complete if you live to watch them die. So, here we go." Tuesday's heart skipped. He was going to kill them all.

Hatter fired into the floor near where Mox stood with his hands in the air. "Moxy by proxy." Hatter laughed when Tuesday screamed. "And Myles to go before I sleep," Hatter recited. He fired into the filing cabinet next to Myles. The ringing metal echo hung in the air, and Hatter repeated, "And Myles to go before I sleep."

Tuesday felt herself starting to crumble. "Let them go! They're innocent!"

"The living are never innocent!" Hatter yelled back.

Tuesday snuck a glance at Mox's gun on the floor where she had dropped it.

Hatter caught her looking, "One move and I will end everything." He produced a tiny remote control from the pocket of his purple vest. "I've got my finger on the button."

Tuesday didn't want to see what the button did. "Hey, let's not do anything—" she stopped herself.

"Crazy?" Hatter finished for her. He cocked his head and pressed something on the remote. Another explosion rattled the building. "Ooh, I hope your...*familiaris* wasn't in that wing!"

Tuesday hoped desperately that Oz would disobey her. *Don't find Myles! Please stay away!*

"We're just here for my sister," Tuesday cried, "Angie is innocent, just like Serena!"

"No one is like Serena!" Hatter fired another round into the ceiling. "Maybe Serena should decide your ending." He spun the cylinder of his revolver contemplatively. "Yes, I like that," he said to himself as he spun the cylinder again. How many shots had he fired? Four? There were two bullets left.

He pointed the revolver shakily at Mox. "Do you deserve to live?"

Mox held his hands in the air, "Listen—"

Hatter squeezed the trigger.

Nothing.

Before anyone could release their bated breath, Hatter whirled toward Myles, "Or you?"

He fired.

Nothing.

Then he swung the revolver toward Tuesday. "She should be angriest at you."

"You're right," Tuesday conceded shakily, staring down the barrel of the revolver. How had it all come to this? Tuesday's nightmares and her search for her sister had led her and her friends to this room, trapped with a demented drug lord playing Russian roulette. "Maybe I deserve to die for what I did," Tuesday continued quietly. "If I could take it back, I would. I've suffered for ten years. I thought I lost the most important person in my life. Just like you did. You were right—I am like you."

The Mad Hatter fired.

Nothing.

Tuesday's mind reeled. She had been spared.

There was no time to be relieved. She had to find Hatter's weakness and get Myles and Mox out of this room. She had to find Angie and Oz. "I saw photos of you and Serena when I was at the Repository," Tuesday ventured. "I could tell she loved you. You said you were going to change for her. To be better." Tuesday knew she was swimming in dangerous waters. "You still can."

"It's too late!" Ben Hatter swung his gun around hysterically, "All the junkies I've created, lives I've drained, destroyed, and ended—it's too late!"

"For them, but not too late for us," Tuesday willed herself to sound confident. "Or for you."

Hatter pointed the revolver at the ceiling directly above himself and squeezed his eyes shut, but didn't pull the trigger.

"The Mad Hatter wasn't a villain," Tuesday rushed on. "It's the queen who cuts off heads. And you don't even have to be The Mad Hatter anymore. You can just be Ben." Hatter opened his eyes but kept his gun in the air. Tuesday couldn't tell if her persuasion was working. She forged ahead, "I don't think you're as crazy as you want people to believe. You want to keep people at a distance so you don't get hurt. I know what that's like, Ben." Tuesday thought she saw a flicker of something in Hatter's expression. He stood frozen for an agonizing few seconds. Maybe she had gone too far by using Hatter's real name.

Suddenly Hatter whipped something out of his pocket and rocketed a surprisingly accurate throw at Myles' head. With his hands still bound under the desk, Myles could only turn away to let the item bounce off his shoulder.

Tuesday stopped herself from grabbing the object as it skidded to a stop. It was Myles' phone. How could she have been so stupid? She'd been texting with Ben Hatter ever since she'd lost Myles at the Repository. His lackeys must have grabbed Myles there, just as they'd grabbed Mox at the airport. It was Hatter's own texts that had led her to him, not Myles'. Myles would never work for The Mad Hatter.

"You doubted," Hatter seemed to read her thoughts. "For more than a moment. How does that make you feel?" He directed the last part to Myles. "To know she thinks so little of you?"

Even with the adrenaline pumping through her body, Tuesday felt a sharp stab of regret. She wanted to blurt an apology for ever doubting Myles, for believing Hatter's niggling, deceitful words, for not noticing the trap in time, and for not returning his kind words.

"Category," Myles spoke for the first time since Hatter had burst in.

Tuesday shot him a look. "What?"

Hatter looked intrigued. "What?"

"Category," Myles repeated.

Trust him. "Okay," Tuesday agreed. She fixed her eyes on Hatter.

"Good words starting with 'ben,'" Myles articulated clearly so Hatter understood the game. "Benevolent."

Tuesday mustered enthusiasm, her heart beating as if it might explode. "Yes! And benefactor!"

"Benefit," Mox added.

"Benediction," Tuesday said. She was tempted to take a step toward Hatter. "In Latin 'ben' means good. You can be good like Serena knew you could be. Even in leading me here, you might have been trying to make me suffer," Tuesday knew this was risky. "And I did. But you also showed me that my sister was alive. You built a connection instead of a wall. You meant to take life, but instead you brought it back."

Hatter seemed to be considering this. He held the remote control in

278

one hand, his fingers caressing the buttons thoughtfully. When he finally spoke, he said, "The best thing I can do is burn this place to the ground."

Tuesday's blood froze.

"The building is a bomb," Hatter said, "Tick, tick, tick."

Tuesday knew he wasn't bluffing. "Ben, before you do anything, I have to tell you—" She had only one card left to play. "I brought her here!"

Hatter looked up, from the remote, his eyes glassy. "Who?"

"Serena," Tuesday answered, proceeding carefully. "You kept her in the little building at the Repository. I brought her so you could be together." This was a lie. Tuesday had grabbed the teapot, which she had guessed were Serena's ashes, so she'd have something to trade in a hostage negotiation. "I put her in a place…where she can watch everything and keep you safe." Tuesday hoped the riddle would appeal to The Mad Hatter.

Hatter responded, "You have five minutes. Get out." At the press of a button, an announcement came through the intercom system, *Five minutes until detonation.*

"Angie and Oz are still here somewhere!" Tuesday nearly screamed.

"Yes. You'll have to choose. Your *familiaris* or your family," Hatter said mildly. "There's not time to find them both." Hatter left the room casually, as if he were not endangering five lives and exploding a school building while committing his own suicide.

Tuesday sliced through the zip-ties to free Myles. Mox swiped his pistol from the floor. "Let's go!" Tuesday shouted as all three of them bolted toward the door.

"He's right, there's no time!" Myles stopped. "Where's Oz?"

"I don't know, and his paw is hurt!" Tuesday wanted to sob. "I told him to find you! Angie is in room 321." Her breath came in shallow gasps.

"Look at me," Myles said evenly. Tuesday did. "You are going to save your sister. Go as fast as you can. Mox is going with you."

"But—" Tuesday protested.

"There's no time," Myles cut her off. "I'll find Oz." Tuesday watched her best friend and Oz's best chance to live sprint down the hallway into the darkness.

Mox grabbed her elbow, "Come on!" They dashed to the nearest set of stairs Tuesday remembered seeing and ran up two flights.

Four minutes until detonation, announced the intercom.

"Can you read the room numbers?" Tuesday asked frantically, searching the classroom doors.

"Angie!" Mox called. "Where are you?" There was no response.

"Look," Tuesday said as she picked up speed, "There's light coming from the room at the end of the hall!"

Tuesday rattled the locked door handle and then backed up as Mox took aim and fired at the handle. Inside the room, Tuesday saw exactly what she had seen in the photo dropped from the drone, and exactly what she had seen when Hatter had broadcast the live feed to Tuesday at the Repository.

It was her sister.

Angie sat with her back to the door, her hands bound to the desk, her white-blonde hair hanging down her back, her chin resting on her chest.

"Angie!" Tuesday ran to her sister's side and drew her dagger.

Angie screamed in surprise, then tried to stand up but fell back into the chair she was tied to. "Alouette? Al, is it really you? What's going on?"

"There's no time to explain," Tuesday snapped the zip-ties from Angie's wrists with her dagger.

Angie threw her arms around Tuesday, "Al, they told me you were dead! I didn't know until the Mad Hatter told me that you were alive! I didn't know whether to believe him!" She was shaking.

Three minutes until detonation.

Or maybe it was Tuesday who was shaking. "I can't believe it's you," Tuesday whispered, feeling Angie's tears on her cheeks. She pulled away, "We need to go. Now!"

"Justin?" Angie cried when she saw Mox. She threw her arms around him too. "Did you guys patch things up?"

"Never mind," Tuesday took Angie's hand and started for the door.

"I've found her," said a voice quietly from somewhere in the room.

"Who's that? Hatter?" Mox asked, scanning the room, his pistol drawn.

Tuesday stopped. "He must be talking through the security system like I did."

"I don't hear anything," Angie said. "But I'm deaf on this side," she covered her left ear. That explained why Angie hadn't answered Tuesday when she'd tried to talk to her through the security system.

"Serena and I are now...secure," Hatter went on. So he'd found the teapot in the security office where Tuesday had left it. "You have two minutes and thirty-six seconds. Then the lark, the pilot, and the angel will earn their wings."

"Am I dreaming?" Angie asked, putting her hands to her head. "Are we going to blow up?"

"Not if we get out of here!" Tuesday shouted, pulling Angie down the hallway with Mox close behind.

The three charged down the stairs.

Two minutes until detonation.

The slow, tinkling, music box song *Alouette* blared tauntingly through the school's intercom system.

Alouette, gentille alouette,

Alouette, je te plumerai.

"Where are they, where are they, where are they!" Tuesday shouted as they ran. She stopped to look down a corridor on the first floor. "Myles? Oz?" she screamed desperately.

"There's no time!" Mox pulled her toward the doors of the school.

One minute until detonation.

They pushed through the doors and raced into the school yard, putting as much distance between themselves and the building as possible in their remaining minute.

Either the blast from the explosion or sheer exhaustion sent them all sprawling into the field as smoke and flames erupted into the night sky.

Tuesday stood up, her chest heaving and her ears ringing. Embers drifted lazily through the air. Mox and Angie rose unsteadily and each took one of Tuesday's hands. They watched the catastrophe together. One wing of the building blazed, and another had already collapsed. The roof caved in on the whole fiery ruin.

"Who were Myles and Oz?" Angie asked breathlessly.

Sixteen

Tuesday and Angie sat reclining under the weeping willow tree near Tuesday's tiny shipping container home on Alabama Hill in Bellingham, listening to the birds in the nearby trees. Angie's husband, Rick, hammered busily inside a second shipping container placed on the plot of land adjacent to Tuesday's. He whistled cheerfully to himself while he finished constructing what was to be his and Angie's new home.

"No one told me it was break time!" Rick pretended to complain. He joined the sisters under the willow tree and kissed his wife on the thin train-track scar behind her left ear. Angie blushed and turned her good ear to Rick, her smile just slightly lopsided, as it always was, looking as if she was about to tell a sweet secret. Their cozy position reminded Tuesday of the photo she'd seen in Hatter's slideshow. Was that really only a month ago?

Tuesday offered Rick a Mason jar of cool honey-sweetened tea. "Have some of this. Angie made it from lemon peel and the chamomile we picked from the herb garden."

Rick was the EMT first on the scene of the accident that haunted Tuesday for so many years. He was the one who brought Angie back to life. A year later Rick and Angie married, vowing to face life's adventures together, for better or for worse. Then things got worse. Soon after the wedding, when Ben Hatter's relentless pursuit drove them from Bellingham into deep seclusion in the Colorado mountains, Angie and Rick were forced to live off the grid with minimal contact to the world beyond the wild.

"Can I just say for the hundredth time in two weeks," Angie rested her head on the trunk of the small willow, "I'm SO glad to be back in Bellingham!"

"That might be the *thousandth* time you've said that in two weeks,"

Rick grinned. "But I'm with you. As much as I love the mountains, nine years of isolation was enough."

"To finally be released from the constant fear of Hatter finding us," Angie put her hand on her heart. "Is liberating."

"And then to discover you," Rick looked at Tuesday, "is icing on the cake."

"She isn't just the icing," Angie protested, "Al is the whole dessert bar: cake, icing, cookies, pie, and ice cream!"

"I think *I* discovered *you*, if we want to be technical about it," Tuesday smirked. She sounded glib, but truthfully, she felt a joy, both foreign and familiar, coursing through her veins again when she was with her sister. And Rick was the cherry on top.

That morning all three of them had gone to meet Justin Mox at his apartment above the lighting shop in Tacoma. They hadn't seen him in the month since he, Angie, and Tuesday had escaped the school building where The Mad Hatter had orchestrated his own spectacular death. Rick had insisted on thanking Mox in person for his role in rescuing Angie.

Tuesday agreed to set up the visit with Mox partly so that Angie and Rick could thank him, and partly out of curiosity. How would it feel to talk to Mox again? She also had one remaining question.

After exchanging initial introductions and pleasantries, Rick expressed his deep gratitude, and Mox brushed it off, as Tuesday knew he would. "My armor was starting to tarnish anyway," he had said.

Before long, Tuesday cleared her throat, "Well, we don't want to impose. And we have a house to build."

"I only have two chairs anyway," Mox responded.

"Go on ahead, I'll just be a minute," Tuesday told Angie and Rick as they said their goodbyes.

Tuesday turned to Mox. "Justin," she found his name on her tongue. Where to begin?

"I need to thank you, too." She shrugged helplessly. " Without you, I never would have gotten my sister back. There's no way to make it up to you. I owe you any favor you can name."

"I'll bank that for later," Mox replied.

Tuesday went on, "Maybe it's weird after all this, but if you're visiting Bellingham, or want to—"

"Birdie," Mox interrupted gently.

"Hang out..." Tuesday was sure this was not the right thing to say to someone who had declared his love for her a short time ago.

"Sometimes people go through too much together to be friends," Mox said.

She had figured he would decline the invitation. Tuesday looked into his eyes and nodded, "A wise lady once told me to be careful digging up the bones of the past. But maybe someday."

"I think that might be the problem," Mox said. "I never buried anything that happened between us."

"I wanted to ask you something," Tuesday said. "Then we can drop all this or never speak again, or...whatever you need."

Mox raised one arched eyebrow.

"Why did you have to turn me in when we stole the answer key for the anthropology final? I think I understand why you left me. But wasn't it enough to just dump me? Why break my heart and then kick me in the ass on the way out?" She'd been waiting a decade to ask.

He waited a moment to reply. "It was a compromise."

"For what? With who?"

"Sharon never liked you," Mox shook his head, "as you've figured out by now."

Tuesday had figured it out. As soon as she had a moment to clear her mind after coming back from Colorado, looking at the wood grain on the ceiling of her tiny home the first night she'd slept there after coming back from Colorado. Long, straight line, swerve to the left, through a smear of pine tar, back to straight. Sharon, the former registrar at Western Washington University. She knew Tuesday's real name, she'd had the opportunity to put the tracker on Oz, and she flaunted a rolling luggage bag made of genuine pangolin leather that could only have come from the National Wildlife Property Repository outside of Denver. When Tuesday had stormed in to confront Sharon, there had been a sign on the door of the empty office reading, "Vacationing in the Maldives, call again soon." Tuesday had gone immediately back to the tiny house where she and Angie spitefully ate all of the Reese's peanut butter cups she'd collected for Sharon.

"Well," Mox continued, "Sharon knew of your...less savory side-gigs. And she was going to rat you out to the police. We compromised. I figured you could talk your way out of expulsion for cheating. Better that than get arrested, charged for dealing, and have to do time. You'd make a terrible jailbird."

"Huh," Tuesday crossed her arms.

"You were better than me then, and you're better than me now. I haven't changed," Mox said. "And I knew from the very first time I saw you with him that you would never belong to me again."

Mox had long known what Tuesday was only just beginning to see. It had taken the terror of staring into a burning abyss without him for Tuesday to understand she loved Myles.

She didn't answer Mox.

With only a hint of bitterness, Mox finished, "So will I come to your family cookouts and birthday parties in Bellingham? Probably not, Birdie."

"Maybe someday, Justin," Tuesday countered kindly. "And maybe Oz was right about you all along."

Under the weeping willow tree, sipping sweet tea with Angie and Rick, Tuesday let her thoughts wander further. She thought she had been in hell that day, watching the building erupt in flames and crumble with Myles and Oz inside. To finally reunite with her sister, to have a family

286

again, she'd risked her dearest friends. And as the smoke from the explosions cleared, Tuesday had dashed back to the razed building in a frenzy. Mox and Angie didn't stop her.

Tuesday had pried pieces of concrete and sheetrock off of the rubble, ripping open the skin of her fingertips, her face smeared with ash and tears. "Myles! Oz!" she screamed. More debris crashed down nearby, sending plumes of smoke and ash into the air. The demolition had been too complete. She would never uncover them.

Then, emerging through the darkness from the other side of the smoldering ruin, was Myles. He was sprinting full speed toward her, carrying a big silver dog in his arms. They had survived—both of them.

As Myles set Oz onto the ground, Tuesday flung herself into his arms, and for the first time, she felt her heart thundering with his. She buried her face in his shoulder and felt his hand at the base of her neck, holding her against him. Both their chests rattled with desperate relief.

"I thought I'd lost you," Myles breathed.

Tuesday didn't let go. "I'm sorry I doubted you," she choked. "I'm sorry I kept you at a distance. I was afraid. I built walls to keep you out."

"I'm in," said Myles.

The familiar sound of a truck's tires brought Tuesday back to the present. Her heart lifted into her throat, as it always did now when she saw Myles.

"I wondered when Prince Charming was gonna get here," Rick teased. "Tell him to have you back by curfew or you turn into a pumpkin!"

Tuesday laughed, not at the joke as much as from delight at having a brother-in-law who said things exactly like a brother-in-law should. Myles stepped out of the truck, dressed in the teal polo shirt that drew attention to his mocha skin and toned biceps. Tuesday's heart skipped.

In the schoolyard while Hatter's headquarters collapsed beside them and the scent of singed cotton lingered on Myles from his brush with death, Tuesday had realized it was time to let herself love. And she knew she had to tell him.

When they were safely back in Bellingham with a moment to themselves looking over the water at Lake Whatcom, Tuesday had confessed, "I should have realized sooner how much I care about you." She took a deep breath before turning to him, "And how much I want to be with you."

Myles balked. Solid, reasonable Myles, who had been quietly and steadily in love with Tuesday for years, balked. The sting of Tuesday's doubt had affected him deeply. After all they had been through, she still wasn't able to trust him, and for a moment she even believed he might have betrayed her to Hatter. Myles held back.

He took Tuesday's hand in his and said, "I don't think I can do this. If we jump, I'm going in with both feet. And I won't be able to stop myself from loving you. That's risky."

It was. Tuesday was impetuous, fiery, and guarded. But then she had always been, and he'd loved her anyway. "Loving anything is a risk," Tuesday had answered. "And I'm ready to take that chance now, so just tell me when you are, too."

A month later, Myles was at the tiny house on Alabama Hill to pick up Tuesday for their first date. It would be a re-do of the surprise date he had tried to invite her to the day she had burst into his trailer during his preparations. Today he had reset the scene, which awaited her at the trailer, complete with warm blueberry cobbler.

"Here comes your chaperone," Angie smiled her lopsided grin.

Oz bounded across the grassy meadow in between the two tiny homes, greeting Myles with his playful bow and high arched tail. There was no sign of a limp in Oz's gait from the glass that had injured him at the Repository. The patches of fur that had been singed before Myles was able to rescue him had already started to regrow. Myles had found the big dog, with the wound in his paw newly torn open, trapped under debris from one of The Mad Hatter's blasts. With seconds to spare, Myles freed Oz and carried him out of the imploding building in his arms. He'd delivered Tuesday's heart. It was the kind of gift that simply had to be accepted, because it could never be repaid.

Tuesday had been on the verge of contacting the World Disaster Relief Organization to officially retire Oz after the explosion almost took his life. But the morning after their first night back in the cozy Bellingham house, Oz awoke and stared pointedly at the hook on the wall where his red vest used to hang, as if to ask what adventures they would meet that day. He wanted to work. So Tuesday conceded, "If you're still in, I'm still in." There had been no WDRO Deliverer assignments in the past month, so they'd been content with more mundane GoferGoods tasks. But she knew it was only a matter of time before she and Oz would be needed. She'd already put in a request for Oz's new red Deliverer vest.

Tuesday's nightmares had vanished. Now when she dreamed, she dreamed of walking through sunny meadows with Oz, laughing with Angie on the wooden stoop of the tiny house, or soaring through blue skies with Myles. After a decade living under a shroud of guilt, she finally felt free to explore Tuesday Devlin—who she was, and who she truly could be.

That evening, with white lights strung along the awning of the trailer, and only the glow of candlelight at the table for ambiance, Tuesday reached down to scratch Oz behind his ears. "Category," she challenged Myles with a wry smile. "The best way to toast our first date."

He thought for a moment, then raised his glass, "To many more adventures together."

Tuesday's stormy eyes met his as she raised her glass, "I'm in."

Acknowledgments

Foremost, I would like to extend heartfelt gratitude to my editor Sittrea Friberg for her guidance and keen eye for language, which vastly improved this book. Her enthusiasm gave me the confidence to follow through and share this book with others. Thank you for being my cheerleader.

Many thanks must also be extended to my beta reader, Lauren Frederick, for her astute suggestions, encouragement, and attention to my audience. She is the inspiration for the line, "Sisters are the best people in the world." I owe Jared Knutson much gratitude for being my gatekeeper, and for suspending his disbelief (even though he doesn't like novels).

The characters and events in this novel are fictional, but I would like to recognize the many people who lent their names or pieces of their personas to my work. Thank you Jody and Erika Coleman, Piper Leiper, Ariel Woodruff, Richard Frederick, Laura Strong, Alexia Culver-Kritsonis, Damian Culver, Selena Kritsonis, and Filomena Kritsonis-Small.

For transforming my vision for the cover into reality, I would like to thank Adam Botsford, who generously donated his time and tremendous skill.

I appreciate Woodward Canyon Winery, Gilman House, The Museum of Glass, Pure Bliss Desserts, Village Books, and The Garden Spot for inspiring some of the venues in this book.

Lastly, because ideas flow more easily when my feet are moving, I am grateful for a shabby pair of size 6.5 Ryka running shoes, which carried me over 250 miles during the months spent writing this book.

About the Author

Suzanne Akerman is a Pacific Northwest zookeeper who loves dancing, good storytelling, and bar trivia. She earned a B.A. in English Literature and an M.A. in Education from Pacific Lutheran University, as well as an M.A. in Biology from Miami University. Her previously published works include poetry in the arts journals *Saxifrage* and *Creative Colloquy Vol. 7*, and an article in the scholarly *Journal of Museum Education*. She has authored several self-published children's books including *Petunia's Big Day* and *Stop the Story!* This is her first novel.

Made in the USA
Middletown, DE
02 October 2021